THE
LIVES WE
LEFT BEHIND

An evocative and charming WW1 family saga

DOMINIC LUKE

Brannans Family Saga Book 4

JOFFE BOOKS

Joffe Books, London
www.joffebooks.com

First published in Great Britain in 2023

Cover art by Jarmila Takač

ISBN: 978-1-80405-723-0

. . . So keen is change, and time so strong,
To weave the robes of life and rend
And weave again till life have end . . .

Prelude to *Songs Before Sunrise*
Algernon Charles Swinburne

CHAPTER ONE

The picnic had been something of a success, but the journey home a disaster. Now, as the sleek black motor sped up the drive in the gathering dusk of the August Bank Holiday, Mrs Eloise Brannan leaned forward on the back seat, waiting for the moment when the house came into view. The motor swung round the sharp turn at the head of the drive. Its headlamps swept across the familiar grey facade. Wheels skidded on gravel as it came to a stop by the front steps. The sound of the engine died.

Eloise sat back. A sense of relief flooded through her. They were home at last.

Roderick had taken the wheel on the last stage of the journey. The way he drove was, admittedly, somewhat slapdash. Her heart had been in her mouth on more than one occasion. It made her, in retrospect, all the more appreciative of their chauffeur, Smith; she had rather taken Smith for granted until today.

Eloise closed her eyes and pressed her fingers against her temples. She could still hear Smith's terrible screams. Poor Smith! What a calamity!

But now was not the time to dwell on it. Her fellow passenger had already jumped out and was holding the door open, waiting to hand her down. She gave him a perfunctory smile as she stepped from the running board. Roderick's friend, Mr Antipov, could be as courteous as the next man when he chose, but there was no consistency in his behaviour; at times, he could be exasperating. He was only young, however — just twenty-four — and he was a foreigner. One had to make allowances.

Eloise paused to straighten her skirts before looking up at the house. It was, if anything, more impressive than ever this evening, etched against a fading sky. So pleasingly symmetrical. Such clean lines. There was a reassuring air of permanence about the place, deeply rooted as it was in the Northamptonshire countryside.

Lights shone in many of the windows; light spilled out from the open front door. Roderick went leaping up the steps, calling for Ordish to have someone put the motor away. (But who, now that Smith was . . . ?) As Eloise looked on, Roderick paused for a moment, framed in the doorway, a tall silhouette with electric light glowing all round him. Her son, she said to herself, and her house. Her house and her son. The sight stirred something within her. Her mind groped for the right words, but there were no words, not for one's deepest feelings: that was why the deepest feelings remained fittingly veiled.

Roderick plunged into the house, still calling for Ordish, and disappeared from view. Where, indeed, was Ordish? And why had the front door been wide open when they arrived? These details niggled as Eloise climbed the steps. Mr Antipov stepped aside to let her go first.

Up in her room, Eloise took a seat at the dressing table and set about removing her hat. As she arranged the hat pins in a neat row, she listened out for her maid who seemed, like Mr Ordish, to have gone missing. Would it really be necessary to ring?

Placing her hat to one side, Eloise sighed. She could not leave the house for so much as a day without things getting slack. No doubt there would be trouble over dinner, too, due to their late return. Dinner was probably all but burnt to a crisp by now. Cook would not be happy. But then Cook could be difficult at the best of times. As for trying to keep the peace between Cook and the housekeeper, Mrs Bourne, this was a truly Sisyphean task. Eloise spent half her life on it.

This was what it took to run a house like Clifton Park. People had no idea.

Eloise leaned forward, massaging her head, trying to ease the throbbing pain behind her eyes. It didn't help that she was thinking still of those screams, Smith's terrible screams. They would haunt her tonight. They would keep her awake. And yet today, on the whole, had gone very smoothly.

It was true that — given the choice — she herself would not have chosen the Eidur Stones as a destination. There was something a little disturbing about them, those ancient, weathered monoliths of unknown purpose. Some, over time, had toppled into the turf. Others still pointed skywards like harbingers of doom. But at least the weather had held, and no one had been bitten or stung, and Cook's well-stocked hampers had been — though she said so herself — something of a triumph; even Mrs Somersby had remarked on the food. (This little success was as good a reason as any as to why one was so forbearing with Cook.)

Only when they were halfway home had things started to go wrong. Somewhere the other side of Welby, the Clifton motor had developed a flat tyre. The cortège of three cars had come to a halt on a gentle downslope. Smith had set about changing the wheel. This, by rights, ought to have taken a matter of minutes. Eloise was no expert, but she knew that detachable wheels were one of the selling points of BFS Motors, something her late husband Albert had been working on at the time of his death five years ago. Smith, however, had run into problems. A nut or bolt had jammed and wouldn't come loose. He'd crawled half under the machine, attacking the offending part with a spanner, whilst the other men gathered round and offered advice, as men were wont to do.

One booming voice had risen above the rest: Colonel Harding's. The Colonel had spent twenty years denouncing motor cars as the work of the Devil, only to undergo a recent road-to-Damascus conversion. He was now, in his own eyes at least, as much an expert on motors as he was on everything else. He had interfered. He had known best. He had tried to teach Smith the job that Smith was paid to do.

But for all the Colonel's meddling, it was not he who'd courted disaster. It was his elder son, Charles. Whilst Smith was busy with the Clifton motor by the side of the road, Charles Harding — a pale imitation of his father — had started tampering with the Colonel's machine. Somehow he had contrived to release the brakes. The Colonel's motor had begun to roll down the slope. It rolled slowly at first but with gathering speed, scattering the men grouped around the punctured wheel and — there was no getting away from it — rolling right over Smith's outstretched legs.

Sat at the dressing table, Eloise pressed her palms against her brow, as the memory of Smith's screams focused the pain in her head into a point right behind her eyes. She felt decidedly queasy. The poor boy's agony (he was just nineteen, a child really) had been only too audible. All the same, she'd not made a fuss; she had no time for women who made a fuss, women who were prone to fits of the vapours and to dosing themselves with sal volatile. Eloise shunned such attention-seeking behaviour.

There'd been mayhem in the leafy country lane. Most of the men had gone haring after the runaway motor. Most of the women had stood around shrieking. The dreadful commotion had been made all the worse by that squalling child, the Colonel's tiny grandson. (So ill-considered, to have taken a child of that age on the picnic without a nanny or nurse. This sort of lapse had rather put Eloise off the Colonel just lately; this — and other reasons.)

It was Roderick who had taken charge. He had helped lift poor Smith into Mrs Somersby's motor and ordered the chauffeur to find the nearest doctor. He had also sent people in search of a horse or two to pull the Colonel's machine out of the ditch where it had ended up. He had even replaced the punctured wheel himself. 'I used to mend my own bicycle. A motor can't be all that much different.' A resourceful, no-nonsense sort of boy, so very like his father.

Dorothea had gone with Smith in the Somersbys' motor. She was a sensible girl who could always be relied on; she'd be missed when her visit to Clifton came to an end. But that day was fast approaching; she would soon be heading back to Hamburg and her husband. Why Albert's niece had married a German, and not some nice, respectable Englishman, remained a moot point. But what was done could not be undone, and Dorothea seemed happy enough in her choice.

Eloise sighed once more and opened her eyes. She looked at the door. It remained resolutely shut; there were no footsteps in the corridor outside.

She couldn't wait any longer. She would have to ring for her maid. She would have to ring.

This was how slack things had got in just one day.

* * *

Roderick was standing by the cabinet brandishing a soda siphon as Eloise entered the drawing room. Dorothea and Mr Antipov were side by side on the settee. Her daughter Elizabeth, who had not come on the picnic, was sprawled untidily on the couch. The French windows were wide open and the curtains not drawn; cool air seeped in from the August night outside. A bright white moon, not far from the full, was climbing the black sky.

The drawing room was comfortingly familiar; if there'd been changes since Eloise's childhood — the electric lights, for instance — there was still more that remained the same. She pulled the bell cord, adjusted the delft vase to its correct place on the sideboard and took a seat in the Eugenie armchair.

'A drink, Mother?'

'Not for me, Roderick, thank you.' Eloise turned to her niece. 'You're back then, Dorothea. How is poor Smith?'

'We took him straight to Dr Camborne here in the village. We decided that would be quicker than searching for a doctor where we broke down.' (Dorothea's 'we' no doubt embraced the Somersbys' chauffeur.) 'Dr Camborne insisted on keeping Jeff at Maybank tonight. I offered to stay, but he said there is nothing more I can do at present; poor Jeff is in no danger. Dr Camborne gave him something to take away the pain and he'll put splints on both legs, he said.'

'Never mind all that!' Elizabeth blurted out. 'What about the—'

Eloise cut her daughter short. 'Please don't interrupt, Elizabeth. Let Dorothea finish. You were saying, Dorothea?'

'There's not much more to tell, Aunt. Dr Camborne thinks there's every hope of a full recovery. It all depends how the bones heal.'

'If they heal.' Roderick, having replenished his drink, crossed the room and leaned against the piano. 'Smith's legs were more or less squashed flat. He'll probably never walk again.'

'Oh, Roddy,' cried Dorothea, 'don't say that! Dr Camborne told me—'

'That old quack! He'll end up sawing both legs off above the knee. You know what he's like.'

'You really shouldn't exaggerate, Roderick,' Eloise gently admonished her son. 'Arthur Camborne is more than capable. He has been the family doctor for over forty years.'

'Exactly. He's old hat. Past his best—'

Elizabeth jumped up, interrupting again. 'What about the war! Does nobody care about the war?'

Eloise winced, rubbing her temples. 'Don't shout, Elizabeth! What are you fussing about?'

Roderick said equably, 'I expect she's referring to the war in Europe, Mother.'

'Not that again. It's nothing. It will all blow over.'

Roderick swirled the drink in his glass. 'I'm not so sure, you know.'

Dorothea looked up at him. 'That's not what you said the other day, Roddy. The other day you said—'

'The great catastrophe!' cried Elizabeth dramatically. 'The great catastrophe has come upon Europe — that's what it says in the newspaper!'

'She's right, you know.' Roderick sounded almost apologetic. 'I didn't get to read *The Times* in all the rush this morning, but having glanced through it just now—'

'There's more!' exclaimed Elizabeth. 'Something Billy told me, Billy Turner. He went to Northampton today and—'

Eloise cut her short again. 'That's enough, Elizabeth! That's quite enough. How many times must I tell you not to be so familiar with the servants?'

There was a sudden silence and Eloise wondered if she'd spoken rather more sharply than she'd intended. She looked round at the young people. They all appeared busy with their own thoughts. Elizabeth had sat back down, and was rocking back and forth on the couch, even more dishevelled than usual. Roderick, leaning against the piano, frowned down at his drink as he swirled it in his glass. Dorothea stared pensively at the fire screen. As for Mr Antipov, well, one could not help feeling that he was making mental notes the whole time; his eyes — they were a bluey-grey, very pale, almost unnerving — missed nothing.

The door opened. The tall footman came in, responding somewhat tardily to the summons of the bell. With his arrival, an air of normality returned to the room.

Eloise addressed him. 'Ah, John. The French windows are open. Will you shut them, please?'

'Yes, ma'am.'

'The curtains, too.'

'Yes, ma'am.'

'And, John — I shouldn't need to ask.'

'No, ma'am. Sorry, ma'am.'

'When you've finished here, you may tell Cook we are ready for dinner.'

'At once, ma'am.'

* * *

At dinner, Eloise did her best to fend off the subject of war but it was as hopeless as King Canute trying to hold back the tide. She began to wonder if she might have underestimated the gravity of the situation. She had not been keeping pace with events; her mind had been elsewhere these last few weeks, making preparations for Dorothea's visit, organizing the village fête, not to mention today's picnic and all it entailed. As she listened to the talk round the table, she did her best to piece things together. Germany, she gathered, had declared war on Russia and then invaded Luxembourg. This was in *The Times*, apparently, so it must be true, though what Luxembourg had to do with it not even Mr Antipov could say. There was no mention of Austria and Serbia, where the whole sorry business had begun, but Elizabeth complicated matters still further by bringing in Belgium — some titbit she'd picked up from the stable boy, Turner, who'd heard it in Northampton on his day off.

'Billy said if the Germans won't back down—'

'An ultimatum, you mean?' questioned Roderick. 'There's nothing in any of the papers about an ultimatum.'

'But it's what people are saying, Billy told me.'

Eloise's mind wandered. She wished Elizabeth would behave with a little more decorum; at the age of fourteen, it was about time. Instead, here she was, talking at the top of her voice, waving her arms about — all most unladylike. Also, in the drawing room earlier, Eloise had noticed the footman dart a reproachful glance in Elizabeth's direction as he closed the French windows, a glance which suggested he'd closed the windows once already and that Elizabeth had been meddling and fiddling and making extra work for everyone, which was only too typical.

Eloise sighed, put her knife and fork down; she really wasn't hungry. Everything that had happened today — it was enough to put anyone off their food. The accident loomed largest of all. Smith's family would have to be informed. And Smith would obviously be incapacitated for some considerable time. How would they manage without a chauffeur?

Just as Eloise's head was starting to throb again, Roderick suddenly changed the subject and began to recount an amusing incident at the Eidur Stones that afternoon, when Charles Harding had inadvertently sat on a Victoria sponge. The mood round the table was instantly lightened; Eloise breathed a sigh of relief. She rather suspected that Roderick had steered the conversation away from the war on purpose. He could be quite masterly when he put his mind to it. How many other boys of twenty-one would show such tact?

'Did you notice,' he continued, getting into his stride after the success of his story about the Victoria sponge, 'how the War Bore monopolized Miss Harding the whole afternoon?' (The War Bore was Roderick's name for Mrs Somersby's son, Mark, who had served in South Africa.) 'I could see Miss Harding's eyes slowly glazing over.'

'Oh, Roddy, you do twist things!' laughed Dorothea. 'She was hanging on his every word! I wouldn't be surprised if she wasn't a little in love with him.'

'How could she possibly be, Doro? The man is dull as ditch water. If I hear once more how he single-handedly raised the siege of Mafeking . . .'

Eloise permitted herself a brief smile. To hear Roderick and Dorothea squabbling amicably at the dining table was almost like old times; if only Dorothea didn't have to leave!

But there was no point wishing for the impossible.

* * *

Elizabeth, after dinner — and despite her protests — was despatched to bed; Dorothea went up 'to tuck her in', a habit from the old days. One had hoped over the years that some of

Dorothea's common sense might rub off on Elizabeth. There was not much sign of it.

Eloise went down briefly to the kitchen, to thank Cook for dinner. Not strictly necessary, of course, but they had been rather late returning, and Cook had worked miracles to ensure the food didn't spoil. Cooks weren't ten-a-penny these days; a good cook was worth her weight in gold. And Eloise always kept in mind one of her father's favourite maxims: *a well-placed word works wonders.*

Back in the drawing room, she found Roderick and Mr Antipov deep in discussion (Dorothea had not yet returned from seeing Elizabeth to bed). Taking a seat, Eloise watched the young Russian pacing up and down, one hand in his pocket, the other waving in the air, emphasizing the points he was making. Such energy and passion seemed almost improper in the sedate surroundings of the drawing room. His foreign accent made ordinary English words sound rather strange and, well, almost disreputable.

It had always seemed odd to Eloise that Roderick and the Russian should be such fast friends; they appeared to have little in common. But Roderick had a penchant, going back to his school days (if not before), for surprising friendships. He'd often taken up with boys whom Eloise called, in her own mind, Roderick's waifs and strays. Boys from the village. Boys from school. Boys — like Mr Antipov — from Oxford. Some of these boys visited Clifton only once, then disappeared. Others lasted rather longer. That plump boy, for instance, with the double-barrelled name, terribly shy, rather hard work. Or the boy who liked poetry and struck Eloise as being somewhat highly strung. Mr Antipov, however, was the first foreigner among Roderick's succession of friends.

He was a most singular young man. Eloise could not make up her mind about him. His clothes tended towards the threadbare and were frequently creased. He forever had his nose in a book. He left a trail of books wherever he went. And he wrote things down. He wrote on margins, he wrote on flyleaves, he filled little notebooks with those peculiar Russian hieroglyphs. She couldn't begin to imagine what it was all for.

As he walked restlessly back and forth, Mr Antipov repeatedly brushed back his floppy, flaxen hair. His rather low-pitched voice gave his words a certain gravitas.

'Ordinary people do not want war. Is only governments who want war.'

'Nobody wants a war, old man,' said Roderick mildly, lolling on the couch. 'But if war comes along—'

'Is impossible! There will be no war! Working men will not fight, working men will go on strike, and without working men there are no armies and war cannot be.'

'Another of your pipe dreams, Antipov. Too late, in any case. The fighting has begun. The only uncertainty now is what our bungling government will do. I've rather come round to the idea that England must be in it, if we don't want to lose our good name forever. The Germans need taking down a peg; that's been obvious for some time.'

Eloise was perturbed to hear Roderick talking like this, almost as if he welcomed the prospect of war — a war he'd professed not to believe in only a few days ago.

'You mustn't say such things in front of Dorothea,' she cautioned him.

'Of course I won't, Mother. Why do you think I changed the subject at dinner? But I'm afraid Doro will have to face facts sooner rather than later.'

He was right. War talk was fast becoming impossible to avoid; even on the picnic, mention had been made. But though Roderick's matter-of-fact attitude was not entirely soothing, at least he was not afraid to take matters by the scruff of the neck, the way his father always had.

This reminder of her late husband made Eloise think of something he'd been in the habit of saying whenever faced with a seemingly intractable problem. *It'll all look different in the morning.* Wise words, and particularly apt after a day like today.

11

Eloise got to her feet. 'I'll bid you both good night, I think.'

But once in bed, sleep proved elusive, as it often did. Little incidents, which passed unnoticed during the day, loomed large as she lay awake in the dark. There'd been some discussion on the picnic — out of his earshot, of course — about the Colonel's sudden change of heart vis-à-vis motor cars. Mrs Somersby, it was, who'd suggested that the Colonel was anxious to appear up to date. 'There's someone he is trying to impress,' she'd said, 'and we can all guess who!'

But, really, said Eloise to herself as she lay flat on her back with her hands folded on her breast, Viola can't have meant me. She can't possibly have meant me.

And yet—

Eloise closed her eyes, but there was nowhere to hide. She had no choice but to admit that all this awkwardness stemmed from her trip to Scarborough last summer.

She had felt somewhat under the weather last summer: not sleeping, plagued by headaches. Insomnia was nothing new. She'd suffered with it intermittently for years. Sometimes it was less severe, sometimes more. Last summer had been particularly bad and Dr Camborne had recommended a complete break, a rest cure. Colonel Harding had stepped forward with an invitation from his eldest daughter, Mrs Varney. She and her husband had taken up residence in Scarborough some years ago, and would be delighted to welcome Eloise as a guest. And so Eloise had arranged a short visit — a fortnight at most. But somewhere along the way, this fortnight had become a sojourn of three months.

The Varneys had been kindness itself; they had pressed her repeatedly to postpone her return to Northamptonshire and Eloise had let herself be persuaded, for the sea air really had been doing her good; she'd felt quite revitalized. To be free, for once, of all her responsibilities had been a novel experience. That was not to say she hadn't given Clifton Park a thought; in fact, she'd found herself talking about it a lot, reminiscing with her hostess — for Mrs Mortimer Varney of Scarborough had once been Miss Charlotte Harding of Newbolt Hall (the house where the Colonel lived), and she'd known Clifton Park in its heyday. She had known Eloise's father, too. She remembered him well. So few people now did.

Eloise had been nearly a month in Scarborough when Colonel Harding arrived out of the blue. There was no reason, of course, why the Colonel shouldn't visit his daughter. He no doubt visited her on a regular basis. But thinking things over as she lay sleepless in the dark, Eloise couldn't help feeling that the Colonel's arrival ought to have been the signal for her to depart. That was not to say she'd intended any encouragement by staying; the very idea was preposterous. She did not stand in need, at her time of life, of the attentions of any man. She was a widow, and a widow she would remain. But she could see in hindsight that extending her visit to the Varneys might have given Colonel Harding the wrong impression. She'd been endeavouring to put him right ever since — which made Mrs Somersby's remarks all the more galling.

No doubt all would be forgotten in time. Meanwhile, no good would come in dwelling on it, certainly not at this time of night. Eloise sighed and emptied her mind as best she could, then she waited stoically for sleep to take her.

* * *

She slept in the end: for several hours, as it happened. She woke from long habit at her usual time. Slipping from between the sheets before her maid came, she knelt on the floor, facing the bed like an altar. She closed her eyes and placed her hands together, praying as she'd prayed every morning for nearly fifty years. She prayed for her mother, as she had been taught to when a little girl, the mother she had no memory of and of whom no image existed. She prayed for her dear, departed father, and for Albert, who was also gone. She prayed for Roderick and Dorothea and Elizabeth, asked

13

God to bless them and keep them safe. And she thanked the Lord for his divine bounty — of which Clifton Park was not the least.

On her knees in the void — the empty dark behind her eyes — she left a pause after her last amen, as she always did, as if waiting for an answer. When a child, she really had expected an answer. She'd expected God to speak to her. He never had.

Eloise opened her eyes. She waited a moment, then levered herself up (oh, her poor knees!) and got back into bed. Pulling the covers straight, she waited for her maid to bring the tea.

* * *

On entering the breakfast room, Eloise found *The Times* spread across the satinwood table whilst Roderick and Mr Antipov continued their argument from last night. Elizabeth was poring over a page detached from the paper. Dorothea was eating toast. Her face was rather pinched and pale beneath her mop of dark curls.

Eloise took her place. 'Must we have war talk at breakfast? Please put that newspaper away, Elizabeth.'

'Handle it with care!' Roderick ordered. 'You don't know the trouble I had in getting it!' He'd been up with the lark, he said, and when *The Times* failed to appear, had gone in search of it. 'They'd none at the village shop, so I drove into Lawham. There was a place on the High Street with what seems to have been the last copy in existence. Some other chap claimed to have seen it first. We had a boxing match over it. I won on points.'

By now, halfway through breakfast, the precious newspaper had been picked over and devoured, and its news was already stale. Roderick was hungry for more up-to-date information; he'd learned nothing in Lawham. But Lawham was a backwater, incurably behind the times.

'Even the stable boy has more idea of things than anyone in Lawham, or so Eliza tells me.'

'Billy is not a boy!' Elizabeth protested. 'He is twenty-five years old.'

'Boy or man, he had the right idea yesterday, going to Northampton. That's the place for news.' Roderick jumped up, rubbing his hands together. 'I'm off there now, to see what's what. The banks won't be open, I know that much. The bank holiday has been extended until Friday and that wouldn't happen for nothing.'

He hurried out of the room, followed by Mr Antipov. Elizabeth half rose from her chair, as if she had a mind to run after them. Eloise caught her daughter's eye. Elizabeth sank back down. She began picking at the remains of her breakfast.

Having finished her tea, Eloise laid her napkin aside and went to the window. There were spots of rain on the glass: a passing shower. (They had been lucky with the weather on the picnic yesterday.) The upper branches of the age-old cedar tree were raised against a grey and overcast sky. After a while she heard the sound of an engine and one of the Clifton motors come speeding from the direction of the stable yard. Roderick at the wheel, Mr Antipov in the seat beside him. Spraying gravel, the machine rounded the cedar tree and accelerated down the drive, disappearing behind the line of evergreens.

Eloise lingered by the window a moment longer, watching the rain on the glass; she heard behind her Dorothea get up from the table.

'I suppose I ought to pack.'

'Pack? Why must you pack?' exclaimed Elizabeth. 'You can't be thinking of leaving! Oh, Doro, you can't, you mustn't! You promised to stay for Roddy's birthday!'

'That was before . . . all this.'

All this, thought Eloise. But what was all this? Nothing that need concern them yet, she was sure of that. For once, she found herself in accord with her daughter: Dorothea must not think of leaving before her time.

Turning from the window, Eloise said, 'I wonder, Dorothea, if I might ask for your help? There's the matter of

Smith. I rather think he should come to Clifton for the time being. It's the least we can do.'

'Oh, Aunt, how terrible of me! I'd almost forgotten poor Jeff. Of course he must come here. I will see to it at once.'

All thoughts of packing were forgotten — for now at least — and Dorothea hurried away to make arrangements for Smith's removal to Clifton. Elizabeth went trailing after her, eager to 'help'.

Left alone in the breakfast room, Eloise gathered up *The Times* and took it into the parlour next door. She sat down at her bureau, opened the newspaper and looked almost reluctantly at the headlines.

THE GERMAN MENACE
EUROPE UNDER ARMS

Her eyes ran down the page. She read of the breathless anticipation in Europe, of France and Russia waiting anxiously for Britain to act. She read of crowds gathering in London, a concourse of people at the gates of Buckingham Palace in the evening. The King and Queen and the Prince of Wales had appeared on the balcony. The Prince had waved his hand.

'The Prince waved his hand . . .' Eloise murmured. She lowered the newspaper and took off her spectacles. A handsome and upstanding boy, the Prince of Wales, much like Roderick. But really and truly, it was all too incredible! Sat here at her bureau, with letters to answer and the accounts to look over, she couldn't quite believe in the crowds on Trafalgar Square, or the King and Queen on the balcony. The distant fighting in Europe was even less real, like something out of a story.

There was a knock at the door, discreet but firm. Mrs Bourne, of course. She always came at this hour. Whatever might (or might not) be happening elsewhere in the world, nothing interrupted Clifton's established routine. Eloise was thankful of the excuse to put the newspaper aside as the housekeeper entered the room. Mrs Bourne was dressed in black, with a bunch of keys at her belt. Roderick called her, behind her back, the Dreadnought — and there was indeed something majestic and indomitable about her: she was the unvarying Clifton routine personified.

In her familiar, clipped tones, Mrs Bourne gave her daily report. There was nothing untoward, unless it was that Mrs Roderick had not taken any breakfast this morning and was feeling out of sorts.

Mrs Roderick. Roderick's wife. No doubt, in time, one would get used to thinking of him as a married man, but it had only been six months and one was apt to forget. But that was neither here nor there. Eloise turned to matters at hand; the newspaper was on her desk as a reminder.

'It seems there is to be a war, Mrs Bourne.'

'I had heard it mentioned, madam.'

'We ought to be prepared.'

'My thoughts exactly, madam.'

'A list, then, Mrs Bourne. One can't go wrong with a list.'

* * *

A single list proved inadequate. It was necessary to draw up several: supplies they would need, tasks to be completed, all sorts of contingency plans. Mrs Bourne's well-known attention to detail was as invaluable as ever. Before the lists were begun, a telegram was despatched to Mr Smith, informing him of his son's accident, the message carefully couched so as not to raise undue alarm.

And so the morning passed in what, for Clifton, counted as a blur of activity. Luncheon was announced almost before Eloise knew it. There was lobster. But Roderick and Mr Antipov were not yet back. They returned later, arriving from Northampton with armfuls of newspapers, and brimming with all sorts of reports and rumours. These were discussed at length in the drawing room before dinner.

'It seems the government really has issued an ultimatum,' said Roderick. 'Everyone is saying so. If the Germans won't respect Belgium's neutrality, then England will take all necessary steps. But if the late editions have it right, the Germans are in Belgium already.'

'I don't understand, Roddy!' said Elizabeth. 'Everyone keeps talking about Belgium. What has Belgium to do with it?'

'I expect it's some plot cooked up by the Teutons, to get at France.'

'Oh, Roddy!' Dorothea looked at him, wide-eyed. 'A war between England and Germany? It's too horrible to think of!'

The Russian interjected. 'Do not worry, Frau Kaufmann. There will be no war. Workers will not fight. In Northampton was big demonstration—'

'Half a dozen people on Market Square!' scoffed Roderick. 'And they were blaming Russia for the war. Russia is Serbia's catspaw, they said.'

'Russia, is true, must take share of blame.'

'What does it matter who's to blame?' Roderick spoke rather sharply. 'This is no time for niceties. Your country is under attack. You ought to show a little loyalty, a little patriotism.'

'Patriotism! You talk to me of patriotism!' Mr Antipov was scathing. 'Patriotism is trickery, is ploy to dupe workers into fighting rich men's war. Workers will gain nothing from war. Workers should not fight each other. Working men of every nation must join together and rise up against oppressors!'

This sort of talk was Mr Antipov's stock-in-trade. Eloise was used to it by now. She didn't take much notice. Young men were all the same. They liked to draw attention to themselves. They liked to make a mark. Mostly, they grew out of it.

It was time to go through to dinner. Ordish's measured announcement brought a welcome lull in the conversation, which had been growing rather heated. Eloise hung back as

18

the others made their way across the passage to the dining room. A moment later, Roderick reappeared in the doorway. Their eyes met.

'What is it, Mother?'

'Dorothea, this morning . . . she was talking of . . . of packing . . . of leaving.'

'She will want to get back to that husband of hers.'

'Yes, of course. But . . .'

They looked at each other. His dark eyes were impenetrable.

After a moment he nodded. 'Don't worry, Mother. It will all turn out for the best. You'll see. Let's go through now. The others are waiting.'

* * *

'Why is this happening? It has come out of nowhere.'

Dinner was over. They were back in the drawing room. Eloise watched from the Eugenie armchair as Dorothea moved restlessly round the room. Roderick, too, was on his feet, leaning against the piano. Elizabeth was in bed, Mr Antipov elsewhere.

'Why, Roddy? Why are England and Germany at loggerheads?'

'To be honest, Doro, it's been on the cards awhile.'

'You said it would blow over. You said there wouldn't be a war.'

'A fellow can change his mind.'

'So you think there will be a war?' Dorothea fingered distractedly a brooch fixed to her blouse just below the stand collar. 'I'm sure that nobody wants a war. I certainly don't. And I know Johann will hate the very idea. Johann likes England, he admires England. I can't tell you how disappointed he was when he couldn't come with me on this visit. You don't want a war either, do you, Roddy?'

'It's not a question of what I want or don't want. The fact is war looks increasingly likely. That doesn't mean we

19

have any quarrel with your husband, Doro. I mean to say, he's more or less family now.'

'He's my family, he's everything to me. Which is why I must go home at once.'

'You'll find travel very difficult, if not positively dangerous.'

'I don't care how difficult or dangerous it is. I want to go home.'

'That might be impossible. Ships are being diverted, frontiers sealed. And even if you did reach Hamburg, what then? The German authorities would look on you as an enemy and lock you up.'

'Oh, Roddy, do you really think so? Are things really that bad?'

'You should stay here, Doro, until the dust settles. I'm sure your husband would tell you the same. He'd not want you to take unnecessary risks. Come now, Doro! Don't look so glum! There's still every chance all this sabre-rattling will come to nothing. But even if there is a war, it won't last long. Think of that business between the French and the Prussians forty years ago. Your Frog governess told us all about it when we visited her, if you remember: all that gumph about Alsace and Lorraine and the Battle of Sedan, and how her father was besieged in Paris. That was Europe's last major war, and it was a very short war. All wars are short these days. A matter of months at most.'

'Months!' Dorothea stared at him in dismay.

'It will seem like no time, I promise. You'll be back with your only beloved before you know it. What are a few months apart, when you've the whole of the rest of your lives to spend together? At least you'll be safe here at Clifton. You'll be safer than if you went back to Germany and got locked up. And it's not as if you need to worry about your husband: he won't be in any danger. He's a doctor — all but qualified. His job is to save lives, not to take them.'

Dorothea wrung her hands. 'I wish I knew what to do for the best. If only there was some way I could talk to

Johann. I'd feel so much better if I could talk to him.' She glanced at Roderick. Her eyes lingered. Her expression slowly changed. 'You never answered my question. Do you want this war? I believe you do.'

'That's absolute rot, Doro!'

'Is it? Do you remember the day after I arrived from Hamburg? We took Hecate for a walk up Rookery Hill; you must remember. You said you wanted more from life. You wanted a big adventure. Well, now you've got it.'

'I never said I wanted a war!'

Eloise could not help thinking that Roderick's protests rang a little hollow. She wondered if Dorothea was right, and that Roderick actually wanted there to be a war; few people knew Roderick as well as Dorothea. As she pondered over this, Eloise found herself gazing at the painting on the wall opposite, a classical Italian landscape, leafy, arcadian, at peace. Almost it seemed to be taunting her, a vision of perfection forever out of reach.

Roderick was trying to steer the conversation back in the direction he wanted. ('We're talking about you, Doro, not me. We're talking about what's best for you.') Eloise stirred and got to her feet.

'That's enough for now, Roderick.'

'But, Mother, I'm only trying to—'

'Yes. I know. But Dorothea must make up her own mind.' Eloise turned to her niece. 'Dorothea. Whatever you decide, please remember that you have a home here too. There will always be a place for you at Clifton.'

'Dearest Aunt, you've always been so kind. And you, Roddy . . . I'm sorry. I know you're only trying to help.'

There was a sudden silence. Eloise and Roderick were both watching Dorothea. All three of them were now on their feet, standing in different parts of the room, frozen in place, as if on stage with the curtain about to come down.

Dorothea sighed and the moment passed. Clutching her brooch again, she said slowly, 'I think . . . I think I have to stay here for now. I don't see that I have any choice. I must stay until things become clearer.' But she bit her lip, as if still in doubt.

Eloise felt the need to escape for a moment from the tension in the drawing room. She excused herself, went to the parlour, turned on the electric light, sat down from habit at her bureau. But she felt strangely out of place, and the parlour looked different somehow: she was not used to being here at this time of day.

The lists she'd compiled with Mrs Bourne earlier were spread across the desktop. Eloise fingered them absently, as she thought about Dorothea's husband and wondered if he would really think it best that his wife remain in England. She had met Johann Kaufmann only once, when he came to Clifton for his wedding two years ago: a very handsome young man, pleasant, well-mannered, conscientious. His father had also made a good impression, had seemed every inch a gentleman. Was one now meant to look on these people as enemies?

Men made such a fuss. They made too much of things. Politicians, leader writers — they were all the same. Even Roderick couldn't resist creating a furore. But when it came to the present crisis, Eloise felt that it was Mr Antipov — Mr Antipov, of all people — who spoke the most sense. One didn't give much credence, of course, to his high-minded talk of the working men of Europe joining as one, but he was surely right to suggest that war was something of an anachronism in the modern world. People in this day and age — it was 1914, after all — were too sensible, too civilized, too advanced, to have recourse to something as barbaric as war. Except at the benighted fringes — the Balkans and so on — Europe had moved past that stage; even Roderick had been forced to admit that the last major war had been over forty years ago.

The world was a different place now, different to the world she'd grown up in. Cooperation between nations blossomed as never before. Nations were inextricably linked in all sorts of ways: by trade, by travel, by postal services. Look at Dorothea, a perfect example: an English girl married to a German boy, equally at home at Hamburg or at Clifton. Then there was Mr Antipov himself, who'd travelled from far-flung Russia as if it was nothing. Was all this progress to be swept away in a moment of madness? Eloise refused to believe it. Europe, in a strange fit of absent-mindedness, had strayed to the very brink of disaster — or so the newspapers would have one believe — but common sense would surely prevail. Now that everyone was alive to the danger, they would all take a step back. The 'great catastrophe', as Elizabeth had so melodramatically called it, would be averted.

In which case, there was no need for these lists.

Eloise gathered the lists together. She searched out a box of lucifers. Crossing to the empty fire grate, she stooped to set fire to the offending papers, then stood back. But as she watched the flames leap, and the papers curl and blacken, she was overtaken by a sense of unease. She glanced at the window. The curtains hid the night from view, but she was aware suddenly of the darkness outside.

The last flame died. The lists had crumbled to ashes. Eloise turned away from the grate, a little ashamed now of her showy act of destruction. She couldn't imagine what had come over her. But all this fuss, it was a fuss over nothing, she had convinced herself of that. Europe would step back from the brink. There wouldn't be a war.

There wouldn't be a war.

CHAPTER TWO

Mr Smith arrived the next morning not long after breakfast. Eloise received him on the doorstep; it would have seemed unfeeling, under the circumstances, to have had him ushered into the house by Ordish. She shook his proffered hand and held it a moment, so as best to convey her deepest sympathies.

'I came as soon as I could, Mrs Brannan. Your telegram . . .'

'You were not unduly alarmed, I hope. But you will want to see him at once.'

'If it's no trouble . . .'

Mr Smith, for some reason, always reminded her of Lloyd George, with his grey hair and bushy grey moustache, his modest origins, his wizardly reputation: a reputation for motor-car design, in Mr Smith's case, rather than political guile. Eloise today was also struck by how long in the tooth he looked, like a man in his sixties rather than his fifties. He followed her into the hallway, holding his hat in his hands.

Dorothea stepped forward. 'I will take you up, Mr Smith.'

'How is he, Miss Ryan?' (In his anxiety, he'd obviously forgotten that Dorothea was now married.) 'How is my boy?'

'Jeff is going on very well, all things considered. We brought him here yesterday and made him comfortable. But the doctor is due any moment; he will be able to tell you more.'

Their voices faded up the stairs. Eloise thought it best not to accompany them. There was nothing more unseemly than people crowding into a sickroom as if it were a peep-show. As she made her way to the parlour, she reflected on the fact that Mr Smith showed no outward sign of his genius, less so today than ever.

Genius. That was the word Albert had used. Without Mr Smith, Albert had often asserted, there would have been no BFS Motor Manufacturing Company, for BFS was built entirely around Mr Smith's designs.

Albert's successful motor business had come about by chance, a chance meeting on a train. That, anyway, was the story as Albert told it. Not that there had been anything unusual in Albert taking the train; after moving to Clifton, he had travelled daily by rail to his work in Coventry. But when in a contemplative mood, Albert had liked to pick out a pattern in life, a series of turning points, which he saw as the workings of fate. How else to explain Mr Smith being in that particular compartment, on that particular train, on that particular morning?

'What was it, Ellie, that prompted me to start up a con-versation, when I hate talking to strangers on trains? It was fate, Ellie: fate. Like me and you. That was fate, if you like.'

He had been referring to the party where they'd first met, a party at her cousin Clara's house in Coventry; a party now lost in the mists of time, the cousin long since dead. Looking back, Eloise seemed to recall there'd been some sort of hint or suggestion that she might consider a match with Clara Galbraith's son, David. She'd been twenty-six and still unmarried, with time ticking on and her options growing ever more limited. Had this been spelled out to her, or had it merely hung over her like a question mark? All she recalled with any certainty was that she'd been very reluctant to go to the party. Coventry was so far away, she'd got nothing to wear, she'd not liked to leave Father when he was ill. But

Father had pressed her to go, and his wish had ever been her command, so she'd gone to Clara Galbraith's party. She had not thought much of Clara's son, but she had met there a man named Albert Brannan who was of rather more interest.

Less than a year later, they'd been married.

Immersed in a flood of memories, Eloise sank down absent-mindedly onto the sofa instead of taking a seat at her bureau, and she tried to pinpoint exactly what it was that had made Albert stand out in the crowd. He'd been taller than most, and well-built; rather stern, rather gruff, very plain-spoken; proper in his manners, but not highly polished. This was just a first impression, however. There was much more to him. His generous nature, for example. His generosity had often gone unnoticed because it had been of the most unobtrusive kind. It had shown itself — to take just one instance — in the recognition he gave to Mr Smith; he'd even made Mr Smith a partner in the motor business. Mr Smith, like many geniuses, had been as poor as a church mouse, and he might well have lived his whole life in penury, his talents undiscovered, had it not been for Albert and their 'chance meeting' on a train. After Albert's untimely death, Mr Smith had taken over as managing director of the BFS Motor Company, a position he still held. He owed his advancement in great part to his designs, of course. But those designs would have languished on the drawing board forever, had it not been for Albert; in many respects, it was true to say that Albert had made Mr Smith the man he was.

And what manner of man was that, precisely? This posed something of a problem. Mr Smith's position in society was distinctly ambiguous. He was not exactly one's employee, yet not entirely an equal. Matters were still further confused by his habit of making his sons work their way up as he had, which was why young Jeffrey Smith was here at Clifton at all.

Perhaps Mr Smith's status wasn't really important. That was what Dorothea would say. But old habits died hard, and Eloise liked to have such things clear in her mind.

Albert had approved of Mr Smith's methods with regard to his sons. 'It will do those boys a power of good!' But that did not mean Albert had envisaged a similar arrangement for his own son. Eloise was not entirely sure what Albert actually had envisaged for Roderick; he'd died very suddenly when Roderick was still a schoolboy. He'd never raised any objections to the idea of Roderick's going up to Oxford. But after Oxford, what? No doubt, in Albert's calculations, the businesses had figured largely in Roderick's future. But whatever Albert's plans for Roderick's future, it had surely never crossed his mind that they would be interrupted by war.

Eloise sighed. She could ignore them no longer, the headlines she'd read in this morning's *Times*:

WAR DECLARED
BRITISH AMBASSADOR TO DEPART BERLIN
BRITISH ARMY BEGINS MOBILIZING

Yesterday, it had still been possible to believe this would never happen. Today, it was beyond all doubt. The war had begun.

* * *

Mr Smith stayed upstairs with his son until luncheon. By the time he took his place at table, he seemed much more like himself. He'd seen Jeff, he'd spoken with Dorothea and with the doctor, he now knew all the facts. Mr Smith was like Albert. He preferred to deal in plain facts.

'So very good of you, Mrs Brannan, to take such care of Jeff,' he said as the hors d'oeuvres were served.

'It's the least we could do, Mr Smith. How did you find him?'

'Ah, well, you know Jeff, he's never easy to please, always grousing about something. His older brother, now — Stan — he's just the opposite, so easy-going that he needs a kick up the backside now and then. Curious, isn't it, how children can be so different. You must see it yourself, Mrs Brannan, with your two: very unalike to look at, your lad dark and your girl fair. I've five kids, as you know — two girls, three boys, the youngest just six — and every one of them is different. Jeff's number three and he's more trouble than the rest put together. Typical of Jeff to have got himself in a scrape like this. But it's set my mind at rest, seeing him for myself, and having a word with the doctor. And now I must be getting back as soon as lunch is over. Mrs Smith will be worrying. She was all for coming with me, but I said to her, "Hannah," I said, "you're in no fit state; you'll only make yourself bad again." All the same, I daresay she'll want the boy moved as soon as possible; she'll want him under her own roof — you know how mothers are.'

The hors d'oeuvres were removed, and Cook's braised chicken was carried proudly in. Cook was also a genius of sorts, especially when it came to chicken. Wielding his knife and fork, Mr Smith approached his portion with all due reverence. He pronounced it delicious after the first mouthful.

'Such wonderful meals you always serve, Mrs Brannan. I will never forget when I first came to tea — I came to discuss my designs with your husband, must be a dozen years ago now — I'd never seen so many sandwiches and cakes, and all of them quite delicious.'

Mr Smith was loquacious on many subjects, but as lunch progressed it was war talk that came to dominate at the table.

'Ah, yes, the war,' he said. 'Bad business, that. Won't be good for trade, mark my words. I was thinking, on my way down this morning, that it might be as well to put the new Mark VI on hold. We hoped to have it ready for the Motor Show at Olympia this autumn, but with all this ruckus going on, people will have other things on their minds than motors.'

'This war will be the making of us,' Roderick announced. 'It's high time England was shaken up a bit. The old ways of doing things have become stale and tired.'

'War brings only destruction,' said Mr Antipov.

'War brings out the best in people. Self-sacrifice. Heroism. Nobility. Everything that's needed to make a fresh start.'

'Nothing will truly change until capitalist system is abolished.'

'Listen to the fellow — the rot he comes out with! I do believe you're cracked, Antipov.'

'The carapace of my indolence has cracked,' said the Russian. 'Time for talking and thinking is over. Now is time for action.'

He used such extraordinary words, thought Eloise, 'carapace' and 'indolence' being only the latest examples. One noticed these unusual words all the more because of his foreign accent. His accent always grew more pronounced when he was impassioned, and his voice got deeper.

Roderick paused, his fork halfway to his mouth, and he looked at the Russian rather sharply across the table. 'Now is the time for action, eh? Is that what you told my wife, whilst you were ensconced with her all morning?'

'Rosa believes as I do, that war is criminal madness.'

'Rosa has enough to cope with, without you going on at her.'

'She likes to talk, she gets bored otherwise.'

'Too much excitement is not good for her, in her condition.'

'She is not ill, she is pregnant. This does not affect her mind.'

'I think I know what's best for my own wife.'

'Marriage is bourgeois despotism.'

Roderick said coldly, 'If you insist on taking that tone, Antipov, then I suggest you take it amongst your own people — though I don't suppose your utopian tosh will go down any better in Russia than it does here.'

Roderick and Mr Antipov glared at each other.

It was not unusual for them to cross swords. They spent most of the time at Clifton arguing about one thing or another. No doubt they'd argued at Oxford, too, which was where they'd first met. Their arguments sometimes got heated, but always ended amicably as a rule. Today, though, Eloise sensed there was more of an edge to their exchanges than usual; nor was she the only one who'd noticed this, judging by the sudden silence round the table.

The Russian was the first to look away. With a single shrug, he seemed to shed all his pent-up aggression, and when he spoke again he appeared perfectly calm.

'Is true that people in Russia are no wiser than people in England. I'm sure Russian people welcome war, though it will bring only disaster to Russia, as the last war did. What will happen then? I need to see for myself.'

'What do you mean, Kolya?' cried Elizabeth. 'You can't be thinking of leaving us!'

He smiled at her. 'We have talked of this, Leeza. I must go home one day.'

'One day, yes — but not now. Oh, please, not now!'

'Mr Antipov,' Dorothea broke in, 'surely it's too dangerous to travel?'

'I do not think is any big danger, Frau Kaufmann. Britannia rules the waves; this is correct aphorism, yes? And German emperor, he will not risk favourite toy, the Kaiserliche Marine, in open water. So to travel by sea, it is safe, I think.'

Roderick threw down his knife and fork. 'Of all the confounded nuisances, Antipov! Of course it's not safe to travel, any fool can see that.' He gave the Russian a hard stare before turning to Dorothea. 'Don't listen to him, Doro. He hasn't a clue what he's talking about — as usual. His head's in the clouds.'

Eloise decided it was high time to bring some order to proceedings. The conversation was getting out of hand. She was disturbed, too, by the way Elizabeth was gazing wistfully at the Russian; their use of nicknames just now — Kolya, Leeza — hinted at a level of intimacy of which Eloise had been unaware.

Her portion of chicken finished, Eloise placed her knife and fork at a precise angle on her plate and announced smoothly, 'I do believe Cook has strawberries for us.'

There was silence. She glanced round the table. Everyone seemed lost in thought — all except Mr Smith, who had a bemused expression on his face as he looked from one person to the next.

Finally, he spoke.

'What lively discussions you have at the meal table!' he said. 'Lively indeed!'

* * *

Mr Smith departed directly after lunch; Roderick drove him to the station. Eloise repaired to the parlour, having letters still to write. Barely had she put pen to paper when the front door bell jangled. A moment later, Mrs Somersby was announced.

She came sweeping in. Her vast hat, with ribbons and feathers, seemed to fill the parlour. She stood for a second, poised in the centre of the room, her hand resting on the long handle of her umbrella, then she sank slowly onto the sofa in an attitude of exhaustion.

She must apologize, she began, for calling at this hour. She had been impossibly busy all day, but she felt she simply must snatch a moment to enquire about the boy — how was the boy, the chauffeur? A ghastly business, most unfortunate. But the war — one couldn't ignore the war — what did Eloise think of the war? It almost beggared belief that this preposterous government had tried to keep England out of it. Thank goodness sense had prevailed! Now the whole sorry mess in Europe could be settled properly.

Mrs Somersby went on without pause. She was just this minute back from Lawham. She'd thought it prudent to stock up on essentials. She had taken the matter in hand herself — not everyone was lucky enough to have a housekeeper as reliable as Mrs Bourne. But what a morning! Lawham was teeming. All decent manners had gone out the window. And the cost of everything! Prices had doubled overnight — quite scandalous! Thankfully it would all soon be over. Mark had said — and Mark should know, with his military experience — that continental conscripts would be no match for a professional army like Britain's. The British boasted superior training, superior equipment, and had learned invaluable lessons in South Africa. Mark, naturally, had been in contact with his old regiment. His expertise and experience would be much in demand. He'd received no word as yet, but—

Mrs Somersby broke off, grasped her umbrella, got to her feet. She must go. She had a hundred and one things to do. She did hope the poor boy — the chauffeur — got better soon. If she could be of assistance in any way . . .

She departed in a flurry, like a great bird taking flight, leaving a gaping silence in her wake.

Eloise picked up her pen, then hesitated, deliberating. She pushed her correspondence aside. She took out some blank sheets of paper. In light of what Mrs Somersby had just said — and given today's headlines — she felt she might have been somewhat premature in burning those lists yesterday.

She set about reinstating them.

* * *

The lists were ready, her correspondence completed; Eloise had spent the afternoon profitably, despite Mrs Somersby's interruption. She took the letters, sealed in their envelopes, through to the hallway. There were peonies in a vase on the table; she rearranged them properly, and moved the vase an inch to the left where it ought to have been. The slow ticking of the grandfather clock was the only sound.

She stepped back from the table. The vase was in its place, the letters were ready for posting on the silver salver (Ordish would see to it). Glancing at the time to see how long until tea, she suddenly became aware of soft and furtive footsteps in the side corridor, as of someone anxious to go unobserved. Her suspicions were aroused. She waited. A moment later, Roderick appeared, treading warily. When he caught sight of her, he stopped dead.

If he was dismayed to see her, Eloise had the greater shock. She felt, for a second, almost giddy. Her son's face grew blurred in her vision as she tried to take in his dishevelled appearance. There were cuts and grazes, a swollen eye, a split lip. His hair, always meticulously neat, was tangled and matted. There was dust and dirt on his clothes. His jacket was torn at the elbow.

Roderick recovered first. He drew himself up and made an attempt, using both hands, to smooth his tangled locks. 'No need for any fuss, Mother. I'm all in one piece.'

He tried to get away, but she swiftly took hold of his arm. To have hold of him steadied her. She became business-like at once.

'You must let me attend to your cuts and bruises.'

'Mother—'

'Roderick, I insist.'

She was determined and he knew it. He stopped trying to pull away, he hung his head, he allowed himself to be led across the breakfast room and into the parlour. As Eloise pulled the cord, Roderick took a seat on the sofa.

Needing a moment to marshal her thoughts, Eloise crossed to the window. There was a tight feeling across her chest as she looked out at the lime trees that rose up from a riot of rhododendrons; a faint breeze stirred their upper branches. Slowly, her eyes focused in on a dim reflection in the glass: Roderick on the sofa behind her. How had he ended up in this state? He had gone to the station with Mr Smith and come back looking as if — well, as if he'd been in a war.

Still facing the window, she said, 'Who did this to you?'

'No one.'

She turned and looked at him. He was exploring his elbow gingerly, a grimace on his face. She caught his eye and held his gaze. He looked away.

'If . . . if you must know, it was that oaf Carter. He was waiting for me on the other side of the village when I came back from the station. He came out of nowhere. He must have been hiding in the hedge. He stood right in the middle of the road. I had no choice but to stop.' Roderick's hands bunched into fists and he said savagely, 'I shouldn't have stopped. I should have run the swine down.'

'Carter?' Eloise was trying to put a face to the name. There were Carters in the village, she knew that much; a rather unfortunate family. Both parents had died, and the children had been left to fend for themselves. Albert, for some reason, had got involved, had done his best to help them, providing the eldest boy with a job in Coventry, whilst one of the girls had been taken on as a kitchen maid here at Clifton. Then there was the boy who'd worked in the gardens as an assistant to Becket. That had not turned out well. The boy had been dismissed for stealing. But all this was long ago, before Albert died.

'Carter?' Eloise repeated. 'Do you mean the gardener's boy?'

Even as she spoke, it came back to her: it was Roderick who'd caught Carter helping himself to vegetables from the garden. Surely Carter didn't still bear a grudge after so long — eight years, was it?

'Roderick?' she prompted.

Before he could answer, someone knocked at the door and the housemaid, Hobson, came in.

'You rang, ma'am?'

'Hot water, please.' Eloise watched with irritation as the girl's eyes slid round to gawk at Roderick in all his disarray. 'A face cloth, Hobson,' said Eloise sharply, 'and some towels. Ointment too. At once.'

'Yes, ma'am.' Hobson curtsied, retreated.

'I don't understand, Roderick,' said Eloise as soon as the door was shut. 'What has Carter to do with you?' A sullen youth, she seemed to remember.

'It's not important, Mother.'

'But he can't be allowed to get away with it. He must be held to account.'

'I'd much rather you left it alone, Mother.'

'I don't see why.'

'Because . . . because it's not as straightforward as it sounds.' She gave him a look and he added hurriedly, 'Carter has got it into his head that I . . . that Hobson . . . that we . . .' Roderick swallowed, scowling hard, but Eloise remained silent, waiting, and he was forced to go on. 'Hobson is his sweetheart, you see, so some people might think him justified in . . . in . . .'

Eloise tried to take it in. Hobson? The girl Hobson? The housemaid? She'd been in this very room only a matter of moments ago. But surely Roderick didn't mean—

She looked searchingly at her son, wanting more than anything to be mistaken. He avoided her eyes. He looked shifty — guilty.

She had to sit down quickly on the stool by her bureau. She found that she was breathing heavily.

Roderick again took her silence as interrogative and he blundered on. 'She . . . she more or less threw herself at me, Mother. What was I to do? I know it was wrong, but somehow I . . . I couldn't help—'

He stopped abruptly as the door opened once more. Hobson was back. Eloise watched narrowly as the girl put a steaming bowl on the table, along with cloths, towels and a jar of ointment. She was a village girl, Hobson; she'd been at Clifton six, maybe seven, years. But Eloise had very little to do with the housemaids; they were Mrs Bourne's province — although now Eloise came to think of it, she seemed to remember the housekeeper reporting on more than one occasion that it had been necessary to pull Hobson up. 'Slovenly' was one word Mrs Bourne had used, 'impertinent' another.

The girl appeared to sense that she was being scrutinized. Colour flared in her cheeks. She slopped the water, all fingers and thumbs. She kept her head down.

'That will be all, Hobson,' said Eloise coldly.

'Very good, ma'am.' The girl scrambled out of the door. She seemed to leave behind her a trail of slipshoddiness, like the track of a snail.

Eloise sat down next to Roderick on the sofa. She reached for a cloth, wetted it. She held the cloth ready but she hesitated, her hand hovering in mid-air. She couldn't help feeling there was suddenly something different about Roderick, something more than the cuts and bruises, the dirt and the dust. It was like a glaze, a film, smeared over him: the taint of impurity.

She pursed her lips, tried to reason away her distaste. It was the shock of it, that was all. The shock of seeing him in this state. The shock of finding out that he — that he—

But you knew, said a voice in her head: blunt, precise, scrupulous.

No. She shook her head. No.

Yet even as she tried to deny all knowledge, she saw in her mind's eye the girl Hobson coming out of Roderick's room at a time of day when she had no business being there.

But that was months ago. It meant nothing. She had not given it a thought since.

All the same, she knew.

Oh, yes, yes, very well, she knew! She knew what men were like. She had not been deaf and blind all these years. She knew about those demons inside them, their fleshly cravings. The strongest of men could be weak when it came to those demons. Even Albert . . . even Albert . . .

Her skin crawled at the thought of it, the gross indignity of her wifely duty. Albert's kisses had seemed always to taste of stale cigars. His bushy moustache had chafed her skin. He'd grunted softly in the dark, like a boar in search of truffles. No words had ever been spoken during the unseemly act, nor in its immediate aftermath; it was never named, never alluded to. But it was always there: that coarse side of life was always there. And there were times when all the trappings of modesty and decency and respectability seemed too thin a veneer to veil such things from view.

Perhaps she was too fastidious. Perhaps other women found it less onerous. She couldn't say for sure. She only knew how she felt about it. She couldn't help how she felt about it. That was the way experience had shaped her.

And now her son — her own son — was enmeshed in all that too.

The scrupulous voice was uncompromising: she knew what men were like, why should she think her son would be any different? He wasn't, and she knew it. She'd seen the girl Hobson come out of his room, and he'd got Rosa with child when they weren't even betrothed.

Eloise straightened her back. She did what was needed, dabbing at Roderick's injuries with her cloth, gripping his chin with her free hand to keep his head still, and holding her inner self aloof.

'Ouch . . . ow! Mother, that hurts!'

'Keep still, Roderick. I must clean your wounds.'

She rinsed the cloth, then hesitated. Blood streaked the water and slowly mixed with it, turning it pink: his blood, her blood — for he was flesh of her flesh.

For a split second she saw in the water, as in a mirror, a vision of herself, younger, radiant, sat up in bed with a child in her arms. She had never liked that house on Forest Road in Coventry where she'd lived for a time after her marriage; it had never seemed like home. But that summer afternoon, the day Roderick was born, her drab little bedroom had been transformed, had been full of light and colour, as if she'd fallen into a Renaissance painting: the very image of the Madonna and child. Was it blasphemous to think so? Yet Mary, first and foremost, had been a mother too.

Eloise stirred the blood-stained water. The image shivered and dissolved and was gone. She rinsed the cloth and slowly wrung it out. She raised her eyes, and there he was sitting beside her, the child she'd held in her arms, the child grown strong and tall — grown very tall, over six feet; a man with broad shoulders and a strong jaw, with big hands and hairy wrists. His eyebrows, when he frowned — he was frowning now — almost met above the bridge of his Grecian nose; his eyes were dark and fathomless. What was he thinking about? Would she even want to know? On Saturday, he would turn twenty-two; it was twenty-two years since she'd held him on that August afternoon in Coventry. He was no longer a blameless babe-in-arms — but he was still her son.

She took hold of his chin once more, but gently this time, and she took extra care as she dabbed at his cuts and grazes. His fine, manly face was bruised and marred; she worked to repair it, feeling beneath her fingertips the warmth of his skin and the roughness of his shaven bristles. There was blood on his collar, on his tie, on his waistcoat; he was holding his arm as if it pained him. She eased off his jacket. She rolled up his sleeve. His elbow was a mash of skin and blood.

She rinsed the cloth again, applied ointment with a delicate touch — which made him wince nonetheless. But he did not complain now, sitting still and biddable, and staring down at the carpet.

After a time, he swallowed — it sounded loud in the hush — and he spoke again at last. 'I . . . I've been an idiot, Mother. I've let you down.'

'Everyone makes mistakes, Roderick.'

'I mean to redeem myself.'

'What's done is done. It shan't be mentioned again.'

'But if I'm to make you proud—'

'I can't think what you mean.'

'I must do my duty.'

'There's really no need. The matter is closed.'

'Mother, you know what I'm talking about. I can't sit back and do nothing. That would be . . . it would be dishonourable.'

'You can't simply drop everything, Roderick. You have a wife, there's a child on the way, there are your father's factories.' Everything had been arranged. He was to go daily to Coventry, to learn about Albert's businesses. He would, in due course, take Albert's place at the helm. It was what Albert would have wanted. 'You can't change your plans at this late stage.'

'Father's factories have managed perfectly well without me up to now, Mother. They can manage a little while longer. I spent so much time in the OTC at school; it would be a waste not to put all that training to good use.'

'Fighting must be left to the professionals.' Eloise found herself echoing Viola Somersby's words from earlier. 'They have conscripts on the continent, conscripts will be no match for the British army.'

'The professionals may need some help before they're done. But I need to get in quick. This hullabaloo won't last long. No one has anything to gain from upsetting the balance in Europe — not even the Germans. What'll happen is this. We'll all head out to Belgium, we'll bag a few Teutons, then the whole bally circus will be closed down and there'll be some sort of conference to iron things out. I'll be back before you know it.'

Eloise pursed her lips but said no more. He would only dig in his heels. She knew him too well.

She sat back, her work done. He got to his feet.

He paused a moment in the doorway. 'By the way, Mother, you needn't mention any of this to Doro — the fisticuffs and so on. She's always had a soft spot for Carter. She hates it when he and I come to blows. She has enough to worry about just now.'

He spoke as if it happened all the time — fighting with Carter — but probably he was harking back to his youth. He'd been rather a lively little boy. Nanny had struggled to keep him in check.

Left alone in the parlour, Eloise remained seated on the sofa. She wondered why Roderick was so keen to fight. She thought of his words at luncheon. This war will be the making of us. It's high time England was shaken up a bit. Was life really so stale that it needed 'shaking up'?

She looked at the table in front of her, where the bloodstained cloth and the bowl of murky water were evidence of Roderick's cuts and bruises. If such damage could be inflicted in a simple fist-fight, what injuries might he sustain whilst 'bagging a few Teutons in Belgium'?

But it wouldn't come to that. Mrs Somersby was surely right. The army did not need enthusiastic amateurs. Let Roderick find that out for himself.

In the meantime, Hobson would have to go. Eloise was quite decided on that.

* * *

In days gone by, Dorothea would have known there was something amiss; she had a sixth sense for such things. But at dinner that evening, there was no sign that her suspicions had been aroused and she passed no comment on Roderick's cuts and bruises. No doubt he'd offered her some explanation or other, which Dorothea appeared to have accepted at face value.

The problem of Hobson remained. Some pretext could be found for dismissing her, but she would not be entirely out of the picture, living as she did in the village. If she chose to tattle about her liaison with 'Mr Roderick', there was nothing anyone could do to stop her. This was why locals were always best avoided when it came to hiring staff: there was always the danger of one's private business becoming the subject of general gossip.

Eloise knew this. She knew it well. But sometimes the temptation was too much, when there was a reservoir of willing workers on one's very own doorstep. She had succumbed to that temptation more than once over the years. Now she was paying the price.

* * *

As it happened, the immediate problem of getting rid of Hobson more or less solved itself. When Mrs Bourne came to the parlour after breakfast next morning, the first item on the agenda was that Hobson had handed in her notice.

'She's getting married, or so she informs me, though to look at her you'd think she was being sold into white slavery. All puffy-eyed, she is, and miserable as sin. But there it is, madam. I'm afraid we'll be a housemaid short again.'

Hobson's decision was unlikely to go unnoticed. Sure enough, it was discussed round the table at luncheon.

'Daisy told me all about it,' said Elizabeth.

'If you are referring to the nursery maid, her name is Turner,' Eloise corrected.

'Well, I call her Daisy. Daisy once told me that Susie Hobson was waiting for someone better than Nibs Carter. Susie wants to marry the Prince of Wales, Daisy said.'

'Am I to understand that Hobson is to marry the Carter boy?'

'Of course, Aunt,' said Dorothea. 'Susie and Nibs have been sweethearts ever so long. I know, Eliza, that Susie is something of a flibbertigibbet, but I'm sure deep down she's as fond of Nibs as he is of her. They are made for each other.'

Eloise passed no comment, but she had her doubts. Why on earth would Carter want to marry Hobson when he knew exactly what sort of girl she was? And he did know, for that was why he'd attacked Roderick. Not that Carter himself was much of a 'catch'. Eloise remembered him as a sullen youth with an insolent, lopsided smile.

What good could come of such a marriage? Yet Dorothea seemed to think it a match made in heaven.

Roderick had nothing to say on the subject and he ate his lunch in silence.

* * *

Only after lunch did Eloise brave the newspaper, which she found in the morning room. It bore all the signs of having been pulled apart and reassembled several times. She opened it warily. The Germans, a headline announced triumphantly, had been repulsed from Liège. But, really, truly, where was Liège? Somewhere in far-off Belgium. Liège, Belgium: they bore no relation to daily life. What concern of Roderick's was Belgium?

Eloise put the paper aside, took off her spectacles, pressed the backs of her hands against her aching eyes. So much had happened this week — the fête, the picnic, Smith's accident, Roderick's misadventure, the onset of war — and it was still only Thursday. No wonder her head was throbbing. She got to her feet and glanced out of the window. A change of scene might do her good: a breath of fresh air, a walk round the gardens, it was just the thing.

She walked slowly along the cinder paths. The August afternoon was warm, but not hot, and rather overcast; the grey clouds hinted at rain. If she'd hoped to take the edge off her mood, she was sadly disappointed. She felt only a sense of frustration, seeing the gardens as they were now, and comparing them to how they'd been in Father's day. There was an undeniable air of neglect. Here, for instance, was the old croquet lawn, almost unrecognizable, overgrown and full of weeds with molehills disfiguring the once-smooth surface. The boundary wall, in places, had crumbled almost completely away; trees were encroaching from the Pheasantry. But what else could be expected from a gardener as old as Becket? He had to be eighty at least. He was half blind, partly deaf, rheumatic. There was a boy to assist him, it was true, but in Father's day there'd been a whole troop of boys; there'd been a head gardener, too, and an under-gardener, and there'd been a donkey kept in the stables, solely to pull the roller and the grass-cutting machine.

Yes, the gardens had been neglected. There was no denying it. For a time, the house had been neglected, too, during Father's last years and after Frederick had inherited. Following Frederick's untimely death, Eloise had returned from Coventry with Albert to Clifton and they'd been appointed guardians to Frederick's young son, Richard. Eloise had been painfully aware of the house falling into rack and ruin, but nothing could be done, Richard's trustees proving most niggardly. In the end, Albert had paid for the repairs; he'd paid out of his own pocket, another example of his oft-overlooked generosity. He'd done so for her, for his wife: her gratitude had been the only return he could hope to make. No one could have foreseen that Richard would die unexpectedly aged fourteen and that Clifton would pass, beyond all expectation, to Eloise.

Surveying the derelict croquet lawn, Eloise felt she ought to have given the gardens some thought before now. Money was no longer any object. The estate, it was true, brought in very little, but Albert's businesses had been doing well for years.

Roderick had talked yesterday of his duty to king and country, but there were other kinds of duty, equally important.

'One doesn't own a place like Clifton,' Father had often said. 'One merely holds it in trust, to pass on to the next generation.'

A new gardener, then, said Eloise to herself. Someone who could restore the grounds to something of their former glory. Becket needn't be ousted entirely. Indeed, he was as much a part of Clifton as the fixtures and fittings; he'd been here longer than anyone could remember, since Great Uncle Edward's day, before Eloise was even born. She happened to share a birthday with him, and when she was a little girl he'd got into the habit of presenting her, every year on the day in question, with a rose from his own cottage garden. This had become a tradition: every year a rose (except for her time in Coventry — but that could be safely forgotten), and now that she was mistress, she always reciprocated with a small token — tobacco perhaps, or a warm scarf for winter — always gratefully received.

So Becket must stay. Becket and his wife could keep their little cottage. The new gardener could be lodged — where? And how to go about finding, in this day and age, a gardener of Becket's calibre? Eloise sighed. Her fantastic schemes for restoring the gardens were already bogged down and she had more pressing needs: a replacement chauffeur, a new housemaid. There was always so much to do, which was why she couldn't afford to fritter an afternoon away on a fool's paradise.

She retraced her steps, purposeful, and only gradually became aware of voices ahead. The path from the croquet lawn curved through shrubbery towards an ornamental pond and a pergola. She could see the pond ahead, but not the pergola, where — by the sound of it — two people were sitting and talking. One of the voices was unmistakeably Mr Antipov's. The other was Rosa's. What was Roderick's wife doing out of bed? She'd been feeling under the weather these last few days; little had been seen of her.

It was impossible to pass without them seeing her. Why this should matter, Eloise couldn't say, but she found herself hesitating on the path and listening; she had no choice but to listen, when they were talking so publicly.

'Why must you leave England?' (Rosa's voice.) 'You have so many friends here. We don't want to see you go. How will you get to Russia, in any case?'

'Maybe is impossible. I do not know. I try.'

'But we need you, Kolya. We need you more than ever. Leo will need you, and Tom. They won't want to fight. There will be others from the Thursday Evening Club who feel the same. We should arrange a meeting. We can talk it over. We can decide what best to do to stop this terrible war.'

'No more talk. Is time for action. War will be . . . catalyst. Is this correct word, yes? In Russia last time, during war with Japan, there was revolution. I was there, in Petersburg. I was fourteen years old. Revolution that time failed. Perhaps now will begin new revolution.'

'Won't a revolution be just as destructive as a war?'

'To build new and better world, old world must first be destroyed.'

'Why not build a new world in England?' Rosa sighed. 'Oh, but what's the use? I can't organize meetings, I can't do anything — not whilst I'm tied down with this baby. Everything's going up in flames, and I'm trapped here in this backwater.'

'Then leave this place. Come with me.'

'How can I, when I'm . . . when I'm like this?'

'Baby is not handicap. You are not helpless because of baby.'

'But look at me! I can barely walk. My feet ache. My back aches . . .'

Eloise did not stay to hear more. She returned to the croquet lawn in a state of some agitation. Mr Antipov had said:
Come with me. And Rosa had not replied: *I can't, or I mustn't.*
She'd said: *How can I?* Almost as if, had she not been with
child, she might actually have considered it. Surely even a girl
such as Rosa wouldn't walk out on her husband after a mere
six months of marriage? Did she really find it so onerous,
living here? Did Clifton really seem so oppressive?

More disturbing to Eloise, however, was the hope which
had leaped in her own heart at Rosa's words. But to want
Roderick's marriage to fail was not only foolish and unfor-
giveable, it was in every way beneath her.

Roderick had been adamant about the marriage. He'd
come to her in the parlour last December and told her of
his plans. He'd trampled down all her reasoned objections.
He'd insisted there was no alternative. And Eloise, despite
her misgivings, had been forced to admit that he was doing
the honourable thing, now Rosa was with child. Better, of
course, if he'd not got in such a situation in the first place.
But— 'Boys will be boys,' as Albert used to say of Roderick's
childhood scrapes and misadventures.

Eloise had been aware, that day in her parlour, of the full
force of what she privately called her son's 'iron will'; she'd
felt it again yesterday, though rather more veiled, when he'd
spoken of going off to fight. He was more than capable of
managing his own wife — even when his wife was someone
like Rosa. So it was best all round not to interfere.

Eloise collected herself. She swept along the cinder path.
But when she reached the pond and the pergola, the bench
there was empty, almost as if it had been empty all along,
almost as if she'd imagined the whole thing.

* * *

Having dressed for dinner a little early, Eloise took her time
going downstairs, and thus it was that she noticed, on the
half-landing, what looked very much like a film of dust on the

portrait of Sir George Massingham, her great-great-grandfather on her mother's side, red-faced and resplendent in a large white wig. She ran her finger along the frame. Dust, undeniably dust. This was too bad; it was lax, it was slapdash. She would need to have words with Mrs Bourne.

Entering the drawing room, she found that she wasn't the first down.

'Good evening, Rosa.'

'Hello, Mrs Brannan. I thought I'd come down to dinner this evening, instead of eating in my room. I'm feeling much better.'

'Good. I'm glad.'

Eloise crossed the room and sat down on the couch by the French windows. This was not her usual place. She couldn't think why she'd sat here. What was it about Rosa that threw one out of kilter?

Eloise glanced at her daughter-in-law, who was stood on the Turkish carpet in front of the fire screen. Rosa's dark hair was rather carelessly dressed, heaped up on her head with strands hanging down. Though firmly of English descent, she had something of an olive complexion, which made her look almost foreign, even a little exotic. A dash of powder, a hint of lipstick, only added to this impression — as did her clothes, loose and brightly coloured and decidedly bohemian. As Eloise looked on, Rosa grimaced and rubbed her back, sticking out her swollen belly, making it obvious.

Belly. The word presented itself. It seemed to fit. But it was not a word that would have been used in the drawing room in Father's day.

'Roderick takes an age to get ready.' Rosa made conversation. 'Everything has to be just right. He's rather a perfectionist, I'm afraid.'

Thinking of the dust on the picture frame, Eloise said, 'There is nothing wrong in being punctilious. It's all too easy to let things slide, but that way leads to chaos.'

Rosa laughed. 'I hardly think the world would end if Roderick's tie wasn't perfectly straight, or if his shirt cuffs showed more than an inch. And there are some things that simply can't be helped. His black eye, for instance. He makes such a fuss about it. He thinks it spoils his looks.'

Rosa caught Eloise's eye, as if to include her in this mockery of Roderick and his ways, but Eloise could not imagine Roderick making 'a fuss'; he was not the type. And he was right about the black eye: it did spoil his looks.

'I offered to cover it up with some face powder,' Rosa added in the same tone of levity. 'You can imagine how that went down! Actually, I'm rather fond of his black eye. It makes him look disreputable, as if he were a highwayman or a buccaneer. Needless to say, I've no idea how he came by it. I'm his wife, but he tells me nothing.'

Eloise passed no comment and patted her hair, a habit left over from the days when she wore pads in her coiffure and it was necessary to check periodically that they weren't out of place. No doubt Rosa thought such hairstyles as antiquated as Sir George's white wig.

Rosa was watching her, no longer smiling. 'I may know nothing about Roderick's black eye, but you obviously do.'

There was a pause, as if Rosa expected her to say something, but Eloise could not think of anything she could say that wouldn't betray Roderick.

Rosa evidently drew her own conclusions. She turned away. 'Never mind. Keep your little secrets. I'm really not interested in playing games.'

'I can't think what you mean.'

'Tell me, why is it you dislike women who think for themselves? I've often wondered.'

'I have never said anything of the kind. But I do think there's a difference between a woman with a mind of her own, and a woman who thinks the world's in her debt, simply by dint of her sex.'

Rosa did not reply. She seemed disinclined to continue the discussion, which was most out of character. She grimaced again, rubbing her belly.

47

Eloise was displeased with herself. If Rosa was a little touchy tonight, it was only to be expected, given her delicate condition. Why get so vexed with her? Why let this happen again and again? True, they had different opinions, Eloise was ready to admit that, but it wasn't as if she subscribed to the view of women as weak and feeble creatures. Just the opposite. And often she saw the sense in Rosa's arguments, even when she didn't wholeheartedly agree with her.

Sometimes it seemed to her they contradicted each other simply from force of habit.

Rosa broke the silence. 'I think, after all, I'll have my dinner upstairs.'

She was about to take her leave when the door opened and Roderick came in.

'Where are you off to?'

'I'm going upstairs.'

'But you've only just come down.'

'I . . . I don't feel well.'

'Is it the baby? Do you need the doctor?'

'No, it's not the baby, do stop fussing. Everything is not always about the baby. There's more to me than the baby.'

Rosa brushed past him and left the room.

'Good Lord,' said Roderick, blinking. He shut the door, which Rosa had left open, then crossed to the sideboard, saying placidly, 'I swear she gets more fractious by the day. I'll be glad when this infernal child finally puts in an appearance, then we can get back to normal. What was it set her off this time?' He glanced at Eloise, his hand on the whisky decanter. 'Mother?'

Eloise kept her peace.

* * *

Next morning, at breakfast — everyone was present except Rosa — the newspaper once again was prominent on the table and its contents the only topic of conversation. A Royal Navy cruiser named HMS *Amphion* had been sunk by a mine off the east coast with the loss of over a hundred lives. A British battleship sunk in British waters with British men aboard. The war, which yesterday had seemed so remote — distant Belgium, unknown Liège — had suddenly come a step closer.

Eloise took her place at table. A note from Viola Somersby awaited her: an invitation to a first aid class at Brockmorton Manor.

'First aid!' scoffed Roderick, busy eating.

Dorothea, about to take a sip of tea, looked at him across the top of her cup. 'I think it's a sensible idea. First aid may come in useful. I shall certainly go.'

'Me too!' cried Elizabeth, with her mouth full. 'I want to learn first aid!'

Helping himself to more bacon, Roderick relented a little. 'If you like, I'll drive you both to Brockmorton, before I go off to make enquiries.'

'Enquiries about what?' asked Dorothea suspiciously.

'About how best to do my bit. To fight for brave little Belgium. To avenge the dead of the *Amphion*.'

Dorothea put her cup down with a clatter. 'It's no laughing matter, Roderick Brannan.'

'I'm deadly serious, Doro. A chap must serve his king and country.'

Eloise rearranged her napkin, watching her son, her niece: Roderick's country was England, that went without saying, but what about Dorothea? Did she still feel English? Or did she now consider herself German? Could one be both?

Such thoughts — such talk — at the breakfast table was rather disconcerting. Also, Roderick was being less than tactful with Dorothea. But perhaps he felt that being tactful was no longer entirely possible. The way things were going, one soon wouldn't be able to say anything in front of Dorothea.

Roderick threw his knife and fork onto his empty plate, and jumped to his feet as he swallowed his last mouthful. 'Come on then, you two: Doro, Eliza! It's time to go!'

Eloise said, 'Do finish your breakfasts first, all of you.' Roderick had cleared his plate, but Elizabeth's remained laden, and Dorothea, by all appearances, hadn't eaten anything at all. But Eloise could see she was swimming against the tide.

She tried one last tack. 'We haven't yet talked about your birthday tomorrow, Roderick.'

'My birthday's hardly important in the scheme of things, Mother. This is no time for trivia. There's a war on.'

Roderick hastened from the room; Dorothea and Elizabeth trailed in his wake. Their voices faded. Silence fell. Eloise slowly stirred sugar into her tea. This war. It was nothing but a nuisance. It had quite upset the usual routine. And now Roderick's birthday looked likely to be spoilt, on top of everything else.

She looked down at her tea. She didn't really want it.

As she put her cup and saucer aside, she became aware with a start of surprise that she wasn't alone. Mr Antipov was there. She'd forgotten Mr Antipov. He'd not said a word since she came into the room and he continued to sit there in complete silence. She found this faintly disturbing. Her eyes lingered on him. What was he thinking about? But she couldn't begin to guess. Those pale, grey eyes of his were utterly unfathomable.

* * *

The morning wore away. The house grew very quiet — so much so that Eloise, sat at her bureau, found herself side-tracked, listening for the slightest sound instead of paying attention to household affairs. But when her ears did finally pick up a faint humming noise, it took her several moments to place it. A motor engine, outside. Was Roderick back already? Perhaps he'd discovered that he wasn't needed, that the war could go on very well without him.

As she got to her feet, she found her mind racing ahead. All this silly talk of adventure could now be set aside. Plans, at last, could be made. There was Roderick's birthday tomorrow, there was the imminent child; the child's arrival would usher in a new routine, a routine which included Roderick going daily to Coventry to prepare for the day when he finally took the reins of his father's businesses.

Eloise checked herself. She was getting too far ahead. Nothing was decided yet.

She went through to the breakfast room, next door, which had been swept clean of all signs of their meal. The satinwood table gleamed. The japanned chairs were neatly pushed under. Everything was as it should be. A window had been left ajar, to let in some fresh air, and Eloise went over and looked out. A motor car with the hood down stood by the front steps, shuddering slightly as its engine ticked over. Eloise knew nothing about motors, but even she could see that this wasn't the latest model, the Mark V, the one Roderick had driven off in earlier. This was an older version, kept as a spare. A man was sat in the driver's seat. As she watched, he threw the door open and jumped out. It was Mr Antipov in his travelling clothes.

Puzzling though this was, it was nothing compared to the amazement she felt when she saw Rosa emerge from the house a moment later and struggle down the steps. Rosa was dressed in a buttoned coat and a flowerpot hat, and she was manhandling a heavy-looking bag. Mr Antipov ran to take it from her.

Eloise could just about hear their conversation above the grumbling noise of the motor engine.

'You are ready?'

'Yes.'

'This is what you want? You are sure?'

'Quite sure, yes.'

Mr Antipov led the way towards the car but Rosa, instead of following, hesitated on the bottom step. Mr Antipov turned back, her bag still in his hand. His keen eyes looked her over.

'You do not say truth. You are not "quite sure". You worry about baby, yes?'

'Of course I'm not worried about the baby. It's not due yet. And when it does come, I'm sure I'll cope. Women give birth in the most appalling conditions: in slums, in caves, under the open sky. They manage. So shall I. I am not a china doll, Kolya.'

'Then you will come with me?'

'Yes.'

'You will come to Russia?'

'Not to Russia, I never said that; I've made no promises. I need to get away first. I need to go somewhere I can think. I can't properly think at Clifton. I can't breathe. Once I've had a chance to talk to Maggie — and to Leo and Tom and the others — I'm sure I will have much more of an idea of what I ought to do. I've left a note for Roderick, explaining. It's not as if I'm leaving forever.'

Rosa appeared to be talking as much to herself as to Mr Antipov — as if, despite her words, she hadn't yet made up her mind whether to leave or not; her whole demeanour was hesitant and undecided. She stepped down onto the gravel, heavy and clumsy-looking, and she winced, swaying and unsteady on her feet.

'Give me your arm, Kolya. Help me.'

The Russian put her bag down and hastened to her side. As he took her arm, a look of concern crossed his face.

'You do not look well, Rosa. You have turned white.'

'I'm perfectly all right. Please don't fuss. Why must men fuss?'

Eloise had remained frozen in place all this time, standing to one side of the window looking out slantwise, but as her eyes followed Rosa's slow progress towards the motor car, some sixth sense told her that something was wrong. Rosa hobbled across the gravel, clutching Mr Antipov's arm. She was obviously in some discomfort. Mr Antipov opened the passenger door. Rosa lifted her foot to the running board — and then, without warning, she staggered back, letting out a sharp cry of pain. Doubled over, she clutched her belly and looked likely to fall.

Eloise did not hesitate. She acted at once. She got outside just in time, just as Rosa's knees were buckling. Mr Antipov was stood gaping — ineffectual, as men so often were in a crisis. Eloise ignored him and took charge of her daughter-in-law.

'Where is the pain?'

'Here — and here. It's — ouch, ow—'

Rosa's eyes rolled. Sweat ran down her face. She sagged in Eloise's arms.

Eloise's calm appraisal of the situation left no room for panic. Was there something seriously wrong? Perhaps not. Childbirth itself was explanation enough. She remembered, only too well, her own first time. A fatuous Coventry doctor had said to her, 'Soon be over,' and, 'You won't remember a thing.' So much did he know.

Mr Antipov finally found his voice. 'Rosa! What is happening?'

Eloise fended him off, holding Rosa, shielding her. 'Haven't you done enough? You must leave her alone now.'

'She is needing the help!'

'Not from you. There's nothing you can do.'

Eloise spoke sharply, annoyed with him, with all men. Why did they think it their prerogative to interfere in matters of which they knew nothing? But this wasn't the only reason she was sharp with him. Even in the midst of this emergency, she still had enough wits about her to see that he harboured certain feelings for Rosa. If she'd suspected this before, she was certain now; it was obvious, written all over his face. For a split second, she wondered what it was about Rosa that men found so alluring — Roderick, the Russian, and others too no doubt. Perhaps a woman could never hope to understand.

Eloise dismissed such speculations almost before they'd formed. She said to Mr Antipov firmly, 'Roderick will be back at any moment. I can't imagine what he'll make of all this. If you were intending to leave, perhaps now would be the best time.'

Mr Antipov stepped back smartly, almost as if she'd hit him. He looked at her for a moment intently, almost resentfully. A sudden spasm passed through him. His face cleared. He drew himself up.

'Yes. Yes, I understand. Is finish now.' His eyes were grey as flint. His voice was even more low-pitched than usual. 'I have been weak. I have lived comfortable life. I have let personal feelings get in way. From now on, I must be single-minded. I must untie my hands. Hereinafter, all that matters is the cause.'

Eloise was not exactly sure what he meant by 'the cause': they espoused so many different causes, the obsessive, earnest youth of today. Seeing him so stern and unbending, she felt there was something unconscionable about him, and for a moment she was almost afraid. All his talk of revolution and destruction: how much of it did he actually believe? How far would he go in the name of his cause?

But this was Clifton, not the setting for some fantastic conspiracy. He was Roderick's friend, not a snake in Eden. And the way he'd got his tongue around the word 'hereinafter' — the way he'd produced it with a little flourish — reminded her once more of his boyish enthusiasm for discovering new and obscure English words. He was only young, just twenty-four, still on the cusp of manhood. He had so much to learn.

All her fear, all her irritation melted away, and she said to him, crisply but not unkindly, 'I will look after Rosa now. She will come to no harm.'

He hesitated for a second, then he bowed to her. He could be like that at times: oddly, disconcertingly, formal.

'I apologize, Mrs Brannan, if I make trouble. Is not my intention. I will go. But first, I must say thank you. You are good person, generous, you make me always welcome, I always feel at home here. This will I never forget.'

There was no mistaking his sincerity. She was startled by his words, pleased by them. Yet she knew so little about him. She wished she knew him better. But it was too late now. She sensed that he'd burned all his bridges. Somehow she knew she would never see him again.

Rosa moaned in pain. At once, Eloise forgot everything but the present emergency. She looked round helplessly with Rosa shaking and sobbing in her arms, but just then Mr Ordish appeared, prompt as ever when needed: almost no time had passed since Eloise first hurried out of the house.

'Ordish. There you are. Mrs Roderick is not feeling herself. We must get her upstairs, and then send for Dr Camborne at once.'

'Very good, madam.'

He came running down the steps. They managed Rosa between them. Eloise barely noticed Mr Antipov turn away and climb back into the motor.

As Rosa was half-carried over the threshold, the footman appeared, followed by Mrs Bourne. Maids came running. All at once, the hallway was alive with people.

The front door was still wide open, but with so much noise and confusion, Eloise afterwards could not be entirely sure if she ever did hear the sound of the motor fading away down the drive.

CHAPTER THREE

Mrs Viola Somersby had, in her time, been the subject of a rather unusual number of fantastic stories. Eloise, for no reason she could think of, found herself considering some of the more absurd of these stories as she sat in the morning room listening to Viola expound on her self-styled 'war work'. It had sometimes been suggested, for instance, that Mrs Somersby kept a crippled husband locked away in the attics at Brockmorton Manor — or, more shockingly, that she'd divorced him. There wasn't an ounce of truth in any of this, of course. Viola was a widow. She'd been a widow since—

But Eloise could not pinpoint the exact date when Mr Somersby (not a cripple) had passed on; it must be — what? — twenty years ago at least. Which would account for the event being so hazy in her mind, Eloise realized, for twenty years ago she'd been in exile in Coventry following her marriage to Albert. True, news had continued to reach her from what she'd never ceased to think of as home, but there'd seemed little point in dwelling on it when (as she'd supposed) she had left Northamptonshire for good.

But if many of the stories concerning Viola Somersby were patently false, others were less easy to dismiss. It was hinted in certain circles that she'd once been intimate with a gentleman who, on occasion, had played vingt-et-un with the Prince of Wales. Nor was he the only gentleman whose name had been linked with Mrs Somersby down the years. In fact, one had always taken it as read — and with very little justification, Eloise had to admit — that Viola Somersby led something of a fast life. Viola had done very little to substantiate such an impression, but neither did she refute it. An air of mystery wafted round her, as faint and delicate as her scent.

The plain truth was simply this: that people were only too ready to repeat all manner of fanciful hearsay about the chatelaine of Brockmorton Manor, because they found her intimidating. They were intimidated, and they resented it. They sought to cut her down to size. Such was human nature.

Eloise, too, had been overawed in the early days of their acquaintance, Mrs Somersby being older, more worldly, undeniably handsome, and — it had to be said — sometimes rather acerbic. But sat with Viola now, all these years later, in the morning room at Clifton, one felt very differently about her. A four-year age gap no longer meant so much at their time of life. And though Viola remained a fine-looking woman, there was something a little desiccated about her these days. Her regal face had a pinched look, her skin was of a parchment complexion, and her once-elegant neck now looked rather thin — some were spiteful enough as to say scraggy. But if the years were taking their toll, perhaps it was little wonder, for Viola's life, whether fast or slow, had not always been a bed of roses. She'd lost two of her five children — both died young, though few people now remembered — yet she'd never fed off such tragedy. She went through life unbowed. Eloise was always reminded of that poem — how did it go? — something about treating triumph and disaster just the same: that was Viola in a nutshell.

Since the beginning of August, Viola had thrown herself into her 'war work', as she'd been explaining at length — knitting and sewing for the soldiers, learning first aid, singing patriotic songs, flying the flag. But she paused now in her monologue, smoothing her skirts, glancing out of the window, visibly gathering her thoughts. Eloise wondered if this might be an opportune moment to change the subject. Yet what other subject was there, apart from the war? The war came into everything.

'The Germans,' Eloise ventured to say, as the pause unexpectedly began to stretch out, 'seem rather more tenacious than one might have hoped.'

The Kaiser's armies were reported to be fighting stubbornly, though quite where they were fighting was not entirely clear. One moment they were said to be within thirty miles of Paris, the next they had been driven back almost to their own frontier.

'*The Times* gives so little away,' Eloise added. *The Times* — and every other newspaper. There'd been vague hints today of a violent battle in progress, the outcome in the balance. A certain phrase amid all the verbosity had lodged in Eloise's mind: 'the fog of war'. That was exactly how it felt — that one was blundering about in a fog, with no clear idea of what was happening.

'The newspapers? My dear Eloise, I never take any notice of the newspapers.' Mrs Somersby dismissed the press in the same imperious tone with which she'd dismissed many a mere mortal down the years. 'People are so much more reliable than print. I depend on Mark. He's au fait with all the latest developments. He has complete confidence in the regular army. There's some grand strategy, he assures me, yet to be revealed. In Mark's view, these new armies of Kitchener's are quite unnecessary — just a sop to public opinion.'

'Where is Mark now?' It was only polite to ask.

'At the south coast. His experience of the South African war is invaluable, of course, and he's been called to train the volunteers. They are all quite hopeless, so he informs me. Roderick, I believe, is also at the south coast?'

'Yes, he is. He was able to secure a commission in the Northamptonshire Regiment.'

Eloise glossed over the fact that Roderick's battalion was indeed part of Kitchener's new armies — the new armies which were merely a sop to public opinion — nor did she mention Roderick's letters home, in which this much-vaunted fighting force came across as the epitome of muddle and confusion. The men lacked uniforms, let alone rifles. They were sleeping in tents and cooking over open fires. The beach was their only parade ground.

Reading Roderick's letters — his large, sloppy handwriting — it was easy to imagine his disparaging voice, his scornful smile. All the same, he professed to be enjoying himself. A most singular experience, he called it: all the holiday atmosphere of the OTC summer camps in his schooldays, coupled with the organized chaos of the village fête. Eloise had been rather stung by this slighting reference to Hayton's annual fête, of which she was a leading light, but she'd forgiven Roderick his impertinence, for in the same letter he'd told her that the new armies would not be ready for months. At this rate, he'd lamented, the war would be over long before he got anywhere near the fighting. Though she'd been careful not to say so in her reply, Eloise could only regard this as welcome news.

Roderick had been gone nearly four weeks now. He was sorely missed, of course, but there'd always been certain times through the year when his absence was expected — term times at school and, later, Oxford. It would be a different matter if he wasn't back for Christmas, but Christmas was more than two months away; general opinion was that the war would be over by then. Some people were bullish at the prospect of an even earlier victory. The Austrian emperor was about to sue for peace, they insisted; the Kaiser was teetering on the brink, soon to be toppled by his own subjects; the Russian steamroller had all but reached Berlin. Eloise could not help but wonder if this great battle, currently being fought in the fog of war, might represent some sort of final denouement.

Her mind went back to the day of Roderick's departure. There'd been quite a crowd at Northampton's Castle Station.

A carnival atmosphere had prevailed. Soldier volunteers had crowded the carriages of a train stood at the platform. They'd hung, grinning, out of the windows, as women plied them with chocolate and cakes and lucky white heather. Children had raced up and down, waving little flags. A silver band had been playing.

At the sound of a whistle, the last doors had been slammed shut. The silver band had struck up 'Auld Lang Syne' as the locomotive belched into life. The carriages were showered with flowers. Roderick had elbowed his way to a window and leaned out, waving, as the train slid out of the station. Chugging, rumbling, clanking, it had snaked under the road bridge, rounded a bend, and swiftly disappeared. Off he'd gone, that jubilant September afternoon — her boy, her son, just twenty-two — off he'd gone to war, a war that had been unimaginable only weeks before.

'Such a pity,' said Mrs Somersby, 'that he had to go away so soon after the birth of his child.'

'At least he was here for the baptism.'

'Ah, yes, the baptism. I was sorry to have missed it. Couldn't be helped, I'm afraid. I had a . . . an appointment in town — in London — which I couldn't put off. But anyway, you're a grandmother now — as am I.' (Viola's elder daughter was a mother of two.) 'The child has been named Katherine, I understand? Katherine with a K. Not a name that runs in your family, I would have said.'

'No, it's not a family name.' In truth, Eloise had no idea where Katherine had come from, whether it was Roderick's idea or Rosa's. 'I don't see the need,' Eloise added, 'to blindly follow tradition.'

Viola laughed. 'Goodness me! What would your father say if he could hear you now? But you're quite right, of course. I don't believe in tradition either — only in some things.' Smoothing her skirts once more, Viola said in all innocence, 'When was it they were married, Roderick and his bride? It seems only yesterday.'

'It was January.'

'January? Well, well. How time flies. Old age, I suppose.' Viola laughed again.

'The child came early, of course. Brought on by the war, Arthur Camborne says.'

Dr Camborne had indeed (when prompted) described the birth in those very terms. He had also remarked that the baby was uncommonly large. But Viola surely knew — she had no need to ask — that not much more than nine months had passed even now since Roderick's marriage, and the 'early' baby was already several weeks old. Eloise was grieved to be reminded of this. She cautioned herself, too. Her old friend and neighbour should never be underestimated. Viola Somersby was still more than capable of letting off a sly arrow or two.

To all appearances, though, butter would not have melted in Viola's mouth today and, as if to belie Eloise's suspicions, she began talking about the new and harmonious spirit sweeping the nation. This was also a favourite theme of the vicar lately in his Sunday sermons. All divisions, all bitterness, had been healed, he said, since the outbreak of war. The endless bickering over Home Rule, the seething discontent amongst the workers: none of this seemed important anymore. The country was as one. The kingdom truly united. It was a new dawn.

Which was all very well as far as it went, thought Eloise, but this talk of a new dawn was somewhat premature. When the fighting was over, when the men were back home — only then could one begin to look to the future again.

Mrs Somersby got to her feet, all bonhomie, gathering her hat and her gloves, making ready to leave. Eloise rose too and rang for Ordish. He answered the summons with his usual alacrity, ready to show the visitor out. Mrs Somersby sailed from the room. Her voice resounded in the corridor.

'And how are you, Ordish? Mrs Brannan has just told me your news. It was the last thing I expected. What made you decide, after all this time? Ah. Your nerves. How awful for you. But what a lovely day! The weather this week has been quite perfect . . .'

Viola was gone, her voice had faded away, but her spirit still lingered in the morning room and, as Eloise returned to her seat, certain of Viola's remarks echoed in her head.

. . . How time flies . . . what would your father say . . . I never take any notice of the newspapers . . . you're a grandmother . . .

A grandmother, thought Eloise. Was that really possible? It hardly seemed possible.

I am fifty years old, she reminded herself. But that didn't sound right. She couldn't be as old as fifty. She didn't feel fifty. And she certainly didn't look her age; people often remarked on it.

She heard the sound of a motor outside as Viola was driven away (but Viola always bought BFS machines, she was loyal like that) and then silence fell: an odd sort of silence, almost watchful, as if the very walls were listening. Eloise, who knew Clifton inside out — every room, every corner, every stone — did not recognize this odd, watchful silence; it seemed something new. Could it be that houses changed over time, the same way people did? It was an unsettling thought.

Unsettling. An apposite word, when there was so much that needed to be settled. She'd yet to appoint replacements for Smith and for Hobson. Good, reliable servants were increasingly rare and hard to find. And now Ordish, too, was leaving.

Yes. It was true. After all these years, Ordish had handed in his notice. His nerves couldn't stand it anymore, he'd said. What it was exactly that his nerves couldn't stand had not been made clear. He'd never struck Eloise as the nervous type. She'd always thought of him, when she thought of him at all (he was a most unobtrusive man), as being steady, unflappable, a mainstay — the perfect foil for the hustling, bustling efficiency of Mrs Bourne. Eloise had assumed she knew Ordish as well as anyone but, when interviewing him about his decision to leave (she'd not been able to persuade him to reconsider), she had found herself at a loss, as if addressing a perfect stranger: a most disconcerting experience.

Ordish's imminent departure threatened to throw the house into disarray. It sometimes seemed to Eloise that she'd spent half her life trying to get Clifton into some sort of order. There'd always been something to upset her arrangements: she became enceinte with Elizabeth, Dorothea arrived out of the blue, Albert suddenly passed away, Dorothea departed for Germany, Roderick made a hasty marriage, war broke out. And that was not to mention the servants; the servants were a world of trouble in their own right. She had an uneasy feeling that Ordish would not be the only one wanting to leave in the near future. The tall footman would surely feel it his duty to join up. A strapping lad like Turner in the stables must be eager to do his bit. How would one manage in the event of a mass exodus?

Eloise could think of one possible solution. Mrs Somersby's mention of London just now brought to mind the London house that Eloise had inherited from her husband: 'Albert's folly', she'd called it, when he bought it on a whim (most out of character) in 1904. She'd soon grown used to it. London had a certain allure, and visits were easier with a house of one's own. They'd spent time there, the whole family, each summer, and at Easter too on occasion, but it was now two years since they'd last stayed there. Might it be a good idea to make use of the London house whilst the war was on? There would be several advantages. A smaller establishment could be run more cheaply and it would need less staff. The house had never been let; they could move there at once.

But was London quite safe? Paris, it was reported, had been bombed from the air by German aeroplanes. The Germans also had those strange gas-filled contraptions — dirigibles — which they called 'Zeppelins', and which they might use with lethal effect. Mrs Somersby had mentioned in passing that lights were now dimmed in London; this suggested that the authorities were taking the threat of an aerial attack seriously, though Viola had not seemed unduly concerned and it had not kept her away from the capital. What had she been doing in town? No explanation had been given. It was not like Viola to be so reticent.

Eloise sighed. She was letting her mind wander. What did it matter why Viola had been in town? As for going to live in London, it was out of the question. Clifton Park could not simply be shut up and abandoned. The London house might be cheaper to run, Eloise admitted, but she wasn't on the verge of penury just yet. Economies could be made, if and when economies were needed. Mrs Bourne was an expert in that department, knew how to get the money's worth out of anything, whether a tin of polish or a housemaid.

But none of this was of pressing importance and Eloise got to her feet, for she had work to do, the household accounts to inspect, correspondence that needed attention. Also, in a moment of madness, she had agreed to study a voluminous first aid manual that Mrs Somersby had left with her — heaven only knew why. Yes. There was work to do. And yet Eloise found herself lingering in the morning room, adjusting the curtains, fingering the leaves of the potted plants on the jardinière, passing from one thing to another, restless. She glanced up at a painting on the wall, a picture of a racehorse — the painting unlikely to be a genuine Stubbs, in Albert's opinion; Roderick said the same. Yet Father had been so sure. He had been adamant. Could Father really have been so wrong?

The glossy brown horse in the painting looked lean and sleek and powerful; its glinting eye seemed almost alive. When a little girl, Eloise had fondly imagined a resemblance between this aristocratic beast and her first pony: a staunch, solid, safe animal — or perhaps not always so safe, the way she'd ridden him. She remembered the feel of the wind in her hair and the breathless exhilaration of speed, as she crouched low in the saddle, leaning hatless over the pony's neck, digging in her heels and making him gallop faster, faster — everything her instructor, Clifton's head groom at the time, had told her not to do. When finally she'd come skidding to a halt back where she'd started, more by luck than judgement, the groom had glared at her, silent and reproachful.

But Father had laughed. 'That's my girl! That's my Ellie! How fierce you looked, just like an Amazon warrior — my own little Amazon.'

The pony was long gone, the head groom was gone too (there was no head groom in the stables now), and Father lived on only in memory; her riding days were long over, too. But as Eloise turned back to the window and glanced out at the spreading cedar dappled with golden autumn sunshine, she felt an echo of that old yearning for the wind in her hair and the fields spread out before her. Her riding days were over but she still had the use of her legs. Why not go for a walk? It was a long time — too long — since she'd ventured further on foot than a brief turn around the gardens. A walk would blow the cobwebs away, rid her of her restless mood. She might even go as far as the village. Why not?

On her way upstairs to put on her outdoor clothes, she almost imagined that her heart skipped a beat at the prospect of faring afield. But that was just silly. The heart of a fifty-year-old woman — a widow, a grandmother — did not skip. The girl she'd been, growing up in the 1870s — Father's 'little Amazon' — had been tamed and domesticated long ago: squeezed into stays and corsets, trussed up with knotted laces, wrapped in endless layers of clothes (one had worn so many clothes in the 1870s). That girl had gone, never to return.

* * *

Picking her way up the worn path, taking care on the uneven slabs, Eloise approached Hayton church via the side gate, having walked across the fields from Clifton. The church stood big and grey and solid amid the grave-strewn grass. Its squat, crenulated tower was draped in a thin morning mist that still lingered here in the village, obscuring the brightness of the day. There'd been a funeral at the church earlier, but it would be over by now; she was safe to go inside.

The funeral had been the subject of some discussion at breakfast that morning. An old woman had died in the village, an old woman of ninety-two, who'd lived her entire life in Hayton.

'I really ought to go,' Dorothea had said, 'and pay my respects.' She had been dressed accordingly, all in black.

Whilst walking across the fields, Eloise had tried to remember the old woman's name. It came to her now, here in the churchyard. Mrs Franklin, that was the name, or Mother Franklin, as Dorothea had called her: old Mother Franklin.

'You must know her, Mama!' Elizabeth had exclaimed. 'Everyone knows her! She's old, and wrinkled, and has no teeth. Can I go to the funeral too, Doro?'

'I'm sure Dorothea would rather go alone.'

But Elizabeth had insisted and there'd been a last-minute scramble to find some black ribbon for an armband. Dorothea and Elizabeth had set off, hand in hand, into the mist which, at that hour, had only just begun to clear.

Ninety-two, said Eloise to herself, making some quick calculations as she picked her way up the path to the church. The old woman had been ninety-two. That must mean she'd been born just two years after Father, yet she'd outlived him by more than twenty. Remarkable to think they'd both begun life in a world before Queen Victoria. Their memories, indeed, must have reached back as far as George IV. Mother Franklin's long life had encompassed the whole of Victoria's extended reign. Father, on the other hand, had not lived to see the Diamond Jubilee. What if he hadn't died? What if he'd lived until he was ninety-two, or longer? He might easily have been alive even now. One could not help but feel cheated, thinking of all those extra years.

Might-have-beens: they served no useful purpose. Father was dead, so was the old woman, that was all there was to it. Most probably, there was no one left in Hayton now who could remember the reign of George IV. And so a line had been drawn, marking the end of an era. Had Dorothea felt this, sat in church for the funeral? Perhaps not. The young had too much future ahead of them to bother unduly with the past. Eloise was sure that she herself had never given

George IV so much as a thought when she was Dorothea's age.

Reaching the church porch, Eloise lifted the latch and gave the heavy wooden door a push. It groaned as it slowly opened. She stepped inside the cold and silent church, and then hesitated. Now that she was here, what next? Why had she come? To commune with God? She glanced up at the vaulted ceiling: here in St Adeline's, one was exposed to God's unblinking eye — the stark, public God of the Sunday service, not the private God one prayed to every morning.

Her footsteps echoed as she walked along the nave. How quiet it was, how gloomy. The misty daylight was further muted by the stained-glass windows. She thought of the baptism that Viola Somersby had been unable to attend, the baptism of Roderick's first child. Nor was Viola the only one. The church had been half empty. Only to be expected, perhaps, under the circumstances. It hadn't detracted from the sense of occasion. The genial old vicar — he'd been at Hayton nearly a decade now — had struck exactly the right note, Eloise had felt. And the timeless rites — the rich and beautiful prose of the King James Bible — never failed to move her.

She ran her hand round the carved stone of the font. It was a gift from one of her ancestors: Sir John Massingham. (But there'd been two Sir Johns, and she never could remember which of them had made the donation, the seventeenth-century Sir John, or the eighteenth. Father could have told her.) Here they'd stood, grouped round the font on the day of the baptism, the vicar and the child, the proud parents, the godparents. Dorothea was one of those; Rosa's stern and colourless friend, Miss Ward, another. (Miss Ward came of the Miltons, a family with no pedigree to speak of, but reputed to be fabulously rich. Iron, was it? Or coal? Such question marks niggled.) Katherine's third godparent was a young man named Gosse, a friend of Roderick's from Oxford days — the Honourable George Gosse, to give him his correct title.

'A fellow like George is just the ticket,' Roderick had said. 'He'll give Katherine a boost in life.'

Mr Gosse had presented the child with a case of finest port — a sort of joke, Roderick had explained, going back to their time at university; there'd also been a munificent cheque to go with it.

Little Katherine had resented the whole procedure, the holy water most of all. The church had resounded to the sound of her infant rage. Roderick had been rather amused, Rosa less so. None of Rosa's relatives had been in attendance. Eloise was not even sure they'd been invited. In all the haste to make the arrangements before Roderick went away, Eloise had rather lost track of such things.

'I'm so sorry,' she'd ventured to say, as they left the church that day, Katherine quiescent at last, 'that your family could not be here.'

'Oh, well.' Rosa had shrugged. 'It's only a christening.'

Only a christening. That was Rosa for you. That was young people all over. Bohemian. Iconoclastic. A pampered generation.

Until now.

Leaving the font, Eloise went on to the pulpit and slowly climbed the creaking wooden steps. A bulky antique Bible had been left open on the bookstand. The parchment pages crackled as she turned them. She stilled her hand. Her eyes lingered on the page, on the centuries-old lines of print.

The Lord at thy right hand shall strike through kings in the day of his wrath. He shall judge among the heathen, he shall fill the places with the dead bodies; he shall wound the heads over many countries.

The words grew blurred in her vision; her thoughts were blurred too, running into each other like ink in the rain. So much for clearing the cobwebs.

She closed the heavy book; its front cover fell into place with a dull thud that echoed around the silent church. Holding the rail, Eloise descended the pulpit steps. She went back in her mind to the baptism, and to Katherine, who had very nearly been born on Clifton's front steps — for it had been a swift and straightforward birth; very different, Eloise admitted, to her protracted struggle in the little front bedroom on Forest Road, which had resulted in Roderick.

As she walked back though the nave, Eloise wondered if there hadn't been a change in Rosa since Katherine's birth. Certainly she seemed more settled now, though she had her own ideas about motherhood and wouldn't follow the proprieties. She refused to have a nurse, proposed to look after the child herself. This would have been unimaginable for a woman in Rosa's position twenty and thirty years ago.

'The old ways are the best,' Father had often said. In this case Eloise wasn't entirely convinced. What if she'd had more of a hand in raising her own children? But back then it would never have crossed her mind.

Katherine didn't sleep in the nursery. A cot had been installed in the room Rosa shared with Roderick. Roderick had objected. The child's squalling kept him awake, he said. He'd taken to sleeping in one of the guest rooms. But he didn't rein Rosa in. He let her have her head. And he was immensely fond and proud of his daughter. He definitely had a way with her. She would lie uncomplaining in his arms, as she did for no one else, whilst he told her to her face what a damned nuisance she was.

'You've turned the whole house upside down. A fellow can't get any peace, morning, noon or night. That's girls for you. Girls like nothing better than a fuss. A pity you're a girl. I rather wanted a boy. When you popped out — a girl — I'd a good mind to send you back where you came from.'

If Rosa seemed more settled, Katherine had surely played a part in that, but Mr Antipov's departure could not be unconnected. Mr Antipov had been a disruptive influence: not just with Rosa but with Elizabeth, too. On balance, it was better he was gone, for all that he was missed. There'd been something strangely appealing about him, Eloise had to admit as much; Elizabeth had actually shed tears over his going.

Roderick had been less perturbed. 'It's a rum business, his leaving like that, taking one of the Clifton motors, then abandoning it at Welby station. But he's a foreigner, and there's no accounting for foreigners. Perhaps he's come to his senses and gone to fight for Mother Russia; one can but hope.'

Eloise had her doubts about this. The Russian had always seemed the sort who would stick to his principles, and she rather admired him for that, even when those principles were entirely fanciful. But who could say what a boy like that would actually do when (or if) he got home? He'd remained an enigma to the last.

Eloise could only imagine that they'd never know what became of him, which seemed a pity. But that was the way of the world. Loose ends abounded.

Roderick knew nothing of his wife's failed plan to leave Clifton, that much was obvious. Amid all the chaos of Katherine's precipitous arrival, Eloise herself had brought in Rosa's bag from the front steps, and she'd unpacked it, too. It was whilst she was unpacking the bag that she'd come across the note Rosa had left for Roderick, sealed in an envelope and propped on their dressing table. Without thinking, Eloise had picked it up and put it in her pocket. Only later had it occurred to her that her actions could be construed as deceitful, covering up Rosa's intended flight, keeping Roderick in the dark. That had not been her intention. That had not been her intention at all. She'd quite expected Roderick to be in full possession of the facts before the day was out: if Rosa didn't tell him outright, then one of the servants seemed sure to let it slip and he'd find out that way. But the whole affair had quickly been forgotten — by Eloise as much as anyone — and the days and weeks before Roderick's departure had been taken up with Katherine, and the baptism, and his securing a commission. Eloise had never found time for a quiet word with her son and Rosa's letter remained unread. Eloise had it still, locked in a drawer in her bureau. Perhaps it would be best now simply to destroy it.

Eloise reached the main door of the church and opened it wide, then she paused and looked back — looked at the rows of empty pews, at the high stained-glass windows, at the expectant pulpit with the antique Bible on the bookstand. The words she'd read there were still echoing in her head.

. . . The lord shall strike through kings in the day of his wrath . . . he shall fill the places with the dead bodies . . .

She shivered all over and quickly turned her back on it all, pulling the door shut behind her.

Stepping out from the porch, she found pale sunlight now shining dimly through the thinning mist. She left the path and walked, step by step, across the shorn grass and the fading vegetation, weaving between the gravestones. She came to Albert's last resting place. It was marked by a grey stone with a simple carved inscription.

ALBERT HENRY BRANNAN
1846–1909

It had always seemed to her significant that one of Albert's names should be the same as Father's. It had seemed, in the days of their courtship, something more than a coincidence — though no one, as far as she knew, had ever called Father 'Henry'. He'd been known to close acquaintances as 'Harry', and this usage had gradually spread far and wide. He'd come to be known as 'Old Harry' in his later years, something of a local character, larger than life. Which was why his last, lingering illness, that so diminished him, had seemed unwontedly cruel.

These days — older, wiser — Eloise was rather less credulous and tended to dismiss her previous fancies. The confluence of the names was not really such a coincidence. Henry, after all, was not an uncommon name: eight kings of England, the current and previous prime minister, and her neighbour Lady Fitzwilliam's only son, all called Henry. As, indeed, was Roderick. But Roderick's middle name had been chosen purposely, in honour of both his father and his grandfather, a recognition of his family heritage.

Eloise, with her gloved hand, brushed the dirt and grime from the top of Albert's gravestone. Her venerable

71

Massingham forebears had ornate memorials inside the church, but Albert, she knew, would much have preferred this, his modest resting place out in the churchyard. He'd hated all fuss and frippery. Although he'd known his own worth, he'd never gone in for self-aggrandizement.

A mostly rational man, he'd poked gentle fun at her 'Henry' illusions, yet he'd never quite lost his belief in the pervading influence of fate. 'Me and you, Ellie. That was fate, if you like.' How many times had she heard him say that?

But if their meeting at Clara Galbraith's party in May 1890 had indeed been preordained, then fate wove a most tangled web, as she'd explained.

'Cousin Clara is the daughter of Father's sister, who married young and against her family's wishes.'

'Why is it so many women are won over by wastrels?' Albert had been thinking of his own sister, Dorothea's mother.

The case of Father's sister, however, was different. She'd not married a wastrel. She'd married a man who had later become quite eminent — a Member of Parliament, no less. But he'd been a Liberal — or a 'Whig', as they were called in those days — whereas the Massinghams, puritanical Parliamentarians in the distant past, had become respectable Tories by the 1830s.

'Ah, the murky world of politics. It's divided many a family, Ellie.'

'Father gave the matter a lot of thought in his later years. He came to regret the schism. Family is more important than anything, he often said.'

But, by then, it had been too late to heal the rift with his sister: she was long dead. He'd made overtures instead to her children, Eloise's cousins, who were all much older than her, Clara being one of them.

'I see now where this is going, Ellie.'

'If the rift had not been healed—'

'You would not have been at that party in Coventry, and we would never have met.'

'True, Albert. But, equally, if there'd been no rift in the first place, Father might not have been so assiduous in cultivating my cousins. It was Father who insisted I go to the party, when I was reluctant.'

'Well, there you have it! Fate, Ellie. Fate!'

Cousin Clara had married a man of property named Galbraith in the 1860s, and they'd set up home in Coventry. Liberal and forward-looking, they'd not concerned themselves overmuch with good breeding. Albert — hard-working, self-made, an entrepreneur — had been just the sort of man they admired, the sort that England needed in the modern age. Eloise had found Albert a very different man to Father — very different to all the men of her acquaintance — but she'd been drawn to him from the outset. Not that she'd held out much hope that anything would come of it. It hardly seemed possible that a man as eligible as Albert should have reached the age of forty-four unattached. And, indeed, he hadn't. But here again, fate — or blind chance, or providence, or whatever one wished to call it — had played its part. By the spring of 1890, Albert Brannan had been a widower for some ten years.

Standing all these years later by her husband's grave, Eloise wondered if people would think it odd that she'd never been curious about Albert's first wife, that she'd never felt any jealousy; but most people had no idea there'd been another wife at all. Albert had never spoken of his first marriage. He'd not been one for looking back.

She could just imagine what he'd say, if he were here now.

'You and your family history, Ellie! You spend half your life in the past.'

'It's the past that makes us who we are, Albert.'

'But it's the future that counts, Ellie. The future.'

Eloise touched the gravestone one last time then took her leave, walking round to meet the main path that led down to the lychgate. The gate clicked shut behind her. She was standing on the High Street. She was used to seeing it on

Sunday mornings, with people making their way home after church, and the Clifton motor waiting to whisk her home. Today, the street was quiet and empty, the only sign of life a dog, a rather mongrelly-looking thing, walking haughtily in the middle of the road. As she watched, it paused to sniff a certain spot on the ground, circling round the place with its nose pointed down, as if puzzled by something. Losing interest in whatever elusive scent it had detected, it took to its heels, loftily ignoring Eloise as it lolloped off on business of its own.

The village green was across the road, a triangular space of grass with an old well in one corner, and a rustic bench beneath a tall sycamore whose twisted branches were laden with fading yellow leaves. The green was bounded by the High Street and by School Street, and by a path that slanted between the two, running past a large, ivy-fronted house where the Miss Evanses lived, aging spinsters, these days seldom seen.

Eloise was about to turn away when a girl appeared from the direction of School Street and came racing across the green, kicking up the winged seeds which had fallen in numbers from the sycamore.

'Mama! Mama!'

The girl waved with one hand, holding on to her hat with the other, and Eloise realized that it was Elizabeth. Of course it was Elizabeth. Who else would be in such a tearing hurry? Who else would present such a dishevelled appearance? Her hair was escaping from under her hat, her black armband had slipped down to her elbow, her unbuttoned coat was flying out behind her. Dorothea, all in black, followed in her wake at a more dignified pace.

Elizabeth came up in a breathless rush. 'Mama! What are you doing here? I saw somebody come out of the churchyard, but I didn't expect it to be you! We went to the funeral, Doro and I. There was a coffin. There was a wreath. We went afterwards to Mrs Harris's house. She lives in a cottage, it's very small, and there were lots of people squashed in—'

'The family invited us back.' Dorothea joined Eloise and Elizabeth. 'I thought it only polite to look in for a moment.'

'Mrs Harris?' Eloise queried.

'The youngest of Mother Franklin's daughters,' Dorothea explained, as if it hardly needed saying, as if everyone knew, though Eloise was sure that she herself had never heard of Mrs Harris before.

Elizabeth prattled on. 'Mother Franklin has lots and lots of children. They paid for the coffin and the wreath, and the plates of ham and bread-and-butter for afterwards. Mother Franklin has hundreds of grandchildren as well, and thousands of great-grandchildren. There was a pot of tea and there was a cake, and Dorothea got given a present. Show her, Doro! Show Mama the cup!'

It was nothing more than an old pewter mug, rather stained and dented, but it might have been the Holy Grail by the way Dorothea handled it. 'This was among the bits and pieces I rescued from Mother Franklin's cottage on the day of the Great Fire. Mrs Harris said her mother particularly wanted me to have it.'

'What was the Great Fire?' asked Elizabeth.

'The Great Fire of Hayton,' said Dorothea. 'It was a long time ago — you were very small, too small to remember. But you must have seen the burnt-out cottages, opposite Mr Lines, the butcher.'

'Those bits of ruins, all grown over? I thought they'd always been like that.' Elizabeth lost interest in the Great Fire. 'Why are you here, Mama? You never come to the village!'

'I thought I would take a walk, to—' Why should anyone find this surprising? '—to blow away the cobwebs.' And it was quite untrue that she never came to the village, when she came every Sunday.

Why was it one could not do anything a bit different — a walk on a sunny day — without being made to feel . . . to feel what, exactly?

But whatever it was, this feeling, it melted away like the morning mist almost at once. The sun was shining brightly now, the High Street glowing with autumn gold, and Eloise found herself smiling at her daughter, at her niece, the one rosy-cheeked from running and all dishevelled, the other serene and sensible and so widely well-loved that she'd been presented with a special cup — a pewter mug which, whilst it was only really fit for the rubbish, had nonetheless been the treasured possession of a woman old enough to remember the reign of George IV.

'Shall we go back?' said Eloise. 'We don't want to be late for luncheon.'

From the High Street, they walked up a little path that ran between the low stone wall of the churchyard and the high brick wall surrounding the vicarage garden. After several yards, the two walls drew apart and the path ran across a patch of long grass which was scattered with blue speedwell and bounded by a hedgerow on the far side where red campion was growing in the shade. A stile led into Row Meadow and they climbed over it, one after the other, leaving the village behind. Eloise walked at an easy pace beside Dorothea, retracing her steps, following the footpath as it gently rose and fell over the field's low, grass-grown ridges, whilst Elizabeth ran ahead towards the next stile in the next hedge, where a line of age-old elms were still in leaf, their fading crowns raised against a pastel-blue sky.

Dorothea was brimming with all the latest village news. The young shopkeeper, Cardwell, had joined the army, leaving his married sister in charge of the shop; Hobson, the erstwhile maid and now married to the Carter boy, was already 'in the family way' (Dorothea used the village parlance). Eloise soon got lost amongst the many different names and the tangled relationships, but she didn't interrupt, for it warmed the heart to see Dorothea more like her old self.

Dorothea was a blessing, made herself useful in any number of ways. She'd always been good with the staff, settling petty quarrels, soothing ruffled feathers. She took charge of Elizabeth, she helped Rosa with the new child. And she'd travelled up to Coventry with young Smith, to deliver him back into the bosom of his family, where his legs were slowly healing, though not without complications, according to Mr Smith's latest letter (it was feared one leg might end up shorter than the other). If Dorothea was quieter at times, if she was more pensive than in the old days, it wasn't unexpected, for she had to be missing her home in Germany and her husband. But she didn't make a fuss — she'd never made a fuss over anything — and just how deeply the separation was affecting her could only be guessed at.

It was odd, thought Eloise as she looked at the elms and the blue sky, and felt the warmth of the autumn sun: it was odd how little one really knew about people, even the people one had known for years (Mr Ordish, still a mystery after twenty years' service; Mrs Somersby, wrapped around with so many tall stories). Then again, thought Eloise, what did anyone really know of her — of Eloise Brannan? Very little, in fact. Almost no one now remembered her childhood; her exile in Coventry was largely forgotten. And some things no one else knew of at all. Some things would always remain hidden.

They reached the next stile. As Eloise climbed over with a helping hand from Dorothea, Elizabeth came running back towards them, her hat dangling and bouncing on her back, and her hair flying.

'Doro! Doro!'

Eliza would turn fifteen in a week or so. She really ought to have been at school. There was an academy for young ladies in Northampton that Elizabeth had attended since last autumn, but when the new term started a few weeks ago, she'd flatly refused to go, and Eloise had not thought it worth arguing. It was so much easier to simply turn the girl over into the care of Dorothea, as had happened in the past. Dorothea, down the years, had been both nurse and governess to Elizabeth; she'd slipped so easily and naturally into the role that one had never thought to question it — not until Dorothea got married and went away. Elizabeth's education, to speak the truth, had been somewhat slapdash all along, but it was rather too late in the day to do much about it now.

'Doro! Doro! I nearly forgot! We didn't tell Mama about Joey Atkin. We must tell her about Joey Atkin.'

Eloise knew that Atkin was the name of the village blacksmith, once a familiar face at Clifton, in the days when the stables were less empty. Joey, it transpired, was the blacksmith's son, who'd joined the army years ago, not long after the South African war. He was, in fact, one of those professional soldiers who, according to Mrs Somersby, were so markedly superior to continental conscripts; he was, or he had been. For Joey Atkin was dead. He'd been killed in France aged twenty-eight.

As they made their way across the meadow known as Coney Close, Dorothea delved into her encyclopaedic knowledge of the village to supply further details of Joey Atkin's life. An only child, he'd been expected to follow in his father's footsteps as a blacksmith, until he'd happened to see some marching soldiers in Lawham, newly returned from the victory in South Africa, and he'd been bitten by the army bug. His father had been much aggrieved when Joey joined up. To add insult to injury, Dorothea added, the unfortunate blacksmith had later lost his apprentice, too — a lad named Young.

'I'm afraid that was Uncle Albert's doing. Uncle Albert lured Linus Young away to work in one of his factories. I remember Mr Atkin saying at the time that if Linus wanted to give up a good trade for the latest fad and fancy then it was his lookout. Actually, it proved a wise move for Linus. He's done very well for himself. He's chief assistant to Mr Simcox now.'

How Dorothea knew all this, Eloise could not begin to guess. Her own acquaintance with the village paled into insignificance next to Dorothea's. As for Albert's businesses, she had only a very vague idea of their structure and operation. With the factories as far distant as Coventry, it was all too easy to forget about them altogether. She knew Mr Simcox, of course, Albert's associate and right-hand man, but she couldn't ever remember that she'd heard mention of anyone by the name of Young.

'Mr Atkin fully expected Linus to come back to the village with his tail between his legs, but of course he never did,' said Dorothea. 'That left Joey. Mr Atkin still had hopes of Joey. He thought Joey would return to the family trade, once he'd had his fill of soldiering.'

'But Joey won't ever come back again,' said Elizabeth, wide-eyed and solemn. 'And now the war is real. When it's someone we know, that makes it real.'

Elizabeth was exaggerating; they had not known the Atkin boy — not really. All the same, there was something in what Elizabeth had said. This was not distant Belgium or unknown Liège, or even a ship sunk off England's coast. This was one of Hayton's own sons. Hayton was now within the war's long reach. And with Roderick in uniform, the war was even tapping at the windows of Clifton itself.

Eloise paused on the path to adjust her hat. Dorothea walked on a little way, before stopping to wait. They had reached Horselands, the last field before home, brown and empty since the harvest. The path ran like a stretched ribbon between the stubble until it disappeared into the clump of trees known as the Pheasantry. (But pheasants were no longer raised there. The old gamekeeper was long gone and had never been replaced. Albert, in any case, had never really taken to the country pursuit of shooting. That had been Father's métier.) Beyond the trees, there was a glimpse of Clifton, of its roof and chimneys, and a hint of grey wall: it spoke to Eloise of her parlour and the work she'd left undone this morning; of the drawing room and its glowing fire (always the best in the house); of luncheon being prepared in the kitchen, and the table in the dining room laid ready.

With her hat pinned back in place, Eloise was about to re-join Dorothea, when a flicker of movement caught her eye. A bird, it was, rising out of the trees of the Pheasantry, disturbed no doubt by Elizabeth's rampaging approach. Eloise watched as the bird flapped its wings and ascended into the pale sky, before gliding away towards the line of tall evergreens that marked Clifton's long driveway, their ragged crowns wreathed in lingering mist. The bird, to Eloise's eye, was a tiny blur of black and white. A magpie, she thought. Yes, definitely a magpie.

Something stirred in the recesses of her mind, one of those scraps from early childhood which persist in the memory — a fragment, a moment in time, detached from all else. She must have been very young. She'd been walking in the gardens, holding someone's hand. Whose hand? She could not recall. Some long-forgotten nurse or nanny. What she did remember very clearly was standing on the edge of the lawn and watching magpies hopping and flitting and chattering beneath the mulberry tree. She remembered her forgotten companion repeating an old rhyme, as they stood there side by side.

One for sorrow
Two for joy
Three for a girl
Four for a boy . . .

Eloise remembered that she'd needed help in counting the birds. 'One — two — three.' She had pointed with her finger, marking each bird off. 'Four — five — six.' Six magpies. Six for gold. She had clapped her hands with delight. But the magpies, taking fright at this noise, had flown chattering away, leaving her crushed with disappointment.

Odd, that she could still feel after so long the sharp sense of disappointment. The disappointment remained, when so much else had faded away. But that was the way with memories. So often, when one took them and shook them out, they proved to be as full of holes as moth-eaten clothes.

Hesitating just a moment longer in the thin autumn sunshine, amid wide and empty Horselands, Eloise followed the magpie with her eyes as it skimmed along the line of evergreens until, no more than a speck now, it dipped down and disappeared into the Spinney.

It was one magpie, alone.

'One for sorrow,' Eloise murmured, still thinking of the old rhyme.

One for sorrow.

CHAPTER FOUR

'Damn and blast! So much for a peaceful leave!'

Roderick struggled out of his greatcoat, fierce in his annoyance. Eloise had not waited with the others in the drawing room, but had ventured into the hallway to greet him, impatient for this, their first meeting in three long months. She found herself face to face with a different Roderick to the one who'd departed from Castle Station in September. Here was Second Lieutenant Brannan, looking fit and healthy and more handsome than ever. He was in uniform, his face was rather tanned — and he had a moustache! Eloise was rather taken aback by the moustache — by his language too, damning and blasting under the hallowed portals of Clifton Park. As he kissed her cheek in a decidedly swashbuckling manner, she could only pity any poor German soldiers who happened to come up against him; they would surely crumble in the face of such a fine specimen of English manhood. Not that Roderick was likely to come up against any Germans in the near future, or so he'd lamented in his letters home. He would remain safe in England for some time to come. To know this afforded Eloise considerable comfort; she need have no apprehensions about his immediate future. And so nothing could spoil this homecoming. In time, one might even get used to the moustache.

Eloise took Roderick's arm. They left Crompton — the rather diminutive, middle-aged replacement for both Ordish and the footman, Basford — shaking out Roderick's dripping coat and wiping, rather fussily, a speck from his military cap. In the drawing room, the fire was blazing, the fire that was always the best in the house. The wet and dismal December afternoon, fading towards dusk, was banished beyond the steamed-up glass of the French windows.

The others were waiting, queuing to greet him: Dorothea, Elizabeth, Rosa. He turned to Rosa last of all, kissed her on the cheek, but not in a swashbuckling way. He exchanged a look with her, brief yet somehow lingering.

Rosa might have made more of an effort, thought Eloise. She could have put on a decent frock, she could at least smile. But Rosa was a young woman of the modern type: they never put themselves out; they thought it beneath their dignity to make any effort for a man, a result of their suffragist views. Mrs Pankhurst had a lot to answer for.

Roderick settled himself between Rosa and Dorothea on the settee. He stretched out his long legs. His black boots shone. The tea things were on the table. Eloise poured, and piled a plate for him with sandwiches and cakes.

'Really, Mother,' he said, talking and eating, returning to his grievance, the news that Eloise had thought it best to break to him straight away, 'you could have put them off. The last thing I want whilst I'm home is to have the place turned upside down for a wedding.'

'If I'd known you were coming, Roderick, then of course I'd never have agreed to anything of the sort. But it's all arranged now. There's no getting out of it.'

'But why on earth did you say yes in the first place? The Somersbys of all people!'

'One could hardly say no. Brockmorton Manor is unin-habitable, by all accounts, water everywhere. Something to do with the pipes. Viola was beside herself.'

'Couldn't they postpone until the Manor is serviceable again?'

'There's no time. Mark Somersby is going out to France next week.'

'To France? At his age?'

'He is only thirty-five, Roderick. Not decrepit quite yet.'

'Well, lucky old him! Lucky old War Bore! He gets to go to France, whilst I kick my heels on the south coast! It's too bad!'

Roderick reached casually for yet more cake. For some reason, this brought a smile to Dorothea's lips: a smile, Eloise judged, of fond remembrance, something from their shared past. Elizabeth, meanwhile, was unusually quiet, watching her brother with wide eyes as if she couldn't quite believe it was really him. Eloise could understand why. His uniform, like his moustache, took some getting used to.

As she presided over afternoon tea, enthroned in the Eugenie armchair, Eloise did her best to damp down any exasperation at the way things had turned out. Mark Somersby's marriage to Eileen Harding had coincided most unhappily with Roderick's first home leave. By rights, of course, what Eloise in her own mind called 'this farrago of a wedding' ought to have been held at Newbolt: the ceremony at Newbolt parish church, the reception at Newbolt Hall, the bride's family home. Eloise had never learned exactly why — in Mrs Somersby's words — this was 'quite, quite out of the question'. Possibly it was a mere contrivance, to give Mrs Somersby complete control over the arrangements. Colonel Harding, a widower, was no doubt only too happy for someone else to take charge, and his rather timid daughter, the bride-to-be Eileen, was hardly likely to raise any objections. But once Brockmorton Manor had become off limits, the 'farrago' ought to have been transferred, bag and baggage — and without further ado — to Newbolt. Eloise had not stopped to consider this, when offering Clifton as an alternative. She had simply felt she should do all she could to help, times being what they were. It was too late now to have second thoughts, and it would have seemed churlish to express her chagrin at the way things had turned out.

Roderick, however, for all his complaints, did not seem unduly upset. Having drunk three cups of tea, having finished off most of the remaining sandwiches and all of the cake, he now got to his feet, yawning and stretching, his fingers, from Eloise's perspective, seeming almost to scrape the ceiling. (Was it possible to still be growing at the age of twenty-two, to be getting even taller?)

'I suppose I ought to go up now and make myself presentable,' he said. 'I feel as if I'm caked from head to foot in mud. There's so much mud in camp, it's impossible to avoid getting filthy. I do hope, Mother, you've arranged something decent for dinner. You can't imagine how much I've missed our good old Clifton dinners.'

Watching him leave the room, Eloise was more than ever vexed that they'd not had more notice of his coming. Everything could have been arranged properly. They'd have been able to make the most of his time at home. But something, at least, could be done about dinner. It was even worth the risk of upsetting Cook.

* * *

Roderick, now in ordinary clothes, ruled the roost at dinner. Even Rosa listened with rapt attention, for all that she'd mocked him earlier: when Crompton appeared in the drawing room to announce dinner, Rosa had stood aside at the door and bowed her head to her husband.

'Make way for the conquering hero!'

Roderick's eyes had sparked at her, then he'd laughed.

He'd yet to do any conquering, he told them over dinner. He was more of a hero-in-waiting. But there seemed little that was heroic in the muddle and confusion he described as the soup plates were cleared away. His newly formed battalion, after departing from Northampton, had arrived on the south coast in mid-September to find nothing made ready. There'd been too few tents and too few blankets, and only one dilapidated old shed to serve as both the officers' quarters

84

and their mess. Endless drill had been the only training, the only uniforms a temporary blue outfit which made the men look like convicts. Wooden dummy rifles had been handed out to serve as weapons; they'd mainly been used to fix up clothes lines. Washing and bathing was done in cold water, or in the sea. Their parade ground was a pebbly beach. In the balmy days of early autumn, all this had seemed a marvellous adventure. Then the rains came, and the camp turned quickly into a quagmire.

Weeks passed. Nothing happened, nothing changed. Incessant rumours did the rounds. They were going over to France next week — or next month — or never. They were being kept back to fill in the trenches at the end of the war. They'd been overlooked completely; everyone had simply forgotten they were there. The latter seemed most likely, given the chaos.

'There's only one thing we aren't short of, and that's musical instruments. The local Northampton papers, in their infinite wisdom, got up a campaign and, thanks to the overwhelming generosity of the public, we now have the world's supply of flutes, drums and trumpets. A battalion band has been inaugurated. The noise it makes is guaranteed to put the Hun to flight — should we ever get anywhere near the front line.' Roderick gave a sardonic smile as he reached for more bread sauce to go with his roast pheasant. '"Gentlemen in England now a-bed,"' he quoted, '" shall think themselves accursed they were not here."'

'You seem very cheerful, Roddy, despite it all,' said Dorothea.

'I'm enjoying myself immensely. One even gets used to the mud after a time. But from next week, we shall be living in the lap of luxury. We are going into billets. Why we couldn't have been billeted from the start is a mystery. That's the army all over.'

'You certainly look well on it, muddle or no muddle.'

'I feel well, too, Doro, fit as a fiddle. I'm straining at the leash, of course, but one must just be patient.'

'Being patient,' said Rosa, 'is not exactly your forte.'

He grinned at her across the table. 'How well you know me, darling.'

Dinner was over. They returned to the drawing room for coffee. The fire had been built up and the curtains closed. The electric lights were glowing. The war, which had loomed so large during the momentous events of August and all through thrilling September, seemed now, on this dark December evening, impossibly remote. In spite of the many auguries of doom, they'd barely been touched in their corner of Northamptonshire. There was the blacksmith's son, of course. But, when all was said and done, he was just one boy out of a whole village.

Roderick was of the opinion that the war had got 'bogged down and boring'. All the fun had gone out of it. Neither side had much left to gain. Perhaps it really would be over by Christmas.

'I jolly well hope not,' he added. 'Not before I've had a chance to be "up and at 'em". Do you know, all this time spent kicking my heels, it reminds me of school, of biding my time until I had a chance at the House Eleven. I used to dream in the dorm every night of the House Eleven.'

The Eleven, the Fifteen: one was the cricket team, the other rugby football, but Eloise could never remember which was which and she didn't like to show her ignorance by asking. Roderick had made quite a name for himself playing games at his school, Downfield, she knew that much.

'I was a hopeless little squirt, of course, when I first went up to Downfield,' he continued, 'but I had ambitions. Raynes was head of house and captain of the Eleven. We considered him a god among men. But he wouldn't so much as consider me until I was in a fit state — and quite right, too. I had to wait a devil of a time to get on the team. I thought my chance would never come. And it's the same now, waiting to get out to the front. The only difference is that the Eleven was always there, from one year to the next, whereas the war . . . well, all I can say is that I'll feel an awful slacker if I don't get to do anything. I say. I wonder whatever happened to old Raynes? We rather lost touch.'

Roderick blew out his cheeks, looked round at them.

'Enough about the war. Let's talk about home. What have you all been doing since I went away? I feel horribly behind the times. My offspring has grown so much, I barely recognize her.'

'A nurse is what Katherine needs.' Eloise couldn't stop herself from bringing up this bone of contention. Rosa was adamant that Katherine did not need a nurse.

'Oh, I don't know, Mother. If Rosa's happy to skivvy, then let her, I say.'

'Being a mother,' Rosa corrected, 'is not the same as being a skivvy. Motherhood is a vocation, not a line of work. And you really shouldn't be so scathing of "skivvies". You couldn't live as you do without them — none of us could.'

'Is that right? I do so love it, darling, when you start on with all your socialist nonsense. So very droll, and most entertaining. It's the reason I married you.'

Rosa raised an eyebrow. 'The only reason?' she said drily.

'There may have been others. I forget.'

He grinned at her, in the same way he'd grinned at dinner when she made the remark about his lack of patience, but this time he looked, if anything, even more wolfish; there was a glint in his eye that seemed entirely out of place in the chaste surroundings of the drawing room.

'Now I come to think of it,' he added, holding Rosa's gaze, 'you did scrub my back most satisfactorily when I was in my bath earlier. Such a good little wifey, you are! Did you used to scrub Father's back, Mother, when he was in his bath?'

Eloise did not deign to answer. The question seemed to her almost indecent. Roderick's short time in the army appeared to have coarsened him. Rosa obviously thought so, too. She, at least, had the good grace to blush.

'You can scrub your own back next time,' she muttered, giving him a hard stare.

Roderick was unabashed. His grin grew ever wider until it broke off into a yawn. He yawned like a cavern, then he said rather sleepily, 'I say, is it true Ordish has left us? It was in your letter, Mother, and in yours, Doro, but I couldn't quite believe it. Ordish has always been here. He's been here forever. He'd no business leaving. You might have tried to keep him. Who is the midget that's replaced him? And where's John?'

'Crompton is not a midget, he is almost as tall as I am,' said Dorothea, taking Roderick to task as she'd done so often down the years — though rather less forcefully than she might have done. 'As for Basford, he's gone, he volunteered.'

'And his name is Herbert, not John,' Elizabeth interrupted. 'It's rude to call him John.'

'I agree, Eliza,' said Rosa. 'Not to call a person by their right name — it's somewhat medieval, if not positively despotic.'

Eloise wondered if this jibe was directed at her, tit-for-tat after her earlier comment about employing a nurse. But Rosa didn't understand about the rituals that grew up over time in a house like Clifton; she didn't realize what those rituals meant to the place. The footman wasn't called 'John' on a whim. It was tradition, the name a title, a badge of honour, a sign of acceptance. Any footman worth his salt would be proud to be John, and rightly so — to be the latest in a long line of Johns stretching back into the hallowed years. The most recent John had looked the part too, so tall and personable: the very embodiment of 'John'. A pity he'd decided to leave, but inevitable, the way things were.

If Rosa didn't understand all this, she at least had the excuse of being an outsider. Elizabeth, born and bred at Clifton, had no such excuse. Why must she be so contrary? She said, in her own defence, that she was only doing as Dorothea did. But there was a world of difference. Being overfamiliar always came with a risk, yet somehow Dorothea got round it. When Dorothea called the servants by their Christian names, it sounded natural; it was entirely unaffected. She never lowered herself. She didn't try too hard. She never came across as ingratiating, the way Elizabeth did. But Elizabeth appeared to revel in being contrary, all the more so now she had Rosa to encourage her.

Eloise, nonetheless, thought it wisest to let Rosa's remark pass. It wouldn't do to get into a quarrel — or what Rosa called 'a discussion' — on Roderick's first night home. In any case, it was a moot point, as there was no John now. Crompton, being a replacement for Ordish as well as Basford, did not qualify.

Roderick got to his feet, yawning hugely again and not bothering to cover his mouth. 'If it's all the same to you lot, I think I'll turn in. I've been awake since the crack of dawn and I'm about ready to drop.'

He said goodnight. Rosa did too. Watching them go, Eloise was irritated by the way Rosa seemed to find it necessary to follow Roderick around as if she were his dog, Hecate — or as if she were a grasping child, wanting more, more, more; wanting Roderick all to herself.

Catching sight of her daughter, Eloise said crisply, 'It is time you were in bed too, Elizabeth.'

'Oh, Mama—'

But Eloise would brook no argument.

Dorothea went up with Elizabeth as usual (did a girl of fifteen really need 'tucking in'?), but before she left the room, she looked back and said, 'Oh, Aunt! Isn't it wonderful having Roddy home?'

As Dorothea closed the door behind her, Eloise was suffused with warm feelings towards her niece, whose love for Roderick was pure and unselfish — an honest love — not that of a grasping child.

But it wasn't entirely fair to be so hard on Rosa. Dorothea certainly wouldn't think it was. Roderick was Rosa's husband, after all; she had first claim on him. That was what Dorothea would say. Why couldn't one be more like Dorothea, Eloise asked herself: unselfish, forgiving, endlessly patient?

They had been much in each other's company these last few months. They had often sat in the drawing room of an evening, just the two of them, whilst Rosa was busy elsewhere, upstairs with the baby, or reading in the library: a distant presence in the house. They had found comfort in each other, or at least Eloise liked to think so; she hoped Dorothea felt as she did, but it was not always easy to tell.

Dorothea had been desperately worried for a time about her husband, and what he would think of her decision to stay in England. Then a letter had arrived, a letter from Johann which he'd sent via Switzerland, forwarded by the proprietor of the Gasthaus where Roderick, Dorothea and Elizabeth had stayed during their continental holiday in 1910. It was at this Gasthaus that Dorothea had first met Johann; they'd returned there two years later on their wedding trip. That the proprietor should put himself out and act as intermediary in Dorothea's correspondence with Hamburg was most considerate of him, though not at all surprising. People often went out of their way to help Dorothea.

Letters to and from Johann were subject to lengthy delays and the attentions of the censor. Eloise could only imagine what those letters contained, but it seemed that Johann approved of his wife's decision to remain for the time being in England, which had set Dorothea's mind at rest somewhat, but to be apart couldn't be easy. Dorothea, of course, didn't complain.

Eloise had always thought of Johann Kaufmann as level-headed and dependable. That didn't change just because of the war; he was still the same man. But he was German — there was no getting away from it — and that made things awkward. Still, there was no need to think of him as the enemy, not exactly. Eloise gathered that he was serving in some sort of medical corps — or whatever they called such things in Germany — which meant that when (or if) Roderick reached the firing line, Johann would not be among those trying to kill him.

Eloise shuddered. Why dwell on such things? It was far too morbid. Roderick wasn't at the front, he was safe in England. He was safe and at home, taller and stronger and more handsome than ever — and with a moustache! Eloise furrowed her brow. Roderick's moustache, new and unexpected, gave her nonetheless a strange feeling of déjà vu. Albert had worn a moustache, of course, but his had been thick and bushy and grey, quite unlike Roderick's neat, trimmed production.

Eloise suddenly realized. It wasn't Albert she was reminded of, seeing Roderick's moustache. It was Frederick — her brother, Frederick.

Poor, dear Frederick, who'd been dead these nineteen years.

* * *

Eloise next morning, after breakfast, repaired to the parlour to examine the household accounts. Vigilance was needed. The staff were apt to be profligate. They used cloths, dusters, tins of polish as if they grew on trees. Today, though — and despite careful scrutiny — she could find no evidence of waste. How, then, to explain this figure here? Why was it so high?

She sighed, taking off her spectacles, rubbing her temples. The accounts would have to wait. She would unravel them later. More pressing was yet another missive from Viola Somersby. Some might have accused Mrs Somersby of being over-particular, but Eloise was determined that there should be no cause for finding fault with Clifton as a setting for the wedding reception.

She was about to make a start on a response, when there was a knock on the door. She looked up, exasperated, hating any interruption when she was working. But when the door opened, it was Roderick who came in, and Eloise put her work aside at once. One had to make the most of Roderick whilst he was at home.

He looked much more like his old self this morning, apart from the moustache. He'd always taken pride in his appearance. His tie was perfectly straight, his dark hair brushed and brilliantined, his face — tanned from so much outdoor living — scrubbed and shaven.

'What-ho, Mother. Keeping busy?'

He thrust his hands into his pockets as he walked round the room, his arms holding his jacket open, a loop of watch chain gleaming on his plain grey waistcoat. He came to rest by the window and she sensed that he'd come to her with no particular purpose in mind. For some reason, she took pleasure in this. She joined him by the window and they watched the rain come down.

His hand went up to his moustache, perhaps to check it was there, for the novelty of it must not yet have worn off, but the mannerism reminded Eloise sharply of Albert, who'd had a habit of smoothing his moustache in exactly the same way. Roderick resembled his father as much as anyone. For all his moustache reminded her of Frederick, the two of them were not otherwise alike. Frederick had been slim, slight, fair-haired; Roderick was tall, dark, athletic. She liked to think she could see something of Father in him. Certainly he had her father's pride and self-assurance — his occasional haughtiness, too.

Roderick's voice broke in on her thoughts. 'What a filthy day. Absolutely filthy. I'd hoped for a hack on Conquest, but not in this. Thank God we're moving into billets next week — the camp will be uninhabitable.' He frowned, touching his moustache again. 'What's all this I've been hearing from Rosa, Mother? Something about Doro and the police. I'm sure Rosa must have it wrong.'

'No, Roderick, I'm afraid it's true. Dorothea is required to register with the police.'

'What on earth do the police want with Doro? Explain, Mother!'

'It came as a shock to us all, but Dorothea is married to a German and so she's considered an enemy alien. As such, not only does she have to register with the police, she also has to obtain official permission before she can travel.'

'An enemy alien? But that's absurd! I've never heard any-thing so ridiculous!'

That had been Eloise's immediate reaction, too. Deeply offended on Dorothea's behalf, she had even gone so far as to write to David Galbraith, the son of her long-dead cousin Clara and the man she might have married. She'd kept up a desultory correspondence with him over the years, as one did with distant relatives, and this had finally come in useful, for David Galbraith was now high up at the Home Office — a 'pen-pusher', as Albert would have put it — and she'd felt sure he could offer expert advice on Dorothea's situation. He'd not proved very comforting. He'd made it plain in his reply that, as the law stood, Dorothea, in marrying Johann Kaufmann, had immediately, automatically and irreversibly lost her British nationality.

Eloise had been astonished. It was unbelievable. The possibility had never so much as crossed her mind, neither at the time of Dorothea's wedding, nor in the years since. This ignorance of the law now seemed a terrible oversight. Why hadn't they known? Surely someone should have told them?

But even if they had been told, would that have made any difference? On balance, Eloise did not think that it would. How could anyone in 1912 have foreseen the future consequences of Dorothea's marriage? As far as Eloise was aware, no one back then had seriously suggested that a war with Germany was at all likely; it had not been so much as a distant threat on the horizon.

'Doro? An alien?' Roderick protested. 'Good Lord, Mother, there's no one more English than Doro! That doesn't change, just because she married a Hun, and if the law says so, then the law's an ass.'

David Galbraith had been adamant, nonetheless. There could be no exceptions and no extenuating circumstances.

Of them all, it had been Rosa who was most outraged. Here was yet another example, she'd exclaimed, of society's unjust treatment of women. You could be sure that a man marrying a foreigner would not likewise be robbed of his nationality. In a flurry of righteous indignation, Rosa had proposed writing to the newspapers, getting up a petition, organizing a march with placards and slogans — all the old tactics from her suffragist days.

Roderick nodded vigorously. 'Good old Rosa! She's absolutely right. Something must be done.'

'I thought so, too, Roderick.' For once, Eloise had found herself in complete sympathy with her daughter-in-law and had even seen some merit in her crusading ways. 'But I'm afraid that creating any fuss would do more harm than good.'

That, anyway, had been David Galbraith's response, when Eloise had suggested adopting Rosa's strategy. In the light of current public opinion, he had put it tactfully, it might be unadvisable to proceed in that line.

Eloise had taken his point. Whilst it was plainly preposterous to hold Dorothea to account for the Kaiser's crimes, there was no denying her married name or the fact that, legally, she was German. To the world at large, this was all that mattered. There was widespread feeling against the Germans. One met with it everywhere, even amongst one's own acquaintance — Mrs Adnitt, for instance, whom Eloise saw at church every Sunday.

'I simply refuse to be served anymore by German or Austrian waiters, and if a waiter claims to be Swiss, I demand to see his passport. One can't be too careful.'

'I had no idea you dined out so often, Mrs Adnitt.'

'Well, no, we don't, Mrs Brannan, but that's beside the point. It's the principle that counts.'

Dorothea's name was never mentioned in exchanges such as these but the implication was there. That Dorothea could remain oblivious to this hostility was out of the question, though she never spoke of it. She had, however, shown very little enthusiasm for Rosa's proposed campaign, as if she knew it would be unavailing and perhaps even counterproductive. Any suggestion of letters and petitions had been quietly dropped.

'All this was going on,' said Roderick, 'and I knew nothing about it. None of you mentioned it in your letters.

But what I really can't understand is why Doro isn't more upset about it. I'd be jolly well furious if it was me. I am furious!'

'Getting worked up won't do any good. I'm sure Dorothea knows that.'

'Yes, well, perhaps you're right, Mother. But we mustn't leave her to brood on the injustice of it. She needs something to occupy her mind. Mention was made of nursing. That could be just the ticket.'

'Nobody has mentioned it to me. Would it be wise?'

'Come, Mother. You know how she likes to make herself useful. I think Mrs Somersby's first aid classes have given her ideas. Also . . .'

'What is it, Roderick?'

'Nothing, it's nothing. Except . . . well . . . I think it would mean a lot to her if she was doing work along the same lines as that husband of hers.'

His tone was casual, as if he was talking extempore, but Eloise wondered if Dorothea might have confided in him — or was it that he simply understood Dorothea better than anyone? Either was possible. They were very close, the two of them, always had been, more like brother and sister than cousins. Which was not to ignore the fact that he'd resented her very much at first, when they were children and Dorothea had turned up at Clifton out of the blue. But it had not taken Dorothea long to change his opinion of her. She'd not set her sights on him, of course; nothing like that. She'd never been sly or calculating, didn't have it in her. She won people round simply by being herself.

Roderick ventured, 'I imagine she'll have to do some sort of training — if she wants to be a nurse, that is.'

'Haven't you been listening, Roderick? Dorothea can't go anywhere, for training or anything else.'

'Not without official permission, you said.'

'She needs a permit to travel. She can't stay the night under another roof without the proper authorization. Some parts of the country are completely forbidden to her.'

'Places where there are docks, I suppose, or army camps, in case she's a spy or saboteur.' Roderick grunted in disgust. 'It's grotesque, to have Dorothea treated like a common criminal. Surely we can do something? Can we not write to Cousin David again? I know you'd rather she stayed at Clifton, Mother, I know how much you rely on her—'

'That is neither here nor there. What is best for Dorothea: that's what is important.'

'Yes, of course. And she'd still be in England, even if she went nursing, that's the main thing.'

'She could not very well go back to Germany.'

Roderick said, after a pause, 'I'm not so sure about that, Mother. People still get about. We . . . we may have laid it on a bit thick back in August when we persuaded her to stay.'

He made the word 'persuaded' sound almost disreputable, as if they'd acted dishonestly in some way, as if they'd been complicit in some crime. He'd also made sure to say 'we', Eloise noted, thereby implicating her in — in whatever it was they were meant to have done.

But all they had done was present Dorothea with the facts.

Eloise experienced a twist of irritation as she watched the rain teeming down, dripping off the bare branches of the lime trees, making the rhododendrons sag, but she could not remain annoyed with Roderick for long. A vast and indefinable feeling swelled inside her; she felt it like a pain across her chest. It left her, for a moment, breathless, speechless.

Rain beat ever harder on the window. A blur of water obscured the dismal view. She wanted nothing more than to go on standing there, alone with her son, but Mrs Somersby's missive was lying on her bureau and could not be ignored. The wedding loomed large as the big day grew ever closer.

She sighed. 'Well, Roderick, if there's nothing else, I really must get on.'

* * *

96

After the service in Brockmorton's tiny church, the congregation crowded into their cars and carriages and descended on Clifton. The gravelled space in front of the house, the stable yard, the track that led past Becket's cottage: all were clogged with parked vehicles. Guests hurried indoors out of the rain (it was raining again, such a wet December); Crompton, in the hallway, collected coats, hats and umbrellas, assisted by one of the housemaids. People spilled from room to room, as the house slowly filled. Lavish flames danced in the fireplaces. Electric lights banished the gloom of the winter afternoon. Clifton had not seen such a gathering since Dorothea's wedding nearly two and a half years ago — or perhaps longer than that, going back to Father's famous parties in the 1870s and the 1880s.

The bridegroom was in uniform, Roderick also. Of the two, Roderick was younger, taller, leaner; virile and very handsome. Mark Somersby, by contrast, looked a little portly and . . . well . . . the words 'slack' and 'grooved' sprang into her mind, but Eloise was not sure what she meant by them. Was she trying to say 'complacent'? But that was not quite right either. Mark Somersby was too dispassionate a man to seem complacent.

The bride, Colonel Harding's youngest daughter, was almost a dozen years her new husband's junior. She was rather plain, rather shy, seemed overawed by the occasion. Eloise could not help wondering if a girl like Eileen Harding would have made a more suitable bride for Roderick than the one he'd chosen. But whatever one might say of Rosa, she certainly stood out in the crowd. With her dark hair and rather Italianate looks, and a mouth red with lipstick, she was — if not the best-looking girl present — certainly the most striking.

'Your daughter-in-law always wears such interesting clothes,' remarked Mrs Somersby, regarding Rosa across the room. 'She reminds me of a gypsy, or something equally exotic.'

No one would ever have said that Viola Somersby dressed like a gypsy, though her clothes, always fashionable, often edged towards the flamboyant — her hats in particular. Today, however, her hat was unexpectedly subdued, with a narrow turned-up brim and a single feather. In her role as the bridegroom's proud mother, she swept from room to room, greeting all and sundry with great effusion, so that Eloise was left feeling rather like a guest in her own home.

The father of the bride was equally impossible to ignore; Colonel Harding's booming voice could be heard at every turn. Eloise was much relieved to find that he showed no sign of partiality towards her today. She was, indeed, more and more inclined, after so long — four months since the picnic — to dismiss Viola Somersby's insinuations as entirely mistaken — if indeed Viola's remarks had been quite as pointed as Eloise remembered.

The Colonel, on leaving church, had laid claim to Mark Somersby with a manly slap on the back, immensely pleased with his martial son-in-law. 'But one of my other daughters married a general, don't you know, so you must be on your mettle, young man!'

His daughters, the Colonel was proud of. His sons, less so. The elder, Charles, was a disappointment to him, unmarried at thirty-seven and with an undistinguished military career already behind him. Charles's younger half-brother, Julian, was more of a mystery. Eloise knew little about him. He'd gone to school at Harrow. He'd got married in the same year as Dorothea. What else? Roderick had a habit of calling Julian Harding 'the housemaid's son'.

'Colonel Harding's second wife was his housemaid before he married her, everyone says so.'

'Who is "everyone", Roderick?'

'Oh, you know, Mother. Just — everyone.'

When and where this canard had first arisen was impossible to say, but it was remarkably persistent, even though there was not a grain of truth in it. Colonel Harding was the last man on earth who'd marry out of his caste. Julian was not a housemaid's son. But certainly he wasn't a man who made much of a mark.

This was certainly not true of Roderick. He'd been something of a hit today. People were drawn to him. He charmed them by not being charming. Old ladies were shocked by his forthright views, and took great delight in being so shocked. Young girls listened to him shyly with shining eyes. Men found in him a congenial companion. His uniform gave him an added cachet; a uniform was fast becoming de rigueur for any young man worth his salt.

One had no qualms about Roderick. Elizabeth was a different matter. Eloise looked around the room, sought out her daughter. What was it Mr Smith had said back in August about one's children being unalike? Not that Elizabeth wasn't handsome in her own way, and there was a sort of giddy charm about her. She'd never been neat and tidy like Roderick, but she looked almost presentable today. Her new frock, with the narrower skirts that were now à la mode, certainly suited her gangly figure. All the same, Eloise couldn't help noticing loose strands of hair hanging down, a trailing sleeve (was it torn in some way?), mud on her court shoes. In many ways, she was still very much a child, but a child fast approaching the dangerous threshold of womanhood. Men's eyes had begun to stray in her direction; Eloise had noticed it particularly today. One could only be thankful that she didn't seem to realize. She looked right now as if she was lost in a world of her own, as she so often was. What did she find to think about? What was she thinking about now, as she fingered the Chinese fan on the sideboard? It was not good for a girl of her age to think. And why must she always fiddle with things?

'She reminds me—' Mrs Somersby, glass in hand, reappeared at Eloise's side. 'She reminds me, your Elizabeth, of you as a girl, Eloise. She has your hair, of course, your nose, too, and that joie de vivre I remember so well in your youth. She's a most spirited child. If only Cecily showed such spirit.' Mrs Somersby sipped her drink, lamenting her younger daughter, who was known as something of a mouse. 'How very young they are, my Cecily, your Elizabeth! Oh, to be that age again! To have one's life before one! How is it we have got so old, Eloise?'

Old, thought Eloise: did Viola really feel so old? Eloise was sure she did not feel old herself. Fifty was not old — not compared to Colonel Harding or Dr Camborne, who were both in their late sixties now, as was their friend and neighbour Lady Fitzwilliam.

'Dear Alice!' cried Mrs Somersby. 'It seems only yesterday we were first introduced to her, this new young wife of Sir Joseph at the Grange. But don't you find—' Viola swapped her empty glass for a full one, as Crompton passed by with a tray — 'that Alice is becoming rather vague? I noticed it earlier. She seemed to have little idea who was marrying whom. Of course, she's had a lot to cope with: Henry's accident, Henry confined to a wheelchair, her only son. When I think how I would feel if it was Mark . . .' Mrs Somersby shuddered and took a long sip of her champagne — gulping, almost.

Across the room, Colonel Harding was still holding court, his booming voice rising above all others. 'Now, as I was saying, every summer, at Simla—'

Mrs Somersby raised an eyebrow as she swallowed more champagne. 'Listen to him! Isn't he louder than ever? And those tales of India! How many times have we heard them? Even now, I haven't the first idea where Simla is. But credit where credit is due. There's nothing vague about the Colonel. He's on the button, sharp as a knife — even at his age. He'll go on forever, I should think. I have to keep reminding myself that we're family now, he and I. We're related. His Eileen, my Mark . . . But there it is. Mark is settled. I've only Cecily to marry off. Only Cecily left.'

Mrs Somersby's glass, Eloise noted, was already half empty. She seemed determined to be the life and soul today. Her hat might be more modest than usual, but her personality was as large as ever. There'd always been times when Viola Somersby might have been said to have trod a rather thin line; somehow that line seemed thinner than ever today.

Mrs Somersby was called away. Eloise stood alone amid the crowd in the drawing room. She sensed that the day had gone as well as could be expected, under the circumstances. Viola could surely have no cause for complaint. Even so, looking round, Eloise could not help but feel there was something ad hoc about it all, like trying to fill a vase with too few flowers. Had anyone else noticed? She listened in, with some trepidation, to the conversations going on around her, but could hear nothing about the day's arrangements, nor was anyone passing comment on Clifton. Most of the talk was — inevitably — of the war, which was in its 136th day (the newspapers were keeping count). Even Dorothea was alluding to the war, and she usually avoided the subject; the rector of Brockmorton, who'd conducted the marriage service earlier, was listening to her with a distracted mien.

'. . . The boy is just fifteen years old. His parents are naturally anxious to have him home. If you could help in any way . . . as a man of the cloth, your voice would carry weight . . .'

Eloise recognized the theme. Dorothea, recently, had taken up the case of a boy from the village, a boy named Cheeseman who had enlisted without telling anyone. He'd given a false age. The recruiting officer — recruiting officers were said to earn a shilling for every man they signed — had turned a blind eye. Now that the mistake was out in the open, one would have thought the boy's release a matter of routine, but all Dorothea's efforts on behalf of his family had so far come to nothing.

Not everyone approved of Dorothea's involvement, Mrs Adnitt for one.

'If a boy wishes to do his patriotic duty, then he ought really to be congratulated, not thwarted. I can't think what anyone would hope to gain, making a fuss about it.'

Eloise could tell, simply by looking, that the rector of Brockmorton was of a similar opinion. One could see him thinking up excuses as to why — alas! — he'd have to pass this over.

With her attention focused on Dorothea, Eloise only gradually became aware of another conversation nearby, a little group standing by the piano, amongst whom was Giles Milton: he was married to Mrs Somersby's elder daughter, Julia. Under discussion were the German raids on the east coast. The raids had been reported in great detail in this morning's newspapers. Eloise had been shocked to discover that Scarborough had been targeted, bombed from the sea: Scarborough, a place she'd visited as recently as the summer before last. Churches had been hit, and a hospital — houses too; four people had been killed in one house alone. Much damage had been inflicted to buildings on the sea front, where she'd often walked with Mrs Varney. The Grand Hotel, where they'd sometimes taken lunch, had been hit as well.

Giles Milton was indignant. England, under attack! Ordinary people cut down in their own homes! It was monstrous! It was scandalous!

'Where was the navy in all this, that's what I would like to know? Where was the Royal Navy? We have the world's most powerful navy, and yet the Hun was allowed to steam right across the North Sea and murder innocent Englishmen with impunity — and they got away scot-free! It's a national disgrace.'

Eloise listened with growing dismay as Giles Milton ranted on. A man in his thirties who spoke with a lisp, he happened to be uncle to Rosa's friend Miss Ward, as well as being Mrs Somersby's son-in-law. In addition, he was in charge of the BFS motor showroom in London — which made him, in effect, as Eloise reminded herself, one's employee. Why the son of a millionaire should want to work in a motor showroom was another matter altogether, though Giles had always been something of a motor enthusiast; maybe, as a sixth son, he could not entirely rely on his father's largesse.

He was finding fault now with the government as well as the navy: the government's lamentable failure to issue clear instructions as to how people should behave in an emergency.

Was it any wonder that chaos ensued during the raids? There'd been panic. He had it on good authority — despite what the papers were saying — that there'd been considerable panic. And what was the prime minister doing? Nothing. Absolutely nothing. The man was a liability, a drunkard by all accounts (one heard whispers, living in town; one mixed with those in the know). The prime minister had dithered in August over the simple act of declaring war, which was unforgivable in itself. Now he was dithering again, when he should be taking the lead.

Giles Milton was talking at the top of his voice as he approached his peroration. There happened to be a lull at the same moment, one of those natural pauses which can occur in a crowded room; even Colonel Harding had fallen silent. Giles Milton's lisped words carried clearly right across the room. Everyone seemed to be listening in the sudden hush.

'We have reached a critical moment. The barbarians are at the gates. We must act, and act now, or else Rome will burn. By Rome, I mean London — England — the Empire: I am being metaphorical. Rome, I say, will burn, unless we take decisive steps to defend ourselves. The best form of defence is attack, as every soldier knows. We must take it to the Hun. We must give as good as we get. The more we kill, the better. Slaughter the swine, that's what I say. Slaughter the bally lot.'

Dorothea had her back to Giles Milton but she was standing so close she could not fail to hear: she bore the brunt of every hate-filled word. Eloise could just about see her niece's face. It was completely expressionless. But there was an emptiness in Dorothea's eyes, as if she'd withdrawn deep inside herself. Only someone who knew her well would have noticed.

Eloise did not stop to think. She swept a path through the crowd. 'I must ask you, Mr Milton, to please moderate your language.'

'Moderate my language?' He looked at her in puzzlement. 'I beg your pardon, Mrs Brannan, I don't quite . . . ?'

'We do not use language like that in this house.'

'Language like what? Oh, I see. You mean "Hun", "swine", "barbarian". But — Mrs Brannan — that's exactly what those scoundrels are. There aren't any other words to use.'

Eloise drew herself up, stood tall and straight as she looked him up and down. Slowly, deliberately, she said, 'Mr Milton. We are English. That means we are civilized. We uphold good manners. We believe in fair play. It's in our blood. It's the very essence of what it means to be English. We must never forget it. Now, more than ever, we must be true to ourselves.'

The lull deepened to a gaping silence; one could have heard a pin drop. Eloise stood her ground, watching colour flare into Mr Milton's cheeks. His mouth opened, as if he was about to make some crushing riposte, but she caught his eye and he seemed to think better of it. He bowed his head. He muttered a few words that might have been a brief apology, then shuffled quickly away.

The silence stretched out, unnatural now. Eloise felt as if a spotlight had fallen on her, so that she stood illuminated, alone, with a ring of people in the shadows all round her, every last one of them watching her. This breathless hush seemed to last an eternity but, in truth, not much more than half a minute passed before a few murmured voices were heard. The sound swiftly swelled like a rising tide. In half a minute more, it was as if there'd never been an interruption at all.

Roderick appeared as if from nowhere. 'Mother! You were magnificent! You put that damned fool in his place — because that's what he is, a fool, an idiot, a prize idiot. Fancy talking like that in front of Doro! I never did understand what Father saw in Giles Milton.'

'But, Roderick, your father—' Eloise broke off, not sure what she wanted to say. She couldn't help thinking that Albert would have handled the situation much better, made less of a scene. As for Giles Milton, he must have something about him, if Albert had shown him favour.

But none of this was important. There were more pressing matters. 'Where is Dorothea? Did you see where she went, Roderick?'

'Leave Doro to me, Mother. I'll see she's all right. You stay and enjoy your triumph.'

Roderick shouldered his way across the room and disappeared into the passage. Eloise composed herself, smiling at the people round her. Many smiled back, and nodded, but with some she met resistance: they avoided her eye. She became aware — there was no mistaking it — of a certain amount of sympathy in the room for Giles Milton's sentiments and, concomitant with that, umbrage at the tone of her intervention. It was disconcerting, came as a shock, to feel herself out of step, when usually she epitomized the prevailing mood.

She felt in need of a moment's peace, to gather her thoughts, but there were people everywhere; she couldn't get away from them. Even in the side corridor there was discreet but constant traffic, to and from the closet. Lest anyone mistake this as her own destination, Eloise swept past the closet and through the door at the end of the corridor that led to the back stairs. A further door opened onto a dull and dingy passage, with the laundry room on one side, and the generator room on the other. This passage was really part of the stable block, rather than the house proper; yet another door at the far end opened onto the stable yard itself. The tradesman's entrance, as it had always been known. Albert, in his plain-speaking way, had simply called it the side door.

Eloise, as she walked along this short passage, could just imagine what Albert would have made of today's festivities. Fuss and palaver, he'd have said. Typical of Viola Somersby, he'd have added. They'd not got on, in the early days, he and Viola; she'd been pointedly condescending about that bicycle maker from Coventry, whilst Albert had thought her ridiculous, with her airs and graces and her fancy hats. Over time, there'd been a change. They'd grown to respect — even to like — one another. Albert, in his later years, would have found today's fuss and palaver highly amusing. He might even have enjoyed it.

Warmed by these recollections of her husband, Eloise opened the side door and stepped outside for a breath of air. The stable yard seemed very quiet after the cacophony indoors. The brick-built stable buildings, all in darkness, enclosed a damp and muddy yard. Rain glistened on the cobbles. One or two motor cars were parked here, higgledy-piggledy. Out beyond the arched entrance, there were other motors, and a carriage or two, all silent and still, as if they'd been abandoned. There was no sign of life. The drab December day, which had never really got going, was fading already to a grey twilight.

She was about to go back inside when her eye caught a flicker of movement. The stable yard wasn't quite as deserted as she'd thought. Peering through the gloom, she recognized, with a start of surprise, her daughter. Of course it was Elizabeth. It would be. There'd never been such a girl for turning up where she was least expected — where she wasn't wanted, where she didn't belong. What in heaven's name was she doing out here in the drizzle? She would make a terrible mess of her brand-new cream frock, trailing the skirts through the muck on the cobbles.

Eloise realized that Elizabeth wasn't alone; there was someone with her. He wasn't easy to see in the half-light. His sludge-brown jacket and grey corduroy trousers blended in with the gloom. A big cap was jammed on his head. He had hobnailed boots on his feet. The stable hand, Turner.

A local lad, Turner. Born and raised in the village. He'd worked in the stables at Clifton since he was a boy — a dozen years or so, all told — and he'd grown into a rather brawny young man, though only of middling height. Eloise found him somewhat dour in disposition, taciturn too. But no doubt Elizabeth did enough talking for the both of them. They did not appear to be talking just now. They were standing still and silent in the deepening dusk, almost invisible. Eloise felt there was something almost suspect about it, their stillness, their silence.

Her mind went back to the summer before last, the summer when she'd spent a month in Scarborough. She'd returned to reports of Elizabeth running wild and being over-familiar with the servants; Turner's name had been mentioned. Eloise had thought it necessary to take her daughter to task. But if she'd spoken to Elizabeth once about talking to the staff, she'd spoken to her a hundred times: it went in one ear and out the other. Eloise had also had words with Turner, though she'd never before had cause to find fault with him. Roderick described him as 'a steady sort of fellow, honest as the day is long', which was praise indeed, coming from Roderick. But Roderick's opinions, at the time, had carried less weight than usual, for Eloise had not been best pleased with him. She'd relied on him being home all summer so that he could keep an eye on his sister, only to find when she returned from the east coast that he'd been absent much of the time, off gallivanting — chasing after Rosa, Eloise rather suspected, looking back. And so, when she interviewed Turner, she'd been rather sharp with him, reminding him of his responsibilities. There'd been nothing in his demeanour to suggest he was anything other than contrite. Which only confirmed her suspicions that the blame lay mostly — if not entirely — with Elizabeth.

In all likelihood, therefore, there was nothing in it, this little tête-à-tête in the stable yard. Turner knew his place and Elizabeth, though forward in some ways, was still in most respects a child. At the same time, Eloise could not forget what she'd noticed earlier, the eyes of men turned towards her daughter. Men were becoming aware of her. And Turner — conscientious beyond reproach though he might be — was, nevertheless, a man. Men could not help themselves, even if it was no more than a glint in their eyes. And this meant that these cosy little chats in the stable yard would have to be nipped in the bud.

Now was not the time, however, with the reception ongoing. And this certainly wasn't the place. The stable yard was in the working part of the house, the servants' domain, what Father had called 'the offices'. If she must speak with Turner, she would do so on her own terms, in the parlour. Also, she would need to tread carefully where Elizabeth was concerned; her daughter could be most contrary, digging in her heels, if not handled right.

Leaving the stable yard, Eloise made her way back into the house. The side corridor was almost empty now; only Mark Somersby was there. She smiled at him briefly and made to walk past, but he stood in her way.

'I wonder if I might have a word in confidence, Mrs Brannan?'

She was rather taken aback, couldn't imagine what business Mark Somersby had with her, unless it was to thank her for her help in arranging the wedding. But that hardly required this cloak-and-dagger approach.

'Very well, Mr Somersby. Shall we step in here a moment?'

She opened the door of the blue room, a room that was not much used these days and tended to get overlooked. As soon as they were inside, Mark Somersby turned to her in a state of some anxiety.

'I want to ask of you a very great favour, Mrs Brannan, if I may. Would . . . would you keep an eye on Mother, whilst I'm away? I'd feel so much better if I knew someone was watching over her. There's Cecily, of course, only . . . well . . . she's so young. And there's my wife, Eileen.' He stuttered a little over the words 'my wife'. 'But Eileen's new to it all, she's still getting used to the Manor and to Mother, it wouldn't be fair to burden her.'

Eloise waited patiently for him to get to the point. He'd never struck her as a man to fuss over nothing; neither was his mother someone who needed watching over.

'It would be a weight off my mind if—' He swallowed and ran a hand through his hair. 'Mother is . . . is ill, you see. There's a cancer. She's been attending a specialist in Harley Street. He's not been very encouraging. I rather think, reading between the lines, that there's nothing much anyone can do. Mother, of course, would much rather people didn't know. She's not even told Cecily. I don't think she'd have told me, if I'd not realized something was wrong. I winkled it out of her, rather. She won't have any fuss, Mrs Brannan; she wants to carry on like normal as long as she can. She made me give my word that I'd keep all this to myself. Naturally, I'd never betray her trust under any other circumstances. But I'm going away — there's no helping it, not with the war and everything — and I just thought there ought to be someone on hand who knows the truth.'

Eloise was shaken by his words, so unexpected, so shocking, disturbing the long peace of the blue room. A cancer? And yet Mrs Somersby looked no different, seemed no different, unless—

There had been something rather brittle about her today. Eloise had put it down to the pressure of events. The wedding. The broken pipes. Mark's imminent departure. She hadn't, for one moment, imagined there was anything seriously amiss. It all fell into place now: the way Viola had reached for another drink, the way her glass was so swiftly emptied. Her every look, her every gesture: it all made perfect sense. Yet such was her poise, such was her pride, that anyone who hadn't known her at least a quarter of a century would have noticed nothing.

Eloise quickly collected herself. 'Mr Somersby, you may be sure I'll do everything I can—'

He interrupted her, over-eager in his relief. 'It's jolly decent of you, Mrs Brannan, jolly decent indeed. I felt sure I could rely on you. "There's no one better when it comes to the pinch," I said to myself. I shall feel so much easier, out in France, knowing you're keeping an eye on her. You . . . you won't, of course, say anything to anyone? Not to Mother — especially not to Mother.'

'I give you my word, Mr Somersby.'

Her word, it seemed, was enough. He thanked her again most profusely, then hurried back to his guests before he was missed.

Eloise lingered a moment in the blue room, wondering what, in all honesty, she could do to make a difference. I shall feel so much easier, he'd said. But what real comfort could there be, if his mother was dying?

Eloise slowly became aware that she was staring at the glass cases housed here in the blue room — at the stuffed wildlife inside them, the kills of long-forgotten shooting parties, preserved for all time. Glazed eyes stared back at her, fixed and lifeless, yet faintly unnerving, as if in some mysterious way the unmoving corpses were still sentient, still aware; frozen in place, yes, but watching, watching, watching, always watching; watching, as the endless years rolled by.

She walked from one glass case to the next. Her thoughts turned back to Viola Somersby, whom she'd known all her life. After so many years, Eloise would have said she knew Viola inside out, but she had seen a new side to her today. Not her courage in facing her illness; Eloise had always known she had courage. It was the nature of that courage which was so unexpected: a quiet, personal courage, incongruous in a woman as outgoing as Viola Somersby.

So very cruel, to be thus afflicted. So very cruel of God — or Fate — or the random workings of chance, whichever it happened to be (it hardly mattered).

Eloise came to a halt, gazing almost as if hypnotized into the glassy brown eyes of a fox in one of the cases, a fox which had one paw forever raised above a litter of artificial dead leaves. There seemed something almost sinister about it, and she shuddered and turned away. As she shut the blue room door behind her, Eloise could not help thinking that Viola was not alone in her affliction. There was a cancer in everything just now. There was a cancer at the very heart of life.

The war was a cancer that had far from run its course.

* * *

As there was to be no wedding trip, there was no big send-off; the afternoon had no final act. Instead, people slipped away a few at a time. The reception meandered inch by inch to an end, until there were no guests left. The last of the motor cars and carriages faded into the wet and miserable December evening.

Next morning, directly after breakfast, Roderick departed for the south coast once more.

CHAPTER FIVE

The price of coal was quite shocking.

Sat at her bureau, Eloise put on her spectacles and inspected the coal merchant's bill for a second time, to make certain there was no mistake. The numbers were clearly written. But the cost must have increased by at least a quarter in the six months or so since the war began.

It was not just coal. Prices were increasing all round, so much so that her accounts had become almost unmanageable. She had to check everything twice. No figure was ever the same.

Eloise put the coal merchant's bill aside. There would be no problem in settling it. There need be no concern on that score just yet. But if prices continued to rise at the same steep rate, she would need to keep a sharp eye on expenditure. Revenue from the Clifton estate barely covered running costs, but that was nothing new; it had been the same for years. Of more concern was the decline in Albert's businesses since the start of the war. Mr Smith and Mr Simcox kept Eloise informed, Mr Smith the general manager of the motor-making business, Mr Simcox in charge at Albert's other factory that used to produce bicycles and now made motor components. The war looked likely to offer new opportunities, they'd reported, but this required changes that would inevitably cause some temporary dislocation. In addition, they'd already lost a number of employees to the military — some of them their most valuable men — and this would only get worse as the war continued (the war had not ended at Christmas). Eloise did not pretend to understand even half of the difficulties they faced but she had every confidence in them, Albert's chosen right-hand men, and she'd written to tell them so.

She took off her spectacles and rubbed her temples. Her head was starting to ache. She had done all she could today. The accounts, and all other money matters, would just have to wait.

Tidying her desk, she uncovered the newspaper lying quarter-folded in one corner. The words 'KILLED IN ACTION' and 'DIED OF WOUNDS' jumped out at her. There was something grotesque in seeing those headings on the front page of *The Times* alongside the customary births, marriages and deaths. She could not imagine ever getting used to it. Thankfully, she had no fear of seeing Roderick's name in those lists, for he was still safe on the south coast. He'd been there five months now. His sense of adventure, and the general holiday mood, were both wearing thin — or so she gathered from his letters home — but he was sticking at it, he said. If his country required him to be 'bored out of his skull for months on end' (as he put it), then he would do his best to bear it. To Eloise's mind, it was far better he was bored than facing such danger as — she squinted without her spectacles, trying to make out some of the many names in the KILLED IN ACTION column, but not wanting to see them too clearly — as Captain Hartwell or Lieutenant Bond or—

But the list went on. There was no need to read it to the end. Eloise wondered if Captain Hartwell's mother, or Lieutenant Bond's, had seen her son's name in this morning's *Times* and suffered a sharp reminder of her loss.

Eloise dismissed such macabre thoughts. She picked up the newspaper to tidy it away — and even as she did so, another name came swimming up at her out of the blur of print: the Earl of Denecote.

She looked again. Was it true, the Earl of Denecote dead?

Slowly — almost reluctantly — she picked up her spectacles and put them back on. She read, in the regular DEATHS column:

DENECOTE. On the 16th February, at Ashby Hall, Northamptonshire, JONATHAN GEORGE MUIR HUNTLEY, 8th Earl of Denecote, aged 59. Funeral at—

She took off her spectacles. The words grew blurred once more.

With her spectacles in one hand and the newspaper in the other, she sat staring into space. They'd got his name wrong. It was George Jonathan, not Jonathan George. Possibly no one now remembered. He'd always been known by his second name — many men were, it was far from uncommon — and that was how he'd been introduced to her, as Jonathan, a friend of her brother's. In those days, long before his father died, George Jonathan Muir Huntley had been Viscount Lynford. He'd been Viscount Lynford most of his life. Seeing the substantive title in the newspaper — the Earl of Denecote — Eloise still thought automatically of the father, rather than the son.

She'd noticed the old earl's name in the newspapers on occasion right up to the time of his death. His last public appearance, as far as she knew, had been four years ago, when the Parliament Bill had been going through the House of Lords. He'd been one of the Ditchers, implacably opposed to any watering down of their lordships' prerogatives. A man used to getting his own way, he'd been on the losing side in that battle, a bitter pill to swallow. He'd died a few months later. His title had passed to his only son. And now the son, too, was dead.

Poor Jonathan! He'd not had long to enjoy his inheritance. His father had been earl for fifty-seven years, Jonathan not even three.

The newspaper fell from Eloise's hands. Putting her spectacles aside, she got absently to her feet, drifted across to the window, looked out at the lime trees whose leafless branches were like dark filaments against the marbled grey sky. A robin was hopping by the rhododendrons, its breast arrestingly red. The grass was wet from recent rain.

'How long,' Eloise murmured, unaware that she was talking out loud. 'How long . . . ?'

Turning away from the window, she went to the camel-back sofa and sat down, gazing at the glowing fire where tiny flames were licking the piled coals (the price of coal . . . shocking). She added up the years. She reached a total of forty. Forty years, more or less, since she'd first met Jonathan Huntley, her brother's 'ripping new chum' from Oxford, or 'the Varsity' as Frederick jauntily called it. They'd been inseparable back then, Frederick and Jonathan: some people, thinking themselves original, had even taken to calling Frederick 'David'. But it was a different epithet that finally stuck. Joined later by a younger friend, Philip Milton — one of the Miltons of Darvell Hall, and an elder brother of Mrs Somersby's son-in-law Giles — they'd become known as 'the Three Musketeers'; again, hardly original, but altogether apt.

Who was it first called them the Musketeers? Ah, yes. Lady Fitzwilliam, of course: Alice Fitzwilliam, back then the young new wife of their neighbour, Sir Joseph Fitzwilliam. She was now a widow in her sixties and 'getting rather vague', as Viola Somersby had remarked back in December. Alice's sobriquet for the three boys had stuck, and soon everyone knew of the Musketeers, three friends who'd first met at Oxford — except that it wasn't Philip Milton whom Frederick and Jonathan had met at university, but the eldest Milton boy, the heir; they'd not met Philip until later, another detail that, like Jonathan's proper name, had become obscured by the passing of time.

The eldest Milton brother (Eloise groped for his name, couldn't lay hold of it) had been a high-minded boy, some even said priggish; he would never have involved himself in the Musketeers' less edifying escapades. For they had been rather wild, the Musketeers, rather reckless, bordering at times on the disreputable, so much so that Father had been very worried for a while about Frederick and what might become of him. Two significant events had changed the course of Frederick's life. He had fallen in love with, and then married, Jonathan's sister, the Lady Emerald; and he had been taken up as protégé by Sir Joseph Fitzwilliam, who had mapped out for him a career in politics. Sir Joseph, in the 1870s, had been their local Member of Parliament, but he'd lost his seat in the election of 1880, the election in which Mr Gladstone had carried all before him. Ill health thereafter prevented Sir Joseph's active participation in politics and he'd chosen Frederick as his proxy.

Staring into the fire, Eloise was aware of her mind tidying all these memories into neat compartments, in the same way that she tidied the papers on her desk and placed them in the drawers of her bureau. The mind also searched for a pattern to events, and thus found pleasing symmetry in her recollection of her own first romantic involvement. Frederick had married Jonathan's sister. And she, Frederick's sister, had fallen in love with Jonathan.

Eloise shifted on the sofa. Fall in love: a ridiculous phrase. Fall suggested a degree of immediacy and happenstance which she had never found love to possess. Whatever her tidy mind might now want to tell her, she had not fallen in love at the time of her brother's wedding in September 1880; she had merely come to recognize certain feelings which, beyond doubt, had been growing and developing over many years, ever since she'd first got to know Frederick's dearest friend. There was another fallacy, too, which she felt ought to be denied: the tendency to ascribe far too much to the changing power of love. She had indeed changed around that time. She had ceased to be Father's little Amazon. She had become interested in clothes and jewels, had wanted to appear a young lady. But this would have happened anyway. It was called growing up.

Having cut love down to size, Eloise got to her feet, for there was nothing more needed saying. But the past was not done with her yet, and she stood where she was, in the middle of the room, thinking of her relationship with Jonathan Huntley in the early 1880s. It hadn't really been a courtship, it hadn't been anything like that; she'd not felt the need to define it or to justify it, or even to admit what was happening. With Frederick married to Lady Emerald, and the two of them living at Clifton, it was only natural that Lady Emerald's brother should have been a frequent visitor. He and Eloise had met as a matter of course; no one had taken much notice. Even Father's suspicions had not been aroused, not until the letters started coming.

Taking a seat once more at her bureau, Eloise searched through the drawers until finally she found in one of them, pushed to the back and left there as if by oversight, several bundles tied with yellow ribbon: all of Jonathan's letters from the 1880s, written between visits. Why had she kept them? It was a question of no importance. She dismissed it. She picked up the bundles, one after another, turning them over and over in her hands. From one of them, she slipped out a letter at random. She unfolded it and glanced at the page, the once-familiar handwriting. Her eyes were caught. She reached automatically for her spectacles. Words, phrases, whole sentences, resolved out of a blur of ink.

> *I dream of you. You are always in my dreams. And such dreams they are! I see you at times in red, dressed all in red, a violent red, red like blood. Or it might be green, a green more verdant than the brightest spring. I call out to you but you turn away. You leave me. I am left to wander alone in strange lands far away, always searching for you, never at peace. I stumble on forsaken palaces in the midst of steaming jungles. I scour every room. Your face stares out at me from*

the walls. I see your face at every turn, multiplied a hundred, a thousand times. Then again, I find myself at dusk on some fire-blackened heath stood beneath a sky streaked with such colours as I've never seen before, vivid and vibrant and nameless. I fall to my knees. I call to you. I shout your name aloud. My voice echoes to the empty heavens. But you do not come. You do not come.

She lowered the letter onto the dark polished wood of her bureau. It was true, he'd insisted, every word: she really did haunt his dreams. She haunted his every waking moment, too. She was on his mind, day and night. To a young girl — a girl not yet twenty — all this had been flattering, exciting, puzzling too, even a little disturbing. She'd wondered if all men were haunted by such fantastic dreams. Was Frederick? Was Father? She measured all men against Father and, more often than not, found them wanting, but Jonathan was different, a man out of the ordinary; the usual standards didn't seem to apply to him. Blue-blooded, tall, handsome, a man of the world, she'd found him incredibly alluring. But also, she'd felt, he was rather dangerous. There was something almost unearthly about him, as if he was more than a man, as if he had in him a touch of the mystic, the visionary. Reading the letter now, however, after so long, she found it rather troubling than alluring. Certainly, the dreams he described were not the dreams of a man at peace with himself.

How much had Father known of all this? How much had he guessed, how much had he suspected? He'd cautioned her, whether because his suspicions had been aroused, or for some other reason, Eloise had never been sure. It was true that Father, by then, had taken against the Huntleys. Partly this was because he'd never got on with the old earl (the feeling had been mutual), but also it was because of Lady Emerald and her behaviour.

What did any of this matter now? It was ancient history. Eloise took off her spectacles and folded the arms. She put the letters away and shut the drawer with a decisive snap.

But her tidy mind hated loose ends and it ran on a moment longer, bringing the story to a rapid conclusion. Jonathan had proposed. She had refused him. He had gone away at once. She had not seen him again for seventeen years. And now he was dead.

So that was over.

She got to her feet, but as she did so she caught sight of *The Times* still lying on the desk with the death notices uppermost. She hesitated. She could not make up her mind: should she go to the funeral or not? If only Dorothea were here. Dorothea always knew the right thing to do. But Dorothea was in London. A way had somehow been found around the obstacles in her path, and she was now training to be an auxiliary nurse.

But even had Dorothea been available, this was too delicate a matter on which to ask her advice. It would have required all manner of explanations, raking up the past for no good purpose. Eloise hesitated just a moment longer but indecision was not in her nature and she quickly made up her mind. Jonathan's last rites really would be the final word, drawing a line under a chain of events that had begun forty years ago, making an end to it. So she would go to the funeral.

She would go.

* * *

Eloise, all in black, lingered in the churchyard after the last of the mourners had gone. It was a churchyard very different to Hayton's, set high on a rise and beset by tall evergreens. She followed a cracked and mossy path round to the back of the church itself, where — as she remembered — one might catch a glimpse, through the box trees, of Ashby Hall, down in the valley. Seen from up here, one got little idea of its size. The sweeping drive, the vast facade were hidden. Only the roofs of the palatial east wing and a few of the upper windows were visible. Eloise found that even this limited view was much narrower than she remembered. The box trees had grown since the 1880s.

She halted a moment beside the long and drooping branches, surveying the distant Hall which had once been full of warmth and light and countless people, but was now shut up and deserted. Inside, it must be as cold as a sepulchre on this bleak February afternoon.

She held her breath a moment, listening for any hint of an inner voice saying to her, *The house, the estate, the title: all that could have been yours.* It would have been an unworthy thought. But the thought was not there. There was no voice. There were no feelings of regret.

She shivered in the chill winter air. Turning up the collar of her coat, she began to retrace her steps.

She had been surprised — indeed shocked — by how few people had come. The church had not even been half full. The Huntley family, once pre-eminent in the county, once prolific, had dwindled now almost to extinction. The last remnants had gathered today, with one or two family friends, and a handful of grandees. Eloise had recognized hardly any of them. Philip Milton, now the last of the Musketeers, had not come.

The coffin had been draped in a silk and velvet pall, with a single tribute of flowers. It had been carried up from the now lifeless Hall by a handful of estate workers. Eloise had not joined the procession. She had waited at the church. She had sat near the back during the service. Afterwards, outside, she had stood a little apart, watching the short ceremony at the graveside. The grandees at length had moved off. This had been the signal for the rest to disperse. Eloise, from her vantage point, had watched them all go, until only two remained.

There he is, she had said to herself: *Jonathan's son.*

He was perhaps twenty-eight or so, of average height, rather pale and thin, in uniform (so many men were these days); he was a major in the army as well as an earl. His countess was called Eugenia; their son, aged five, had been left at home in London; they would not be living at the Hall in the foreseeable future. All this Eloise had gathered from the whispered conversations among the lesser mourners, and from the pronouncements of the grandees, not whispered.

The new earl had played his part throughout. He'd made a point of addressing each and every mourner as they left. He'd exchanged a few words and thanked them for coming. Last of all, and a little diffidently, he'd approached Eloise. She'd stepped forward and introduced herself.

'Mrs Brannan? Of Clifton Park? Forgive me, but I don't believe we've ever . . . Oh, yes, of course, Uncle Fred, I remember Uncle Fred. I was only a boy when he died. And you're Uncle Fred's sister. Have I got that right? So good of you to come. Do you know, now I come to think of it, I believe Mother once took me to Clifton Park. I must have been six or seven. I don't recall that I met you there . . . Ah, I see, in Coventry, that would explain it. And now you're back at Clifton. How jolly! Such a pity about Uncle Fred. He died too young — his boy as well. Did you know my mother at all, Mrs Brannan? You never met her, you say? Sadly she's no longer with us. She died when I was sixteen. Grandpa took charge of me after that. I'm afraid he and Father did not get on. Perhaps you didn't know, but it was Mother's last wish to be buried in the churchyard, not in the family vault; the catacomb, she called it. "Don't let them bury me in the catacomb, Tommy!" she said to me. "I can't bear the thought of the catacomb." I did as she wished, of course; Grandpa was very understanding. And when it came to the point, we — that is, I — felt that Father wouldn't want the vault either. He would want to lie next to Mother.'

Eloise had wondered about the mother, Jonathan's American wife, said by some to have been an heiress. American heiresses had been rather in vogue in the 1880s. What Jonathan's son could not possibly know was that his father had once said, in the drawing room at Clifton (this was twelve years ago), 'If I couldn't have you, Eloise, then it didn't really matter who I married, I simply wasn't interested. I chose the first passable woman who smiled at me. A terrible mistake. We've not made each other very happy. Oh, Eloise, think how different our lives could have been, if only you'd said yes all those years ago!'

Some people, Eloise supposed, might have expected her to have feelings of jealousy towards Jonathan's wife. She had none. She'd never felt anything for the American heiress, and they'd never met. 'You have a heart of ice,' Jonathan had accused her on another of his visits to Clifton a dozen years ago.

Though she'd never given much thought to the wife, she had been curious, on and off, about the son. Meeting him at long last, she'd been inclined to feel sorry for him. His smile had seemed to her somewhat forlorn. He'd looked altogether lost, this unremarkable young man who was almost the last of the Huntleys.

The new countess, waiting by the gate, had called sharply, 'Tommy, darling, we don't want to miss the train.'

Those few, brisk words had been revealing. It was all too plain that the countess piped the tune and 'Tommy darling' danced to it. Eloise was reminded of Frederick and Emerald, whose relationship had worked that way too. The countess, like Lady Emerald, looked to be some years older than her husband.

Jonathan's son had shaken her hand, then his wife had ushered him away. Eloise had been left to linger alone in the churchyard. Now it was time to go.

Huddled in her coat, she hurried along the path. By the gate, she paused for a moment to finger a cluster of red berries on a holly bush, almost the only splash of colour on this drab winter afternoon; she fingered the berries with her gloved hands then she turned away, walking through the gathering gloom back to the motor parked in the lane.

* * *

The chauffeur had taken a wrong turn. Eloise had her doubts that he knew exactly where they were; they'd been touring the byways of Northamptonshire for some time as the last of the daylight faded and the countryside slipped into a bleak, wintry dusk. She regretted all the more the loss of young Smith. He'd been a little rough round the edges, but he'd always found his way.

The motor pressed on through the deepening dusk, and her fingers and toes slowly grew numb from the cold. Her thoughts went back to the churchyard, and to Jonathan, whose fingers and toes would now always be cold, his lips, too — those lips that had kissed her long ago in the billiard room at Clifton, her first proper kiss.

She had found it impossible this week, since reading the notice of his death in *The Times*, to keep Jonathan at bay. In her mind, she returned repeatedly to the early 1880s, when she'd first begun to understand the true nature of her feelings for the dashing young viscount. She had desperately wanted to know how he felt about her. She'd tortured herself, hoping, doubting. And then, in the billiard room, during one of Father's famous parties, Jonathan had kissed her, thereby erasing every last shadow of doubt.

His lips had not been cold that evening.

The summer of 1885; she'd just turned twenty-one. Father had been celebrating the fall of Mr Gladstone, the Liberal Government having lost a vote of confidence in the Commons. To his many supporters, Mr Gladstone had been revered as 'the GOM', the Grand Old Man, but Father detested him and joined other detractors in calling him instead Gordon's Own Murderer: General Gordon had been killed at Khartoum in January that same year. Mr Gladstone, all these years later, was now as dead as General Gordon — they had both passed into history — and the summer of 1885 seemed an age ago, almost another world. It was sobering, sat in this motor, watching the headlamps sweep a path through the winter dark, to think of that other world, where there'd been no motors, and no electric lights, not at Clifton anyway. Thirty years separated that day from this, yet Eloise remembered it as if it were yesterday. Her brand-new evening gown had been trimmed with bows, had a fringe decoration.

She'd worn it with long white gloves, silk flowers in her hair, a velvet ribbon at her throat.

'Ravishing! Scrumptious!'

She had laughed out loud at Jonathan's ostentatious and extravagant praise. But, later, he'd added in a whisper, meant for her ears alone, 'I can't keep my eyes off you,' and there'd been something in the tone of his voice that made her heart beat fast, that made the colour rise in her cheeks.

All evening long she'd been aware of him, aware of his eyes on her, making her skin tingle. Finally, they'd found themselves alone, as if by accident, in the billiard room. He'd told her then that he loved her. He'd taken her in his arms. He'd kissed her.

Girls these days would no doubt think her naïve, that she'd found it so intoxicating, that she'd been shaken by it too, a single kiss. They would be astonished, also, that it had taken Jonathan so long to get round to it. Modern girls would think so, girls like Rosa — Rosa, who'd been in a delicate condition on her wedding day, so fast was she, and so forward. But in the 1880s, there'd been no girls like Rosa.

That was not to say young people at the time had all been perfect. There'd been whispers, for instance, about the Musketeers; stories of drinking and gambling and philandering, and veiled allusions of even worse excesses. But people were apt to exaggerate. People liked to add spice. There was no good reason to think that the three young friends had been quite as disreputable as rumour suggested. Certainly, Eloise had never been able to believe it of Frederick. If Frederick had indeed fallen from grace, it was because he'd been led astray, not from natural inclination; and to be led astray was surely wrong-headed rather than wicked. As for Jonathan, he'd always liked to dice with danger, there'd always been that side to him; he'd been hot-headed, devil-may-care — he'd admitted so himself. Which left Philip Milton. But who could say what Philip Milton had been capable of? Eloise had come to have her suspicions, and not without reason.

She shivered inside the cold motor, holding the collar of her coat close round her throat, and gazing out at leafless hedgerows passing in a shadowy blur. High in the sky, a first faint star glimmered where the tattered clouds were thinning. The star seemed to keep pace with them as the motor swept down a long, dark lane. Like the star, remote but diamond-bright, the fervour she'd felt in the weeks and months after Jonathan kissed her shone clear in her memory, where much else was dark. Wrapped in her own affairs, she'd barely been aware of Frederick's political ambitions building up to their first real test, the general election that November.

Father had never had much time for politics, but he'd encouraged Frederick in this new venture, sensing perhaps that it would give his son a focus that might otherwise have been lacking. Frederick's wife had felt differently. She had pouted and complained. 'Why are you always so busy these days, Freddy? I never get to see you anymore. Can't you make time for me? Freddy, I'm bored!'

Thus it was that Lady Emerald alone had been glad when, despite his best efforts, Frederick had failed to get himself elected. His mentor, the ailing Sir Joseph, had been bitterly disappointed. Father's primary concern had been that Frederick might slip back into his old ways. As for herself, Eloise remembered only the astonishment she'd felt that her peerless brother could fail at anything.

Frederick had shrugged off his defeat. 'Politics is a waste of time. I'm not cut out for it.'

'Don't give up yet, my son,' Father had urged. And Sir Joseph: 'Your time will come.'

But Frederick said, 'There won't be another election for years. I can't wait that long.'

As it happened, the next general election was as soon as the following July, but by then Frederick had abandoned politics for good. In the aftermath of defeat, he had been determined to enjoy himself. Just before Christmas, there'd been a ball at Darvell Hall, a grand if rather gaudy affair. (The Miltons were nouveau riche. Such distinctions had mattered in those days, had somehow been more obvious.) Frederick, enjoying himself a little too determinedly, had got rather tipsy. His wife had been less than impressed with him. One of her headaches had come on; not that she was a sal volatile sort of woman, but she'd liked to be the centre of attention, and her headaches had invariably served a strategic purpose. She'd prevailed on Philip Milton to take her home. Frederick had begged her to stay. She'd shaken him off. She'd shaken him off rather vigorously. Frederick had lost his balance, fallen against a console table, and cut his cheek open. Unrepentant, Emerald had taken her leave. (She had not pushed him, she'd insisted later, that was a lie. He'd been too drunk to stand. Everyone knew that Frederick Rycroft could not hold his liquor.)

Eloise had been blissfully unaware of all this. She'd been taken up with dancing. She'd danced with Jonathan many times that evening. She'd been the envy of the other girls, for Jonathan, at thirty, had been in his prime: handsome, dashing, and perhaps just a little disreputable, enough to make him intriguing as well as eligible. Their preoccupation with one another had not passed unnoticed, had been remarked on, but this hadn't seemed to matter. Let people say what they liked! Everything soon would be settled. An unspoken proposal already hung in the air between them. Jonathan had only to give it voice.

Not until the ball was over, and she was getting ready to leave, had Eloise discovered that Emerald and Philip had gone already, and that Frederick was — not to put too fine a point on it — blind drunk. She'd watched, shivering in the cold night air, as Jonathan and the coachman bundled her brother into the carriage. Frederick had passed out even before they started off.

She remembered sitting opposite him. She remembered seeing him with his head lolling and his mouth open, his face flushed, his cheek smeared with dried blood where he'd fallen and cut himself (he'd borne the scar ever after). A frosty night, she remembered, and the carriage window kept slipping open, as they jolted over the ruts and potholes on the back roads between Darvell Hall and Clifton. But what did a bit of cold air matter? She'd barely noticed it. Music had still been playing in her head; she'd felt herself spinning and wheeling as if still dancing. When Jonathan, sat beside her, put an arm round her, it was the culmination of her evening. Nothing else was wanted to make it perfect.

But that wasn't the end. Jonathan, in the confines of the carriage, had begun to kiss her over and over. These were different kisses to the kiss in the billiard room all those weeks before, which had seemed so intoxicating; that kiss was chaste by comparison. Whether it was the way he was kissing her, or for some other reason, she'd found herself pressing her body against him, she simply couldn't help it. Daring, brazen, she'd even kissed him back. She'd been swept away by that same feeling which, as a little girl, had made her dig her heels in her pony's side and ride, ride, ride like a mad thing, ignoring the head groom and making Father roar with laughter — his little Amazon. She'd known it was naughty to be so reckless and disobedient, whether riding her pony too hard or kissing Jonathan, but why shouldn't she be naughty once in a while, why shouldn't she? If Frederick, a grown man of twenty-nine, could get falling-down drunk and make a spectacle of himself in public, then she saw no reason why she shouldn't kiss Jonathan in the privacy of the carriage.

Jonathan kissed her lips. He kissed her cheeks, her nose, her ears. There came a subtle change. She began to feel — as she'd never felt with her pony — that it was all happening a little too quickly, that she no longer had hold of the reins, that all she could do was cling on as she was carried off into the unknown.

Jonathan kissed her arms, kissed her shoulders. (She'd been wearing — she remembered it clear as day — a new off-the-shoulder ballgown of striped taffeta, with frilled decorations and a delectably long train. She'd had on her long white gloves that reached to her elbows. Her upper arms and her shoulders had been bare.) He kissed her neck, her throat.

Like a dog, he licked her. He ran his soft, wet tongue along her collarbone, and up her neck as far as her ear, leaving a trail of saliva, cold on her skin. This was more than naughty. It was beyond all her experience. Beyond anything she'd ever imagined. She was not sure that she liked it. Even a bold and fearless Amazon would surely baulk at this.

Ever more avid, his hands moved all over her in the rocking carriage. His fingers, like wriggling worms, burrowed into her clothes. His hands pushed deeper inside her gown. Breathing heavily, crushing her skirts, he climbed astride her, groping her and fondling her, weighing her down. She was frozen in place, struck dumb. She couldn't account for this sudden, terrifying change in him. Perhaps he was drunk. But surely even drink did not have this effect.

It was then that she remembered her brother. She'd been able to see him over Jonathan's shoulder, slumped in the seat opposite, so close she could have reached out and touched him. But even as she made mute appeal with her eyes, willing Frederick to wake up and save her, she suddenly realized how she must look, her hair loose, her frock down to her elbows, her breasts half-bare, Jonathan climbing all over her. She felt it would destroy her, for Frederick to see her like this, to witness her degradation, to carry this image in his head ever after.

Don't wake up, don't wake up! Please don't wake up!

She repeated the silent words over and over like a prayer. She kept her eyes firmly fixed on Frederick's sleeping face. The carriage rattled on through the endless night.

In the cold motor car nearly thirty years later, Eloise shuddered, a creeping sense of dread taking hold of her. She could not help but wonder what else might have happened — what further, terrible indecencies she might have been subjected to — had not the lights of Clifton swung suddenly into view through the carriage window. Up to that moment, she'd been drowning, sinking slowly into a smothering darkness. In the nick of time, she was saved, she was home, her ordeal was over.

With an effort, Eloise banished the memory of that evening back into the recesses of her mind, where she'd kept it safely quarantined these thirty years. She tried to empty her head, as the motor car forged on through the dark winter countryside. The incessant noise of the engine was almost soothing after her discordant, disquieting thoughts. But at least she could console herself that no one else now knew what had happened on that carriage ride from Darvell Hall. To think that people knew would have been like being violated all over again. She'd never spoken of it to anyone, and she felt sure that Jonathan would have kept quiet. His death was the final reprieve. The secret was safe forever.

She looked through the window, searching for the star she'd seen earlier, but the shifting, formless shapes of half-guessed clouds now covered the darkling sky. She watched the clouds, still clutching the collar of her coat, and asked herself if she'd really been so ignorant at the age of twenty-one, ignorant of the ways of men.

Only a few months earlier, the newspapers had been much agitated by shocking revelations of the unspeakable exploitation of young girls in London. Parliament had been moved to pass a law to protect such girls from the ravages of certain depraved and immoral men. Eloise could not say she'd been unconscious of the scandal. But it had happened in London, distant London. London was a law unto itself; a modern-day Babylon, to hear Father talk. There was surely no such stain on the wholesome English countryside. Yet suddenly, in the days after the ball, she'd become aware of impropriety on every side, or so it had seemed. The under-gardener had been discovered kissing the laundry maid in the ironing room. Dr Camborne had spoken in veiled terms, at luncheon one day, of the problem of misbegotten infants in the village. And there was something else, something she'd noticed before, but that only really made sense to her after the scales had fallen from her eyes. Looks exchanged. Meaningful smiles. Sudden silences when she came into a room where they were sat together. There'd seemed only one explanation. Lady Emerald and Philip Milton were lovers.

To have such suspicions of her own brother's wife had seemed terribly wrong, but she'd become worldly wise over the course of one evening and she could no longer ignore what was under her nose; she could not turn the clock back to the days of her innocence before the carriage ride from Darvell Hall. With both Jonathan and Philip Milton guests at Clifton — under the same roof as her — she could not wholly avoid them, and the house had felt oppressive, her stomach forever in knots. She'd taken refuge, as often as she could, in the gardens, despite the December cold. Her winter coat that year had been a warm one with a deep fur collar, and there'd been a matching muff. (Odd, that she remembered so clearly her clothes of yesteryear. But the new gown she'd worn on the night of the ball — the new gown she'd been so proud of — had languished in her wardrobe, never to see the light of day again.)

Sat in the motor car as it swept through the endless dark of the February evening, Eloise pictured the crisp winter afternoon, just a few days after the ball, when she'd walked on the lawn near the mulberry tree. One of her clips had fallen out. Her skirts had started to drag. It was whilst she was searching the grass for her clip that Jonathan had come to her.

He came to her. He tried to kiss her. She wouldn't let him.

She distanced herself, telling the story in silent words as if it had happened to someone else. (But of course she had not let him kiss her — how could he have thought that she would?)

He was taken aback but it didn't put him off, and right there by the mulberry tree he asked her to marry him. She had waited so long for him to ask her. But it was too late. She turned him down.

Pulling the collar of her coat ever closer round her throat — lamenting the warm fur of thirty years ago — Eloise repeated her last words, emphatic. *He asked me to marry him. I turned him down.*

How could she have done otherwise? Yet, at the time, her feelings had been confused. She'd wondered if she might somehow be to blame for his behaviour. She wondered if she was too fastidious. He'd certainly acted as if nothing untoward had happened, unless he'd forgotten about it — or was it that she'd dreamt the whole thing? But it hadn't been a dream. She knew that much. And would an innocent man, she'd asked herself later, have taken her rejection of him so finally?

Her saying no to him would have been the end of it, had the proposal not somehow become public knowledge (Eloise suspected Lady Emerald). The local rumour-mongers had cast around for some sort of explanation for what they saw as her inexplicable refusal. They'd seized on her father's growing antagonism towards the Huntleys.

'Old Harry and his pet hates! He's implacable! The railways, Mr Gladstone — now it's the Huntleys. Everyone knows Miss Rycroft dotes on her father; she would never go against his wishes, whatever her feelings for Viscount Lynford. That's why she turned his lordship down.'

Over time, this speculative guess had come to have the verity of an established fact, for no one ever denied it, least of all Eloise herself. But the rumour-mongers knew nothing of the carriage ride from Darvell Hall.

No sooner had he been rejected than Jonathan departed Clifton. Eloise had not seen him again for a very long time. She'd heard tell of him now and then in the years that followed. He'd gone to America. He'd married an American heiress. Later, he and his wife had returned to England. Soon after, Eloise had seen an announcement in the newspaper, the birth of a son and heir, the only child of the marriage: the boy she'd met for the first time today.

Seventeen years went by. In the autumn of 1902, Jonathan had turned up at Clifton out of the blue. He said that he'd come to see his nephew, young Richard, by then both an orphan and an invalid.

Eloise shifted on the back seat of the motor car as it made its measured way through the winter evening, for she was cold and uncomfortable, and she'd been sitting too long in the same position, her legs starting to cramp. Her thoughts had taken a painful turn. She was remembering, not the remote 1880s, but events of a dozen years ago — and they were events which had caused a rift between her and Albert, the only serious rift in their eighteen years of marriage.

After his first, unexpected visit, Jonathan had called again, for a second, a third, a fourth time. He'd gradually changed his story. It was not just Richard he came to see. It was her, too. It was mainly her, it was only her; she alone mattered. Why had he let her slip through his fingers? He'd been a young hot-head, too easily discouraged.

She'd reproved him, of course. She'd told him in no uncertain terms that she wouldn't permit such talk.

'When did you become so cruel, Eloise? You have a heart of ice! Can't you see how much I adore you?'

He'd told her that she looked the same as she'd done twenty years ago; she'd hardly changed at all. But he had been a shadow of the man she remembered: pale and drawn with sunken eyes, listless and seedy-looking. The ravages of long-thwarted love, he'd insisted. Eloise had been more inclined to put it down to his continuing dissipations — for it was only too clear that, unlike Frederick, Jonathan had never mended his ways. She'd begun to wonder if those whispers about the Musketeers that she'd never taken much notice of might have more than a grain of truth in them; all those tales of drinking and gambling and womanizing — and hints of other, even darker habits. She thought of those rapturous, otherworldly letters he'd sent her long ago. Had they been written in the intoxication of love, or under some other, more sinister influence?

By the time of his visits in 1902, Jonathan's father — the stiff and abstemious earl — had finally lost patience with his son and cut him off without a penny.

'My damned father! The world's worst miser! How I hate him for what he's done to me! But my life would never have got in such a muddle if only you'd married me, Eloise. You'd have kept me on the straight and narrow. Instead, I live in penury, pining for what might have been.'

She'd lent him money, even though she knew he was unlikely ever to repay her (he hadn't). She'd lent him far more than she ever dared admit to Albert. Whether Jonathan had asked outright, or whether she'd offered, she could not now remember, but it had become part of the pattern of his visits, her repairing to the parlour to write out a cheque, her handing it to him without a word as he got up to leave.

Albert had been hurt, puzzled, angry, when he learned what his wife had neglected to tell him: that Viscount Lynford had become a regular visitor at Clifton. Albert had demanded an explanation. But how could she explain her actions to him when she hardly understood them herself? And so Albert had taken himself off to Coventry in high dudgeon, to stay with Mr Simcox. Eloise had followed him a few days later. Not that she'd doubted he would return sooner or later, but she hated things to fester.

Albert had not, in his heart, suspected her of anything improper, nor did he believe she'd deliberately deceived him, though he'd made a show of accusing her of both. Perhaps what had most stung him was how it might look to other people, especially those who knew Eloise's history with Viscount Lynford. Usually, Albert didn't 'give a damn' what people thought, but there was no accounting for the vagaries of male pride.

Albert had not known everything; he'd only heard the bare bones of the story of their courtship, her and Jonathan. But he'd not needed to be told what sort of man Jonathan was.

'Why, Ellie, why? Why would you have such a man in the house?'

'He's an old friend of the family. He's Richard's uncle.'

Was that all? Was there not some small part of her flattered by Jonathan's protestations of undying love?

No. Not that. Then what? Why had she not followed the old earl's example, and cast Jonathan aside? Was it simply weakness? Had she been too weak to show him the door — just as she'd been too weak to fight him off in the carriage all those years ago?

But when she had ventured to suggest that she'd shown weakness in entertaining Jonathan's visits, Albert had cut her short.

'Weak?' he'd cried. 'Good grief, Ellie, you're not weak, where'd you get that idea? There's not an ounce of weakness in you — unless you count pity as a weakness.'

He was right, of course. He'd seen it at once. Albert knew her better than she knew herself. If anyone was weak, it was Jonathan; he'd always been the same, too weak to resist temptation, too weak to curb his baser passions and prevent them gaining mastery over him. How sad it was — tragic, even — that a young man of such promise and distinction should fall so low. She'd felt that strongly in 1902 — for she had grown in the years since they'd last met, and he had diminished. On that carriage ride from Darvell Hall, she'd been innocent and ingenuous and unprepared, but seventeen years later she was a wife, a mother, the custodian of Clifton Park — at the height of her powers — whilst all Jonathan had left was the terrible waste of a life unfulfilled. Of course she'd pitied him. Albert had been right about that, too.

And so they'd come through that crisis, because of Albert's clear thinking. From the very first moment she'd met him, she'd known she could rely on Albert, she could trust him, which she'd never felt with Jonathan.

She noticed that there were now lights outside the motor car, the glow of lamp-lit windows. They were passing through a village, and it was a place she recognized, the village of Welby, what little there was of it: just one main street; the Railway Inn; the station. Already they were leaving the lights behind, passing under the bridge which carried the main line down from London, heading out into the darkness once more. But Hayton was not far off now and, after Hayton, Clifton and home.

She went back in her mind to what she'd been thinking about. Eighteen years, she said to herself. Eighteen years she'd been married to Albert, until the day the footman burst in on her in the parlour — the most recent John, it had been, the one who was now in the army: Herbert Basford, to give him his proper name, which Dorothea preferred and Rosa insisted on. He'd only been with them a matter of days back then.

'Ma'am! Ma'am! Come quick! It's the master. There's something wrong.' Poor boy. He'd been terribly shaken.

She'd found Albert where he'd keeled over on the settee in the drawing room, mute and in pain, his body twisted, his face grey, eyes wide and staring, the breath rattling in his throat. She'd sat with him until the doctor came. Arthur Camborne had arrived post-haste from the village, but it had all been over by then. Albert was dead. His heart, Dr Camborne said. There was nothing anyone could have done.

Albert's death came barely a week before his sixty-third birthday, which was no age at all. Eloise still had, in a drawer of her bureau, the pair of gold cufflinks she'd been going to give him.

Eloise shook her head, as if to free herself of this spider's web of memories. She'd spent so much time these last few days looking back — beginning and ending with death: Jonathan's, Albert's. And perhaps that was only to be expected when there'd been a funeral looming. But now the funeral was over and she was nearly home and it was time to look forward again. The motor was passing through Hayton. Soon the long beam of the headlights would search out the turning to Clifton.

She faltered for a moment. It had been such a long journey home, she felt quite drained, and she wondered how she would find the strength to go on. But in a minute or two, the house would come into view and the motor would pull up by the front steps. Despite the detours, she would be just in time for dinner. Crompton would open the door to her, perhaps there'd be a letter from Roderick, or news of Dorothea. Up in her room, with the fire lit and the curtains drawn, she would divest herself of her mourning and dress for dinner, then she would go downstairs and pick up once more all the threads of her day-to-day life.

CHAPTER SIX

When, towards the end of May, Mrs Adnitt and Mrs Lambell from the village had called at Clifton about the church fête, August had seemed an age away.

'First things first.' Mrs Adnitt had taken a seat on the sofa in the parlour and set about removing her gloves finger by finger (she always came to Clifton 'properly dressed'). 'Ought there to be a fête at all this year?'

'What Sybil means to say,' Mrs Lambell had elucidated, 'is would it be quite proper? It does seem rather frivolous to be talking about the fête, after everything that has happened recently.'

May, it was true, had been a dispiriting month. A hopeful British attack on the Western Front had unaccountably stalled; the reason, it was discovered, was a shortage of shells. The newspapers had trumpeted 'the shell scandal' and there'd been a public outcry: something must be done, heads would have to roll.

Heads did not roll. They increased in number instead. A coalition government now ruled with an unwieldy Cabinet of twenty or more. Mr Asquith remained prime minister.

All through the weeks of wrangling, the daily casualty lists had continued. As if this catalogue of death was not enough, by a cruel twist in mid-May there'd been a dreadful rail smash near Gretna Green, over two hundred lives lost. Crueller still, many of the victims turned out to be Scotch soldiers on their way to the front. Their names would never now appear in the newspapers under the heading 'Killed in Action'; they had perished instead in a pointless accident. Pointless, Father would have added, but entirely predictable; he'd always said railways were the work of the Devil.

So much tragedy had seemed at times hard to bear. One began to doubt that anything would be gained by going on with the war. But just as one was doubting, the Germans proved once more why they had to be stopped. Already in April they'd stooped to using poison gas; in May they plumbed new depths. On the seventh of that month, they'd sunk the passenger liner *Lusitania*; scores of civilians had drowned. And then, just a few weeks later, the Zeppelins returned. Zeppelins had already bombed several coastal towns. This time London came under attack. More innocent civilians had died. Would the Germans stop at nothing? Was this really the same country from which Johann Kaufmann came, Dorothea's quiet, polite husband, and Johann's father, every inch a gentleman? Could Dr Kaufmann possibly condone the use of poison gas and sky bombs?

Next to all this, the church fête had seemed a paltry matter.

'No one would blame us if we cancelled,' Mrs Lambell had ventured.

'That's all very well,' Mrs Adnitt had said. 'But is it not our patriotic duty to carry on as normal in the face of this enemy onslaught? Our boys in the fighting line expect it of us; it's what they are fighting for.'

Mrs Adnitt might have sounded somewhat pompous, but that did not make her wrong. Eloise, indeed, had been aware that she'd said something in a similar vein on the day of Mark Somersby's wedding last December. The annual fête might seem of little importance, but sometimes it was the little things that mattered. A decision had therefore been made. The fête would go ahead.

In May, August had seemed an age away, but now August was here. It was the day of the fête, the Sunday before the bank holiday, and Eloise was on her way to the village in the best Clifton motor, dressed for the occasion and ready to do her duty.

* * *

The motor car swept into the village and drew up by the green. The best Clifton motor still looked the part, though it was two years old now; production of a new BFS model had been indefinitely suspended, just as Mr Smith had predicted last summer. The rather elderly chauffeur, who was proving a less than satisfactory replacement for Smith, fumbled with the door. Eloise stepped out onto the grass.

The other members of the organizing committee were waiting to receive her. Known simply as 'the Committee', this body was something of a village institution, with Eloise the unofficial but acknowledged head. Other members included the genial old vicar and his hospitable wife; Mrs Adnitt, a woman of big words and grand ideas who lived at The Hawthorns, one of the larger houses in the village; and Mrs Lambell, whose husband was headmaster of the village school. Unassuming, but pragmatic and indefatigable, Mrs Lambell was unlikely to talk portentously of 'our boys at the front', as Mrs Adnitt did; but had she done so, it would not have been empty rhetoric: all three of her sons had volunteered in the early days of the war.

With Eloise's arrival, proceedings got underway. The vicar said a few words, declared the fête open, then Eloise led the Committee on a tour of inspection. It was Mrs Adnitt who'd dubbed this year's event 'a homage to England'. The bunting was red, white and blue, and there were rather more flags than usual — mostly Union Flags, but also the flags of the Allies: of France and Russia and Belgium, and one said to be the flag of Serbia, though there was some doubt about that. Providentially — and to Mrs Adnitt's immense satisfaction — there was also a man in uniform, symbolic of all England's fighting men: Mrs Lambell's youngest boy had arrived home on leave only yesterday. Here on the green, there were several stalls as usual — white elephant; tombola; bread and cakes; jams, preserves and pickles — as well as the coconut shy, a marquee for the flower show, and an area roped off for games. The teams were already lining up for the first round of the tug-of-war.

The fête, as ever, was split in two. Away from the green, in the more genteel surroundings of the vicarage garden, seats had been set out for those wishing to enjoy music and refreshments. The Miss Evanses had emerged from hibernation to run the tea stall as usual, more doddery and decrepit than ever, fumbling the cups and saucers, spilling the milk and sugar — but the fête wouldn't have been the same without them.

The Committee was always much in demand on fête day — there were last-minute hitches to deal with, contests to judge, prizes to give out — and Eloise was kept busy for the next couple of hours.

* * *

The sun was glowing behind a thin veil of cloud, the air was still and warm, the vicarage garden lush and green and verging on the overgrown. Eloise sat down with a cup of tea on a cast-iron chair, glad to take the weight off her feet at last and snatch a moment to herself.

The vicarage was set at an angle to the High Street, and was walled off in its own grounds. The rear elevation faced the churchyard, its brick-built facade festooned with ivy; French windows opened onto a flagstone patio crammed with terracotta pots. At any other time, thought Eloise, this back garden would have been a tranquil place, but today the door in the end wall, which served as a shortcut to the church, stood open, so that people could circulate freely between the green and the vicarage garden; as well as the tea stall, there was music in the form of Mrs Lambell's daughter's violin. From the green came the faint clamour of other, and rather more raucous, amusements; the tug-of-war was still in progress by the sound of the shouting and cheering: Wilmot's Farm against Manor Farm against Home Farm, the Red Lion versus the Barley Mow. The teams, as they lined up on the green earlier, had looked a little depleted this year, with so many young men missing, but apart from that, and the flags, it could have been any other year.

Eloise watched people coming and going as she drank her tea. She could name only some of them; Dorothea would have known them all (but Dorothea was still in London, nursing). A young woman in a threadbare frock was shambling across the lawn with a child on her hip; Eloise recognized her as Hobson, the erstwhile maid, now Mrs Carter, of course. The child, Eloise judged, looked six months old at least, which perhaps explained the girl's rather precipitate marriage last year. Not that one was in any position to cast aspersions, when one's own grandchild—

But people now had more important things to worry about than counting the months between Roderick's marriage and the birth of his daughter.

Eloise raised her cup to her lips to sip the last of her tea, but paused in the act, watching as Mrs Carter met Rosa coming the other way. Mrs Carter stuck her nose in the air and tossed her lank hair, ostentatiously turning her head away — 'uppity' was the word that came to mind. But Rosa did not seem to notice, deep in conversation with a friend from her Oxford days who was staying with them at Clifton just now. If Rosa had any idea of Roderick's philandering, she covered it well, but Eloise was of the opinion that Rosa had not been told, by Roderick or by anyone else. What suspicions Rosa might harbour was impossible to know. Eloise had not forgotten Rosa's words in the drawing room a year ago: *I may know nothing about Roderick's black eye, but you obviously do. Never mind. Keep your little secrets.* It was a secret Eloise would much rather not have had to keep.

Eloise's fingers tightened on her cup. She wanted to jerk Mrs Carter away from Rosa, felt the urge to slap the hussy, who seemed intent on rubbing Rosa's nose in it, her sordid assignations with Roderick. Rosa's ignorance of the affair left her somehow exposed, defenceless. She had on today a plain blue frock, almost presentable, which had none of the defiance of her usual, bohemian style.

The moment was fleeting. Roderick's two women passed each other and moved apart, heading in opposite directions. Eloise relaxed her grip on her cup, turned her attention to little Katherine, who was doddering along between Rosa and the Oxford friend, clinging to their hands, mouth puckered in concentration as she placed one unsteady foot in front of the other. Next Saturday would be Katherine's first birthday; Roderick turned twenty-three the day after. He would not be home for either occasion. Eloise's thoughts softened towards her son as she thought of other birthdays of his she'd not spent with him. She'd missed a good many, one way or another. Yes, he'd been at home last year, but his birthday had been rather overlooked, what with the outbreak of war and the birth of his child. The previous year, she'd been in Scarborough; the year before, his birthday had come in the aftermath of Dorothea's wedding. He'd spent his eighteenth on holiday in Europe with Dorothea and Elizabeth; his seventeenth had seen him in Shropshire, staying with a school friend, that plump boy whose name escaped her. Only his nineteenth birthday had been celebrated properly, only one birthday out of the last six: the year of the hot summer, the summer before he went up to Oxford. There was always next year, of course. But the future was far too uncertain to offer much of a consolation.

Eloise got to her feet, adjusting her hat, pinning it at the right angle, and feeling with her hand to make sure the bow was still in place. She left the cup and saucer on the grass beside her chair, not wanting to run the risk of another rambling conversation with the Miss Evanses. Her skirts skimmed across the lawn as she made her way unhurriedly round the garden with the mournful tones of Mrs Lambell's daughter's violin to accompany her. Rather a dirge, this tune. Not exactly the right sort of thing for the occasion. Music, Eloise had to confess, was one of the failures of this year's fête. There was always something, despite the careful planning. What could they do next year by way of music? They'd once had a barrel organ, another time a German band. But a German band was out of the question, of course, even if there were any left in England.

As Eloise reached the patio, Elizabeth came galloping into the vicarage garden, looking particularly gangling and awkward today — and she would dash about as if she hadn't a minute to live. Fingering the smooth green leaves of a bay tree in a pot, Eloise watched as Elizabeth made a beeline for a rosy-cheeked, middle-aged woman standing with a cup of tea and listening to the music. Colour flushed into Elizabeth's cheeks as a torrent of words poured out of her; Eloise could not hear what she was saying. The woman Eloise now recognized as Mrs Turner listened to Elizabeth gravely until, finally getting a word in, she broke into a beaming smile and patted the girl's arm, quickly putting Elizabeth at her ease — making her laugh, even — as if it was the most natural thing in the world. Perhaps it came with practice, for Mrs Turner had — how many children? Dorothea would know. All Eloise could say for certain was that several of the Turner children had worked at Clifton down the years; there was a girl there now, employed as the nursery maid, and there was the boy, of course, who'd been for so long a fixture in the stables; their father was an agricultural labourer.

Eloise pursed her lips, thinking of the boy, Turner, whom she'd seen alone with Elizabeth in the stable yard last December. Was Elizabeth asking for news of him?

Eloise had breathed a sigh of relief when, some four months ago now, Turner handed in his notice. He was off to join the army — the cavalry — in order to 'do his bit', as the expression was these days. But even with Turner gone, Eloise had not forgotten what she'd first noticed in December: that other men beside him had begun to notice Elizabeth. Right here and now, for instance, the Lambell boy, over by the wisteria, eating cake that was crumbling in his fingers, was watching Elizabeth across the garden with what seemed to Eloise a look of appraisal.

'What a mess he's making with that cake!'

Eloise was joined on the patio by Mrs Lambell, who was gazing indulgently at her son.

'He always was a messy eater, the dear boy. I say "boy", but he looks very grown-up in that uniform. I do worry about him. I worry about David and Wallace as well, of course, but Rawdon's always been the baby of the family. You must know what it's like to worry, Mrs Brannan. You must worry about Roderick. How is Roderick?'

'Very well, thank you. A letter came just the other day. He's at Woking now, in training with his battalion. There are replica trenches, he tells me: exact copies of the trenches at the front.'

'Rawdon, too, is still based in England. His regiment, or corps, or whatever it's called — I get these military words mixed up — has been sent overseas, but they had too many officers. Rawdon was surplus to requirements and left behind. He was most disappointed. He can't wait to get going.'

'Roderick is the same.' 'Champing at the bit' were the words he'd used in his letter.

'They were great friends at one time, Rawdon and Roderick.'

'Yes, I seem to remember.'

'They used to play cricket together.'

'Did they?'

'Oh, yes. They played cricket in Row Meadow, played for hours on end. Many's the time I had to send Maisie, our maid, to fetch Rawdon for his dinner.'

Eloise had only vague memories of Roderick's friendship with Rawdon Lambell; it had reached a natural end, she rather thought, when Roderick went away to prep school. She knew that cricket had always been a passion with Roderick, but cricket 'for hours on end' in Row Meadow? Eloise knew nothing of that. Roderick had never told her — which wasn't entirely surprising. He'd always been a self-contained little boy, who kept things close to his chest. 'A handful', Nanny had called him.

Nanny had reported regularly from the nursery. 'Such a handful, madam, and so naughty at times. I'm afraid I had to beat him again today. It's the only way he'll learn.'

Necessary, no doubt. Nanny knew best. But Eloise was sure she could not have stood and watched whilst Roderick was beaten, still less have beaten him herself. And what had Nanny been thinking, to let Roderick roam the countryside seemingly at will, playing cricket for hours on end? It was too late to ask her now. Nanny had departed Clifton years ago.

Had Rawdon also been a handful? One wouldn't think so, to look at him now. If Mrs Lambell was fortunate today, having Rawdon home on leave, she'd been equally fortunate in the past, when her son came home from school every afternoon; whilst Roderick was away at boarding school, Rawdon had been a day boy at — where was it? Eloise forgot.

Rawdon licked the last crumbs off his fingers. He was stood by the far wall; somewhere the other side of the wall was Row Meadow, where he'd played cricket. He was talking now to his sister, who'd taken a break after the mournful dirge she'd been playing. She had her violin in one hand, her bow in the other, and she was laughing at something her brother had said; they looked easy in each other's company. There was less of an age gap, Eloise judged, than between Roderick and Elizabeth. Did Mrs Lambell find her daughter as troublesome as Eloise found Elizabeth? It was one thing for Roderick to have gone gallivanting round the countryside when a boy, but for a girl such behaviour was unwise — dangerous, even. Mrs Lambell would surely agree.

It was on the tip of Eloise's tongue to ask, but something held her back. She had a certain position, she had responsibilities. She was here today, not as a widow and a mother, but as a member of the Committee and the mistress of Clifton

Park; she felt it beholden on her to keep a little aloof, just as Clifton was set apart from the village. A silly idea, perhaps — Dorothea might think so, Rosa definitely would. But these social distinctions were real, and they mattered, however much Rosa liked to pretend they didn't.

'I was talking just now,' said Mrs Lambell, 'to your daughter-in-law's friend — Miss Ward, is it?'

'Yes, that's right. Her mother is one of the Miltons of Darvell Hall.'

Miss Ward was a plain and rather serious young woman. She'd arrived only yesterday. Her train had been late, dinner delayed in consequence. The London stations, she'd said, were positively overflowing with bank-holiday trippers. Hayton, with its fête, was not alone, it seemed, in carrying on as normal.

'Such odd ideas she has about the war,' Mrs Lambell went on. 'That's what comes of an Oxford education, I suppose. Don't misunderstand me, Mrs Brannan. I'm not against girls being educated. I want the best for my Stella. But I shouldn't like to see her at a university. My children laugh at me. They call me old-fashioned. Perhaps I am.'

'I think we are all a little old-fashioned at our time of life, and somewhat set in our ways. But I like to think we still have something to offer.'

'You're right, of course. You so often are.' Mrs Lambell sighed. 'To think it will be a year, come Wednesday — a whole year since the war began. No one dreamed of it lasting a year. And now here we are, twelve months later, and no one can say when it all might end. I'm glad, though, that we decided to go ahead with the fête. It seems fitting, somehow. I'd even go so far as to say it's been a success. So, yes, we old fossils still have our uses! Well, if you'll excuse me, Mrs Brannan, I see that Stella is going to play again. I haven't had chance yet to watch her play.'

A little crowd had gathered around Stella Lambell. Eloise looked on from the patio, conscious of her isolation, but pleased too, for the fête was a success; Mrs Lambell had said so — all their efforts had not been in vain.

Stella played a rather jaunty tune this time, a jig. As Eloise listened, a great throaty cheer went up on the green, one team no doubt having just bested another in the tug-of-war. The sound of cheering and the sound of the music mingled for a moment, and rose up and up, to be lost far above in the cloud-strewn August sky.

* * *

Another fête had come and gone, and now August was half over. Miss Ward, with her Oxford ideas, had been nearly three weeks at Clifton. Today was the third Saturday of her visit. For dinner this evening Cook had prepared roast duck.

Miss Ward, on previous visits, had been Rosa's staunch ally, but this time Eloise sensed a certain friction between the friends, a rift that, in hindsight, had begun as long ago as Katherine's christening last autumn. Rosa had ventured to suggest back then that, although all wars are an evil, some wars might be a necessary evil. Miss Ward had condemned such apostasy in no uncertain terms, and she appeared to take great pleasure now in raking over those old arguments — if she took pleasure in anything (she was a rather humourless young woman). Clever talk was always the centrepiece of any meal with Miss Ward; Cook's excellent roast duck was eaten almost as an afterthought.

'I really am appalled, Rosa, that you should allow yourself to be taken in by all this jingoistic nonsense — you of all people! You used to be so clear-headed! You do realize that you are repudiating everything we ever agreed on at the Thursday Evening Club?'

The Thursday Evening Club was a sort of discussion group, as Eloise understood it, that Rosa and Miss Ward had attended in London. From what Miss Ward said, it seemed now in abeyance; there had not been a meeting for months.

'Just because we don't meet, doesn't mean we should abandon all our principles! I know for a fact that Leo and

Tom and Aidan are still of the same mind — Leo, Rosa, your own brother!'

'We were too simplistic,' Rosa argued. 'It's all very well saying there oughtn't to be any wars, but there is a war, it's happening, we can't ignore it. You have to admit, Maggie, that the Germans haven't behaved very well.'

'Don't tell me you actually believe all those stories of German brutality?'

'Are you saying they're fabricated?'

'That's beside the point. Even if there's a grain of truth in them, it's unlikely that one side should have a monopoly in wickedness. War itself is wicked: it's an outrage against our common humanity.'

'The Germans are despoiling France, they are kill-ing English civilians from the air.' (There'd been another Zeppelin raid only a few days ago.) 'It was they who began the war, with the conquest of Belgium by force of arms. Are we to stand by and let them get away with it?'

'Is that what we're fighting for — for Belgium?' asked Miss Ward scornfully.

'Well . . . yes . . . I suppose so . . . amongst other things.'

'Don't be so naïve, Rosa! The war is not about Belgium. The war has become an end in itself. No one knows anymore what it's for. All that matters is victory, victory at any price. And the price gets ever higher. That's why we've got National Register Day tomorrow.'

'What is National Register Day?' Elizabeth dared to ask. She'd been looking from Miss Ward to Rosa and back again, as she tried to follow the argument.

'It's a ploy, a trick,' said Miss Ward. 'A way of putting pressure on men to enlist. Coercion, that's what it is. A first step on the road to conscription. But if the government thinks people will stand for conscription, then they're wrong. If they try to bring it in, they will split the country.'

'But, Maggie, if conscription is necessary—'

'Oh, do wake up, Rosa! There's never been conscription in England. It's one of our basic freedoms. We're told that the war is to protect our freedoms and to defeat German militarism. But if we replace our freedoms with a militarism of our own, what's the point in fighting at all? Leo understands this, Tom and Aidan too. I expect Kolya feels the same, wherever he is. Kolya would be ashamed of you, Rosa!'

Rosa flushed at this but said no more. There was silence round the table, as Crompton collected the plates.

Later, in the drawing room, when Miss Ward had gone to fetch a book from her room, Rosa said, 'Maggie can be so intractable. But she will be gone soon. She is leaving the day after tomorrow.'

She almost sounded glad of it.

* * *

The Times, which in Father's day had been ironed and stitched each morning and kept in perfect order, was now pulled apart and spread around the morning room by Rosa and Elizabeth in daily pursuit of the latest news. The maids, tidying up, never put the pages back in the right order, which was most disconcerting when one came to read it later. Not that there were quite so many pages to sort through these days. Newspapers were decidedly thinner than they'd been before the war.

Eloise put *The Times* aside and sifted through the other newspapers piled beside her on the chaise longue. Rosa insisted on taking *The Manchester Guardian*. She said that *The Times* was much too pompous and served merely as a mouthpiece for Lord Northcliffe. Eloise had wondered if *The Manchester Guardian* might perhaps be a paper that Rosa's father had worked on, but it turned out that he'd never been printed in any of the newspapers one might have heard of, which rather led one to question if he'd been a proper journalist at all.

Taking off her spectacles and holding them in her hand, Eloise stared into space as she reflected on the fact that she knew very little about Rosa's background. Roderick showed scant interest in such things. Where Rosa came from didn't matter to him. Perhaps his was the right attitude. One couldn't help being curious, all the same.

Eloise had met Rosa's family — such as it was — only once, more than a year and a half ago, at the wedding in Tonbridge. Rosa's father, the putative journalist, was dead — as was the mother, for that matter — which left just Rosa herself, an elder brother, a younger sister, and two maiden aunts. It was the aunts who lived in Tonbridge, and it was they who had organized the wedding. Somewhat fusty and set in their ways, the aunts were otherwise perfectly respectable. They'd been most anxious to point out that what they called 'Rosa's little foibles' came from her father's side. Eloise had been given the distinct impression that the aunts believed their dear younger sister (Rosa's mother) had married a man who was beneath her, though for their sister's sake, and in the spirit of Christian forgiveness, they'd always done their best to get on with him. When their sister passed away — tragically young — they'd felt it their duty to do what they could for her poor, motherless children. But their brother-in-law had been a most obdurate man. He'd accused them of interfering, he'd distanced himself and his children. The aunts had been forced to look on from the sidelines.

The aunts had picked their words carefully, had uttered no infelicities, but Eloise could easily imagine that when their brother-in-law also passed away, some six years after his wife, they'd seen it as an opportunity to bring their nephew and nieces in from beyond the pale. Rosa and her brother, however, had proved equally as headstrong as their father. Neither of them had been of age when their father died, but they'd refused point-blank to leave London. They wouldn't even send their little sister Carla to be looked after in Tonbridge. All that was left to the aunts was to offer advice and guidance, and pray that things would turn out well. There must have seemed little hope of that, or so Eloise surmised, when their nephew announced that he intended to become an artist, and Rosa took herself off to Oxford; even Mrs Lambell had baulked at the idea of a university education for a girl. But then Rosa had met Roderick. Marriage to a man like Roderick, Eloise had been given to understand at the time of the wedding, was better than anything the aunts could have hoped for with regard to their benighted niece. Eloise, looking at it from the other side, could only agree. Of course, she'd not said as much.

Roderick. Everything always came back to Roderick. Eloise's thoughts were never far from him. Was it really eight months since they'd seen him last? It felt more like eight years. He'd never been away from home so long, not in his school days, nor when he was at Oxford. There'd been a letter a few days after the fête raising hopes that he might soon get leave. Then he'd written again. His leave was cancelled, he was going on a course instead. There'd been no more talk of leave since then. The one consolation for his continued absence was the fact that, in all these months, his battalion had done nothing more dangerous than digging part of London's outer defences; and the most excitement they'd had was to be inspected by an endless procession of dignitaries: Lord Kitchener one week, the King and Queen and Princess Mary the next. But now—

Eloise put her spectacles back on. She picked a newspaper out of the pile beside her, one of the local Northampton dailies; the Northampton papers often carried news of Roderick's regiment. She found the paragraph she was looking for and read it once more:

A large number of men of the Northamptonshire Regiment left Castle Station on Tuesday . . . they went off in good cheer . . . friends and family saw them off at the station . . . there were many tearful partings . . . when we shall see them again nobody knows . . .

She lowered the newspaper to her lap and took off her spectacles; her eyes focused on, but did not take in, the rich patterns and deep colours of the wallpaper across the room, above the line of the dado. Those men departing from Castle Station, they'd been luckier than Roderick, they must have been home on leave; now they were returning in haste to their battalion. They were returning en masse because, as Roderick had written in his most recent letter, 'We have at last received orders to proceed to France. I needn't tell you, Mother, how bucked up we all are!'

This letter had arrived three days ago, and the men had left Northampton on Tuesday. Which meant — well, what did it mean? Could it be that Roderick was in France already? Had enough time passed for that? There was no way of knowing. Not until his next letter came.

When would his next letter come?

* * *

The village of Brockmorton was not much more than a mile from Clifton when taking the old bridleway across the fields, but it was rather further by motor, a journey which involved a detour to the old turnpike, a Roman road, in order to reach the narrow lane which wound its way to Brockmorton, and then on to Broadstone and Willbourne. As she was driven back along this lane after calling at Brockmorton Manor, Eloise almost wished she had come in the old landaulet with the roof down, for it was a glorious afternoon, more like high summer than September. The grass verges were lush and green, the hedgerows still in full leaf; an occasional ash tree, its leaves sparkling in the sunlight, cast dappled shadows over the neglected-looking meadows. To her left, the land rose in long, gentle slopes towards the hump-backed summit of Duncan's Hill. To ride as far as Duncan's Hill on her pony had been the height of adventure when she was a girl. There was a splendid view from the hilltop. With her back towards home, she'd looked out over unknown lands, yearning to explore, torn between her desire to go on and the knowledge that she'd already come much further than she was allowed. How wild she'd been, how fearless! It made her smile to remember.

Not far from the lane, on the lower slopes of the hill, stood one of the ventilation shafts for Duncan's Hill Tunnel:

a simple, round, red-brick structure that looked rather like a giant chimney, an unexpected sight in such bucolic surroundings. She'd always thought it faintly sinister. Certainly, there was something disconcerting in the fact that, hundreds of feet below, trains were constantly hurtling through the smoke-choked darkness, their whistles wailing in the wind of their speed.

Father had been able to remember when the tunnel was built; he'd been but a boy at the time, newly arrived at Clifton in the 1830s, adopted as heir by his Uncle Edward, last of the Massinghams. Work on the tunnel had been plagued by roof-falls and quicksand. The rough-and-ready navvies who built it had also been cause for concern. On one occasion, they'd rioted in Welby village and the militia had to be called out to restore order. Father had spoken of this; he'd also spoken of a most dangerous game the navvies had dared to play. Dicing with death, they'd challenged each other to jump across the openings of the half-built ventilation shafts, where one slip would result in a terrifying plunge into darkness: one small slip, and a man's life would have been over. Eloise as a girl had wondered what on earth made them do it. She'd wondered how it would feel. She'd asked herself if she would have the courage to try. She'd rather thought that she might. Oh, yes, she'd been wild and fearless back then.

Fearless, she now said to herself, or naïve? It made no difference either way. The young would not be told. They thought themselves immortal.

The ventilation shaft was left behind as the motor car continued on its way. The sun was shining brightly, the countryside green and peaceful; it looked almost unchanged since the days when she'd ridden here on her pony. Brockmorton Manor had also looked the same as always. The broken pipes were now repaired. There was no sign of the damage they'd caused last winter. When she visited the Manor these days, Eloise was mindful of her conversation with Mark Somersby on the day of his wedding, but if she half expected to find Viola shrivelled and shrunken and racked with pain, the reality always proved otherwise. Nonetheless, she could not help but look for signs. Was Viola keeping to her chair more than usual? Was that a grimace as she reached for her tea? In truth, there was nothing, no hint at all that she was ill. On the contrary, she had looked today the very picture of health, as if she was blooming instead of fading — rather like this burst of summer in September. She'd been rapturous over Mark's new-born son, just a few days old. The boy was named Maximilian.

'Not a name that runs in the family.' Eloise had bitten her tongue, but too late. One had grown so used to the cut-and-thrust of conversations with Viola Somersby that the habit died hard, especially when the memory of last autumn still rankled: Viola's visit to Clifton a few weeks after Katherine's christening and the pointed remarks she'd made. (Unlike Katherine, Maximilian Somersby had been born in due time, a respectable nine months after the wedding last December.)

'No, not a family name.' Cradling the infant, Viola had laughed, as if she too remembered last autumn and now renounced such pettiness; the room had fairly rung to the sound of her unaffected laughter. 'Not a family name, but it suits him. He looks like a Maximilian.'

There was no telling when Mark could hope to meet his firstborn. He'd not been home since his wedding. All the talk of his 'going to the front', however, had proved to be somewhat wide of the truth. He had a staff posting; his work kept him well behind the lines.

'We have sent him some pictures. A photographer came from Lawham to take them. Maximilian behaved himself admirably — didn't you, my brave little man, my little soldier!' Mrs Somersby had looked up from the child she couldn't stop cooing over. 'How is Roderick faring with the Northamptons?'

'He is in France, that is all we know.'

'Mark could tell us more, I'm sure, but I expect it's all top secret. He's very guarded in his letters home.'

'Roderick is the same.' But Eloise had learned to read between the lines of Roderick's letters; she'd had plenty of practice down the years.

The motor jerked and swerved, jolting Eloise out of her reverie and throwing her around in her seat. She was sure she heard, muffled by the glass partition, Smith in the driver's seat cursing. There was no denying that the drive to Brockmorton and back had been far from smooth; Eloise questioned the wisdom in offering Smith his old position. But it had seemed the natural thing to do, when he wrote to her from Coventry. 'Dear Mrs Brannan,' he'd written in an ill-formed and laborious hand, with great curved letters. 'Dear Mrs Brannan—'

But the exact wording was neither here nor there. The gist of it was, that he was bored at home, couldn't find work that suited, and had no hope, given his damaged leg, of following his elder brother into the army. He often thought of his time at Clifton, he'd written, would like to come back if at all possible. Eloise had been happy to accommodate him. She'd lost all confidence in his replacement since the roundabout journey on the day of Jonathan's funeral. Also, she felt obligated. Smith had been in her service at the time of the accident; she had a certain responsibility towards him. That he was the son of the man who'd helped make Albert's businesses such a success ought not to be forgotten, either.

Only when Smith returned to Clifton, keen as mustard, had she discovered that he now walked with a noticeable limp. One leg was shorter than the other, he'd explained: something to do with the way the bones had healed. It would not be a problem, he'd insisted. But Eloise could not help wondering, as he chauffeured her back from Brockmorton, whether his leg made driving rather too difficult.

Her mind went back to the beginning of the journey to Brockmorton. They'd stopped off in Hayton so she could visit the post office. She'd taken to posting letters to Roderick by her own hand. Silly, perhaps, but it made her feel one step closer to him.

Mr Downie had greeted her from behind the counter. 'Hello, Mrs Brannan. Another for Master Roderick, is it? How is he getting on, if you don't mind me asking?'

'He's doing very well, Mr Downie, thank you. He's in France now.'

'In France, is he? Ah. I see. Then I'll make sure this gets off as soon as maybe. You can rely on me, Mrs Brannan.'

'I know I can, Mr Downie, and it is most appreciated. Good afternoon.'

She'd stepped out of the post office, pulling on her gloves. The motor had been parked near the duck pond. Three ways met in a loop round the pond, a place known in the village as 'the Circle'; here was found, beside the post office, the school and the headmaster's house where the Lambells lived, and the smithy, to which Joey Atkin would never now return to take up his father's trade. Smith had been stood by the Jubilee Oak, a sapling still in full leaf; he'd been talking to a girl — a laughing, vivacious-looking girl, tossing her hair. He'd come hastening back as soon as he caught sight of Eloise, doing his best to disguise his limp, but the sharp-eyed girl had seen and — by the expression on Smith's face — he knew that she'd seen. The girl had given him a particular look, tossing her hair one last time before going on her way, sauntering up School Street with a basket on her arm.

Smith had opened the door for her. Eloise, as she smoothed her gloves onto her hands, had asked, 'Who is that girl, Smith?'

'It's Annie Britten, ma'am.'

'What were you talking about?'

'She was telling me about Billy Turner, ma'am.' Just before he closed the door, Smith had added with unmistakeable bitterness. 'Billy Turner's sent a letter home.'

Eloise pursed her lips as she remembered this exchange. She could see Smith through the glass partition as he drove them back from Brockmorton Manor. He sat stiff and upright in his seat, his shoulders tilting one way, then the other, as he manoeuvred the steering wheel and reached to change gear. She'd noticed earlier, when he was limping round the duck pond, that his chauffeur's uniform, once a snug fit, now rather hung off him. He hadn't got his old strength back; perhaps he never would. He must think himself disregarded because of it. The army didn't want him. And the Britten girl? Eloise had seen the way the girl looked at him, a look of disinterested pity mixed with unwitting disdain. How many other young men would come to know such looks, as they returned from the war maimed, crippled, mutilated?

Eloise had no time to pursue these thoughts, for they were home now, the motor pulling up by the front steps. Smith limped round to hold the door open. His face appeared rather pale beneath the peak of his black cap; he winced a little as he stood to attention whilst she got out.

'Does your leg still give you pain, Smith?'

'No, ma'am. Not at all.' But he was speaking as through gritted teeth.

She hesitated a moment, watching him close the door. To offer sympathy to a proud boy like Smith risked offending him, but to keep quiet and make allowances would be insulting. It was best always to be direct.

'I'm afraid this won't do, Smith. You can't quite manage the motor anymore.'

'Oh, ma'am, I can, really I—' He broke off and clenched his jaw, staring straight ahead, and finally muttered, 'Yes, ma'am.' He was being honest with her, as she'd just been with him, even if he couldn't bring himself to say in so many words that driving made his leg hurt.

'If driving is out of the question, we must think of something else.'

'Ma'am.'

He could only have been disappointed but he did his level best not to show it. His attempt at unconcern made him look morose; some people might have mistaken him and been offended, but Eloise knew better than that. She respected him for at least trying to be stoical.

'Don't worry, Smith,' she said crisply. 'I won't let you down.'

Something in the tone of her voice caused him to glance up at her from under his cap. His glance lingered and a questioning light kindled in his eyes, but then he seemed to remember himself and quickly lowered his eyes. He scowled, colour flaming in his cheeks, and turned away to get back in the driver's seat.

Eloise swept up the steps. Crompton was waiting in the hallway to take her hat and coat. She removed her gloves, too, wondering if she'd done the right thing where Smith was concerned. Maybe he'd have been better off staying in Coventry, where his family could look after him. But that wasn't what he'd wanted, and he was here now, so she had to make the best of it. What could she find for him to do? She couldn't begin to think of anything.

Handing her gloves to Crompton, it crossed her mind that Father would never have taken such trouble with a servant. Albert, however, had always been ready to help those who showed willing, and Dorothea was sure to approve of her aunt's consideration. Perhaps Dorothea might have some idea of how Smith could be usefully employed. In the meantime, a new chauffeur would need to be found; Eloise's heart sank at the thought of having to go through all that again.

'It's one thing after another, Crompton.'

'Madam?'

'Oh, don't mind me. I'm just thinking aloud. Now, you've got my hat, yes? You will be careful with the feather, won't you? And then, when you're ready, it's time for tea, I think.'

'At once, madam.'

* * *

Roderick was in France. Exactly where in France, it was impossible to say. His letters gave little indication, except to suggest he was not anywhere near the front line at present

157

(but for how long?). Such caginess was no doubt necessary, in case his letters fell into the wrong hands. Some people gave no credence to the spy mania — a fuss over nothing, they said — but spies really had been apprehended, and some even sentenced to death.

Sat with her spectacles and her embroidery in the drawing room where the French windows gave plenty of light, Eloise found herself counting the days since Roderick's last letter, the months since his last leave. The past she could quantify in this way, but the future — the future was incalculable. She had no idea when she might expect to see Roderick again. All she could do was wait, as time stretched out elastically. But was it not a woman's lot to sit and wait?

She felt she must look a picture of concentration, sat focused on her sewing, but her restless mind was elsewhere, and she found herself thinking of the day she'd sent Roderick off to prep school for the first time. He would have been eight years old. He'd seemed to her very young and ill-equipped for such a big step. She remembered the way his lip trembled when he came to say goodbye; he'd done his best to put a brave face on it.

'I know I must go, Mother . . . mustn't I?'

His dark eyes had looked up at her in mute appeal, betraying his innermost feelings. She'd felt unutterably cruel.

Albert did not miss much. 'Why put yourself through it, Ellie?' he'd asked when Roderick had gone. 'The boy, too. How about we send him to a day school instead, like his little friend, the Lambell boy?'

'But, Albert, surely you can see that's out of the question? We aren't the Lambells.'

Albert had left it at that. In his early years at Clifton, he'd made every effort to fit in, to play the role thrust upon him. Later, growing more confident in his position, he'd begun to suit himself much more. He'd given up shooting, for instance, and Father had considered shooting a prerequisite of any country gentleman. And Albert had never gone hunting: he couldn't ride, for one thing, but he'd disliked the sport from the start. And so it had been Colonel Harding who'd taken Roderick under his wing when the time came.

'Good grief, Ellie! Look at the poor boy!' Albert had been indignant when Roderick returned from his first time out with the hounds. 'He's covered from head to foot in mud and blood. It's fox's blood, he tells me. They smeared it on him. Tradition, he says, after a first hunt. Tradition! To be daubed in gore like a savage! So this is country life, eh? Hmm? Hmm?'

Eyes focused on the point of her needle, Eloise saw in her mind's eye Roderick as he'd looked that day, and she had to admit that Albert had not been entirely wrong: their son had indeed looked like a little savage. But Roderick had taken to hunting like a duck to water and his eyes had shone as he regaled them with every detail of the thrilling experience, puffing out his chest. He'd looked every inch the heir to the Massinghams, who had been country gentlemen par excellence.

But if Roderick wasn't Rawdon Lambell, he wasn't really a Massingham either. Why shouldn't he have gone to a day school? Why hadn't Albert insisted? Because Albert had respected her so much, that was why. He'd trusted her to do what was right. For all he fulminated against outmoded traditions, he'd not looked for wholesale change, not in the way Rosa professed to.

Eloise wondered how she would have felt if Roderick hadn't gone to prep school, if he'd not gone on to Downfield either. How would she have felt, for that matter, if he'd chosen not to go hunting — or if he hadn't volunteered last August? Wouldn't she have been, in some measure, disappointed? But hunting was one thing, war quite another. It would not be the blood of a fox Roderick would be smeared with this time. It would be German blood — or his own.

Eloise gave a start, dropped her needle. How silly; she had pricked herself, so careless. This was what came of letting one's mind wander.

She watched the blood well on her fingertip, a shiny red droplet — as if summoned into existence by her thought of foxes' blood and the blood of Germans. She was mesmerized for a moment, until the blood began to trickle down her finger. She snatched her work away just in time — just before the blood dripped — then she sucked up the rest of the red liquid from her finger, for she was not a squeamish woman, she never had been.

She thought of the old fairy tale, the princess who pricked her finger on a spindle and fell asleep for a hundred years. How much easier this endless time of waiting would be if she could sleep like that; to wake, not when a handsome prince chanced by, but when the war was over — and Roderick was home for good.

* * *

You mustn't worry, Mother. I shan't get in a funk, or anything like that. When the time comes, I shall be ready to do my duty and—

And what? She couldn't think, couldn't remember the words.

Eloise opened a drawer in her bureau and took out Roderick's letter that had arrived less than an hour ago, during breakfast. She'd read it half a dozen times already but there were still certain words and phrases that puzzled her.

You mustn't worry, Mother.

Worry about what?

When the time comes . . .

What time?

And why use the word 'funk' at all?

A sense of disquiet took hold of her and she got up abruptly, leaving the letter lying on her bureau. She made her way from the parlour to the morning room. Was there something she had missed in this morning's newspapers?

She went through them all, scanning the headlines. A routine artillery duel on the Western Front. Operations continuing as usual in the Dardanelles. The Germans advancing once more in Russia. Nothing untoward. Nothing out of the ordinary. Perhaps she was reading too much into Roderick's words.

She got to her feet, went to the window. Late September sun gave a golden sheen to the treetops of the Pheasantry. The pale blue sky was streaked with thin white cloud. A serene autumn morning. And yet, beneath the calm surface, it seemed to her there was a breathless air of suspense.

She shook her head firmly, turning away from the window. She was getting as bad as Elizabeth, seeing signs and portents on every side. Lunchtime was getting ever nearer, and she'd accomplished nothing yet today.

She lingered, nonetheless, in the morning room, inspecting the potted plants on the jardinière, rearranging the long-stemmed flowers in the tall vase set in front of the empty fireplace. She looked around the room as if seeking something, but she didn't know what. Her eyes finally came to rest on an old sampler in a frame that had hung on the wall for as long as she could remember. There was a name and a date, in uneven stitching: ANNIE M, 1672. Who was Annie M? Was she one of the long-dead Massinghams? 1672: that was older than the house itself, so maybe the sampler had been fashioned in the old manor house which had once stood on this same spot. Eloise wondered what the old manor house had looked like. She could not recall that she'd ever seen a picture of it. Perhaps there were no pictures.

Closing the door of the morning room behind her, she walked along the corridor and paused in the hallway to watch the ponderous, swinging pendulum of the grandfather clock, as it measured the long, slow minutes: tick . . . tock . . . tick . . . tock . . . All else was still, was silent. Rarely had the house seemed quite so silent. There had been times, by contrast, when it was bursting with life — never more so than during Father's famous parties of the seventies and eighties. Eloise could not forget that she'd once tried to emulate Father's parties, but the whole evening had somehow fallen flat, so she'd never tried again. Strangely enough, on that same evening, Dorothea had first come to Clifton, arriving when the party was at its height. Dorothea and her father had burst through this very door, the door next to the grandfather clock that led into the breakfast room. Eloise opened the door and stepped through. She remembered her first sight of Albert's niece, here in the breakfast room: she'd been next door, in the drawing room; she'd heard the sudden, unnatural silence, and had gone to investigate. Like something out of Dickens, it had been, Albert's long-lost kin appearing unlooked-for out of the dark winter night, the father the worse for drink, the girl dressed in rags. Who would have imagined that such a beggarly little waif would grow up to be such a cherished part of the family?

Eloise passed through the doorway connecting the breakfast and drawing rooms. Here, on the sideboard, were all the family photographs, Dorothea amongst them. But the photographs were in the wrong order; the maids never could put them back correctly after dusting them. Eloise rearranged them: Father, Frederick, Albert, Dorothea, Elizabeth — Roderick. This was Roderick as a fresh-faced boy about to leave for prep school. And this — she put down one photograph, picked up another — was Roderick again, but a more recent picture: Second Lieutenant Brannan in his immaculate uniform, with his cap and his moustache and his dark eyes staring boldly out at her.

She held the framed photograph in both hands, and the words from his letter went through her head once again.

You mustn't worry, Mother. I shan't get in a funk, or anything like that. When the time comes, I shall be ready to do my duty.

* * *

'Nothing more from Mr Roderick today, madam?'

'No, Mrs Bourne. Nothing.' It was days now since his last letter.

The housekeeper had completed her daily report, had received her instructions, but stood paused on her way out, one hand resting on the handle of the parlour door.

'It's . . . it's the waiting for news that's so hard to bear, Mrs Brannan. It's all this waiting that saps the spirit, somehow.'

Having said her piece, Mrs Bourne closed the door softly behind her. The sound of jangling keys dwindled into the distance.

Sat at her bureau, Eloise found herself sorely tempted to call the housekeeper back, to share with her the strain of waiting for news, which so 'sapped the spirit, somehow'. After all, Mrs Bourne was, in a manner of speaking, a part of the family. Almost no one had lived at Clifton longer than Mrs Bourne. She'd watched Roderick grow up from when he was a very little boy; one could even say she had a share in him, that he was partly her boy too: he was the closest she would ever come, at her time of life, to a son of her own.

She would say to her, 'Mrs Bourne.' And Mrs Bourne would say, 'Yes, madam.' And all would be laid bare. They would stand on a new footing. They would understand one another completely.

Eloise pursed her lips disapprovingly. Such nonsense! As if anything would be gained by crossing a line so carefully drawn over so many years. All it would achieve was to destroy the delicate balance they'd built up in their long-standing relationship. Mrs Bourne — Eloise was certain — would not want that, any more than she did.

Reaching for the paper knife, Eloise set about opening her letters.

* * *

The fading gardens had a dishevelled look to them today that only added to the air of neglect. Summer had lingered all through the month of September, but September now was over and autumn at last was taking hold. But Eloise barely noticed. As she walked along the cinder paths, the headlines in Monday's *Times* still loomed large in her mind; presentiment aside, those headlines had been the first real intimation of the great new battle which had lately begun in France.

TWO VICTORIES IN THE WEST
BRITISH ADVANCE ON LENS

She had devoured the lines of print, seizing on every detail. The British and the French had launched a joint attack on the German lines. Large gains had been made. In the days since Monday, the newspapers had enlarged on events, and the names of previously unknown places had come to sudden prominence. Hulluch. Hooge. Hill 70. Loos. They were names that sounded to Eloise's ear unlovely and somehow sinister. She felt certain now that this great battle was what Roderick had been hinting at in his last letter; she felt certain he was involved in it.

In the vegetable garden, old Becket had lit a fire on a patch of bare earth. Dancing flames licked at a pile of dead leaves and cuttings. Smoke billowed and rose high in the still air. Becket, in his cap and apron and his corduroy trousers, poked the blaze with a stick. A little deaf, a little short-sighted, he was not aware of her watching, and he muttered to himself under his breath: 'I don't know . . . I don't know . . . look at this, now . . . what's to do? Oh, me back . . . me poor back . . .' He rubbed his back with a gnarled old hand. He peered at the fire. He slowly shook his head.

She wondered if his back often troubled him. He was over eighty. It was a lot to expect, that he should keep these rambling gardens in order; it would have taxed a man half his age. What he needed was another pair of hands, someone with a bit more about them than the village boy Britten, who dawdled about the place, more a hindrance than a help.

It came to her then, as she stood watching Becket poke the fire. Why not Smith?

Well, why not? She'd long been meaning to find someone to share the burden presently shouldered by Becket, but with one thing and another, and staff to replace in the house, she'd never quite got round to it. This was just the solution. Help for Becket. A position for Smith. Something within Smith's compass. He could be a sort of apprentice. But perhaps he would think it demeaning. It was not what he was used to. Would he feel he was being put out to pasture? Yet he might find it rewarding, if he gave it a try. How best, then, to approach him?

164

A well-placed word works wonders. Father's maxim still held good. It was just a case of choosing the right word. As she wrestled with this problem, Eloise slowly returned the way she'd come.

A sound of running footsteps intruded on her thoughts. She looked up, found that she'd passed through the garden door without noticing. She was standing now in front of the house. The spreading boughs of the cedar tree hung like a low roof over her head. The grey-fronted house cast a long shadow on the gravel in the pale autumn sunshine.

The sound of footsteps grew louder and a boy appeared from the direction of the drive. His booted feet threw up gravel as he ran pell-mell towards the front door. He was in uniform, and he was holding in his hand a piece of paper. Eloise recognized him at once. It was Mr Downie's boy: Mr Downie, the post master. He could only be bringing a telegram.

A telegram.

Her heart stopped. Frozen in place, she watched the boy leap up the steps and reach out to ring the bell. After a moment, the front door opened. The boy held up his burden. (Why should the flimsy telegram seem such a burden? But Eloise knew its significance. She knew what it might portend.)

The telegram was now safely in Crompton's hands, and the boy turned, slipped down the steps, his job done. He ran back towards the drive, heels flying, the burden lifted.

Eloise's knees buckled. The names she'd read in the newspapers over the last few days reverberated in her mind, as if they were being intoned slowly, sonorously inside an echoing church.

Hulluch . . . Hooge . . . Hill 70 . . . Loos . . .

With an effort, she held herself up and compelled herself to move. She passed from beneath the cedar tree. Her skirts swirled across the gravel.

Hulluch . . . Hooge . . . Hill 70 . . . Loos . . .

Raising one foot, then another, she managed to climb the steps. Her legs were leaden.

Crompton had seen her. He was waiting by the door. But he no longer had the telegram. Eloise stepped past him. Rosa was there. Rosa was stood in the hallway. The telegram was open in her hand. She must have come running the instant she heard the bell.

She looked up. Eloise dared not breathe. She searched Rosa's face and, as she did so, every possible eventuality flashed through her mind. It seemed an eternity before Rosa spoke.

'It's from Dorothea. Roderick is in hospital — in her hospital — in London.'

Eloise let out her breath. But at once a new fear seized hold of her. He was in hospital. Maimed, blinded, legless, a cripple?

Rosa read from the telegram. '"Wounds not serious. No cause for alarm."' She looked up. 'Oh! Mrs Brannan! Oh!'

Tears brimmed in Rosa's eyes, and it seemed to Eloise that her daughter-in-law had never looked so beautiful, her olive skin unusually pale, her hair so very dark, her eyes full of emotion. In that instant, Eloise felt as if Rosa had raised Roderick from the dead; Rosa's words had saved him.

Roderick was alive.

CHAPTER SEVEN

Elizabeth being Elizabeth, she was not afraid to ask what Eloise felt they all, deep down, secretly wanted to know.

'What's it like, Roddy? What is war really like? Is it very awful?'

'Deadly dull most of the time, kiddo. One kicks one's heels. One marches from place to place. Nothing much happens.'

There was something paradoxical in the fact that, fresh out of hospital and still convalescing, Roderick looked in the bloom of health. Indeed, he was positively glowing as he lolled on the couch in the drawing room; his arm in a sling was the only sign of his injuries. Dressed in a shirt and a waistcoat, with no jacket and no tie, he looked rather raffish and not a little pleased with himself — and why shouldn't he? Eloise was reminded of an old ancestral tale of the Massinghams that Father had been fond of repeating. A younger son had dared cross the Channel at the time of the French Revolution; after several parlous adventures, he'd finally met his end at the hands of Madame la Guillotine. But Roderick had shown courage the match of any Massingham.

'Weren't you frightened?' Elizabeth persisted, evidently not overawed by her brother in his new heroic guise. 'Weren't you frightened at all?'

Roderick looked round at his rapt audience — Eloise, Rosa, Elizabeth — before replying. 'Going over the top, one gets the wind up, I'll give you that. But I found it nowhere near as nerve-racking as when I went out to bat in the Cricket Cup semi-final of 1908 at school. Those first few minutes against Conway's demon bowler were worse than any Hun strafing.'

'War is like cricket?' Elizabeth, on the settee, seemed almost affronted. 'That's not right! That's not right at all! I was told that—' She stopped abruptly, flushed, looked down at the carpet.

'Oh?' said Roderick. 'Who's been telling you what?'

'No one . . . nothing . . . it doesn't matter,' Elizabeth went on in a rush, 'Will you be afraid to go back, Roddy, now you've been wounded?'

'Rather not, I think. A chap must do his duty. One can't hide at home with the skunks and the shirkers. Besides, I've seen almost nothing as yet. We were dropped in at the deep end, had no chance to get used to the front line . . .'

He broke off, rubbing his wounded arm absently, then smoothing his moustache, silent suddenly, and pre-occupied, staring into space. They sat watching him, waiting. When finally he stirred and looked round, he seemed almost surprised to see them, as if he'd forgotten they were there.

He took a deep breath, leaned forward a little, and said, 'It was like this. We were to be part of the war's greatest battle, that's what they told us: the final act, victory round the corner. My battalion wasn't in the first wave. We were to follow on behind. By the time we arrived, they assured us, the enemy would be in full retreat. Our job was to take up the chase, to push on until our legs gave out, when fresh reserves would take our place and continue the advance. Before long, we'd be at the gates of Berlin, or so you'd have thought from all the talk.

'So much for their plans. Now I'll tell you what actually happened. The battle, as I'm sure you now know, was set to begin on the final Saturday of last month. The Tuesday before, my battalion and I were still forty miles and more behind the front line. We were billeted in a little French village, where we'd marched after disembarking at Boulogne. That Tuesday evening, we finally moved out. We marched six hours that night, nine hours the next. We marched due east, and always at night.

'The big day finally arrived, the day of the battle. The early hours of Saturday morning — it was still dark — found us trying to snatch some sleep in a potato field. We'd had nothing to eat for hours, and there was a gun battery blazing away non-stop in the next field, so you can imagine we didn't get much rest. We moved off at first light and headed for the front line. The battle was raging by then, the wounded pouring back in droves; some of them had turned bright orange because of the gas. One jolly fellow joked as he passed, "Don't worry, lads, there's no more gas, we have swallowed it all." Hun prisoners were being herded, our first sight of the enemy. And it was raining cats and dogs; we were soaked to the skin. To me, it all seemed a terrible shambles, but no doubt the Brass Hats knew what they were about — at least, I hope they did.

'Dusk was coming on when finally we went into battle for the first time. We were sent out to relieve a battalion of Jocks who'd been holding some captured Boche trenches all day. Those trenches were in a terrible state. The water in places came up to one's waist. And you can't imagine the noise, our guns going hell for leather, theirs too; it was never-ending. The vivid flashes as the big guns fired showed like distant lightning on the horizon. Star-shells lit up no-man's land like arc lamps. There were bodies scattered everywhere. All in all, it was like a scene from the end of the world.

'Around dawn, the Hun launched a counter-attack. They drove us out of the trenches. Orders were sent up that we should retake them at once. We'd no bombs left by then, and no water, and no one seemed quite sure what was happening. My company commander rallied us. He sent me ahead with my platoon to lead the way. We went over the top and across some churned-up ground. We'd nearly reached our objective, when some beastly Hun sniper took a pot-shot at me and I caught one in the shoulder. I carried on for a bit, but I began to feel awfully muzzy. Blood was pouring out, and I couldn't use my arm: it had gone completely numb.

'I don't remember much after that, until I came round in the casualty clearing station. Someone had stolen my watch. One of those damned orderlies took it, I expect, whilst I was out for the count. I kicked up a fearful stink, you may be sure, until a doctor came and dosed me with morphia. Everything went muzzy again after that. Do you know, I never did get my watch back. They're nothing but a bunch of thieves, those orderlies.

'I was shipped back to Blighty. It was hell. There was only one saving grace: I was too ill to be seasick. We travelled by train to London, where we were unloaded on stretchers at Waterloo until the platform was overflowing with us. Labels were fixed on each man. I wasn't best pleased, I can tell you, being treated like a parcel. I was all set to rip the label off and throw it away, until I saw the name on it, the place where I was being sent. I could scarcely believe my eyes. It *was* a stroke of luck, ending up at Doro's hospital! I've never been so glad to see anyone.

'And that's about it. They patched me up, kept me in bed for a week or so — as you all saw when you came to visit — and then they packed me off to convalesce. And here I am.'

Elizabeth stared at him solemnly. 'What is your wound like now, Roddy? Is it terrible to behold?'

'There's nothing much to see, kiddo. Rosa will tell you. It's extraordinary, rather, the way one's body heals. I thought I'd be left with a hole the size of a two-bob bit. Funny it should be this arm, the same arm I broke hunting. That was three — nearly four — years ago.' He added, with a wolfish grin, 'You rather liked me, Rosa, I seem to remember, with my arm broken!'

Rosa blushed a little at this but said nothing. Eloise sensed some private joke behind Roderick's remark. She steered the conversation onto safer ground.

'At least this time, Roderick, we had word of your coming. Cook set to work at once. Everything will be just as you like it. There is greengage tart for pudding this evening.'

'Nothing can beat a good Clifton dinner, Mother. You can't imagine the slop they feed us in hospital.' He looked round at them, grinning — a boyish grin this time, with none of his earlier insouciance — and he said happily, 'It's good to be home, you lot, I can't tell you!'

* * *

An endless stream of callers poured up the drive and hung on the bell. They were ushered, in turn, into the presence of the hero, who regaled them with tales of the terrible battle. They were all tremendously impressed; they were pleased with him, pleased with themselves too, as if some of his glory had rubbed off on them. Colonel Harding declared that he'd known all along young Brannan was officer material, whilst Mrs Somersby spoke of him almost as highly as she did of her own beloved son. (Mark Somersby had been nowhere near the battle. His role — what Roderick called 'a cushy number' — kept him well behind the lines.) From the village came the Committee en masse: the vicar and his wife, Mrs Adnitt, Mrs Lambell. Mrs Lambell had news of Rawdon. Surplus to requirements and left behind when his battalion went overseas in July, only a few weeks later he had been ordered to re-join his unit out at the Dardanelles. A posting to the Dardanelles, Roderick affirmed, was most definitely not a cushy number.

'How our fortunes have changed!' said Mrs Lambell to Eloise. 'At the time of the fête, Rawdon was home and Roderick away, now the situation is reversed.'

Roderick and Rawdon had so far both weathered the storm. The news was less good concerning the young village shopkeeper, David Cardwell. He had been killed in action, Mrs Lambell reported, on the very same day that Roderick was wounded. Eloise found this a chilling coincidence, and a stark reminder of what might have happened had the German sniper been more sure in his aim. Life and death, it seemed, was decided these days by a matter of inches.

Word in the village was that young Cardwell's sister had been hit hard by his death.

'Poor woman!' said Mrs Lambell. 'It's only four years since she buried her father, now her brother has gone too — and that's not to mention her son out in France.' All Dorothea's efforts to get the Johnnie Cheeseman released from the army had come to nothing. 'He's only sixteen, still a child,' sighed Mrs Lambell. 'His father says it will make a man of him, but I don't like to think what his mother is going through.'

* * *

'No more visitors, Mother.'

Eloise was walking with Roderick in the gardens, escaping for a time the chaos in the house, where chimneysweeps were at work. Roderick had his jacket half on, one sleeve draped over his wounded arm. There was a gusting breeze; a watery sun shone at intervals between racing clouds.

'No more visitors. I am starting to feel like an exhibit at a zoo.'

'Perhaps it might be wise. You were rather brusque, Roderick, with Mrs Adnitt yesterday.'

'Can you blame me, Mother? You heard her, talking rot as usual. As if Doro wasn't quite right to want the Cheeseman boy sent home. The front line is no place for a lad his age.'

'I'm sure Mrs Adnitt never mentioned Dorothea, nor the Cheeseman boy.'

'She didn't need to. It was quite clear what she meant, all those pointed remarks about German sympathizers trying to deplete the ranks of the British army. And then she had the gall to say that the wives of enemy aliens should be locked up on the Isle of Man like their husbands — and never mind that some of them are English born and bred! But what really riled me was when she started on about Nurse Cavell. I came close then to giving her a jolly good strafing. I'd have been more than brusque, Mother, I can tell you.'

'I don't see why you got so upset, Roderick. All Mrs Adnitt said was that it was wicked of the Germans to shoot Nurse Cavell in cold blood, and she's quite right.'

'There was more to it than that; she was insinuating that Doro is somehow implicated in such frightfulness, that Doro more or less has Nurse Cavell's blood on her hands.'

'That is not what I heard, Roderick. You may rest assured that anyone who actually said such a thing in my hearing would not be welcome at Clifton again.'

'The fault is as much in thinking it as saying it. The Adnitt woman had best watch her step, is all I can say. I shan't be so forbearing next time.'

'That's all very well, Roderick, but I have to meet Mrs Adnitt at church every Sunday, and we serve together on the Committee. Any unpleasantness would make things awkward all round.'

'Dearest Mother. You are admirable in every way. But at a time like this, drawing-room manners simply won't do.'

Eloise was taken aback to find herself being chastized by her son, though it shouldn't really have come as a surprise: he'd always been a forthright boy. But she couldn't help feeling that there was something different about Roderick since he'd come home. He'd changed in some way. How had he changed? She couldn't quite decide.

'Mother, you must never doubt Doro,' Roderick continued to lecture her. 'I'm awfully bucked, you know, having seen her for myself in her hospital. She's an absolute brick. Some of the work she has to do is foul beyond belief, and volunteer nurses are treated worse than slaves, but Doro doesn't say a word, she just gets on with it. And then someone like Mrs Adnitt, who never lifts a finger, thinks she has the right to pass judgement! Mrs Adnitt's not the only one, either. One of the fellows in my ward called Doro a— Well, I won't say what he called her. He wished he hadn't, by the time I'd finished with him, that's all. So Mrs Adnitt should think herself lucky. She got off lightly.'

Eloise did not quite know what to say. Roderick was right about Dorothea — of course he was. But there was no disguising the fact that Dorothea had a German husband, and people saw the Germans in a different light now, after Belgium, after the sinking of the *Lusitania*, after the callous killing of Nurse Cavell. And it was a German — a country-man of Johann Kaufmann — who had fired the bullet which shattered Roderick's arm.

How did Roderick accommodate himself to these changed circumstances? What did he feel for the man who'd shot him? Dare she ask?

Before she could decide, Roderick said, 'Do you imagine those sweeps have finished, Mother? They seem to be taking a devil of a time.'

'I'm sorry about the sweeps, Roderick. It's rather a nui-sance, I know. Now is not their usual time. But everything is out of kilter, and chimneys must be cleaned, war or no war. It just so happens there are rather a lot of chimneys at Clifton.'

'They'd get on a lot quicker if they still used boys. Stuff a few boys up the chimneys and they'd be cleaned in no time.' He took her arm. 'Shall we go in, Mother? I don't care whether they've finished or not. It's getting rather chilly.'

As they turned and retraced their steps, she noticed he was frowning a little, looked rather pale too, and grey about the eyes; he was feeling the cold more than usual, as well. Was this to do with his wound? He was so offhand about it — about everything he'd been through — that she tended to forget how much of an ordeal he'd faced. Like Dorothea, who 'got on with it' at the hospital, Roderick was not one to complain, not when things were serious. If his wound had been no more than a scratch, that would have been different — they'd never have heard the last of it.

This was a rather sobering thought, given how little he'd said on the subject. Eloise also thought of something else as they walked back towards the house. Roderick had spoken of 'the Cheeseman boy' and 'a lad his age', as if there was a vast gap between them, not a mere seven years. But this was part of the change in him, she now realized. Suddenly he seemed a lot more grown-up.

He'd told Elizabeth his wound was nearly healed. Eloise wondered if this was true. She'd nursed a secret hope that the war would be over before Roderick was fit enough to be sent back to France. An end really had seemed in sight when the newspapers first trumpeted the great victory won at Loos, but the decisive moment never quite seemed to arrive, and in the meantime the lists of men killed and wounded grew ever longer, filling two whole columns on the front page of *The Times* each day and running into a third. Have patience, the nation was told. Success would not come all at once. But rest assured, the sacrifices would not be in vain. Yet from what little Roderick had said of such things since he'd been home, Eloise got the distinct impression that the 'great victory' was not all that might be supposed. Roderick had made no mention of seeing the enemy in full retreat; his battalion had not 'pushed on' as they'd been promised. On the rare occasions when Rosa or Elizabeth inveigled him into casting an eye over the papers — which these days he seemed reluctant to do — his only comment was the latest fighting appeared to be in more or less the same place as where the battle began.

Walking back to the house, they'd now reached the space of gravel and the cedar tree. Eloise could hear, from the stable yard, the sound of voices, and the clatter of a cart being loaded. The sweeps, it seemed, had finished at last and were preparing to leave. She led the way towards the front steps, but Roderick came suddenly to an abrupt halt and Eloise, with her arm through his, was forced to stop too.

She realized that he wasn't looking towards the house or the stable yard, but in the opposite direction. Following his gaze, she caught sight of a solitary figure who had obviously just trekked up the long drive and was now walking hesitantly towards the house: a woman wearing a patched frock, with a shawl thrown round her shoulders; her head was bare, her lank hair tied back; there was a gaunt look to her face. She faltered and stopped, looking up at the house as if daunted by the imposing grey facade. She glanced round, as if seeking the courage to go on, and it was only now that she noticed Eloise and Roderick.

Her sudden appearance was so unexpected that it took Eloise a moment to recognize her. It was Hobson, the erstwhile maid — now, of course, Mrs Carter, a wife and a mother. Eloise had last seen her nearly three months ago, on the day of the fête.

Roderick detached his arm. He took a pace forward. In the same instant, the woman who'd been Hobson moved towards him. They both stopped and faced each other across a wide gap.

'What do you want?' said Roderick sharply.

'Oh, Master Roderick, I . . . I only want to know as yer all right. I heard folk saying you was hurt. They're saying all sorts in the village. I've been going out me mind. I had to see for meself.'

'Well, you've seen me, and now you can go.'

She opened her mouth as if to speak, but seemed to think better of it, as if intimidated by his demeanour: tall and stern and imposing. At certain times, and in certain moods, he very much had a look of his father about him.

Carter's wife blanched under Roderick's gaze. Her eyes shied away. She looked up at the house again.

'I never for the life of me thought I'd miss this place, but I do.'

She appeared to screw up her courage and dared to look at Roderick again. This time she held his gaze, even though it made her quail and shrink inside herself.

'It's not just the job. I . . . I miss you and all, Master Roderick — you don't know how much!'

Eloise had been ignored until now, a mere spectator; her mind had gone back to the painful scene in the parlour over a year ago, when Roderick had confessed his entanglement with this unfortunate creature. He'd promised it was over. Eloise had no reason to doubt him. But Susie Carter, it seemed, could not forget.

Eloise roused herself. The situation needed taking in hand. But before she could intervene, events took an unforeseen turn. A young man came running full pelt round the corner from the drive, hotly pursued by another. Both had shabby clothes and muddy boots; one was bare-headed, the other had a cloth cap jammed on.

'She's here, then, is she?' snarled the first young man in a towering rage as he bore down on Susie Carter, who cowered in the face of such a fierce onslaught. 'I told her not to come here. I warned her. I'll kill her this time, that's what I'll do. I'll kill her.'

The second, younger man made a desperate lunge and grabbed hold of the first man's arm, yanking him back. 'Nibs! Nibs! Give over! Let her be!'

'Geroff me, Ned! Geroff! I won't tell yer again!'

'Nibs, I'm begging yer—'

The angry young man was Carter, Eloise realized, Susie's husband, whose nickname was Nibs. The other man had to be his younger brother, Ned; more of a boy, really, than a man: not much more than eighteen. Eloise recognized Nibs Carter from when he'd worked at Clifton. She would not have known Ned but for one thing: the right sleeve of his jacket ended emptily and was tucked up inside itself where his hand and wrist should have been, the hand which had been torn off two years ago by a piece of farm machinery. Dr Camborne had attended the scene; he'd been rather too fond, for a time, of recounting the gruesome story. Ned Carter's disfigurement had made him something of a local curiosity, but now, after a year and more of war, a missing hand no longer seemed so sensational.

Nibs tore himself free from his brother's one-handed grasp and sprang at Susie, seizing hold of her. She tried to shake him off. As they tussled back and forth, Ned hovered nearby, rubbing the back of his neck in feverish agitation, waiting for a chance to intercede.

'Come away, Susie.' Nibs jerked his wife's arm. 'Come away when I tell you, or I'll give you such a trouncing!'

Susie struggled ever more fiercely, twisting and turning as she tried to free herself. 'Leave go of me!' she spat at him. 'Leave go! I've had enough of yer! I can't abide yer! I'd sooner be a slave than be wed to you. We've no money. We live on scraps. I've nothing no more, nothing, only the clothes what I stand up in.'

Nibs jerked her arm again. 'Nothing's all you ever had, you dibby cow,' he bellowed. 'You'd be a sight worse off and all, if I hadn't upped and wed you. You'd be in the gutter, where you belong.'

'I wish to goodness you never had wed me. I wish you'd let me alone. I hate yer! I hate yer!'

The scuffle grew more intense. Nibs now had both hands on his wife, shaking her and pulling her around, whilst Susie flailed at him and kicked him in the shins. To Eloise, the violence seemed all the more shocking when it was set against the hallowed portals of Clifton itself.

Susie at last succeeded in breaking free. She sprang away from her husband and wheeled around at a safe distance, glaring at him with undisguised venom. Raising his fists, Nibs bore down on her.

Roderick stepped smartly between them. Turning to face Nibs, he said, 'What's the matter, Carter? Can't you control your woman?'

His sneering tone seemed more likely to inflame the situation than calm things down, and indeed Nibs Carter advanced on him now with both fists still raised and his eyes blazing.

'This is your doing, you bastard. I oughta flatten yer.'

Roderick didn't flinch, kept his one good arm at his side. 'Go ahead, Carter. Hit me. Hit me, if you're man enough — though I'd have thought hitting women was more in your line. You're a coward, man! You're a coward, or you'd be in uniform by now. The Hun a bit too much for you, is that it?'

They squared up to each other, so close as to be almost touching, their feet firmly planted. Nibs was clearly shaking with rage. His suntanned yet sallow face, with its few patchy bristles, was also now flushed a very deep red, so that an old scar on his forehead showed up startlingly white. Roderick, by contrast, seemed almost preternaturally calm — except for his eyes: his dark, louring eyes told a different story. He was taller than Carter by several inches and had about him the look of a thoroughbred; but Carter was tough, wiry, hard-bitten, and Eloise remembered all too clearly Roderick's cuts and bruises the last time the two of them had come to blows — and back then, Roderick had not been hampered by a wounded arm.

Eloise was desperate to stop them fighting, but what could she do? Susie and Ned seemed frozen in place; she could expect no help from that quarter. Would Ordish hear if she called?

But — wait — how silly of her, what on earth was she thinking? Ordish was long gone. And Crompton, diminutive Crompton—

'The Hun a bit much for you, Carter?'

Roderick seemed determined to goad Carter beyond endurance, but instead his words had an odd and unexpected effect. Carter dropped his fists. He stepped back. The anger drained from his face. His lips twisted in a lopsided smile, dour and contemptuous.

'What do I want with a uniform? Think I'd fight for the likes of you — your lot — stuck-up toffs? King and country? Bah!'

He spat onto the gravel at Roderick's feet, then turned away. Ignoring Susie now, he allowed himself, with one last shrug of his shoulders, to be led away by his brother; Ned took hold of Nibs's elbow, guided him towards the driveway. The two shabby figures swiftly vanished behind the line of evergreens. Roderick stood and watched them go. It seemed to Eloise there was a look almost of disappointment on his face.

Only Susie now remained. Her frock had been torn in the struggle with her husband and was hanging down at one shoulder; it gave her a distinctly slatternly appearance.

'Master Roderick!'

Her pleading voice roused him, but for one moment longer he went on staring after the now-vanished Carter brothers. A shudder passed through him. He drew himself up and turned towards Susie.

'You should go, too. Your husband will be waiting.'

'Him? I don't want him! I want you, Master Roderick. I want you. Why can't we go back to how it used to be, when you loved me?'

'Now then, Susie, you know it wasn't love. We had our fun, but it's over and done with. We've both grown up since then. You have your life now, and I have mine. I've a wife and child.'

'Her? She don't love yer! Not the way I do.'

'I won't have you talking about Rosa. My marriage is none of your business. You know nothing about it.'

'I know enough.'

'Go home, Susie.'

'I know she don't want yer. She were gonna leave yer.'

'Nonsense.'

'Ask Daisy if you don't believe me. It were Daisy what told me. Yer missus, she were ready to run off with someone else. The foreign gentleman, it were, the one with the funny name. She'd packed her bags — the lot. Ask Daisy. Ask Daisy if yer don't believe me. Daisy saw it all. The whole house were in uproar.'

Up to now, Roderick had more or less taken everything in his stride, but this caught him off guard. He obviously thought Susie had got the wrong end of the stick or that Daisy had lied to her, but a seed of doubt had been planted nonetheless.

A succession of thoughts raced through Eloise's mind as, powerless, she watched that seed take root. What had Roderick ever seen in Susie Hobson? Eloise couldn't begin to imagine. She would have liked to believe that the affair was all Susie's doing, that Susie had led him astray — and there was probably some truth in that. But Eloise knew what men were like, and there was no reason to think that Roderick was any different; she knew that men had an inherent weakness, which left them vulnerable to certain artful women — women who understood how to manipulate them. To Eloise's eye, Roderick looked particularly vulnerable just then, with his arm in a sling and doubt written all over his face. Susie had to be silenced, before she did any more damage.

Eloise stepped forward. 'That's enough. That's quite enough.' She took charge, imposing herself. She faced Susie head-on. 'You must leave. You must go back to the village where you belong. Your husband will be expecting you.'

Dishevelled, defiant, Susie flared up. 'I won't. I shan't. I int yer skivvy no more, to be ordered round. You can't boss me now, you frosty-faced old witch.'

Eloise gave her a look of stern reproval, half expecting Roderick to intercede, ready to restrain him if he did, but he seemed not to have heard. Susie for a moment longer stood her ground, wayward and wilful. Then, as suddenly as a candle going out, she wilted. Her head dropped, her shoulders slumped; she turned away without another word. She went limping towards the driveway. She did not look back.

Watching Susie go, it flashed into Eloise's mind that she had not been fair, thinking Susie artful. Susie wasn't shrewd enough or clever enough for that. She wasn't cold and calculating. She lacked self-discipline, that was all. She was still, in some ways, a child. She reached out like a child for what she wanted, without any thought for the consequences, and she never seemed to learn, even when her fingers got burned. Eloise was suddenly aware of the waste of it — that a girl of Susie's spirit should fritter herself away fighting all the wrong battles, battles she could not hope to win, battles that would inevitably grind her down in the end.

Susie finally disappeared from view. The wind gusted. Dead leaves rattled on the gravel.

Bit by bit, Eloise turned to face her son. He hadn't moved. His eyes were flashing dangerously, and he was looking at her — staring at her — frowning so fiercely that his eyebrows almost met above the bridge of his nose, always an ominous sign.

Any sympathy Eloise might have had for Susie Carter evaporated as it struck home what mischief the girl had made.

'What was she talking about, Mother?' said Roderick slowly, deliberately. 'What exactly did *Daisy* tell her? I presume she means the nursery maid, Turner. Where is Turner? She can tell me what she knows.'

'That won't be necessary, Roderick.'

'You explain, then, Mother. You tell me. You must know what happened. The whole house was in an uproar, apparently.'

There was an edge to his voice that made Eloise shiver.

'The Carter girl has it all mixed up.'

'Has what mixed up?'

'It's true that Rosa—'

'Was going to leave?'

'Wanted to go away.'

'With Antipov?'

'They were going to travel together, but I'm sure there was nothing—'

'Why have I never heard about this? Why did nobody tell me? Antipov left more than a year ago. Good God! A year! And in all that time, nobody has so much as said a word.'

Eloise found herself unduly flustered. 'Roderick . . . please . . .'

'Tell me everything.'

'All I know is . . . Rosa had packed her bags . . . she . . . she had left you a letter—'

But here the sweeps' cart came rattling and creaking out from the stable yard, and Eloise stepped back to let it pass. Roderick stepped back too, but the other way, and the cart rolled between them, its wooden wheels scrunching on the gravel. The plodding horse pranced, kicking up the stones.

One of the sweeps, sat up front, flicked the reins and called, 'Whoa, boy! Whoa!' The other sweep touched his cap to Eloise. Their faces, their hands, their clothes, were black with soot.

The cart rounded the cedar tree and turned towards the drive. Eloise looked for Roderick — but he wasn't there; he'd gone.

* * *

She thought he might avoid her, after what had happened. She ought to have known better. He never avoided anything.

Barely had she taken a seat at her bureau, when the parlour door flew open and Roderick strode in.

'There was a letter. You mentioned a letter that Rosa wrote. What happened to it, Mother?'

Eloise was angry with herself for mentioning the letter. That had been a mistake. It was also a mistake to have kept it all this time. But the letter hadn't seemed all that important, until now.

Roderick seized on her hesitation. 'Do you mean to say you still have it, Mother? Yes, I rather think you do.' He loomed over her, thrusting out his hand. 'Give it to me.'

Reluctantly, she searched it out. There was nothing else she could do. She bitterly regretted that she'd never destroyed it as she'd intended. She had only taken it in the first place to spare him. But of course he wouldn't see that, the way things had turned out. He would think she had kept him in the dark on purpose. She wanted desperately to justify herself, but under the present circumstances she felt that anything she said would do more harm than good.

He took the letter from her, barely glanced at it, put it in his jacket pocket. He marched to the door and she thought for a moment that he'd said all he wanted to say, but then he paused and, after a heartbeat, turned back.

'You need not think I'm blind, Mother, you need not think I'm anyone's fool. I know that Rosa was . . . was fond of Antipov. I always knew that. And Antipov doted on her, it was as plain as the nose on my face. I liked Antipov. He was mad as a hatter, of course, and talked the most awful rot, but there was never any pretence with him: what you saw was what you got. I liked him; Rosa liked him. But that's not to say he would have been right for her. He wasn't right at all. She liked the idea of him. She liked what she thought he represented. But she wouldn't have been happy with him, I'm sure of it. That's why I married her. To . . . to save her from herself.'

Startled by his words, Eloise said without stopping to think, 'That's no reason to marry, Roderick! If that's all it was—'

'There . . . there was the child as well.'

'Even so . . .'

Eloise was dismayed by this turn in the conversation. She knew better than to say anything against Rosa; it never did any good, only soured things between her and her son. But she simply couldn't help herself just then, especially as it seemed to her that Rosa was the root cause of all this trouble.

She tried to explain. 'People like Rosa . . . they are . . . eccentric isn't the right word . . . I don't know what the right word is . . . but they are all the same, people of that sort. You know, I suppose, that her brother refuses point-blank to fight for his country — her own brother!'

'I really don't give a damn about her brother!' Roderick burst out, but he quickly checked himself and heaved a sigh. 'Lord, Mother! Must we go through all this again? You didn't want me to marry Rosa. You made that plain. You didn't think her good enough. I sometimes wonder if anyone would be good enough in your eyes, but that's by the by. The decision was made — it was my decision to make, Mother, not yours — and now we have to live with it.'

'Live with it? Is that all your marriage means to you?'

'That's not what I mean. You are twisting my words.'

'I only want what's best for you, Roderick, you must know that.'

'You want what you think is best. But I'm not a little boy now. I'm twenty-three years old. You can't push me around anymore.'

'Push you around? That's most unfair, Roderick.'

Eloise could have said more, but she broke off: anything she said would only make matters worse; there was no talking to him in this mood.

Roderick said severely, 'You ought to have given me Rosa's letter at once. I thought you'd have learned your lesson, after what happened with Doro. You know the trouble it caused, hiding those letters, the ones from her father — destroying them.'

'You father thought—' Eloise began, but Roderick trampled over her.

'Poor old Doro! She's been so good to us — and how do we repay her? I'm as much to blame as anyone, I admit it. I'm the one who persuaded her to stay at Clifton last year when she wanted to go back to Germany. I shouldn't have interfered. But it was what you wanted, Mother.'

'That's quite untrue, Roderick!'

'Is it, Mother? Is it really? You never spelled it out exactly, but I knew what you were thinking; you made it very plain.'

'I'm afraid you're mistaken. If you're under the impression that I—'

'Mistaken, am I? Of course, I would be. It's always someone else. It's never you. You are blinkered, Mother. You only see what you want to see. You won't face facts. Take . . . take Uncle Fred. Everyone knows that Uncle Fred killed himself. Oh, you needn't look so shocked. I've known for years. But you like to pretend that it never happened. You like to pretend that Uncle Fred was a paragon — just as you pretend that Rosa is the opposite. Because it suits you. Because that's the way you want things to be.'

He paused, frowning, and then returned to an earlier remark he'd made — as if he'd been listening afresh to everything he'd said and only now realized how it sounded.

'By the way, you needn't think I only married Rosa so that Antipov couldn't have her. I oughtn't to have said that. There's much more to it. It's . . . it's impossible to explain. But I can't do without her. I can't do without her, and you must just accept it.'

He ended a little breathlessly, as if he'd run out of words, or as if he'd strayed onto ground he wasn't quite sure of. He lingered in the doorway a moment longer; whether he was waiting to see if he really did have nothing more to say, or whether he expected her to speak, Eloise wasn't certain. But before she could even begin to gather her thoughts, he turned and stalked from the room.

* * *

She'd been sitting at her dressing table for a quarter of an hour, waiting for her maid, when she suddenly remembered that it was her maid's half-day. She felt adrift, like an actress on stage waiting for a cue that never came. How silly to have forgotten, when the Clifton routine was her very métier. Quickly, she busied herself, letting her hair down, massaging her face and neck with her fingers.

As she brushed her long, fair hair (there was barely a hint of grey), she tried to compose herself. She was still reeling after her stormy encounter with Roderick.

You are blinkered, Mother. You only see what you want to see.

But that wasn't true. She saw more than he realized. If she kept her own counsel, was that so wrong?

Young people nowadays — they couldn't help but rake things over; they seemed to find it necessary to engage in endless discussion of anything and everything. That was not her way. That was not how she'd been brought up. And it was too late for her to change at her age, even if she'd wanted to.

Her hand faltered and she lowered her brush. Why had Roderick mentioned Frederick? She wished he hadn't. No good was served in bringing up Frederick's tragic end. It had thrown her, she had to admit; she'd been dumbfounded to discover that Roderick was not as unaware as she'd imagined.

Everyone knows that he killed himself.

Everyone? She'd consoled herself that almost no one knew. But people talked. People always talked.

Her eyes slowly focused on her image in the mirror, her hair tumbled around her shoulders, her face pale and drawn. Seeing herself, solid and real, and in such disarray, concentrated her mind. She pinched her cheeks, to put a bit of colour in them; she set about her coiffure. Meticulously, she reassembled the real Eloise Brannan, rolling and pinning her hair, applying the merest hint of powder to her face. She got to her feet, picked out something to wear, slipped it on. Inspecting herself in the tall cheval mirror, she straightened the dress, smoothing out imperceptible creases.

She paused, looked at herself frankly, critically. She wasn't vain, she had no illusions. She'd never considered herself a remarkable beauty. But she liked to look her best. She prided herself on her appearance. She had never let her standards slip.

Sitting down at her dressing table once more, she opened her jewellery box to add a finishing touch. She picked out her sapphire brooch, but then put it down again, thinking unaccountably of the jewels that were gone: Mother's diamonds, for instance, and a certain ruby carcanet that Eloise, as a girl, had thought the most beautiful thing in the world. Father, after Frederick's marriage, had given the jewels to his new daughter-in-law, a matter of some regret to Eloise. Worse had followed. Returning to Clifton Park after her four years' exile in Coventry, and with Emerald in the grave, Eloise had discovered that many of the jewels had simply disappeared. Whether they'd been lost or sold or given away was impossible to say. But the diamonds were gone, and the ruby carcanet, and a little thing like this sapphire brooch could never replace them.

Lady Emerald had always been a greedy woman: greedy for beautiful things, greedy for new experiences. She'd been greedy, too, for her husband's time and attention. She'd bitterly resented Frederick's burgeoning political career during the early years of their marriage. She'd felt herself neglected. Apparently incapable of keeping herself amused, she'd relied on others to stave off boredom. Perhaps if she'd had children, it might have filled the gap in her life, but her son wasn't born until much later.

'Not for want of trying!'

Eloise recalled Frederick's growing exasperation at the pointed remarks of friends and family, who were all awaiting a certain 'happy event'. Emerald had seemed impervious to such comments, but Frederick was more sensitive, and he'd laboured under a growing weight of expectation, fearful of being seen as a failure.

To give Father his due, he'd remained silent on the subject, but Eloise had known, and Frederick must have known too, that Father's most cherished wish was for an heir in the third generation: an heir to establish their dynasty, to make the Rycrofts the new Massinghams.

A son and heir was eagerly awaited on every side. But a son and heir failed to appear.

'Not for want of trying!'

They'd been alone together, her and Frederick, in the drawing room one afternoon. His words had made her blush, hinting as they did at the hidden mysteries of matrimony. She'd not been much more than twenty, still very innocent.

'I'm doing my level best, Maud.' (He'd called her 'Maud', a long-standing joke between them.) 'No one could do more. I wish they'd leave me alone!'

He'd paced up and down, tugging at his hair, as he always did when he was agitated (she'd often thought that the phrase 'tearing his hair out' must have been coined with Frederick in mind). She'd been sitting demurely on the sofa, not knowing what to say. But her silence seemed to soothe him, and after a time he'd given up his restless pacing and his hair-tugging, and he'd come and sat beside her.

'Never mind, Maud. I'll show them yet. Wait till I'm in Parliament! They can put that in their pipe and smoke it!'

But he'd been destined to fall short in politics too.

Frederick had been unfailingly cheerful. He'd never stayed gloomy for long, he'd always been ready to look on the bright side, which made the manner of his death all the more harrowing.

But how much did one really know of people, Eloise asked herself, sat at her dressing table all these years later: how much did one know even of the people one was closest to? She had no idea, for instance, if Frederick had known of or suspected his wife's flirtation with Philip Milton (if flirtation was all it had been). If he had known, might he have laid the blame on himself — on his preoccupation with politics and consequent neglect of his wife? Perhaps that had played a part in his abandoning his political ambitions after the election of 1886. Whether he knew of Emerald's wayward behaviour or not, he seemed only to grow ever more devoted to her, falling over himself to make her happy. She'd played on this; she'd made a show of the power it gave her. She'd taken to kissing him brazenly in public, touching and caressing him too, caressing the contours of his face and ruling him with her eyes. She'd prevailed on him to take her travelling. To travel, she'd said, was all she really wanted. And so they'd begun to spend more and more time abroad.

They'd been married nine years, and they'd just returned from their most protracted trip yet, when the longed-for announcement had come out of the blue: Emerald was with child. Time had been running out by then. Emerald had been nearing forty. And so Richard had arrived not a moment too soon — and to much rejoicing — in the spring of 1890. Only two months later, Eloise had met Albert for the first time; within a year they were married.

Eloise picked up the sapphire brooch once more from her dressing table, and turned it over and over in her hand, as she thought how fortuitous it had seemed, meeting Albert at just the right time. She, too, had not been getting any younger, and she'd no desire to perpetually play the role of Richard's maiden aunt. Also, Lady Emerald, now she was a mother, had let it be understood that she would give up her endless wandering and finally settle at Clifton. She would be its mistress. There wasn't room for another. Eloise had been forced to surrender the role she'd taken on as a stopgap, when it had just been her and Father whilst Frederick and Emerald were away. She'd also given up any slim and secret hope of one day inheriting Clifton Park: Richard's birth had put paid to that (or so she'd thought).

Her wedding had been arranged for March 1891, after a long, hard winter; December, in particular, had been bitterly cold. There'd been a sting in the tail. Gales and snow had swept the country — 'the Great Storm', people had called it — and Eloise had woken on the morning of her wedding to find the world mantled in white. Snow had been shovelled hastily aside so she could walk the path from the carriage to the church. The roof of St Adeline's had been thatched with snow; snow capped the merlons of the battlemented tower. Eloise, in her white wedding dress, amid the white world, had felt like the Snow Queen.

All had seemed settled. Eloise was to live with Albert in Coventry. Frederick had Clifton and his family. Father would be well cared for; already he'd been much recovered after a recent illness. The fillip of his long-awaited grandchild had worked wonders, better than anything the doctors could prescribe.

All had seemed settled. How swiftly things could change.

The sapphire brooch slipped through her fingers, to fall unnoticed on the dressing table; Eloise stared into her own blue eyes in the mirror, remembering how her world had been turned upside down in little more than five years. Not twelve months after her marriage, Father had gone to his grave; his health had rallied only to fail again, and he faded rapidly away. Returning to Clifton for the funeral — she had insisted, despite being seven months enceinte with Roderick — she had found her old home sadly changed.

Father's passing had cast a further pall over a house already beset by tragedy, for the boy Richard had fallen prey to infantile paralysis the previous summer.

'Is there nothing can be done, Frederick?'

'The doctors are quite certain. He is crippled. He will always have a withered leg.'

'I'm so very sorry.'

'Emerald has been badly hit. She suffers most cruelly, can barely look at the boy. You know how she hates imperfection.'

'What will you do?'

'Take her away, straight after Father's funeral. Take her abroad. As a restorative. It's what she needs.'

And so they'd gone; their son they'd left to his own salvation.

Eloise got abruptly to her feet and crossed to the window, opening the curtains a little and looking out at the night. The upper branches of the cedar tree were silhouetted against the dark sky, which was strewn with torn, dark grey clouds. Here and there, high above, in deep pools of blackness, faint stars flickered almost as if they were shivering, cold and alone in the empty heavens.

You are blinkered, Mother . . . you won't face facts . . .

Well, the facts were these. Frederick and his wife had spent more time abroad than they did in England after Father's death. Twenty-one years ago, they'd returned from their latest trip, which also proved to be their last. Eloise, in Coventry, had only been dimly aware that Lady Emerald was ill: some infection, it was presumed, picked up on her travels. Less than a month later, in a mild, wet November, she had died.

As soon as the news reached her, Eloise had hurried to Clifton with Albert, to find her brother inconsolable. Never had she seen a man so bereft and broken. She had been shaken by it.

Albert had done his best to comfort her. 'Fred is grieving, Ellie. It's new and raw just now, and he is suffering, but it will pass. He'll get back on his feet in time.'

After Emerald was buried, Albert had gone back to Coventry — back to his bicycle business and to little Roderick. Eloise had stayed at Clifton a while longer, to support Frederick as best she could, but in the end she, too, had returned to Forest Road.

Winter deepened. The weather had taken a turn for the worse. February had been the coldest in living memory, so cold that the canal had frozen over, leaving the narrow boats trapped in the ice. Frederick had organized soup, sent it down to the boatmen and their families. Having overseen this last characteristic act of compassion, he'd retreated to the library with Father's old shotgun, and there he'd blown his brains out.

'Albert! Oh, Albert! Why ever did I leave him? I will never forgive myself.'

'Now, now, Ellie. Don't be too hard on yourself. If he'd made up his mind, there's nothing anyone could have done.'

For a man like Albert, never daunted by life, Frederick's decision seemed unaccountable; Eloise was not sure she understood it herself. Frederick had been young, not yet thirty-nine. Had he really felt he had nothing left to live for?

A tragic accident: that was the official verdict. But—

Everyone knows Uncle Fred killed himself.

Eloise let the curtains fall back into place, drawing a veil at the same time over her disturbing train of thought. She turned abruptly from the window.

She was ready now. Dressed for dinner. Yet she lingered in her room, strangely reluctant to go downstairs. Why? Was she anxious about coming face to face with Roderick? Surely not. And yet . . . he'd been so angry earlier, in the parlour; she'd never seen him so angry. And she couldn't remember that he'd ever spoken to her quite like that before.

In the gardens that afternoon, she'd had the feeling that Roderick was different, that he'd changed in some way. The temptation was to hold Rosa responsible; the temptation was to see certain parallels between Roderick's marriage and Frederick's, an older woman keeping her younger husband in thrall.

Words came unbidden into her head. She recognized them as a verse from Genesis. How did it go?

'Therefore shall a man leave his father and his mother, and shall cleave unto his wife: and they shall be—'

A noise like a tolling bell broke into her thoughts and she looked up, startled, listening. But no — it wasn't a bell — of course it wasn't. It was the gong, sounding for dinner.

She gathered herself, glanced one last time at her reflection in the cheval mirror. Something was missing. Ah, yes, the sapphire brooch. There it was, over on the dressing table. She picked it up and pinned it on, the finishing touch.

It was time to go down.

* * *

There seemed no rift, outwardly at least, between Roderick and his wife, as they went through to dinner, though he must surely have questioned her by now about the events of a year ago last August. It was not in Roderick's nature to let things lie; he always confronted things head-on. It was absurd, though, to imagine the relationship between Roderick and Rosa was anything like that between Frederick and Lady Emerald: that much was obvious, seeing them in real life. The age gap was less, too: only half that between Frederick and Emerald. And Roderick was not the sort of young man likely to be led by his wife — or anyone else, for that matter. If he really had changed, other reasons suggested themselves beside his marriage, not least the war.

All this was clear to Eloise now. She also saw she had laid an unwitting trap for herself by keeping Rosa's letter; it could only ever have reflected badly on her. Roderick felt he'd been deceived, that she'd hidden it from him, whereas Rosa must imagine that it had been kept to use against her — if she knew it still existed (but she must know, Roderick would surely have told her). Eloise would have liked to explain, but she baulked at raising the subject again, and any explanation at this stage could be seen as making excuses.

There was a strained atmosphere round the table. No one had much to say. Even Elizabeth was uncommonly quiet. Small sounds were loud in the silence: knives and forks scraping on china, Crompton's measured breathing as he cleared the plates. The fish course gave way to fillets of beef, tender, succulent, perfectly prepared. Cook had surpassed herself this last week or so; nothing was too much trouble for the wounded hero.

As they got to their feet and the end of the meal, Roderick flexed his arm. He felt no pain in it now, he said. It was almost as good as new. No doubt he'd be passed fit before long, then he could get back to the important business of giving the Hun a jolly good strafing.

He sounded almost eager to be gone.

* * *

Eloise remained seated in the drawing room with her embroidery after the others had retired, postponing the inevitable moment when she went upstairs to face yet another disturbed night. She knew she would find it more difficult to sleep than ever tonight, after everything that had happened; if only one could switch off one's mind as easily as switching off an electric light.

She sighed and put her work aside. She couldn't muster any interest in it tonight. Taking off her spectacles, she rubbed her eyes, which felt sore and swollen. She really was rather tired. Perhaps she might sleep after all. There was only one way to find out.

In the upstairs corridor, as she was about to enter her room, she noticed one of the chairs askew and moved to straighten it, her skirts rustling softly, her footsteps silent on the carpet, the wall light glowing dimly. She stepped back from the chair, then hesitated. Her eyes strayed to Roderick's door. It was shut fast. She found herself stretching her hand out, not knowing why she did so. Her fingers did not quite touch the polished wood of the door.

Suddenly she stiffened, hearing a faint sound. Someone climbing the stairs, was it? But no. The sound had come from a different direction — from inside Roderick's room.

Therefore shall a man leave his father and his mother, and shall cleave unto his wife: and they shall be one flesh.

Her outstretched hand began to tremble. She lowered it swiftly and pressed it against her thigh. There was no sound now, not a whisper. It could have been anything; wind under the eaves, her imagination — anything.

She turned back to her own door. She opened it, went into her room, and closed the door softly behind her.

CHAPTER EIGHT

'Is that the post, Crompton?' asked Eloise, coming down the stairs.

Crompton paused in the hallway and looked up at her. 'Yes, madam. Only one letter this morning, madam. For Miss Elizabeth.'

So there was nothing from Roderick. It was a week now since his last letter.

From her position halfway down the last flight of stairs, one hand resting lightly on the banister, Eloise could see a solitary letter resting on the salver that Crompton was about to carry into the breakfast room; it was a letter that had every appearance of coming from overseas and was stamped PASSED BY CENSOR. Hope briefly reignited. It was not unknown for Roderick to write to his sister. But the address was written in a hand she didn't recognize — sloping, spidery — and she knew that this was not a letter from Roderick.

Miss E Brannan
Clifton Park
Hayton
Northamptonshire
England

Who could possibly be writing to Elizabeth?

Eloise swept down the last few steps. 'Carry on, Crompton.'

'Very good, madam.'

He opened the door to the breakfast room and followed her in. As Eloise took her place at the table, out of the corner of her eye she watched Crompton present the salver to Elizabeth. The letter was whisked away into a pocket. Elizabeth seemed barely to glance at it, as if uninterested. But there was something furtive in her manner, which served to further arouse Eloise's suspicions. The fact that Elizabeth had shown no curiosity about the letter suggested that she already knew who it was from, was perhaps even expecting it. It was on the tip of Eloise's tongue, as she unrolled her napkin, to interrogate her daughter, but she stopped herself. Such tactics seldom worked with Elizabeth. A different approach was required.

Pushing her misgivings aside for the moment, Eloise applied herself to breakfast. Rosa, she noted, had regained her appetite. She obviously no longer felt sick in the mornings.

Rosa's condition had been the cause of considerable upset. Arthur Camborne had been first to communicate the news, back in December. Rosa, angry, had said that he had no right. It was her business to tell people and Roderick ought to have been told before anyone. She'd refused to see Dr Camborne again; she now went to a doctor of her own choosing in Lawham. No one would ever have described Arthur Camborne as thin-skinned, but it was plain he had felt offended — and no wonder, after serving the family faithfully for more than forty years. Rosa, however, refused to reconsider. Perhaps, if Roderick had been home—

But that was no use. Roderick would only have taken Rosa's side.

Roderick was in France again. After his convalescence at Clifton — during which time he'd filled the house with his presence, eaten like a horse, and got Rosa with child — he had re-joined his regiment at its depot in England, only to be sent back almost at once to the front. A time of waiting had begun again — waiting for letters, waiting for news. Christmas had come, dark, wet and gloomy, the second Christmas of a war everyone had expected to be over before the first. And now it was January; the New Year, 1916, was already two weeks old.

Eating scrambled eggs, Eloise found that Rosa and Elizabeth were talking about — what else? — the war. Elizabeth appeared to have read in the newspaper that half a million men were yet to offer themselves for military service. Prodding a half-eaten kipper with her fork, pushing it around her plate, Elizabeth said, 'How long does it take to count to half a million? It makes my brain ache just thinking about it.'

'I don't believe it's helpful, nor is it right or proper,' said Rosa, 'to reduce people to the level of statistics.'

'Cecily Somersby says that men who aren't in uniform should be handed a white feather.'

'That's not very fair. There can be any number of reasons why a man is not in uniform. He might be working in a reserved occupation — making armaments, for instance.'

'Don't worry, Rosa. Cecily Somersby wouldn't dare give a white feather to anyone. She's far too much of a mouse.' Elizabeth dropped her fork with a clatter and shoved her plate aside. 'Is your brother in a reserved occupation, Rosa? He paints pictures, doesn't he?'

'Leo is an artist, yes. He thinks the war is a terrible mistake. That's why he refuses to fight. In any case, war is inimical to art. You can't create with one hand and destroy with the other.'

'Kolya once said to me . . .' Elizabeth furrowed her brow. 'It was something like this.' She did her best to imitate Mr Antipov's Russian accent. '"The urge to destroy can also be a creative urge." Then he said, "Society must be destroyed to its roots before something new and better can be built." But he was drunk when he said it,' she ended doubtfully.

Rosa paused in the business of eating her breakfast, smiling to herself. 'He used to say things like that when he was sober, too. Not everyone in the Thursday Evening Club agreed with him. We used to have terrific arguments over it.'

'What is the Thursday Evening Club, Rosa? I've often heard about it.'

'It's not like a real club, just a group of friends who meet once a week to talk about art and literature and politics — anything and everything. At one time, there was quite a crowd of us, men and women together, people from different places, from different walks of life. I was still a student when the club began. My friend, Maggie, was at Oxford too — and so was Kolya, of course. Kolya, as you know, came from Russia, there was a young man named Erik from Norway, and Aidan was from Ireland. Aidan used to be a post office clerk, Leo is an artist, and Tom — Tom, in the beginning, worked at the docks. You can't imagine how exciting it was, Eliza — how invigorating — to meet so many different people, to exchange so many different ideas. We felt . . . well, we felt we were involved in something entirely new, something no one had ever done before. We were pioneers, seeking a way to a better world. We had such high hopes.'

'Did Roddy go to the club too?'

'Roderick? Heavens, no! He used to scoff at us, call us cranks.' Rosa went back to her breakfast.

'I don't think you're cranks!' cried Elizabeth. 'It sounds marvellous! I wish I could go to the club. But I never go anywhere.' She sighed. 'Clifton is so dull. When the war began, I thought something would happen — something wonderful and exciting — an adventure. But nothing ever happens at Clifton.'

'You'd have liked the Thursday Evening Club, Eliza. You'd have fitted in — unlike Roderick.'

'You talk as if it is over, Rosa. Has the club ended now?'

'I've not been to a meeting in a long time. London is too far away. I hardly ever go back there. But Maggie tells me there aren't many meetings these days in any case, and fewer and fewer people attend them. I'm not the only one who has moved away. Kolya's gone back to Russia, Erik and Aidan have gone home too. Aidan is lucky: he is safe from conscription in Ireland. But as for Leo and Tom, I'm not sure what this new Military Service Act will mean for them. The government intends to call up the half million men you were talking about, Eliza.'

'So who is this Tom?'

'Tom Hickman, a rather remarkable young man. He's from the East End of London—'

'I've been there! I went there with Doro, to look for her papa!' Elizabeth shuddered. 'We saw horrible places. The people were poor and wretched; their clothes were all rags and patches — some of them didn't even have any shoes.'

'That's the world Tom grew up in. I was the first in our circle to meet him. Back when I was student, I did voluntary work in the holidays. I lectured on history and literature to poor working men. Tom came along to the lectures. He could barely read: he'd not had much schooling. He was very rough and ready, and rather pugnacious too.'

'What does "pugnacious" mean?'

'It means angry and aggressive.'

'Why was he angry?'

'Because he knew so little about life. Ignorance is the enemy, Eliza. Ignorance leaves people feeling helpless and hostile, at odds with the world. Tom was very hot-tempered, but he could be charming, too. I remember he once presented me with a bunch of flowers, to thank me for the work I did. But I was only sorry that I couldn't do more — which is why I invited Tom to the Thursday Evening Club. I knew he'd learn far more from listening to our discussions than I could teach him in a few lectures. After a time, he even came and lived with us — with Leo, Carla and I. He found work as a clerk in an office. He was beginning to fulfil his potential — and now the government wants to carry him off to fight! It's such a waste.'

Listening to all this as she ate her scrambled eggs, Eloise could not help thinking there was something high-handed in Rosa's attitude. It was all very well wanting to help the poor, but there was a thin line between helping and interfering — between education and indoctrination. Left to his own devices, this young working man Rosa was talking of might have been quite willing to fight for king and country, whereas now he risked being branded a coward, because his head had been turned by people who thought themselves cleverer than him.

Eloise remembered Roderick describing the Thursday Evening Club as 'a rabble of malcontents and misfits'. For young men and young women to mix indiscriminately, to call each other by their first names and become overfamiliar, it could only lead to trouble. Rosa would no doubt think this a stuffy attitude to take, old-fashioned, out of date. But the proprieties were there for a reason: not to suppress women, but to protect them. Rosa was glamorizing the unconventional life she'd led before her marriage, which would only put ideas into Elizabeth's head — and Elizabeth was quite troublesome enough already (the mysterious letter, who was it from?).

Her scrambled eggs all eaten, Eloise arranged her knife and fork on the empty plate and said, 'In my opinion, Mr Asquith is quite right to change the law. There are far too many young men who have not attested. They oughtn't to be allowed to shirk their duty. Why should Roderick go and fight, whilst others stay at home in ease and comfort?'

'But, Mrs Brannan, Roderick chose to fight,' said Rosa. 'Leo chooses not to. Isn't freedom of choice what we are trying to defend? I rather think Maggie Ward was right. Coercion and conscription go against the English way of life. It was you who said we should remain true to ourselves — otherwise, what's the point? Not that this war isn't point- less already. Surely it must strike you as singularly futile that Dorothea should spend her days patching up men from the land of her birth, whom men of the land of her adoption have been doing their level best to kill?'

This was Rosa's way: weaving a web of words, trying to confuse, to snare. Eloise stuck to what she was certain of, cutting a straight path through the tangled web.

'We did not ask for this war. It was forced on us. Therefore we must defend ourselves. The Germans cannot be allowed to walk all over us.'

'But, Mama!' cried Elizabeth. 'Not all Germans are nasty! Johann isn't, we know he isn't. Why should we fight Johann?'

'If Johann condones the way the Germans have been behaving, then I'm afraid—' Eloise hesitated. Suddenly it seemed to her that, despite all her vigilance, she had somehow let herself become ensnared. If one spoke against Johann, was it not tantamount to speaking against Dorothea? And one must never doubt Dorothea: Roderick had said so, and Roderick was right.

'What, in effect, you are saying, Mrs Brannan,' Rosa observed, with an air of what Eloise thought of as masculine detachment, 'is that Dorothea's husband should refuse to support the war, and that he would be right to do so. In which case, how would that make him different to Leo? If Johann would be justified in his refusal, why shouldn't Leo refuse too?'

This was easy. Eloise saw at once the flaw in Rosa's argument. 'Because we are right. We are fighting on the right side. The Germans are not.'

A sudden silence fell round the breakfast table. Rosa and Elizabeth exchanged glances. It was as if there was some sort of understanding between them — a conspiracy, almost. Eloise felt herself excluded, isolated.

The silence continued.

* * *

In the parlour a few days later, Eloise put aside a scrap of cloth that had once been a duster, adding it to a pile of rags and broken utensils that she had been inspecting. The servants were apt to throw away perfectly serviceable items in preference for something new: a waste. One had to guard against it. In truth, this could have been left to Mrs Bourne. No one was more stringent than Mrs Bourne. But, as mistress, Eloise felt it beholden on her to keep on top of things. The devil was always in the detail.

She was waiting for Mrs Bourne to return; they had been halfway through their morning meeting when the house-keeper had been called away to some crisis or other in the laundry room. There were matters still pending. The new housemaid, for instance: her trial period was almost over. Was she worth keeping on? She was very young, and rather inexperienced, but there had not been much in the way of an alternative when yet another member of staff had given notice.

Such a nuisance about Kirkham. Eloise had grown used to her. She'd been at Clifton — how long? Five years, was it? But her mother, Kirkham had explained, had written to tell her of new opportunities for work in her home town: Lincoln, was it, or Leeds? Somewhere, anyway, beginning with 'L'. (Really, Eloise was getting to be as vague as Alice Fitzwilliam.)

Yes. It was a nuisance about Kirkham. But Eloise could not blame the girl's mother for jumping at the chance to get her daughter home, nor was it at all surprising that Kirkham wanted to go: the wages on offer in factories these days could simply not be matched. And so Kirkham had gone off to be a munitionette, as such girls were called these days. They made shells and bombs and bullets. Eloise had seen pictures of them in some of the newspapers. She had also seen pic-tures of women in uniform. Some of them looked to Eloise not much younger than her. The newspapers lauded the patriotism of these middle-aged, martial-looking women, but did so in a way that Eloise found faintly disparaging. They'd been dubbed 'Amazons'. It was sad to think that the word 'Amazon' had become a term of mockery. No mockery had been intended when Father used it of her — his little Amazon — all those years ago.

She couldn't help wondering if there might have been a time when a uniform would have suited her. She'd been as bold and fearless as anyone when she was a girl, riding her pony as far as she dared, and much further than she was allowed. The far-flung fields and hedgerows viewed from

Duncan's Hill had certainly not been the limit of her ambitions. When a little older, she'd often imagined herself setting off into the Orient like Lady Hester Stanhope in search of adventure. But the opportunity had never arisen. Perhaps, had there been a war when she was younger, a war like the present war . . .

She rose abruptly from her stool, dismissing these fanciful ideas which only served to lead her up the garden path. Whilst she was waiting for Mrs Bourne, she would do something useful: she would check on the post. Either the post was late this morning, or else Crompton had left the letters on the table in the hall; he sometimes did, if he was busy, keeping them until he had a moment to spare, which was understandable when he was doing the work of two men, taking on Ordish's duties as well as Basford's. But it rather left Eloise in a state of suspense.

There were no letters in the hallway. Rosa was there, however, standing by the front door with her coat on.

'You are going out?' Eloise endeavoured to make conversation.

'For a walk, yes.' Rosa's brief reply seemed designed to cut the conversation short.

'Is it wise to walk so much, in your condition, and in this weather?'

Her words seemed to reverberate around the hallway. Eloise pursed her lips. Why did she always feel so clumsy when it came to talking with Rosa? To mention the weather was particularly silly, when January had so far been unseasonably mild.

Rosa avoided Eloise's eyes. 'I am quite capable of walking to the village and back. I am pregnant, not ill.'

Eloise looked at her daughter-in-law, dressed in her high-collared coat and a flowerpot hat, the baby not showing yet. Rosa was such hard work. It would have been simpler to ignore her. But she was Roderick's wife, and Eloise was loath to give Roderick further cause to find fault, after what had happened during his convalescence last October. Roderick was reason enough not to ignore Rosa, even had it not been the case that to do so would be unthinkably ill-mannered. As Father had often said, 'Manners maketh the man', and never a truer word had been spoken.

Eloise said carefully, 'I am not your enemy, Rosa.'

It was like signalling across a wide sea, they seemed so far apart. But surely Rosa would recognize an olive branch.

'I don't want you to think, Rosa, that—'

Eloise was interrupted by a commotion on the stairs. Elizabeth came stampeding down, her coat half on and her hair tucked untidily into her hat.

'I'm coming, Rosa, I'm coming! Oh, Mama, it's you. I'm going to the village with Rosa. We'll be back later. Goodbye! Goodbye!'

The front door slammed. Eloise was left alone in the hallway. There was no sound but the slow ticking of the grandfather clock.

* * *

Elizabeth's room was in disarray, as expected, clothes strewn across the floor, drawers left open. The bed was unmade even at this hour. Eloise hung back. She'd found the door ajar, like an invitation, but Rosa and Elizabeth had been gone a while now and might return from the village at any moment. How would she explain her presence here, if she was discovered?

But instead of turning away, Eloise went in. She crossed to the window and looked out. She wouldn't be able to see if Rosa and Elizabeth were on their way back, of course, because the window faced away from the village; it commanded a view from the back of the house, where the land sloped down into a shallow valley in which the canal lay all but hidden. Further on, where the ground began to rise again, there was the leafless desolation of Ingleby Wood in winter, skeletal branches etched pencil-thin against a grey January sky. Eloise could never see this view without wondering how it would have looked had the landscaping been completed as planned. Money had run short when the house was being built in the eighteenth century, or so the story went, and the grandly named 'Park' had been scaled down until it was little more than an ordinary meadow, neat and clipped up here near the house, growing ever more unkempt as it sloped gently towards the canal. Eloise, over the years, had come to the measured conclusion that, whatever had been envisaged in the original plans, it could hardly have constituted an improvement on what actually existed. Even in bleak January, the view from Elizabeth's window had a certain austere beauty.

What did Elizabeth see when she looked from her window? What did she feel? What did Clifton mean to her? Dull, she had called it the other morning. Was that really how she thought of it?

Eloise slowly turned, her eyes roaming round the room as if in search of some clue that might lay her daughter bare. There was a book on the bedside table. What was Elizabeth reading these days? The title, *The Story of an African Farm*, meant nothing to Eloise. Written on the fly-leaf was *Rosa Halsted, 1912*. One of Rosa's books, then. Some sort of suffragist polemic, was it? There was a bookmark a few pages in. Elizabeth had not got very far in reading it. That was Elizabeth all over. She dabbled. She didn't see things through.

Replacing the book, Eloise reached down to push shut an open drawer in the bedside table, then hesitated, catching sight of something within. She opened the drawer wider. There was a bundle of letters. She recognized the handwriting on the envelopes. It was the same handwriting that she'd seen on the letter on Crompton's salver a few days ago.

Eloise hesitated again. But she was entitled, as a mother, to inspect her daughter's correspondence, when that daughter was a child of sixteen — just as she was entitled, as mistress of Clifton, to enter any room in the house she pleased. How could there be any doubt of that?

Without giving herself time for further thought, she plucked the topmost letter from the bundle and opened it.

Dear Miss Eliza
You axed me to rite, miss. I have took you at your word. If
I mite be so bold I have put down the directions where you
can send your reply.
Yr obdnt servant
Wm: Turner

Turner, thought Eloise. The stable hand.

She had taken it for granted that Turner's departure would sever all connection between him and Elizabeth. But here was a letter from him, written nearly a year ago. And here was another, and yet another.

They were all from him, the whole bundle; all written in the same clumsy, spidery hand.

Eloise found herself opening one letter after another, quickly scanning their contents with a growing feeling of unease.

Well miss it seems as there's not much call for cavalry just
at present so I will be moved to masheen guns. I did so want
to work with horses as I do at home but they tell me this isnt
possible so I must just make the best of it.

———

We crossed the sea to France in a cattle boat. We was packed
like sardeens. As escort we had 2 destroyers in case Jerry
tried to sink us. I want never to go on the sea again eksept
to come home. We sailed for 6 hours. We come to a place
called LE HAVRE. This is how it is spelt. The Frenchies
seemed pleased to see us. You ort to have heard them cheering
when we marched thru the town We felt like proper hero's.

The letters, Eloise discovered, had been kept carefully in order. They got longer and longer down the bundle.

Last of all was the letter that had arrived only yesterday. It ended:

I can't think how I'd get on miss if not for your letters. They mean the wurld.
You don't know what it's like out here.
To think of you keeps me going somehow. To remember your <u>dear kind self</u>.
I send you all my best wishes.
Yr obdnt servant
Wm: Turner (Billy)

Something slipped from the bundle and fell to the floor. Stooping to retrieve it, Eloise recognized it as a copy of a photograph taken last year to send out to Roderick. She'd arranged for a photographer to come out from Lawham. They'd sat for him in the drawing room, Rosa on the couch with little Katherine on her knee, Eloise standing behind, Elizabeth to one side. In this copy, Elizabeth was missing. She had been carefully cut out, leaving a hole.

There was a rustling sound in the doorway. Eloise swung round. She thought for a split second that it must be Elizabeth, back from the village. It wasn't. Coming tentatively into the room with her cleaning things — brushes, cloths, emery paper, polish — was the new housemaid.

'Beg pardon, ma'am. I didn't know there'd be anyone here.'

'That's all right — Johnson, isn't it?'

'Yes, ma'am.' The girl looked at her anxiously. 'If you please, ma'am, Mrs Bourne said I was to do the bedrooms at once. At once, she said.'

Eloise put the bundle of letters away and closed the drawer with a snap.

'Very good, Johnson. You may carry on.'

She swept from the room.

* * *

The stable yard was deserted — more than deserted. Desolate. Forsaken. There was no sign of life, not even a cat. A mournful place, thought Eloise, looking round in the gusting wind. The winter afternoon was not particularly cold, but very grey and gloomy.

She could not get used to there being no horses. There'd always been horses. No doubt there'd been horses since the moment Clifton was built. True, there'd not been so many in recent years, since Albert introduced motor cars, but three or four had remained to keep the stables alive. Now, even these had gone. They'd all been requisitioned, Roderick's Conquest among them.

It was here in the stable yard, Eloise remembered, on the day of Mark Somersby's wedding, that she'd seen Elizabeth and Turner together, just over a year ago now. Perhaps she should have intervened right then and there, but there'd seemed no immediate danger, and she'd remembered that Roderick always spoke well of Turner, so she'd left things alone. Soon after, Turner had handed in his notice and gone off to join the cavalry (or the machine guns, as it turned out). That had seemed an end to it — until today, and the letters in Elizabeth's room.

Why would a girl of Elizabeth's age and station want to write letters to a servant, a grown man, a farm labourer's son, with whom she could have nothing in common? What, for that matter, did a man in his mid-twenties see in such a childish creature as Elizabeth? Nothing actually improper had happened; that was almost certain. Possibly it was all quite innocent. But if Turner was really the nonpareil Roderick claimed, then he ought to have known better than to overstep the boundaries with his employer's daughter, however innocently. As for Elizabeth, she wouldn't be told; she didn't realize that the rules she railed against were there for her own protection. Society required girls to be innocent, unblemished. This left them vulnerable. They didn't recognize the dangers lurking all around them. There were untold dangers, even in a simple carriage ride home. No harm had come to Elizabeth on this occasion — she'd been in no danger with Turner — but she had to learn that she couldn't carry on as she was.

Eloise sighed, walking across the stable yard towards the arched entrance. She recalled something Viola Somersby had said on the day of the wedding, something about Elizabeth. *She reminds me, your Elizabeth, of you as a girl, Eloise.* If that was so, then Eloise didn't want her daughter making the same mistakes she had. But, really, Eloise couldn't believe that she'd ever been so flighty, so topsy-turvy — so heedless — as Elizabeth. She reached back into her memory, searching for scenes from her childhood that might decide the matter. It must have been somewhere around here — perhaps on this very spot — that Father had lifted her up onto her first pony. How proud she'd been, riding out under the arch led by the head groom. Here, on this little track the other side of the arch that led past the stable block, she'd turned in a circle and ridden back, trembling with excitement.

Eloise looked along the track. It led past Becket's little cottage and ran on to become the bridleway to Brockmorton. She'd ridden that way many a time in her youth but it was years now since she'd made the journey across the fields as far as Brockmorton. She turned her back on the bridleway and walked round towards the front of the house. The garden wall, on her left, slanted away to make room for the circular space of gravel with the cedar tree in the centre; seeing the wall now, it came into her mind that once, long ago — she must have been very tiny — she had trailed her hand along the crumbling brickwork and stopped to watch the wasps nosing into the nooks and crannies. The red of the bricks, the black and yellow of the wasps: the colours remained vivid in her mind. Odd, what one remembered, the most inconsequential things.

She sat down on the old wooden bench beneath the cedar tree, with the gnarled and fissured trunk behind her and the heavy, drooping boughs hanging over her like a canopy. The great, grey facade of the house faced her in all its pleasing symmetry, with its tall pilasters and many windows, and the broad steps sweeping up to the front door with an arched fanlight above. Green ivy was growing up the wall to the right of the door, framing the ground-floor windows on this side. Which of those windows was it that she'd looked out of, one blazing July morning, and seen Frederick in his shirt sleeves with the sun in his hair — his brilliant white shirt, his rich golden hair? This drab January day, dim and colourless, made a mockery of the radiant world of her youth, so bright in her memory.

She gazed up at the grey stonework, the blank windows. She'd always been deeply attached to Clifton: that went without saying. When they'd come to live here, she and Albert, after Frederick's death, Albert had said to her, 'I am beginning to think I married a house as well as a woman.' He'd not been entirely joking.

She'd kept the house in trust, as Father had instilled into her; she'd preserved the house as best she could for the future generations. Indeed, it was in better repair than she could remember, since Albert's renovations a decade ago. Apart from that, little had changed. She'd even demurred at cutting down the ivy. To all appearances, the house was the same. And yet, there was something . . . a sense she had . . . a feeling . . . as if a malaise had taken hold.

But what did she mean by the word 'malaise'? Only that things were different, not how they should be, how they'd always been. Gradually, imperceptibly, the Clifton she'd known in her youth had disappeared.

She shivered, sat on the bench. Unseasonably mild it might be, but it was still January, the depths of winter, and a breeze was getting up, seething in the tips of the trees. Her thoughts turned to Roderick, as they often did throughout the day. He was back with his battalion somewhere in France.

Badly mauled last autumn at Loos, his battalion had been deployed well behind the lines after the battle to be refitted. There they'd remained all through frosty November and into wet December, and there, so far as she knew, they still were. But, sooner or later, they would be sent back to the front line: it was inevitable.

There'd been no word from Roderick for nearly seven days now. Whenever he did write, Eloise felt she could detect a certain coolness in his words that had not been there before. She bitterly regretted that the misunderstanding over Rosa's letter had not been resolved before Roderick left home. Albert would have set it right at the earliest opportunity; he'd never let things fester. He'd have known how to handle Elizabeth, too. Albert's common sense, and his rugged, no-nonsense ways, were sadly missed. But Albert was dead, and she had to carry on alone.

Slowly she got to her feet. Upright, she made her way, as gracefully as ever, across the gravel and up the steps. She opened the door and went into the house.

* * *

Elizabeth came into the parlour reluctantly, warily. 'What is it, Mama? Why have you sent for me? I'm busy.'

Eloise thought it best to get straight to the point. 'These letters must stop, Elizabeth. You will not write to Turner in future. Do I make myself clear?'

Elizabeth flushed scarlet. 'How . . . how do you know about the letters?'

'Never mind how I know, just do as you're told.'

A defiant glint came into Elizabeth's eyes. 'That's not fair, Mama! He's my friend. I have to write to him.'

'Don't be absurd, Elizabeth, of course he's not your "friend". A girl of your age, and in your position, does not have friends of that sort. Turner is nothing to you.'

'His name is "Billy", not "Turner", and he is my friend, he is! I don't care what you say, he is, he is, he is!'

'You know nothing about him. You know nothing about his life.'

'I do! I—'

'You know nothing about men at all.'

212

'Men are just people; they're not bears or lions or . . . or dragons — they're not dangerous!'

'You haven't the first idea what men are really like.'

'Then tell me, Mama. Tell me what's so terrible about them.'

'You wouldn't understand—'

'Yes I would! I'm not stupid!'

'You're too young—'

'I am sixteen years old, Mama!'

'You will do as you are told, Elizabeth, and that's an end to it. I'm saying this for your own good.'

'Eliza, Mama, my name is Eliza. Everyone calls me Eliza, except you. I don't see why you should be different.'

'Please do not shout! It's most unbecoming.'

'But, Mama—'

'Now stop this, Elizabeth. Why must you be so difficult, so stubborn?'

'I'm not difficult, I'm not stubborn!'

'I don't know how else to describe your behaviour.'

'You don't know how I feel. I feel so . . . so useless. I don't do anything. Everyone is doing something. Roddy's gone to fight, Billy too, and Herbert Basford — even Johnnie Cheeseman joined up, and he's no older than I am!'

'Women have a different role. We have to stay at home and keep things going until the men return. What could be more important than that?'

'Doro didn't stay at home, nor Sally Kirkham. Sally's gone to a factory.'

'What's right for Dorothea and Kirkham is not necessarily right for everyone. We all have different roles to play, Elizabeth, the roles God has chosen for us. God must be our guide.'

'There is no God.'

'Don't be silly. Of course there is.'

'No, there isn't. Kolya told me there isn't — and I believe him! Kolya knew everything.'

'Mr Antipov was a very clever young man, I agree. Clever young men like to think they are important. They like to think they are different. They like to ruffle a few feathers. But they don't know everything.'

'But — Mama! How can you believe in something that doesn't exist — how can you?'

'In my experience, the tried-and-tested ways are usually the best. It's not for you to decide otherwise.'

'Why? Because I'm a girl? Girls can be just as clever as boys. I don't see why girls shouldn't do everything that boys do.'

'Men and women have different spheres in life, to which they are perfectly suited. It isn't natural for a woman to ape the ways of men, just as it isn't natural for a man to be soft and effeminate: it's counterproductive, it's unhealthy — it's wrong.'

'Rosa says women are kept in their place unfairly. Rosa says women are . . . are subjugated.'

'That may be her view. It certainly isn't mine. A woman has a realm of her own — her own duties and responsibilities. Why surrender all that in order to usurp a man's place? That is just senseless. Men and women are different; whatever Rosa might say, they are different, it's a simple fact. And, being different, they should each play to their strengths. You have a role to play, Elizabeth — an important and worthy role — if only you'd open your eyes. You shouldn't let Rosa fill your head with all that suffragist nonsense.'

'You're only saying that because . . . because you hate Rosa!'

'Don't be ridiculous. Of course I don't hate Rosa. We may not agree in everything, but that doesn't mean we don't get along. All I'm saying is that Rosa is sometimes mistaken.'

'So are you, Mama.'

'I expect I am. I have never pretended to be perfect. I don't know everything. But I do know more than you, Elizabeth, because I have lived longer. Why won't you listen to me? Why won't you let me help you? All I want is what's best for you.'

'It's you who doesn't listen, not me. I can't talk to you. Rosa is the only one who . . . who treats me as if I'm a real person!'

'That is not the case, Elizabeth—' Eloise began.

But Elizabeth clapped her hands over her ears. 'Stop it, stop it, stop it! I don't want to listen to you anymore! You make my head ache!'

With that, she ran from the room, leaving the door wide open.

Eloise, after a moment, got slowly to her feet and closed the door. Another wasted effort. Elizabeth would try the patience of a saint. But what else could a mother do but persevere? Elizabeth had to be saved from herself — even if Eloise couldn't see how.

It was a task that would take much time and thought.

* * *

Crompton, next morning, brought the post promptly, just as Eloise was taking a seat at her bureau after breakfast. There was nothing from Roderick. Damping down her sense of disappointment, and trying not to wonder what the reason might be for such a long silence, Eloise opened automatically one letter after another, glancing at them perfunctorily and putting them aside.

She was already halfway through a letter from Mr Smith in Coventry, when she suddenly realized it was not the usual report on the BFS Motor Company. Her eyes skimmed back over words she had already read without taking them in.

Dear Mrs Brannan . . . forgive my writing to you like this . . . word came today . . . dreadful blow . . . Mrs Smith is quite overcome . . . daren't leave her at present . . . to tell him in a letter or telegram seems too impersonal . . . hesitate to impose . . . would you be so very good as to—

Eloise put Mr Smith's letter slowly down on her desk and took off her spectacles. She found herself thinking, *If only Dorothea were here. Dorothea would know the right words.*

But Dorothea was not here. This was something she had to do on her own.

She reached for the bell cord but then stopped herself. It would not seem right to summon Smith to the parlour, as if to give orders or take him to task. A different approach was required.

She folded the letter carefully and put it aside. She got stiffly to her feet.

Smith was in the vegetable garden, a rather bleak place this time of year. He was pushing a wheelbarrow along a muddy path, limping, as he always did since the accident. Mud clogged his boots and was plastered up his corduroy trousers. His cap was rather too large for him. A woollen scarf was wrapped round his neck. He did not see her straight away, as she stood there watching him. In those few seconds, she felt the full weight of what she had to tell him.

'Oh . . . Mrs Brannan . . . morning.' Hastily, he put the wheelbarrow down and stood to attention. 'Sorry, ma'am, I didn't see you, I—' He broke off, almost as if he could sense there was something wrong.

'I'm afraid I have bad news, Smith.' Eloise found that words came easily after all. Always, it was best to be brief and to the point. 'It's your brother, Stanley. He has been killed in France. Your father has written to tell me.'

He stared at her, uncomprehending. 'Stan? Our Stan?' He furrowed his brow. He said hesitantly, as if he was afraid he'd misunderstood her, 'Dead? You mean to say he . . . he's . . . really dead?'

'I'm so very sorry, Smith.'

'But he . . . he . . .'

He . . . he . . . These two stuttered words seemed to bring the dead boy into sharp relief. Eloise could see him clearly in her mind's eye, the eldest of Mrs Smith's three sons: a tall and gangling youth, unfailingly cheerful, always grinning and whistling. For a time, he'd been the Clifton chauffeur, 'working his way up' as his father had decreed. He'd not possessed the same gravitas in the position as his younger brother here, who'd taken over from him, but he'd always been a great favourite with Dorothea; in her own inimitable way, she'd never referred to him as 'Smith' but always as 'Young Stan' — 'young' to distinguish him from his father, the elder Mr Stanley Smith. Dorothea would be grieved to hear that Young Stan was dead — and this was a sobering reminder that Dorothea, too, would have to be told the news.

Smith took off his cap and wiped his eyes on his sleeve. 'We . . . we was chalk and cheese, me and him. We never saw eye to eye, not over nothing. And when he came up home in his brand-new uniform, and Ma made such a fuss of him, and he was so bleeding proud of himself, I could have . . . but I never thought . . . I never thought he'd . . . he'd . . . Oh, crikey. What'll Ma do without him? He always was her favourite—'

Smith's face crumpled and his eyes brimmed with tears again. His jaw was now trembling so much that he could no longer speak.

Seeing him in this state, Eloise's first instinct was to turn away, for she'd been brought up to despise any open display of emotion in a man. Weakness, Father had called it. Shameful. Embarrassing to behold. But she stood her ground and, as she watched Smith fighting to regain his composure amid the bleak winter garden — gritting his teeth, blinking back his tears — she found she could not despise him at all: just the opposite. It wrung her heart to see such raw grief in a young man of twenty — a mere boy. She felt immensely proud of him, as he slowly mastered himself.

She was very much taken aback. She'd hardly expected, in performing this unenviable task, to find herself so deeply moved. It left her unprepared. What should she say, what should she do? Dorothea would have been ready with quiet sympathy, soothing, comforting, saying all the right things. But that was Dorothea. No one could match Dorothea.

In which case, it was best to stick to one's own ways.

She was crisp, sensible. 'You will want to leave for Coventry at once. Your parents will be expecting you.'

'Yes, ma'am.' But he didn't move, standing by the wheelbarrow, ankle-deep in mud.

'You should make ready,' she prompted. 'Do you have money for the train?'

'Y-y-yes, ma'am.'

'Very good. Take as long as you need, Smith. Don't worry about us here at Clifton. Come back when you are ready, and not before.'

'Yes, ma'am. Thank you, ma'am.' A shudder ran through him. There was a bewildered look in his eyes. Slowly those eyes came to focus on her. 'Mrs Brannan, I . . . you . . .'

'That's all right, Smith,' she said. 'That's quite all right.'

* * *

Clothes, shoes, hats, gloves had been stored at various times in individual bags and tidied away, to become lost deep in the armoire or at the back of drawers in the Louis XIV commode. Some of the items Eloise was unearthing had not seen the light of day in years. Here, for instance, was the tailored jacket and the long skirt of her riding habit. She measured it against herself in the cheval mirror and judged that she still had the figure for it, but there seemed little point in keeping it now she no longer rode.

Eloise paused, trying to remember when it was exactly she had stopped riding. Around the time of her wedding, she supposed; there had been no horses at the house in Coventry, where she'd begun her married life, and riding had ceased to be part of her routine. Returning to Clifton after Frederick's death, she had always thought she might take it up again one day — tomorrow, next week, at some point in the future. She'd been telling herself that for twenty years, without ever getting on a horse. But now the stables were empty. And even if — after the war, whenever that might be — there were horses at Clifton again, she knew now that her riding days were over.

She glanced at the bracket clock on her dressing table. It was almost tea time. She had wasted a whole afternoon sorting through old clothes. Why? True, Mrs Somersby had asked for donations to help the Belgian refugees, but that was weeks ago — months, even. There was rather less solicitude for the Belgians these days; some people, indeed, felt they'd become a nuisance. In any case, the Belgians would hardly want this hat in the fashion of thirty years ago, or her old riding habit.

There was no time to tidy up before tea. She would have to leave it to her maid. This meant that everything would be put away again, when the whole idea had been to reduce the clutter in her room. Well, it couldn't be helped.

She searched out her best tea gown with a sense of expectancy. After the upset of Mr Smith's letter, and now all this wasted effort, the time-honoured tea-time routine would be welcome respite.

There was no one in the drawing room when she got there. The fire had burned low, the curtains were not yet closed. She was a little early, perhaps.

Crossing to the window, she looked out at The Park, which had all but faded into the winter dusk. The drawing room behind her was mirrored dimly in the glass of the French windows, the reflection overlaid like a ghostly presence on the growing darkness outside. She wondered if Smith had arrived home yet. She could only imagine how afternoon tea would be at Warwick Street today. She had to remind herself that it was real, that the boy Stanley Smith — 'Young Stan' — was gone, dead, killed in the war; somehow it seemed impossible to keep hold of this fact. Would his family feel the same way, that it was all unreal? She remembered what the boy's father had said of him, a year ago last August, after the picnic and the motor accident: that his eldest son was so laid-back he needed, now and again, 'a kick up the backside'.

Young Stan was — had been — twenty-three years old — the same age as Roderick.

Eloise turned away from the window and sat down in the Eugenie armchair. Almost at once, Crompton came in with a tray. He placed it gingerly on the low table — the table which always wobbled a little, ever since one leg had somehow got broken and Ordish had effected a repair. (Ordish had been adept at things of that sort; he'd also handled the tea tray with a lot more aplomb.) Crompton pulled the curtains, shutting out the dismal January evening, then he saw to the fire. Flames leaped in the grate. He straightened up. Would there be anything else? There was nothing else. He beat a retreat, carefully closing the door behind him.

Eloise poured herself a cup of tea. She took a plate and picked out two sandwiches. As she sat down again, she glanced at the door, firmly shut. Where were Rosa and Elizabeth? They were late coming down today.

She bit into a sandwich. It was egg, one of Cook's infinite variety, but Eloise had no appetite this afternoon. Restless, she put her plate aside, her half-drunk tea too, and took a turn around the room: it seemed strangely empty and silent this afternoon, as if it had fallen into disuse. When was the last time the drawing room had seen any visitors? Even Mrs Somersby hadn't stopped by in several weeks. Eloise wondered if an afternoon 'at home' might be in order. She could invite—

But who could she invite? Not even half a dozen names came to mind. So many old friends and acquaintances seemed to have fallen away.

Running her eye over the sideboard, she saw that the delft vase was out of place, the Venetian bottle as well. She reached out automatically to move them, but then hesitated, and her arm fell limply to her side. Why bother to put them back? What was the use, when they would only get out of place again? Oh, what was the use!

She looked at the photographs. Everyone was there, everyone who mattered: Father and Frederick, Roderick and Dorothea, Albert with his big moustache and self-assured stare. What would Albert say to her, if he could speak from the Other Side? What must he think, seeing his family scattered; Elizabeth running wild; Dorothea stateless, an outcast; Roderick estranged and far from home and beyond all protection: what must Albert think? Frederick, too, had reason to reproach her. His cherished son and heir, whom he'd committed to her care, was dead and gone, a name on a gravestone, nothing more. As for the house, her beloved Clifton Park which had been left to her in trust — well, she'd tried so hard, she'd tried so very hard, to keep it all in order, to keep everything in its place (the delft vase, the Venetian bottle). But Clifton had fallen into a malaise, and that was her fault, and her fault alone. All she'd ever wanted was to make Father proud. He wouldn't be proud of her now.

She had failed. She had failed in every way. And — oh! — how bitter it was — so very bitter — to be a failure at the age of fifty-one, to know that her life's work had come to nothing.

The drawing room was empty and silent. The fire was dying down once more. Cups, saucers and plates were set ready, but unused. The sandwiches and cakes were all uneaten. The tea was going cold. Rosa was not coming, nor Elizabeth.

Tea time was over.

CHAPTER NINE

'This is Cartwright, Mother. Lieutenant Cartwright. I met him on the boat coming over. We got talking. He'd nowhere much to go in Blighty, so I invited him to Clifton. I knew you wouldn't mind.'

Roderick, newly arrived, stepped aside as a tall stranger in uniform came in out of the brightness of the May morning, removing his cap as he did so, and looking round at them in the hallway as they looked at him, taken aback by his unexpected presence.

Here was another of Roderick's waifs and strays, thought Eloise; a man he'd known, by the sound of it, for less than twenty-four hours. *I knew you wouldn't mind.* But she did mind. She minded very much.

They'd not had much notice of Roderick's leave. Preparations had been made in a hurry. Now, just when everything was ready, they had this interloper sprung on them, throwing them out of kilter again; it was all the more vexing when she was so uncertain as to where she stood with her son. A stranger in the house would only make things even more awkward. Hadn't Roderick thought of that?

Eloise did not let any of this colour her behaviour. A guest at Clifton was due every courtesy. She greeted him as was right and proper.

He replied, 'I am delighted to make your acquaintance, Mrs Brannan. Your son has been telling me all about you.' And then he took her hand and kissed it.

Eloise was taken aback, unable to decide if this was old-fashioned gallantry or youthful impertinence.

'You will, I hope, forgive my intrusion,' he continued. 'If it's not convenient, my being here, I shall of course leave at once.'

'Don't be such an ass, old chap. You're not going anywhere.' Roderick slapped him on the back, letting his hand linger in order to guide Lieutenant Cartwright forward to where the others were waiting. 'This is my kid sister, Eliza. And this, Cartwright, is my wife.' Roderick moved to embrace Rosa and to kiss her on the cheek. 'Hello, darling. How's my son and heir?' His hand strayed down to caress Rosa's distended belly. 'Clever of you to manage it.'

Eloise was disconcerted by this display — and in front of a stranger! It was indelicate. Indiscreet. Inaccurate, too. The 'son and heir' might well turn out to be another girl.

Roderick seemed impervious, grinning round at them. 'We've arrived in time for lunch, I hope? But first, we must get out of our uniforms. Which room, Mother, for Cartwright?'

Eloise found herself in an unaccustomed fluster. Put on the spot, she could not think. 'Oh dear. Lieutenant Cartwright will think us hopelessly disorganized. But what are we to do? There are two of you, and only Crompton to valet.'

'Honestly, Mother. Cartwright and I have been crawling around for months on end in muddy ditches. We shan't bother about the niceties. Talking of Crompton, where is — ah, Crompton, there you are. Our bags and valises are in the motor. Chop chop. I'm in desperate need of hot water. Where's the Dreadnought?'

Roderick had them all running round. The house had suddenly come alive.

* * *

There were lamb cutlets for lunch. Roderick ate and talked.

'It's rather a stroke of luck, my getting leave like this, when I only went back in December. Cartwright's had to wait for his leave, he's not been home in over a year — have you, old man? An odd thing about the boat we came over on. Quite a coincidence. It was the *Prince of Wales*, serving as a troopship. You remember the *Prince of Wales*, kiddo? It was the boat that took us across the Channel on our continental jaunt in 1910, you, me and Doro.'

'You were seasick,' said Elizabeth.

'He was seasick again,' said Lieutenant Cartwright. 'He turned positively green. I took him under my wing.'

'With it being the same boat,' Roderick continued, 'I was reminded of a certain beastly song I had going round in my head in 1910. "Boiled Beef and Carrots". Ludicrous little ditty. Made my being seasick ten times worse. Mind you, it's no more ridiculous than most of the songs one hears nowadays. The men sing such songs! What's that one, Cartwright, about the mademoiselle from Armenteers? Armenteers: that's how the men pronounce Armentières. It goes something like this:

'"Mademoiselle from Armenteers, parlay-voo—"'

'Perhaps not that song, Brannan,' Lieutenant Cartwright interrupted. 'It might come as something of a shock in company such as this.'

'Roderick likes nothing better than to shock people, Lieutenant Cartwright.' Rosa gave their guest what Eloise thought of as a knowing smile.

The lieutenant smiled back at Roderick's wife. 'He's absolutely unquenchable, I'll say that much for him. Even when he was prostrate at sea, he was the life and soul. I'm just the opposite, I'm afraid: quite disgustingly shy. But I say, Mrs Brannan — and all of you — I wish you'd call me Alex. Rather forward of me to suggest it, I know, but in the circumstances . . .'

Eloise, as she ate her cutlet, studied Roderick's face: every line, every mark, the differences in him, the bags under his eyes, his waxy skin. She had grown used to his moustache. It was not his moustache which made him seem different this time. What, then? Was it that he simply looked tired and rather weather-worn? Or did he somehow seem older, more — what was the word — more mature? Yes, that was it. He seemed more mature, as if he'd grown up a lot since last autumn.

As lunch went on, and despite her continuing absorption in her son, Eloise nonetheless found her eyes straying more and more towards the stranger at the table. Now that he was out of uniform, it was as if she could see him more clearly. He was wearing clothes he'd borrowed from Roderick. They appeared an almost perfect fit, even though Lieutenant Cartwright was, if anything, a few inches taller. He was older, too. Mid-thirties, perhaps. He had brown hair, brown eyes, a rather wispy moustache; his voice had a certain resonance. Somehow, Eloise couldn't shake the feeling that he was making a conscious effort, as if projecting an image of himself. Maybe he was compensating for his underlying reticence, if what he'd said about being shy was true.

Over and above everything else, it seemed to Eloise that she recognized in Lieutenant Cartwright something which she had noticed in Roderick, too. Despite the obvious differences of age and temperament, there was a certain affinity between them. Possibly it was nothing more than that they were both soldiers: even though they were now wearing civilian clothes, the after-effect of seeing them in uniform still lingered.

Eloise grew curious about Lieutenant Cartwright. Had he really nowhere to go, no one waiting for him? She felt she was entitled to make a few polite enquiries. As hostess, it was more or less her duty to show an interest in her guest.

He answered her questions quite readily. He was unmarried, an only son. His people were dead. Before the war he'd been a teacher. He'd held a post in a small establishment in Gloucestershire: a place, he assured them, they would never have heard of; not a school of the first rank, but well-respected in its own little way.

'Cartwright is confoundedly modest,' Roderick interjected. 'I expect this school of his is top-hole. But he'll never let on. You really have to go at him to get at the truth. And the truth is he's been awarded a Military Cross, he's been mentioned in dispatches — he's something of a hero.'

'That's laying it on far too thick.' Lieutenant Cartwright shrugged off their acclamations. 'It was nothing, nothing at all. Anyone would have done the same.'

'What did I tell you?' cried Roderick, delighted. 'Modest to a fault!'

Colour flushed into Lieutenant Cartwright's pale cheeks. His was a modesty obviously not feigned. Eloise felt that he'd passed a test in some way, earned his place at their table.

'What about you, Roddy?' said Elizabeth. 'Would you like a medal as well?'

'I've not had the chance, kiddo. Not since Loos. I've been sitting in the front line, twiddling my thumbs.'

'Now who is being modest!' Lieutenant Cartwright turned to Eloise. 'Let me tell you, Mrs Brannan, that your son has been in the Ypres sector, one of the most dangerous places on the whole British front; yet, to hear him talk, you'd think it was a picnic.'

Eloise smiled warmly at her guest. It was good of him to sing Roderick's praises. And it was good of him to sing them to her, ahead of anyone else.

An unexpected visitor was always an inconvenience. But it seemed that Lieutenant Cartwright would at least prove an agreeable inconvenience.

* * *

Having dressed for dinner, Eloise made her way downstairs only to meet Lieutenant Cartwright on the half-landing. He seemed more relaxed, now that he was rested and refreshed. His brown hair was neatly brushed. He had his hands in his pockets. He was looking at the painting on the wall.

'You have a wonderful house, Mrs Brannan. There is so much to discover. I find something new at every turn. This portrait, for instance.'

The portrait had been there as long as she could remember, but she looked at it now with fresh eyes, gratified by Lieutenant Cartwright's interest.

'That is my great-grandfather, Sir George Massingham, fifth baronet. He was an MP, and the author of several books. The Massinghams were my ancestors. It was they who built this house.'

'Do you know, Mother—' Roderick appeared on the stairs, came down to join them — 'the more I think about it, the more convinced I am that this can't possibly be that Sir George, the fifth baronet.'

'I've never heard anyone say any different, Roderick. My father always—'

'Consider the evidence, Mother. The man in the painting looks to be in his late forties. He's wearing a white wig. But the tax on hair powder killed the fashion for wigs. The tax was introduced in 1795. Sir George the scribbler in 1795 would have been no older than Cartwright here. So whoever this is, it is not he.'

Roderick, having overthrown everything Eloise had always believed about the painting on the half-landing, now turned, grinning, to his newfound friend.

'Tread carefully, old man. If you give Mother the least encouragement, she will whisk you off on a grand tour. You will be taken over every inch of the house and told the history of each ornament and trinket. You will be invited to admire the view from the terrace. You will be informed that the landscaping was never finished, that Capability Brown was called away at a crucial moment.'

'Really, Roderick, I have never suggested it was Capability Brown himself who . . . who . . .' Eloise reached up to pat her hair as she stumbled over her words. She was surprised to find herself so self-conscious, standing there between these two tall young men, being gently mocked by her son.

Lieutenant Cartwright smiled at her. 'Roderick means to make fun of us both, Mrs Brannan. But to speak the truth, there's nothing I'd like more than a grand tour of your home. Please feel free to "whisk me off" at your earliest convenience.'

'Don't say I didn't warn you, Cartwright.' Roderick led the way down the last flight of stairs. 'When is Doro coming, Mother? Tomorrow, is it? You'll like my cousin, old man. Everyone does.' Roderick, in the hallway, yawned hugely. 'I say, let's go in to dinner before I fall asleep. I'm absolutely ravenous.'

* * *

January that year had been unusually mild for the most part, but February had seen the return of winter, and March had been notably cold and wet, ending with a blizzard. The weather had been more settled in April. Not so the news. The Zeppelins had come back; Lowestoft had been bombarded from the sea. General Townshend had surrendered at Kut. And at Easter, a bolt out of the blue: rebellion in Ireland.

Rosa maintained that it shouldn't have come as a surprise. Trouble had been brewing for years. It was only to be expected, she'd said, that the Irish should want a greater say in their own affairs. Eloise had no idea if this was true or not; she always got in a hopeless muddle over Ireland. Wasn't home rule meant to have been the panacea that settled the Irish question — even if that panacea had been postponed until the end of the war? She couldn't help thinking that the Irish were being a little ungrateful — not to mention unpatriotic — in causing such trouble at a time like this. But the newspapers insisted that the rebels were a tiny minority; the bulk of the population remained steadfastly loyal. Not for long, Rosa had remarked, with the government seemingly determined to turn the rebels into martyrs.

At times, Rosa seemed almost to relish being a harbinger of doom.

These events were already fading in the memory as Eloise walked with tall Lieutenant Cartwright in the bright May

228

sunshine; on such a morning as this, it was almost impossible to believe that winter had ever held them in its grip.

'The gardens, I'm afraid, have been sadly neglected,' she explained, as they came to the croquet lawn with its unsightly molehills and trees encroaching from the Pheasantry.

'That's all part of their charm,' said the lieutenant. 'Perfection is often very bland. A few little flaws give interest, add character.'

'An agreeable way of looking at it,' said Eloise, rather pleased.

She led the way across the lawn to the crumbling wall on the far side that marked the final boundary of the gardens. The sun was particularly warm here, where they were sheltered from the breeze. They looked at the view, which was at its best just now in the first flush of spring. Away across the fields, the green slopes of Rookery Hill rose to a tree-crowned summit set against a high blue sky that was streaked by thin white clouds. A blur of rising grey smoke marked the place where Home Farm lay hidden in its little hollow beneath the hill. The village was entirely obscured by the thicket of the Pheasantry on their right; a breeze was rustling in the treetops, leaves fluttering and shimmering.

'Almost all of the land you can see, everything north of the canal and west of the road, is part of the estate,' said Eloise. 'The Clifton estate has been in the family for over three hundred years. I'm not talking about the Brannan family, of course, but of my ancestors, the Massinghams. My father's name was Rycroft, but his mother was a Massingham. "Massingham blood runs strongly in our veins," Father used to say; and I do feel at times more than half a Massingham. I believe they originally made their money in wool.'

There were many stories about the Massinghams. She'd grown up with them. Stories about Sir John, who'd built the house, and who may or may not have been the same Sir John who had gifted the church its font; stories about the second Sir George, Member of Parliament and writer, whose portrait hung on the stairs (or not); stories of the vicissitudes of younger sons, including the daredevil said to have fallen victim to the guillotine. Roderick always scoffed at that particular story, the story involving the guillotine; mindful of this, Eloise did not repeat it now. She pointed out the landmarks instead. She could name every field. The lieutenant was greatly interested in everything he could see.

Eloise couldn't help thinking what a strange quirk of fate it was that had brought Lieutenant Cartwright to Clifton, someone who seemed truly to appreciate the place: one might almost have called his coming here the fortunes of war. Strangely enough, neither Lieutenant Cartwright nor Roderick had talked much of the war since luncheon on the first day, and today the war seemed particularly remote, nothing more than a vague, dark cloud on the far-distant horizon.

Elizabeth alone pursued the subject. Growing bolder as she got used to their guest, she'd gone so far as to ask him at breakfast this morning if he'd killed many Germans. To his credit, the lieutenant had taken the question in his stride. He'd continued with his eggs and bacon, and answered her by saying he had no idea.

'Unlike your brother, Miss Brannan, I didn't take part in the big push last autumn. I was in another part of the line. Time spent in the trenches mostly means keeping one's head down, with never a sight of the enemy.'

That was not to say there was no danger. Eloise had learned from Mr Smith that his son had not been killed in a big set-piece battle, but by a stray bullet to the head. Elizabeth had been tactless enough to mention this. Lieutenant Cartwright, with what Eloise thought of as disturbing honesty whilst buttering a piece of toast, had allowed that men were killed all the time, every day, battle or no battle. There were shells and snipers. There were patrols and working parties. Death lurked round every corner; there was no hiding from it. He himself had been in no-man's land several times — always at night, of course — and on one occasion he'd taken part in a bombing raid on the enemy's trenches. (Was this when he'd earned his medal? He'd not said.)

Elizabeth had been wide-eyed with admiration. 'You must be very brave!'

'Not at all, Miss Brannan. That is to say, I'm no braver than the next man. I simply do what I have to do. Your brother has shown much more courage than I. A skirmish in the dark is nothing compared to going over the top in a great battle like Loos. I only hope I'm equal to it, when the next big push comes.'

This was his modesty speaking, of course. A man with a medal, a man mentioned in dispatches, would surely be equal to anything. Sat at the breakfast table, Eloise had felt that Elizabeth's admiration was in no way misplaced, but she'd also been aware that Roderick, all through the conversation, was unusually silent. It had not escaped her notice, either, that Lieutenant Cartwright, when talking of the next big push, had said *when*, not *if*.

Eloise shivered now, stood there on the croquet lawn, as if a cloud had passed over the sun. But the clouds were too thin and wispy to make much of a difference today, and here, sheltered by the trees, it was almost hot. Her eyes slowly focused back on the view. The sky was a brilliant blue, the fields green and verdant; a chorus of birdsong was floating from the Pheasantry. The war receded once more into the distance.

They retraced their steps. Walking beside the lieutenant, Eloise explained Father's theory that the gardens pre-dated the house, that they'd originally been attached to the old manor house. The two buildings, the old and the new, had occupied more or less the same spot, but there was some evidence to suggest that the manor house had been built on a different axis.

'Ah, I see,' said Cartwright. 'That would explain why the gardens are at an angle to the house.'

'Yes indeed. That was my father's conjecture, anyway. But now, if we turn right here and go through this gap in the hedge, I'll show you the flower garden.'

They found Becket and Smith at work in the flower garden, bickering amiably, as seemed their habit. ('Now then, boy. What you gone and done here?' 'I ain't done nothing, only what you told me.') When Smith caught sight of Eloise and the lieutenant, he touched his cap to them and nudged Becket with his elbow.

Becket peered short-sightedly, muttering, 'Who's there, boy?'

Smith hissed at him, 'It's Mrs Brannan, you blind old bat.'

'Ah. The mistress. Ah.' And Becket gave a slow nod of approval.

'You appear to command their respect,' said Lieutenant Cartwright, walking with Eloise between the flower beds, 'as if you were an empress and they your subjects. I can see you as an empress — someone like Maria Theresa of Austria — and all this—' his arm swept round, taking in the house, the gardens — 'your empire.'

'You taught history, Lieutenant, at your school?'

'Yes. When I had to. Amongst other subjects. That is to say, I don't specialize in history, but I've always been fascinated by Maria Theresa, I don't know why. Perhaps because she was a powerful woman who held her own in a man's world.'

Eloise had to remind herself that he was speaking not of her, but of a long-dead figure from history, of whom she knew next to nothing.

He said, hesitantly, 'You think me presumptuous, Mrs Brannan?'

'Not at all. But my "empire", as you call it, does not really belong to me. I am more of a custodian. My father often said, "One doesn't own a place like Clifton, one merely holds it in trust."'

'Ready to hand on to the next generation?'

'Precisely, Lieutenant.'

'Please. Won't you call me Alex? Or Alexander, if you prefer. Being addressed as "Lieutenant" reminds me too much of — of other things.'

'Very well. If that is what you wish — Alexander.'

'Roderick's a lucky blighter, I must say, being heir to all this! But he's even luckier in the family he has. You all seemed so pleased to see him when we arrived; I noticed it particularly.'

'I am not sure that Roderick would see things in quite that light,' said Eloise, painfully aware that the rift between her and her son had not yet been entirely healed; there remained a certain reticence between them, or so she felt. But it would be incautious of her to allude to this to someone outside the family, and she added quickly, 'What I mean is, you men lead such busy lives. There is always so much more to you than home.'

'That may be true of some men. Too often, such things as home and family are only really appreciated by those who have lost them or who lack them. But I don't think that's the case with Roderick. He couldn't wait to tell me all about his home. He talked of little else the whole time we were travelling together. It became obvious to me how fond he is of you all — and of you in particular, Mrs Brannan.'

Eloise would have liked to believe this; perhaps it really had seemed that way to Lieutenant Cartwright. But how much did he actually know about Roderick? They'd only met for the first time a matter of days ago, and Roderick was hardly likely to open his heart to a virtual stranger — if he ever opened his heart at all.

She wondered if Cartwright had been thinking of himself when he spoke of appreciating what was lost or lacking. When and how had he been orphaned? She might have thought about asking him, had she not just been made sensitive to the fact that there were certain things people preferred to keep to themselves. She would not have dreamed of talking to Cartwright about her rift with Roderick; perhaps he felt the same about his lost parents.

They walked on in silence for a while, leaving behind the spring blooms and the early butterflies, and following the cinder paths back to the doorway in the garden wall. On the space of gravel in front of the house, Cartwright came to a halt, gazing up at the grey facade.

'It's most impressive. Anyone who lived in a place like this couldn't fail to grow up a gentleman.' He glanced at her and added, 'Being the custodian, you must feel at times as if Clifton owns you, rather than the other way around.'

'Most perceptive of you, Alexander. That is exactly how it feels.'

'Rather a heavy responsibility.'

'But a responsibility one is happy to bear. I was born here, grew up here. Clifton is in my blood, you might say. There's nowhere I'd rather be. You must feel something similar about where you grew up.'

'Oh, the places where I lived as a child were none of them as grand as this.'

He seemed not to want to say any more and she wondered if she'd stirred up painful memories. But then he turned to her, smiling broadly.

'I can't tell you what it means to me to be here. I couldn't have wished for anything better. To think I'd never have come if I hadn't met Roderick! And I only met Roderick because of the war. Much as I hate the war, it has brought certain . . . opportunities.'

She had no doubt of his sincerity. He even seemed a little overwhelmed, as if he couldn't believe his luck. But Clifton was a special place, a place that inspired the most intense feelings. And though he'd credited Roderick and the war for bringing him here, she felt he was bestowing gratitude on her too: his smile was like a benediction.

She looked at him with renewed curiosity. He was obviously a very sensitive and understanding young man, and he was brave with it: a decorated soldier. But despite his broad smile, she couldn't help but feel that a faint air of melancholy clung to him, as if he'd known profound sadness in his life. In appearance, he was not immediately handsome; his face was plain and round and rather tanned. But it was this very ordinariness that was in some way attractive, and his deep, expressive eyes only added to his appeal. She sensed a certain reticence in him. And he gave the impression of being somehow unspoilt — if unspoilt was the right word — which made him seem younger than his years. All things considered, he was the perfect guest. How clever it was of Roderick to have found such a new friend!

Eloise suddenly realized that she'd been staring and she turned away, looked up at the house. She also realized that she'd gone too far; she'd let her imagination run away with her. Lieutenant Cartwright saw her as his hostess and Roderick's mother, and that was all. He'd compared her, not to some living, breathing woman, but to Maria Theresa, a figure from history: metaphorical, symbolical. Yet what else could she expect, when she was fifty-one, in the autumn of her years?

She shook herself free of all fancies, and focused instead on the house, which seemed almost to shine in the spring sunshine. She tried to see it as Lieutenant Cartwright saw it, with fresh eyes. There was an innate grandeur to the place which was unmistakeable, but Cartwright had gone beyond that, beyond the bricks and mortar: he saw the place in its true light; he recognized its significance. It was as if he sensed Clifton's very soul.

If even a stranger could see all that Clifton meant, then perhaps she had not failed in her duty quite as completely as she'd imagined. Would Father have thought so? If only one could know what Father would have thought!

But that was surely impossible.

* * *

Dorothea was now home as well. She'd managed to get leave from her south London hospital, though not without difficulty. She didn't say as much. She made light of it. But Eloise could read between the lines.

At dinner that evening, Eloise presided over such a gathering as Clifton hadn't seen in a long time — not since

Roderick's leave in the December of 1914, almost eighteen gruelling months ago. They were all together again around the dining table: Roderick, Dorothea, Rosa, Elizabeth — and one interloper, Lieutenant Cartwright. He was far from unwelcome. Eloise saw him as the grit in the oyster, round which the pearl forms; he was both a focus of attention and also acted as a mirror, reflecting their felicity back at them.

'He's very pleasant company. I'm getting to like him a lot.'

'Who are you talking about?'

'Alex, of course.'

Dinner was over. They'd got up from the table together; there was to be no interval, as in the old days, before the gentlemen joined the ladies in the drawing room. Roderick and Rosa brought up the rear, and they lingered in the passage a moment. Eloise, just inside the drawing room, overheard Rosa's words of praise for their guest.

'There's something about him that's . . . that's almost poetic. As if he were a modern-day Byron. Or, no — not Byron. Keats. He's more Keats than Byron.'

Roderick snorted with laughter. 'You do talk rot! Cartwright is not poetic. That is you being poetic. Cartwright is a hard-bitten soldier.'

'Hard-bitten he may be, but he also has a certain sensitive charm—'

'Sensitive!' scoffed Roderick.

'"Sensitive" is not the same as "weak". But you wouldn't understand that, with your elephant's hide.' Rosa added, 'I don't think he's quite aware of the effect he has. Eliza is dazzled. The maids melt in his presence. I even noticed Mrs Bourne blush today when he was speaking to her.'

'The Dreadnought, blushing? No. I won't have that. The Dreadnought's made of iron.'

'As for the way he flirts with your mother—'

'Now you're being absurd. Flirt with Mother? He wouldn't dare! Would anyone?'

'I have an idea that there isn't much he couldn't get away with, if he put his mind to it. And yet . . . it's funny, but I can't help thinking that he . . . that he's not quite sure of himself . . . as if he's always on his guard.'

'That's not altogether surprising. It takes some getting used to, I don't mind telling you, coming back to Blighty.' Roderick's mocking tone — the raillery — was suddenly missing; he went on in the same serious voice, 'Dressing for dinner, afternoon tea, the company of women — it's all so different to . . . to the other life . . . to our life out there. You can't imagine how different it is.' There was a pause, then he spoke again, but he was light-hearted again now, as if his mood had changed with the flick of a switch. 'If Mrs Rosa Brannan is so smitten with the dashing lieutenant, she ought to go ahead and tell him. Even better, why not simply kiss him?'

'Mrs Rosa Brannan would much rather kiss this lieutenant — even if he hasn't won a Military Cross.'

The voices in the hallway fell silent. Eloise turned away.

* * *

Crompton was clearing the tea things. Another fleeting moment had come and gone. Time was trickling away like sand through one's fingers. All too soon, one by one, they would start to leave: Alexander Cartwright first, then Dorothea, finally Roderick.

Eloise got briskly to her feet, refusing to indulge in such maudlin thoughts; they would only spoil things. All that mattered was the here and now; the future could take care of itself.

The French windows were open wide. She looked out at the bright afternoon. Dorothea, Roderick and Rosa had all disappeared the minute tea was over, but Lieutenant Cartwright was outside, walking on the clipped grass of The Park beyond the terrace, Elizabeth skipping beside him. She was looking up at him, hanging on his every word, laughing, her hair flying in the breeze.

Eliza is dazzled by him . . . Eloise thought of Rosa's overheard remarks of last evening. Not that Rosa always got things right. *The way he flirts with your mother*: that was patently ridiculous.

Why must Rosa be so — so — what was the word? A word to describe the way Rosa stripped the flesh from things, leaving only the bare bones; there was something almost ruthless about it. But when it came to Elizabeth and Alexander Cartwright, Rosa did have a point.

There was no real harm in Elizabeth's infatuation, if infatuation was what it was. It took her out of herself. She needed taking out of herself. And Lieutenant Cartwright would be gone soon enough. He was, in any case, a different sort of man from the stable boy, Turner (there'd been no further letters from Turner since January). Cartwright was a gentleman; he was, in fact, just the sort of suitor who'd make a good match for Elizabeth. But that wasn't really practicable under present circumstances, perhaps wasn't practicable at all. In the meantime, let them walk and talk and laugh. At least Lieutenant Cartwright would take happy memories of Clifton away with him.

Eloise turned from the window and looked round the drawing room, which was deserted now but for her; Crompton had finished clearing away the tea things and had gone. All that remained were a few crumbs on the carpet, a cup and saucer on top of the piano which Crompton had overlooked, and the scatter cushions on the couch all heaped at one end as Elizabeth had left them. The delft vase, of course, was out of place on the sideboard but Eloise felt no pressing need to move it — just the opposite, in fact. She would have liked to keep the room exactly how it was, in all its disarray. She would have liked to pot it, bottle it, preserve it in amber: this precise moment on a May afternoon, with tea just over and dinner still to come and nothing yet set ready for the evening. She was alone right now, but they'd all been gathered together just half an hour ago, they would all gather again when the gong sounded for dinner, and there was no need to look further than that.

Eloise sat down again. She was reluctant to leave, as if she could somehow slow the passage of time by remaining. A faint sound of birdsong floated in through the open window. All else was silent until, at length, she heard Elizabeth and the lieutenant returning; their voices carried before them.

'. . . don't like my moustache? I've grown rather fond of it myself.'

'I didn't say I didn't like it, Alex. I just wondered how you'd look without it.'

'I'd rather not shave it off after taking such pains to grow it. It's not much of a moustache, I'll give you that — a feeble effort compared with your brother's. Rather a poor old show, isn't it: I'm thirty-five years old, and I still struggle to grow a decent moustache.'

'Are you really thirty-five, Alex? Are you really that old? I would have thought you were younger. You seem a lot younger.'

Alex laughed. 'Because I'm so childish and immature?'

'That's not what I meant!' Elizabeth protested, but then she laughed too. 'Oh, you! You're impossible!'

There was a sound of footsteps climbing up to the terrace as they laughed together; then came a pause, the laughter fading, the footsteps stilled. They remained out of sight from where Eloise was sitting.

Quieter now, more sober, Cartwright said, 'I don't feel young, I can tell you that. I feel as if I've lived through half a century in the space of eighteen months. That's what war does to you. It makes you feel old.'

'Oh, Alex! Now it's you who's mentioned the war when you said we mustn't — you made me promise!' Elizabeth seemed to hesitate before adding uncertainly, 'Roddy says that war is like cricket.'

'Does he? I can't think why. I can assure you that war is nothing like cricket — which is just as well: I'd have been out for a duck by now if it was. I can't play cricket to save my life.'

'Don't you play at your school? Roddy played at his school.'

'My school? Oh, yes, my school. Well, I suppose we must play cricket — of course we play cricket — at least, the boys do. But I don't take the boys for games.'

239

'Boys get to do everything: to play cricket, to go to school, to fight in the war — everything! There's nothing for girls. I do nothing, nothing at all. I'm quite, quite useless.'

'That's not true, Eliza. Even I can see you're far from useless, and I've only just met you. You're clever, funny, pretty—'

'Pretty? I'm not pretty! How can you say I'm pretty? My nose is too small, and my chin too pointy, and everything about my face is wrong.'

'Trust me, you are beautiful. As beautiful as Helen of Troy.'

'Now you are making fun of me.'

'Not at all.'

'But you must be. I'm not beautiful, I'm really not. Who is Helena Troy?'

'Not Helena, you silly sausage. Helen. Helen of Troy. The face that launched a thousand ships.'

'I've never heard of her. What ships, and how could she launch them with her face? Oh, I'm so stupid! I know nothing! I used to go to school, but it was a waste of time. All I learned was how to walk properly and talk properly; it was all so silly. I wish I knew things. I wish I could do things. I wish I could do something important. Mama says that girls must stay at home and keep things going until the men come home; she says that's important. I don't see how.'

'Your mother is quite right. It means the world to us — to the men at the front — knowing all this is still here, knowing that you are waiting for us. We think about home all the time. We "dream of home", as it says in the song.'

'Which song?'

'The one about the home fires burning. Don't you know it?'

Elizabeth must have shaken her head no, because after a moment Lieutenant Cartwright began to sing.

'*They were summoned from the hillside*
They were called in from the glen . . .'

He sang well. He had an unexpectedly rich, deep voice which carried clearly through the open French windows. Taking his time, he let each word of the song ripen on his lips before it fell away to be replaced by the next.

> *'There's a silver lining*
> *Through the dark clouds shining*
> *Turn the dark clouds inside out*
> *Til the boys come home.'*

The song ended. The last poignant word — home — slowly faded to be followed by a breathless hush; even the birds had fallen silent. Eloise sat motionless in the drawing room and it seemed to her, at that moment, that the silence would never end.

* * *

They stood on the front steps in the fitful sunshine: Eloise, Dorothea, Rosa. Lieutenant Cartwright, now in uniform once more, took his leave of them one by one. Crompton was loading his valise into the waiting motor. Roderick stood by, ready to drive his newest friend to the station.

Just then, Elizabeth came running from the gardens, dishevelled, out of breath.

'Oh, Alex, Alex, I thought I'd missed you! I went to pick you some flowers, but then I couldn't make up my mind which to pick and I forgot the time and when I remembered it was too late and so all I've got is—'

She held out her hand and slowly uncurled her fingers. Lying on her palm was a tiny daisy, rather squashed.

Cartwright took it carefully from her. 'It's perfect,' he said solemnly. 'It will remind me always of the wonderful few days I have spent here.'

'Must you really go, Alex?'

'Yes, I'm afraid so. There are things I have to do before I return to France.'

'Will you ever come back to us?'

'I hope so, if you'll have me! Now then, what's all this? Don't cry. Don't cry, Helena Troy. Think how lucky we are to have met and to have had this time together, however short.'

He was very good, thought Eloise: very understanding of a young girl's silliness.

Moved by a sudden impulse she did not quite recognize, Eloise said, 'You could always write to the lieutenant, Elizabeth.'

'But, Mama!' Elizabeth gaped at her, surprised, and — Eloise felt — a little reproachful. 'When I wanted to write to—'

'It would be quite in order for you to write to Lieutenant Cartwright — if he doesn't mind, of course.'

'I should like it very much,' he said.

'Would you?' said Eliza. 'Would you really?'

'Of course. Letters from home make all the difference.'

'I'm glad about that! I'm so glad!'

Roderick interrupted. 'Do buck up, old chap. We shall miss your train.'

There was time now only for a few last hurried goodbyes.

'Mrs Brannan, I—' He hesitated, as if he didn't quite know what to say. She wondered if he might take her hand and kiss it, as he'd done on his arrival. Instead, a strange look came over his face, almost as if he was troubled by something. He seemed to be on the verge of speaking, but Roderick interrupted again, impatient, and Lieutenant Cartwright could say no more than 'Goodbye' before he was forced to turn away.

For a second, Eloise was pierced by a sense of disappointment, as if she'd been deprived of something, some last insight or word of compliment. She quickly recovered herself. Lieutenant Cartwright was quite right: it was better to say too little than too much. Overused words and empty phrases, a platitude or a stilted gesture: they would only spoil things. A simple, dignified 'goodbye' was enough. It said all that needed to be said.

Roderick hustled the lieutenant into the motor and then he took the wheel. The engine growled, the tyres scrunched on the gravel. Driving as impetuously as ever, Roderick set the motor spinning round the cedar tree, before it disappeared down the driveway at speed.

* * *

'What was the name of Lieutenant Cartwright's school in Worcestershire?' asked Dorothea over lunch. 'I never did find out.'

'Gloucestershire, not Worcestershire.' Roderick, busy with his soup, didn't look up. 'His school is in Gloucestershire.'

'Are you sure? I thought he said Worcestershire. But I may be wrong.'

Roderick grunted. 'Why this enormous interest in Cartwright? A fellow might begin to wish he'd never brought the blighter home with him.'

'Now don't spoil it,' said Rosa. 'It was generous of you, and considerate, to invite him, when he'd nowhere else to go. Let's leave it at that.'

Roderick eyed her across the table. 'Generous, am I? Considerate?' He snorted with laughter and went back to his soup. 'Rather good soup, this, Mother. Is there any more?'

* * *

'He would have turned seventy this month.'

Eloise stood in front of Albert's grave, Dorothea beside her. The sky was overcast, the afternoon warm and languid. Faint voices of men working somewhere in a field carried on the still air, but their words were too indistinct at this distance to be intelligible. To visit Albert's grave had been Dorothea's idea; it was entirely in character that Dorothea should have remembered Albert's upcoming birthday.

'Seven years since he passed away,' Eloise murmured. 'It hardly seems possible.' But she felt this sounded affected and artificial, and she added, 'It's not like me to be so maudlin.'

'You miss him, Aunt,' said Dorothea gently. 'What could be more natural? After all, you were married to him for eighteen years. I only hope, in time to come, that I can look back on such a long and happy marriage.'

The wistful note in Dorothea's voice stirred in Eloise a long-standing sense of unease. She had not forgotten Roderick's insinuation that, between them, they had persuaded Dorothea to remain in England against her best interests. It was nearly two years now since Dorothea had last seen her husband.

Troubled by her thoughts, Eloise was distracted from her contemplation of Albert's grave and glanced uneasily around her. The churchyard looked rather neglected. The grass had not been cut in a while; beds of nettles were springing up in the far corners. Seeing the nettles, an old memory slowly surfaced, something she had almost forgotten. She'd come to the churchyard once at dusk, late in the summer; this was years ago, around the time she was being courted by Jonathan. She'd been restless and unsettled, her feelings for Jonathan only compounding the heightened emotions and restiveness of youth. No doubt she'd thought the churchyard a suitably sombre and romantic place in which to dream and yearn and sigh.

She'd not been alone for long. She'd seen two furtive figures in the gloaming, carrying between them a spade and a little bundle. She'd watched, unseen, as they hastily buried the bundle, like hidden treasure or a guilty secret. Only later had she come to understand what it was she'd seen: the two shadowy figures had been the sexton and the local midwife, and the little bundle had contained the body of a stillborn child — perhaps one of those misbegotten infants Dr Camborne had once spoken of at luncheon long ago. Eloise had never told anyone what she'd seen, and both the sexton and the midwife must be long dead; perhaps only she now knew that, somewhere in the far right corner of the churchyard, was the last resting place of a pitiable, forgotten child, its grave marked only by nettles.

Strangely affected by this unexpected memory, Eloise found herself turning towards Dorothea and saying, 'Do you ever regret that you didn't go back to Germany in 1914?'

Dorothea appeared to give the question careful consideration before replying. 'I wonder, sometimes, what would have happened if I had gone back, but there does not seem much point in regretting what I never did. The past can't be changed.'

'I can't help thinking that Roderick and I . . . that we had too much influence in your decision.'

'I wouldn't say that. You gave me your opinion, you were trying to help, but in the end it was my choice — mine, and Johann's.' Dorothea paused, staring into the far distance, then she said, as if to herself, 'Perhaps there is no right choice in a situation like that.'

Eloise's eyes strayed back to the gravestone with its simple inscription. Something prompted her to say, 'Have you ever found it in your heart to forgive Albert for burning those letters from your father?' It seemed, somehow, the right moment to ask such a question.

'Oh, Aunt, there was nothing to forgive, not really. Uncle Albert only did what he thought was best. I'm sure he had good intentions. It's not as if Papa didn't know where I was. He could have come back at any time. He didn't. He chose not to. I can't blame Uncle Albert for that.'

'Albert was very fond of you. He thought highly of you. He would be proud of the woman you've become.'

'I like to think so. Dear Uncle Albert!'

They remained at the grave a little longer in silence, before turning away as if by unspoken agreement. Passing down the cracked and uneven path, they let themselves out of the churchyard by the side gate and joined the footpath across the fields to Clifton. Eloise was taken back to the last time she'd walked this way with Dorothea, on a mild October morning eighteen months ago, the day of Mother Franklin's funeral — the day of the magpie in the mist. Autumn then, it was spring now, the fields, the trees, the hedgerows green with new growth, and fallen may blossom scattered over the lush grass where clusters of primroses were sprouting.

Eloise found that Dorothea had taken her arm as they walked; it felt so easy, so natural, that she'd hardly noticed.

'Jeff was telling me, Aunt, of all you've done for him and his family since poor Stan was killed.'

'Jeff? Oh, you mean Smith, of course. But really, Dorothea, I've done nothing — no more than anyone would do.'

'I'm not sure that's entirely true, Aunt. Not everyone would take such trouble.'

'Well, we've been lucky with Smith. Such a conscientious boy. A godsend, really, when good staff are so hard to find; we've never had so few servants. I sometimes wonder how we'll manage. But all that sounds so trivial, compared to what other people are having to cope with: Roderick and Lieutenant Cartwright — you, too, Dorothea.'

'We all have our different crosses to bear. And we all like to grumble at times — Jeff more than most. He always was a prickly sort of boy, but there's a heart of gold underneath. You've made quite an impression on him, Aunt. He looks up to you. He's devoted.'

'That's good of you to say, Dorothea, but I hardly think that's right. I'm under no illusions. I am not the sort of person who inspires affection. Ask Rosa; I'm sure she will tell you. It's the way I was brought up, what was expected: dignity and reserve. Old-fashioned now, no doubt. But I'm not likely to change at my time of life.'

'Dearest Aunt, it's simply not true to say that people aren't fond of you. There's me and Roddy and Eliza, for a start, and I'm sure Rosa will come round. Then there's Jeff and Becket and Mrs Bourne; Lady Fitzwilliam and Mrs Somersby; Dr Camborne — the list goes on.'

Eloise was embarrassed by such talk. She didn't know what to say. She couldn't think how they'd come to it, a conversation as intimate as a confessional. Only with Dorothea was a conversation such as this at all possible. Dorothea approached people without fear or favour, she always had; there was no pretence with her and no affectation. But even Dorothea might have baulked at such talk as this in the old days. She'd grown up since then. She had, these days, a newfound confidence. Adversity seemed only to have amplified her innate good nature, as well as adding to it the wisdom of experience. Sometimes it was hard to believe she was still only twenty-four.

How unprepossessing she'd been on first inspection: a thin and dirty child dressed in worn and tattered clothes, newly abandoned by her father at Clifton! There'd been no good reason why they should have kept her; Albert had less than charitable feelings towards the girl's father, the man who'd eloped with his beloved younger sister. Had some kin-feeling been roused in him nonetheless, so that he hadn't sent the child away? Or had he seen something in her from the start? That was entirely possible with a man who was such a good judge of character as Albert.

And so Clifton had changed yet again. It had changed when Albert came, it changed with the advent of Dorothea. If it wasn't now the Clifton Eloise remembered from her youth, was that really such a bad thing? What she'd thought of as a malaise — was that more to do with the fact she'd not adapted to these changes? Was the malaise to be found not in the house, but in her?

'Are you all right, Aunt?'

They were climbing the stile from Coney Close into Horselands.

'Yes, thank you, Dorothea. Don't worry about me. I'm just a little old, I think, to be climbing over stiles.'

'Oh, Aunt, you aren't old, nothing like it!'

'Maybe you're right. And perhaps I'm not as set in my ways as I sometimes think.'

'Well, of course you're not. I've always known that. You take everything in your stride — even an old stile. Let me help you down. There. We've not far to go now. We're nearly home.'

'Yes. And we shall be just in time for tea.'

* * *

Time flowed ever more swiftly, as the last days of Roderick's leave came and went; time slipped through their fingers and was gone. Lieutenant Cartwright had already departed, and now it was Dorothea's turn to go — to return to her hospital in south London.

They went back to the morning room after seeing her off, reduced in number: just Eloise, Roderick, Rosa, Elizabeth.

'I'm sorry Dorothea had to go so soon, it's been nice having her around,' said Rosa, lowering herself onto the chaise longue. 'I feel I've got to know her much better this time. I do admire the work she does.'

'Nursing isn't a bed of roses.' Roderick was prowling round the room with his hands in his pockets. Rosa looked up at him in some surprise.

'I never said that it was. Nursing is skilled work, tough and demanding. But so is labouring in a factory or on the railways, or even on the land. Women do all those jobs now. Women have really come of age in this war.'

'Dorothea is not just anyone,' said Roderick — rather irritably, Eloise felt. 'Dorothea is a special case.'

'Admirable though she is,' said Rosa equably, 'I think you'll find she's not a special case. Men have always failed to realize how much potential women have. We are seeing now — at last — just what women are capable of.'

Roderick might have been expected to argue the point, but instead he turned away and went over to the window, fiddling with something in his pocket.

Rosa watched him curiously. 'What were you talking about yesterday evening before dinner, you and Dorothea, up in the nursery?'

'Oh, nothing much, this and that,' said Roderick, without looking round. 'Reminiscing, mostly.'

His answer seemed to Eloise deliberately vague. If Rosa thought so too, she passed no comment. 'I wonder if there is anything I could do,' she mused. 'Something useful, like Dorothea's nursing.'

Roderick swung round. 'Your place is here.' He loomed over Rosa. 'Your place is here, with our daughter, and the son and heir to come.' He sat down abruptly, next to her.

Rosa, as always, seemed to relish the prospect of what she called 'a discussion'. 'I am more than just a wife and mother; there is more to me than that. I have other responsibilities, which I have neglected for far too long — my sister Carla, for one. I hear tell that the aunts have carried her off to Tonbridge. I really must see what I can do by way of rescuing her, before she becomes irretrievably conventional. Then there's Leo. He's up before his tribunal soon. I ought to be there to support him.'

Rosa's brother was still refusing to fight, which was a serious matter now conscription was in force. But men like Leo Halsted were in a small minority. Contrary to Miss Ward's confident prediction that conscription would divide the country, there'd been very little fuss over it at all.

'Your brother has brought his troubles on himself,' said Roderick. 'He is a grown man; he doesn't need you to hold his hand. As for Carla, your aunts aren't monsters; they have the girl's best interests at heart. In any case, Rosa, you are in no condition to go gallivanting round the country. You have to think of the baby. You must put the baby first.'

Roderick picked up the newspaper and opened it, discussion over. This time it was Rosa who chose not to pursue the debate. Eloise wondered if Rosa was being so forbearing because of how soon Roderick would be leaving. Eloise also wondered, like Rosa, what Roderick and Dorothea had said to each other in the nursery last evening. He'd never been one to confide in his mother, was even less likely to do so now, with the way things stood between them. As if to underline how far they'd drifted apart, Eloise had found, just now, and to her own surprise, that she had a measure of sympathy for Rosa's point of view on the question of women in wartime. It was perfectly true that women were stronger than men gave them credit for — and this applied not just to women who were nurses and munitionettes, but also to the wives and mothers left at home. Waiting for news in this war required a special strength that was never acknowledged. And all too soon, as Eloise was painfully aware, a time of waiting would begin for her again.

* * *

It was the last evening of all.

Eloise took particular care in dressing for dinner — rather trying her maid's patience, she felt — then hastened downstairs lest she be late. But when she reached the drawing room, she found it deserted. The French windows were still open. She stepped out onto the terrace.

A little shock of surprise ran through her. She wasn't alone, as she'd imagined. Roderick was there. He was leaning on the parapet, smoking a cigarette and gazing out at the view, like the captain of a ship; his eyes searched the far horizon as if he hoped to discover some uncharted land. The sun had dipped already behind Hambury Hill away in the distance on their right. There was a fading light in the sky. The smoke from Roderick's cigarette curled up in the still air. As Eloise moved towards him, he acknowledged her presence with a look, then went back to the view.

Eloise watched the tip of his cigarette glow as he put it to his lips, thinking of how she'd assumed that smoking was a habit he'd taken up since joining the army. But when she'd remarked on it recently, both Rosa and Elizabeth had contradicted her. Roderick had been smoking for years, they said, didn't she know?

He kept things from her. She'd always been aware of that. Smoking, Hobson, what else? In the past, she'd told herself that, if she didn't know every detail of his life, it was probably for the best; what the eye didn't see, the heart didn't grieve over. But now, this evening, she felt differently. She wanted to see into every corner of his life, to know all his innermost secrets.

Foolish hope — and forlorn. For he told her nothing these days, less than ever.

At long last he spoke, breathing out smoke. He sounded so casual, it was obvious he'd not noticed the weight of their silence.

'What I wouldn't give to go galloping over those fields again! I'm rather aggrieved, to think I missed the whole of the hunting season.' (But hunting last winter had been rather in abeyance; he'd missed very little.) 'I wish we needn't have had to give up Conquest. He was a horse who suited me.' He sighed, before adding in a lighter tone, 'I do hope, Mother, next time I come on leave, I shan't find Hecate gone as well.'

She knew she couldn't match his levity, didn't try. 'I hardly think, Roderick, that the War Office will want to requisition your dog.'

'No. No, you're right. It's just horses they want. Horses — and men.' He sighed again, then said, '"When this lousy war is over, oh how happy I shall be . . ."'

His cigarette in one hand, with the other he smoothed his moustache, before running his fingers through his oiled hair, brushing back his neat centre parting. Watching him, Eloise gave a start of surprise. There — and there. Unmistakeable. Grey hairs. Grey hairs mixed amongst the black. How long had he had grey hairs? She couldn't think why she'd not noticed them before. But he was so young — too young to be going grey. What was it he'd been through to give him grey hairs at the age of twenty-three?

She shivered in the cooling air, and looked away.

Silence fell on the terrace once more. The last of the daylight was dwindling fast. Fields, trees, hedgerows were slipping into twilight.

After a long pause, during which she kept her eyes averted, she heard a rustle of movement beside her, and turned in time to see him straightening up, stubbing out his cigarette on the parapet. Tall, he was, and lordly. Immeasurably handsome. Immaculate in his evening wear. He looked every inch a Massingham. He was a Massingham in all but name.

He was heir to all that the Massinghams had ever possessed. And his entitlement came through her. It came through the female line. She would pass Clifton on to him, just as Maria Theresa had passed her empire to her son.

But all this seemed frivolous and footling and of no account, compared to the hard, unyielding reality of him, stood next to her.

He turned towards her as if he was suddenly aware, as if he could sense the ferment of her thoughts. He said nothing for what seemed a very long time. She was conscious of his dark eyes glinting in the half-light. He looked at her intently, as if he was committing her face to memory.

'Mother . . .' He finally broke the silence. His voice was deep and rough-edged; it sounded low and harsh in the gloaming, though he was actually speaking quite softly. 'You'll look after them for me, won't you, Mother, until — until I come back? You'll look after Rosa and Katherine, and the heir to come?'

She nodded, empathic. It was all she could manage.

'I know you find Rosa hard work at times, Mother. But will you . . . will you try with her . . . for my sake? Will you do that?' Without waiting for any sort of answer, he went on, lowering his voice still further, and speaking hesitantly, as if searching for the right words. 'Mother . . . dear Mother. I hope you know . . . you must know . . . no one could ever take your place . . . no one. I wanted to . . . to tell you . . . to make sure that . . . that you know.'

So faint and quiet were his words — and the shadows so deep now on the terrace — that it seemed to her she was aware of him by senses other than sight and hearing. The cool evening air, stirring, brushed against her skin, like the touch of ghostly fingers.

Her every nerve, her every fibre, tingled. She suddenly felt it absurd that she could ever have imagined herself estranged from him. There was a connection between them so deep and primal it was impossible to break. Even so, she'd not been prepared for this. Never, until this moment, had she felt so close to him — never, since the very beginning, the first few minutes of his life, holding him in her arms in that drab room on Forest Road, like a picture of the Madonna and Child.

All this passed in a heartbeat: a fleeting moment. The fleeting moment was gone. There were voices in the drawing room. Sudden light spilled out onto the terrace.

Roderick turned towards the French windows and, in doing so, took a step away from her.

'Here are the girls at last,' he said in his normal voice.

It was as if a spell had been broken; as though she'd stood for a split second on the brink of something unimaginable and now it was beyond reach.

She stirred, moved, put her hand up to pat her hair. What time was it? Somehow they'd got behindhand — and after she'd come down so early, too. Cook would be fretting down in the kitchen. Crompton would be hovering, waiting to show them through.

She followed her son to the French windows. Roderick stepped through into the drawing room, but Eloise at the last moment turned back. The first stars were shining dimly in the pale dark sky. The countryside was at peace in the gathering dusk.

As she stood, hesitating, she heard, faint and far off, from the direction of the canal, the spine-chilling scream of a vixen. At once, she was taken back thirty years. She was a young woman with silk flowers in her hair and a velvet ribbon at her throat. Her brand-new evening gown, with its bows and frills, rustled softly in the quiet of a summer night, as her bosom heaved, as her heart palpitated within her. She was twenty-one years old and she'd just been kissed for the first time. She had just been kissed in the billiard room, and it had sent her into a spin. Overcome by the shock of it, by the thrill of it, she'd taken refuge on the terrace to compose herself, closing the French windows behind her, cutting off the clamour of the party, the music and the laughter and the babble of voices.

She remembered looking up at the glittering stars that evening. She remembered the feeling of something beginning — her life, perhaps, her real life. She had whispered the word aloud, unable to restrain herself.

'Oh, life!'

And that was when she'd heard it, just as she had a moment ago: somewhere in the vast and empty night, a vixen had screamed, as if in reply to her, and she'd shivered all over.

Older, wiser, her feelings all contained — a woman of fifty-one who would never be so rash as to whisper, 'Oh, life!' to the empty night — Eloise waited on the terrace a moment longer, in case the vixen called again, but the enfolding dusk was still and silent once more, the world veiled in shadow.

She breathed in. She breathed out. She turned. She stepped over the threshold and shut the French windows behind her.

* * *

They were waiting on the 'up' platform at Welby station, all four of them, Eloise and Rosa and Elizabeth grouped round Roderick, who stood tall and upright and handsome, impeccably turned out in his uniform, his bags and cases at his feet. The May morning was bright but overcast, and a little cooler than of late. From their vantage point, up on the railway embankment, the surrounding countryside looked green and peaceful. The roofs and chimneys of the Railway Inn peeked between the treetops. The village of Welby was hidden from view.

The station master had huffed and puffed as he lugged Roderick's luggage up the steps, acting as porter. 'Anything for our brave boys, any little service at all!' He'd disappeared now, perhaps to find out when the train might be expected. It was overdue. They'd dragged out their goodbyes and stood now at a loss, not knowing what else to say. A woman wearing a straw hat and a shawl, with a basket on her arm, was watching them from a distance with discreet but keen interest. At the far end of the platform, a boy in boots and a flat cap was kicking his heels, head down, ignoring the world. Other than that, the station was deserted. A far cry, thought Eloise, from the carnival at Castle Station a year and a half ago.

It was Elizabeth who broke the silence. She pointed. 'What are those?'

'What are what?' Roderick craned his neck to look at his shoulder. 'My pips, do you mean? I've two pips now. I'm a full lieutenant. But surely you knew that? I wrote and told you.'

'Did you? I forgot.'

'Forgot your own brother's promotion? Isn't that just like you, with your head always in the clouds! You need some sense knocking into you, kiddo. I shall knock it in myself, just as soon as I've finished with the Hun.'

Elizabeth, against all expectation, raised no objection to this peremptory announcement. She looked up at her brother with a cryptic expression on her face and, after a moment, reached out and took hold of his hand, gripping his fingers rather awkwardly, rather shyly. Roderick made no move to respond, his arm still hanging loosely by his side, but neither did he take his hand away.

'Listen!' he said suddenly, cocking his ear. 'Was that a whistle I heard? It must be the train at last. Well, you lot, you needn't wait any longer, you might as well go.'

'Don't be ridiculous,' said Rosa in a tone of voice that brooked no argument. 'We have come to see you off, and that is what we will do.'

They looked at each other, husband and wife, and then looked away.

The chugging locomotive could be heard clearly now, getting rapidly nearer. Soon it came steaming into the station trailing a line of carriages, heavy wheels rumbling, brakes squealing. The station master reappeared. He began man-handling Roderick's bags and cases.

Eloise found herself standing at the end of a row, with Elizabeth and Rosa beside her. Roderick turned to face them. His smile faded in and out, like sunshine through the clouds.

His dark eyes, beneath the peak of his cap, seemed more impenetrable than ever. The collar of his khaki shirt, and his tie, were spotless. The buttons on his jacket gleamed.

He took his leave of them one at a time, going along the row.

'Be good, kiddo — if that's at all possible.' He touched the tip of Elizabeth's nose, then moved to stand opposite Rosa. Taking off his cap, he leaned forward to kiss her. 'Look after yourself and our daughter. And don't forget to send news of the son and heir. Send word as soon as you can. As for you, Mother—'

He stepped smartly along the row, putting his cap back on. Eloise met his eye. 'Dearest Mother. I shan't be long. I'll be back before you know it.'

As he held her gaze for a moment, it was on the tip of Eloise's tongue to say, 'Do have a good term, Roderick,' the words she'd used so often in the old days, seeing him off to school or college. But it so happened that she couldn't say anything for the lump in her throat.

Roderick swung up into the train. The station master went along slamming the doors — but he closed the last door, where Roderick had got on, almost reverently.

The train was now ready to depart. The station master stepped back and blew his whistle. Eloise, out of the corner of her eye, saw Rosa blinking back tears, her expression set and grim. Elizabeth was unashamedly crying, waving like a mad thing. Eloise held her head high, kept her back straight, more regal and dignified than Maria Theresa.

The train began to move. Hissing, clanking, jerking, it slipped slowly out of the station. Roderick, his head and shoulders framed in one of the windows, was visible just a moment longer, half-waving, half-saluting, then he was gone.

The train gathered speed. It curved away round a bend in the line and swiftly disappeared. Slowly, the sound of it faded into the distance. They were left alone, the three of them, on the otherwise empty platform, as a profound peace settled on the station under a grey May sky.

CHAPTER TEN

Eloise, in the parlour, was reading a letter from Dorothea when Crompton interrupted to announce Mrs Somersby. As Viola swept into the room with her usual flourish, Eloise's eyes lingered a moment longer on a part of Dorothea's letter that described how all leave at the hospital had been cancelled. Was this a sign that the 'big push' was imminent — the next big push, which Lieutenant Cartwright had talked of: the long-awaited attack that was going to win the war?

Viola arranged herself on the sofa. Eloise folded the letter and set it aside. Leaving her bureau, she took a seat opposite her visitor. To Eloise's appraising eye, Viola looked just a little haggard, but she was still dressed with all her familiar aplomb; she was wearing today one of those enormous hats for which she had become famous, this one trimmed with imitation flowers. Her son Mark, on his last leave not long ago, had said to Eloise in confidence, 'Mother's held out much longer than any of her doctors predicted. She has quite confounded all their prognoses. I see no reason why she shouldn't go on a good while longer yet.'

Removing her gloves, Viola said breezily, 'How cold it is! Not like June at all. I was trying to think, as I came up the drive, when I last called at Clifton, and — do you know? — I

257

couldn't for the life of me remember. But that's the way of it these days; it's one thing after another, and no time for the old routines. Now. Please. Do tell. How is Roderick? When you came to see me last month, you were expecting him home, Dorothea too. That must have been nice. Next for you will be your grandchild — it can't be long now. I do admire Rosa, the way she takes it all in her stride. Between you and me, I'm rather envious of your daughter-in-law. She's such a free spirit. My daughter-in-law, I'm afraid, is rather jejune.'

Eloise couldn't help wondering if 'jejune' was preferable to 'a free spirit', but mindful of her promise to Roderick, she said diplomatically, 'Rosa is certainly very modern. It takes some getting used to.'

'Oh, we all have our foibles, more so when we're young; one can't expect the younger generation to have our sense. Young people think they know best, but real wisdom comes with age and experience. All we can do is set a good example — which you do so well, Eloise, as someone remarked to me not so very long ago. Now, who was it, and where? Ah, yes, I remember. The christening. The Colonel's latest grandchild. He has four now, as have I. But, my dear, the christening, what a tawdry affair that was, didn't you think so? Oh, but of course, you weren't there. Let me tell you, you didn't miss much. I'm sure you will do it so much better when it's your turn — which won't be long, as I was saying. But where was I? Ah, yes. Setting a good example, that was it. Someone at the christening, it was — I forget who — but they said . . . well, the gist of it was, how much they admire you, how you always keep up certain standards. You epitomize . . . now, what was it you epitomize? No. It's gone. But you get my drift.'

It was most unlike Viola Somersby to be so vague. Her compliments, too, often came with a sting in the tail, yet there seemed no double meaning in her words today.

A little disconcerted by this unwonted praise, Eloise thought it best to change the subject. With her mind still on Dorothea's letter, she ventured to touch on the postulated 'big push'. Viola had nothing to add. She'd heard nothing on the grapevine, had no inside information. This, again, was unusual. Evidence, perhaps, of her decline? Eloise hesitated to ask after her health, though she was all but convinced by now that Viola was aware that she knew about the cancer; but if that was so, it remained unspoken between them.

The subject of death, however, was obviously not taboo, as Viola's next words made clear.

'My dear. Lord Kitchener. A dreadful shock. One can hardly believe he's gone. The last thing we needed — and coming so soon after that dreadful North Sea affair. What a disappointment that was! The greatest naval battle since Trafalgar, yet it seems to have made not a jot of difference. Really, one expected more from the Royal Navy. Still, one ought to be thankful for small mercies. All those stories of the navy having been knocked about — what a relief to find it was all scaremongering. Anyway, as I was saying: Lord Kitchener. To have drowned on his way to Russia — to have drowned — such an ignoble end, somehow, for a man who was so much of an inspiration. Where would we be without his new armies? Mark tells me they're absolutely essential if we're to win the war.'

Mrs Somersby seemed in no hurry to leave today. Even when she finally showed signs of making ready to go, it was only to sink back down in her seat and start talking again — talking this time, of all things, about her dead children. Eloise could not recall that she'd ever heard Viola talk about them before. There were two, a girl and a boy. What little Eloise knew of them was mixed up with — and mostly eclipsed by — events in her own life. The girl, aged three, had died in 1885, the year of Frederick's failed election, the year of Jonathan's proposal. The boy had passed away nine years later (he'd been eight), when Eloise was in Coventry. She'd received the news belatedly in a letter from Frederick, a letter mainly taken up with Lady Emerald's ills.

'Twenty and thirty years ago,' said Mrs Somersby, 'yet one never forgets.' She sighed, and began once more to gather

her gloves and her bag, this time with an air of finality. 'If you are right about this big push, Eloise, the war may be about to enter its final phase. I have to say, it's about time. Two years is quite long enough. There's one thing, though, of which I'm absolutely certain: we've come too far to think about defeat; the Germans will never get the better of us now.'

She got to her feet. Her face might show the odd line and wrinkle, but there was no denying she had kept her figure, and her long beige coat with a narrow waist showed it off to good advantage. Add to that her majestic hat, and she had an almost monumental appearance as she stood poised in the parlour, taking her leave. She had been talking of England just now — how England would never admit defeat — but she might equally have been talking about herself. One had only to look at her to see that she would go on and on, clinging resolutely to life, fighting the cancer to the bitter end: she would never surrender.

She paused in the doorway as Crompton was showing her out.

'I almost forgot. Many happy returns for tomorrow, Eloise.'

And then she was gone.

* * *

The next morning Eloise found Becket in the vegetable garden. He had ready the usual rose.

'Many happy returns, missus.'

'And the same to you, Becket.' She handed him a little tin of peppermints. He liked peppermints, Smith had told her. 'And how old are you today?' Every year the same words, like a litany.

'Ah. Well. Now you're asking.' He took off his cap and scratched his head. His thinning white hair stood up in tufts. 'I must be eighty, if I'm a day. I've worked at Clifton sixty year — no — it must be more like seventy now, going on for seventy. It were Mr Jephcott as first took me on, when I were no more than a nipper: Mr Jephcott, him as was head gardener to old Sir Edward.'

These were names Eloise had been familiar with since her earliest childhood, though she had not personally known Great Uncle Edward, nor his legendary head gardener: they had both died before she was born.

'I see you're keeping busy, Becket.'

'Aye, missus, I am, I am. I'm seeing what's to do with these here carrots. Nothing's growing in this weather. That's the long and short of it. Nothing's growing.'

'You are always very punctilious when it comes to your vegetables.'

'I do like me vegetables, I do. To my way of thinking, they're just as comely as flowers when they're growing — and there's some utility in 'em, as there ain't in flowers.'

Eloise wondered how many times down the years she'd heard these exact same words. There was something comforting about it, this perennial ritual: vegetables, Mr Jephcott, Becket's long years of service.

'You're quite right about vegetables, of course, but it's nice to have a few flowers about the place, all the same. This is a lovely rose. Quite perfect.' She raised it to her face, breathed in the delicate scent, then added, 'Smith, I hope, is behaving himself?'

'Thinks he knows it all, that one, thinks he's a dab hand, and — my goodness me — never in all my life have I known such a lad for argufying. But I daresay he'll do. Yes. He'll do.'

She left Becket to his carrots and walked back slowly towards the house, holding the rose with both hands, twirling it gently between her fingers. Becket's sixty or seventy years working in the gardens — that was equivalent to a third of Clifton's entire existence. But there'd been other gardeners before him whose names were now forgotten, and even Becket one day would come to an end. The house would outlast him, as it outlasted everyone, even the venerable Massinghams.

She ascended the steps to the front door and paused on the threshold. Holding the rose now in one hand, she reached out on impulse with the other and placed it on the stonework next to the door frame, something Father used to do: 'taking the pulse of the house', he'd called it. When she was a little girl, she'd believed it an act of mystical communion, and she'd wondered what the house was telling him; but whenever she'd tried it for herself, she'd felt only the hard, unyielding stone.

It was Father who'd taught her to venerate the Massinghams, who'd set such great store by tradition, who'd insisted that the old ways were the best; in his later years, he might have been said to have become something of an anachronism. But he'd been a realist, too; he'd known better than to try to hold back the tides of change. He'd accepted Albert without demur — 'He's a man for the future, Eloise. But me, I'm too old to change.' — where the Massinghams might well have looked askance at such a lowborn upstart desecrating Clifton's sacred portals. Father, thought Eloise, would never have been a Last Ditcher, like old Lord Denecote.

How could she be so sure? Well, she'd known Father better than anyone, so of course she was sure. Why, then, could she not be equally sure that Father would approve of the woman she'd become, the woman she was now? Why could she not be sure of that?

She took her hand away from the wall. She opened the door. Holding the rose, she stepped into the house, a woman of fifty-two — fifty-two years old today.

* * *

She had slept intermittently through most of the night but now, in the dead hour before dawn, she was suddenly wide awake, with little hope of drifting off again; her insomnia had not been this bad in a long time.

She lay on her back, completely still, with her hands folded on her breast. Over many years, she'd schooled herself to make the most of her sleeplessness, planning, prioritizing, thinking ahead. But sometimes — when she was particularly tired, and when the night was old but as yet showed no signs of ending — the mind was apt to wander, and it took too much of an effort to drag it back again and again onto the right course.

Her thoughts drifted nebulously over the last few days, back to her birthday on Tuesday, and Viola Somersby's visit the day before. Perhaps it was Viola's talk of her lost children, perhaps it was thinking so much recently about Father, perhaps it was being another year older: for whatever reason, she found herself, as she lay there, thinking about death.

It was strange about death. Such a crabbed, muddled, unsatisfactory sort of ending — whether it was Father's lingering illness, or Albert's life wrenched away in the space of a moment; whether it was Mr Smith's son killed by a stray bullet, or Lord Kitchener drowning in the cold North Sea. Viola's children — the two who'd died — how had they met their end? Eloise wasn't sure she'd ever heard; Viola had not mentioned anything about it the other day. But there were diseases aplenty, and always had been: Eloise thought of her own nephew, who'd died of diphtheria, here in this very house.

Richard. Frederick's son and heir. Though it might be more apposite to think of him as Lady Emerald's child, for there'd been nothing of Frederick in him: a boy with big, dark eyes and long black locks that curled up at the ends — so different to blue-eyed Frederick with his hair of burnished gold. Perhaps it was the stark contrast between father and son which had fuelled rumours that Richard wasn't Frederick's child at all, but the bastard son of an Italian count.

But that was preposterous, the very idea.

Or was it?

Now was the time when doubts crept in, when deceitful voices whispered out of the dark; now, in the dismal hour before dawn, the point at which one's spirits were at their lowest ebb. But the worst was over. Dawn was almost at hand. Already the deepest shadows were beginning their slow retreat to the furthest nooks and crannies. A pale light was seeping into the room, banishing all whispers of doubt.

Eloise sighed, then lay still again, at peace now, the long ordeal of her disturbed night almost over.

The curtains began to glow with the early sun. All the signs were that a bright June morning was getting underway. But no — she corrected herself — not June. Yesterday had been the last of June. And that meant it was July sunshine striking through the curtains.

Today was Saturday. It was Saturday the first of July.

* * *

Mrs Lambell lingered in the breakfast room now that the meeting was over; the other members of the Committee had all taken their leave. With only a month to go, arrangements for this year's fête were already far advanced. (But the Committee had a rather different look this year. Mrs Adnitt had sent a letter of resignation, no reason given. Mrs Keech had been drafted in to replace her.)

'Mrs Brannan . . .'

Collecting her notes together, Eloise got up from the table, leaving the rest for Johnson to tidy up. She waited for Mrs Lambell to continue.

'I couldn't leave without . . . well, I've been thinking about you, these last few days.'

There was no need to ask what Mrs Lambell was speaking of. The newspapers had been full of it.

FIERCE BATTLES
SLOW BUT STEADY PROGRESS

The 'big push' had finally come.

Eloise could only hope her own anxiety didn't show as clearly as Constance Lambell's. The poor woman looked gaunt and drained. Of the three Lambell boys, one was on a course here in England, whilst Rawdon — after the fiasco of the Dardanelles — had been transferred to Mesopotamia. There'd been considerable apprehension over Rawdon just after Easter, with the Turkish advance and fall of Kut, but his battalion had now been moved well behind the lines. The middle boy, however, like Roderick, was out in France; there was reason to believe that both this boy and Roderick were likely to be involved in the thick of the fighting.

'It's most kind of you, Constance, to be thinking of me at this difficult time for both of us.' Under the circumstances, it did not seem out of place to use Mrs Lambell's Christian name. 'I'm afraid there's little any of us can do, except wait and hope.' Eloise evinced a fortitude she did not entirely feel, but now was not the time for what Roderick would call 'letting the side down'.

'That's so true, of course. All the same, one can't help but . . . worry.' Mrs Lambell was apologetic about worrying. She quickly rallied. 'At least we have the fête to keep our minds off it. Mrs Adnitt, I'm told, is dead set against the fête. She thinks it inappropriate. And after she was so adamant last year that it should go ahead! She changes with the wind, that woman. But listen to me, going on. I mustn't keep you. I'll see you at the meeting next Monday, if not before. Goodbye, Mrs Brannan, and God bless.'

She touched, very briefly, Eloise's arm, then turned away. Crompton was hovering by the door, waiting to show her out.

Eloise went over to the window and looked out. Of Mrs Keech there was no sign, but the vicar and his wife were waiting on the gravel beneath the cedar tree for Mrs Lambell to catch up with them. As Eloise watched, Mrs Lambell emerged from the house and descended the front steps. The three of them began to walk together towards the drive, eschewing the muddy footpath across the fields that would be all the muddier after yet another downpour earlier.

Eloise's thoughts returned to the newspaper headlines. Fierce battles. Slow and steady progress. Despite her stout-hearted words to Mrs Lambell, Eloise could not help but wonder how she would get through the coming days.

* * *

The danger lay in just sitting and doing nothing; that only made the long, slow hours even longer and slower. Mrs Lambell had put her finger on it. One must keep busy. Eloise decided to sort out the blue room, something she'd been meaning to do for a long time.

Rain pattered on the window as she stood and looked round at the detritus of the passing years. The stuffed animals in their glass cases, which had seemed to her almost sentient on the day of Mark Somersby's wedding eighteen months ago, were entirely lifeless now: their fur looked rather moth-eaten; their glass eyes were dull and unconvincing. But the glass cases had been carefully dusted, as had all the ornaments on the tables and the sideboard: the majolica-ware and the porcelain, Sèvres and Meissen and Crown Derby. No fault could be found with Mrs Bourne's attention to detail, even if the ever-changing housemaids often failed to live up to the housekeeper's exacting standards.

On the console table, there was a picture in a silver frame of Father. Eloise took it to the window where there was more light. The picture was rather faded. Through a sepia mist, she saw a young-looking Father with a side parting and mutton-chop whiskers. How inordinately fond they'd been of their facial hair, those resplendent Victorian gentlemen!

Eloise lowered the picture, staring blankly into the near distance, seeing in her mind's eye Father in a series of characteristic vignettes: coming downstairs first thing, pausing to tap the barometer in the hallway; reading *The Times* from the back page to the front, in the morning room after breakfast; enthroned at the head of the table every evening at dinner.

The barometer. Where now was the barometer? For so long it had hung on the wall next to the grandfather clock, but it wasn't there now. When, exactly, had it disappeared?

Eloise felt she could hazard a guess. Returning to Clifton in 1895 after her exile in Coventry, she'd noticed one thing after another, all missing. Lady Emerald was to blame. She had been profligate and careless — with her own possessions as well as other people's. She had lost, sold or otherwise relinquished a whole catalogue of Clifton heir-looms: Mother's diamonds, and the ruby carcanet; a Persian carpet from the parlour; the painting of the Flood that had hung in the drawing room; the barometer, too, perhaps. And hadn't there been a silver sugar caster, said to have belonged to Mother's mother? Eloise had looked high and low for it, over many years, but without success. Why did she mind so much about the silver sugar caster? Why did she mind about it so much more than anything else?

The sugar caster was symbolic of everything else that was mislaid, broken or lost. Thus — inexorably, over the course of time — things fell apart in fragments, and life was slowly frittered away.

Rain was blown against the window by a gusting wind, and ran down the glass, obscuring the view of The Park. Eloise turned away, put back the picture of Father, went to the commode and opened one of its drawers. Here, at various times, a jumble of odds and ends had been stored for safekeeping, and then mostly forgotten. There were some Roman coins. There were fragments of pottery. These must be the shards said to have been dug up by Sir George Massingham, fifth baronet, during an excavation on Barrow Hill. Had there been no end to Sir George's talents? Had Sir George been an antiquarian, as well as an author and a Member of Parliament? He'd lived a long life. He'd been baronet for more than half a century, his incumbency almost mirroring the reign of George III: he'd survived the king by a mere three years. Sir George's two sons had both died childless. And so the estate — but not the title — had come, in the end, to Father.

Eloise fingered the fragments of pottery. Were they of any importance? Roderick would know. One could ask Roderick, when — if—

Reaching abruptly into the drawer again, Eloise's hand searched to the very back and found — what? More pottery, was it? Or a small stone? No. It was a fossil. That was what it was. A fossil. Could it be — was it possible, after all this time — but it looked very much like Frederick's fossil, the fossil he'd found the summer before he went up to Oxford. A Devil's finger, country folk called such things. Eloise, a girl of ten or so, had been terrified of it, something that was part of the Devil himself. But Frederick had laughed at her as he twirled the fossil between his long, thin fingers, and threw it up, spinning, into the air before catching it in his hand. It was nothing to do with the Devil, he'd said. It was a — now what was the word he'd used? She couldn't, for the life of her, remember. What she did remember was that Frederick had told her this little fossil had once been attached to a much larger creature, a creature that had lived thousands (or was it millions?) of years ago, a creature of a type that — like the Massinghams — had long been extinct.

To Eloise's childish mind, Frederick's explanation had been even more disturbing than the idea of the Devil. To think that this tiny bit of stone had once been alive: it made her flesh crawl. And her head was sent spinning when she tried to imagine the vast expanse of time since the creature last walked the earth (or swam in the sea — hadn't Frederick told her that it had lived in the sea?).

'I don't like it, Fred. I don't like it.'

'You are silly, Ellie. It's only a fossil.'

He'd poked fun at her, he'd laughed at her superstitious fear, but not unkindly. He'd never been really unkind to anyone in his whole life.

He must have been around eighteen years old that summer, the summer of the fossil. Eighteen had seemed to Eloise incredibly grown up, and her brother the very apogee of young manhood. She'd looked up at him with wide-eyed adoration as he threw the fossil one last time high in the air, following with his eyes the parabola of its rise and fall, before catching it neatly and putting it straight in his pocket. He'd carried it around with him for weeks — for months — maybe even years. She had a vague recollection that she'd caught a glimpse of it much, much later, when Frederick had been fishing in his pocket for loose change. When had that been? And where? But no. The memory was too elusive. It dissolved and disappeared before she could seize hold of it.

She looked down at the Devil's finger lying in the palm of her hand. How had it ended up here, in this drawer, forty years later? Impossible to say. But she found she was not in the least afraid of it now, just the opposite. Almost, she could understand Frederick's fascination. To think that it had survived through such unimaginable wastes of time! Its ancientry alone sanctified it. But also, it having been Frederick's gave it a special significance. Having spent so long in Frederick's pocket, something of Frederick had surely rubbed off on it. In some intangible way, Frederick lived on through this fossil.

Frederick. Poor, dear Frederick. How she'd idolized him, how she'd loved him — despite his faults. For he'd not been perfect. This she'd come to realize as she grew older. He was a man. He'd been prey to a man's appetites. He'd run wild for a time, one of the rakish Musketeers. But even at his most dissipated, he'd never sunk as low as Philip Milton — or Jonathan. And he'd not been permanently corrupted. He'd remained, at heart, a good man.

Eloise went back to the window, looked out through the rain-blotched glass, but instead of seeing the green park and the grey sky, she saw in her mind's eye a blazing July morning more than forty years ago. It would have been about the time when the Devil's finger first appeared.

The window of the morning room was open wide. She leaned right out, standing on tiptoe, balancing her body on the sill, watching Frederick outside on the gravel as he gazed up at the house, unaware of her, rapt in thought, his waistcoat unbuttoned, his white shirt lacking a collar, the sleeves rolled up. Sunshine glinted in his golden hair. His moustache was still something new, an object of curiosity.

When finally he caught sight of her, he broke into a grin, and instantly his whole face lit up. Beckoning with one finger, he called out, 'Come into the garden, Maud!'

She laughed. 'My name's not Maud, you silly!'

He began to walk backwards, still grinning, still beckoning, his shoes crunching on the gravel. Reaching the garden wall, he came to a halt. He flung his arms out, threw back his head, and declaimed:

'*Come into the garden, Maud,*
For the black bat, night, has flown,
Come into the garden, Maud,
I am here at the gate alone!'

His arms fell to his sides. His grin faded. Young and solemn and golden, he stood for a moment framed in the doorway that led to the gardens, then he stepped through it and disappeared, leaving a blank space where he'd been.

The sunlit memory faded. Eloise found herself watching the rain as it ran in long rivulets down the window, Frederick's fossil still in her hand. What had made him so happy that morning? Why had she not followed him into the gardens as he'd wanted? She couldn't say. It was too long ago to remember.

Yes, he'd been a good man at heart, always. Even at the bitter end, his true nature had shone through — in that cold February when the canal was frozen and he'd sent down soup to the boatmen and their families.

'Wasn't that just like him, madam? Wasn't that Master Frederick all over?'

The old housekeeper, talking to Eloise after the funeral, had dissolved into tears as she recalled her master's last moments — the old housekeeper, who'd been with them since Father's day, who'd known Frederick as a boy, who'd felt it impossible to continue at Clifton after Frederick had blown his brains out in the library. She'd retired to a little cottage in Kent bought with her carefully hoarded savings, and Mrs Bourne had taken her place.

Richard had inherited the estate: the boy Richard, not yet five, a sickly child, crippled, a disappointment to his mother who had liked things perfect, unblemished. But nobody, and nothing, had ever lived up to Lady Emerald's expectations. Not Richard. Not Frederick. Not Clifton. Not England itself. Lady Emerald had travelled halfway across Europe looking for — well, whatever it was she'd been looking for, yet to all appearances she had never found it.

Stood by the wet and bleary window, Eloise pictured the boy Richard, black-haired, brown-eyed, so unlike Frederick, so very unlike. Yet Frederick had never evinced any doubt that Richard was his son, as if he'd never heard the rumours concerning his wife and the Italian count.

But had he really been so unaware? What if he had heard the rumours? What if he'd suspected or guessed — what if he'd known — that Richard wasn't his? Perhaps he had known. Perhaps he'd known all along, and it made no difference. As the old housekeeper might have said, it would have been just like him to have loved Richard despite everything: it would have been Frederick all over.

Whatever the truth about Richard's parentage, something of Frederick had rubbed off on him, had lived on in him. But Richard, not yet fifteen, had died on a drab December day a dozen years ago. And so, all that was left of Frederick now were some fading photographs, her memories — and this fossil.

She had not followed Frederick on that summer morning long ago, but she would follow him in the end, she would follow him into that great unknown: death. Whatever death might be like for those who'd departed, for those left behind it was simply this: it was Frederick stepping through the garden door and disappearing, there one moment, gone the next. That was how she thought about death.

Eloise stirred and looked up — as if after a long reverie — and found that the rain had stopped and the day was growing brighter, shining in the water droplets that remained on the glass. She moved away from the window. She put Frederick's fossil back — carefully, punctiliously — where she had found it, and closed the drawer. She turned her back on the blue room, silent and immutable, and left behind all its relics and its memories.

The house seemed oddly quiet as she wandered from room to room, but she saw everywhere signs of the unchanging routine. The newspapers in the morning room had been gathered up and neatly folded, the glaring headlines, the lists of the dead hidden away. In the dining room, the table had been set ready for luncheon. There were fresh flowers in the vase in the hallway.

Slowly she climbed the stairs. In the day room of the nursery, she found Roderick's child playing on the floor under the watchful eye of the nursery maid, who was sat darning.

'Look, Gammy, look!' Little Katherine came tottering over, holding something up for Eloise's inspection. 'Gammy' was her rendering of grandmother.

Taking the toy from Katherine's tiny fist, Eloise found it was one of Roderick's old tin soldiers. Roderick, as a boy, had always favoured his tin soldiers over all his other toys. Eloise had never imagined that he would grow up to be a soldier himself.

Katherine stretched out an impatient hand. 'Give me, Gammy! Give me!'

Eloise gave the toy back to her granddaughter, then went and sat in the chair by the fireplace. She watched the child go back to her game, lying flat on her tummy under the big nursery table, chattering to herself in a language of her own.

Rosa refused to have a nurse or a nanny, compromised only as far as the nursery maid. Rosa wanted to look after her children herself. Perhaps it was the modern way. Perhaps the future belonged to modern women like Rosa. But that did not mean the old ways had to be swept completely aside. Dignity, modesty, good manners, self-discipline: these, surely, were admirable qualities in any age of the world.

Sat by the empty fireplace, Eloise's thoughts went back to Richard, to Frederick, to Father: they were the sum total of the Rycrofts at Clifton. After the long reign of the Massinghams, the Rycrofts had come and gone in little more than fifty years. The Brannans now ruled — for though she had been born a Rycroft, and had Massingham blood in her veins, she bore the name Brannan, and her son was Albert's son. Katherine would be joined soon by a new brother or sister: they were the next generation. What lay in store for them? Who would come after them? How long would the Brannans go on?

A burning desire to know suddenly flared up inside her; there was so much she wanted to know, so much still to come: new generations arising, a whole new world in store, Clifton's long story going on and on. But time was not on her side. She was fifty-two: a widow, a grandmother, in the autumn of her life.

And yet — was fifty-two so very old? Father had lived into his seventies, Becket was still hale at eighty, the old Earl of Denecote — and the old woman in the village, too — had both passed their ninetieth year. Which would give her twenty — thirty — forty more years. Time enough to see her grandchildren grow up, to see Clifton enter the next chapter. For there'd be a new beginning once the war was over — and perhaps that time was nearly upon them; as Viola Somersby had said a week ago, this great offensive might prove to be the final phase.

But the end had not come yet, and to think of the war damped all burning desires, smothered any thought of the future, and distanced the past, so that only the present moment seemed real.

The maid had slipped away for a moment, had left her darning on her empty chair. Eloise was alone with Katherine, whose muttered monologue had now sunk to a barely heard whisper; all else was quiet. As Eloise sat there, at rest, Roderick took shape in her mind, unbidden but not unexpected. She saw him, not as she'd seen him last, in uniform at Welby station, nor as he'd been the previous evening, dressed for dinner and smoking on the terrace; the image that formed in her mind was from further back. It took a moment for her to place it. Yes, of course. The bank holiday before the war, the day of the picnic. How long ago it seemed! The disastrous journey home had felt interminable, but they'd arrived at last and Roderick had gone leaping up the front steps, yelling for Ordish — Ordish, who was now no more than a memory in the house where he'd served for so long. Roderick had paused for a moment in the doorway. She remembered she'd been standing down on the gravel by the motor car, looking up at him, a tall silhouette against the electric light in the hallway. She remembered the feelings that had kindled inside her, feelings for which there were no right words. Sat in the quiet of the nursery, she remembered it all, and her heart thudded inside her chest. Roderick had paused in the doorway, then he'd stepped inside the house and was gone.

Bit by bit, the image in her mind's eye — the image of the empty doorway bright with electric light — slowly dissolved and faded, until it was entirely gone. She was back in the present moment. She sat motionless, gripping the arms of her chair. The silence was now absolute. Even Katherine had fallen quiet.

The silence stretched out in the long, slow hour before luncheon.

* * *

June, by and large, had been unseasonably cold — or so it seemed to Eloise as she sat sewing in the drawing room — and, even in the first days of July, summer had seemed reluctant to show its face: there'd been much rain. But this afternoon the sun was out and the sky mostly blue, and Eloise had opened the French windows to let in some air, as she sat with her spectacles and her embroidery. Crompton was on his half-day, Mrs Bourne running errands in Lawham. Rosa and Elizabeth had gone to the village directly after lunch and were not yet back.

Caught up in her work, Eloise barely heard the front door bell jangle. The faint sound seemed to come from an immense distance. It was of no moment.

After a while — it might have been hours later, for all Eloise knew, she was so absorbed — there came a timorous tap on the door. Out of the corner of her eye, as she concentrated on her needle, she saw the door open by inches. The maid, Johnson, edged into the room.

'Ex-excuse me, ma'am. This has come. A telegram.' Tentative, she held it out.

Eloise had reached a particularly fiddly bit of stitching. Watching the point of her needle, she said, 'Put it on the table, would you, Johnson.'

'Yes, ma'am.' The girl darted forward, placed the telegram on the low table, stepped smartly back.

'Tell the boy there is no reply.'

'Y-y-yes, ma'am. Will . . . will there be anything else, ma'am?'

'No. Nothing else. You may go, Johnson, thank you.'

The door closed softly. The catch clicked. There was a deep silence, broken only by faint birdsong from outside and — here indoors — the sound of thread pulling through fabric.

Eloise's hand faltered. Her concentration had been broken. The telegram was conspicuous on the table. Her mind stretched towards it.

There was barely any need to open it, barely any need to read the words. She knew already what it said. This was not like last time, as long ago as last September: the news that Roderick was wounded but alive. This was very different.

Killed in action.

She felt no sense of surprise, almost as if she already knew, as if she'd known for days, without being quite aware what it was that she knew.

There could no longer be any mistake.

He was dead.

Her son was dead.

She could not, for the moment, think what it meant. All she knew was this: her world was shattered, all hope of happiness ended forever.

She did not go to pieces, she did not weep and wail. She took hold of herself, she sat up straight, she turned back to her sewing. Her needle dipped in and out. Dignity, modesty, self-discipline: these were admirable qualities in any age of the world. They were the qualities Father had most admired. And, as she sat there with her spectacles and her embroidery, she knew beyond all doubt that today, this afternoon, at this cruellest of hours, she was carrying herself in every way exactly as Father would have wished.

He would be proud of her.

Father would be so very proud.

THE END

ALSO BY DOMINIC LUKE

The Joffe Books Story

We began in 2014 when Jasper agreed to publish his mum's much-rejected romance novel and it became a bestseller.

Since then we've grown into the largest independent publisher in the UK. We're extremely proud to publish some of the very best writers in the world, including Joy Ellis, Faith Martin, Caro Ramsay, Helen Forrester, Simon Brett and Robert Goddard. Everyone at Joffe Books loves reading and we never forget that it all begins with the magic of an author telling a story.

We are proud to publish talented first-time authors, as well as established writers whose books we love introducing to a new generation of readers.

We have been shortlisted for Independent Publisher of the Year at the British Book Awards three times, in 2020, 2021 and 2022, and for the Diversity and Inclusivity Award at the Independent Publishing Awards in 2022.

We built this company with your help, and we love to hear from you, so please email us about absolutely anything bookish at:

feedback@joffebooks.com

If you want to receive free books every Friday and hear about all our new releases, join our mailing list:

www.joffebooks. com/contact

And when you tell your friends about us, just remember: it's pronounced Joffe as in coffee or toffee!

Lightning Source UK Ltd.
Milton Keynes UK
UKHW011308130123
415295UK00005B/677